RUINED

A DARK MAFIA ENEMIES TO LOVERS
STANDALONE ROMANCE

M. JAMES

PNK PUBLISHING

1

AMALIE

I savor my very first piña colada, the really sweet and very *strong* beverage that's a perfect complement to the bright Ibiza sunshine. The moment I find myself thinking I'm ready for a second one, a man appears with perfect timing. The sun is now eclipsed by his eight-pack abs and tan hand that just so happens to be offering me another cup of the creamy, icy drink.

"What a nice surprise." I offer a smile and glance upwards to find a broad chest with tan skin and blue eyes as clear as the water outside.

"A pretty girl like you should always have a drink in her hand. And that one looked like it was getting a little low. If you don't remember me, I'm Bradley. You can call me Brad." He flashes his flawless smile, teeth polished to perfection by the dentistry his daddy's money paid for.

I don't remember him. The majority of the people on this yacht are strangers to me. I'm only here thanks to a friend's spontaneity and my own recklessness. All the hallmarks of a perfect spring break.

"Amalie." I turn my head as Brad flops onto the empty lounge chair next to me. I hear the sound of my friend Claire shifting on the other side, no doubt wanting a good view of the conversation that's about to unfold. His smile doesn't falter. "Can I call you Lia?" There's a clear flirtation in his voice as his eyes sweep over my figure that's stretched across the lounge chair.

For once, I'm glad I put so much effort into my looks today. Of course, I'd never admit that to my mother, who has always been so relentless about diet and fitness, and beauty.

"I prefer Amalie," I say with a smile, just enough of an edge to my voice to let him know that I'm not going to make it *that* easy on him. "You'll have to get to know me better before we talk about nicknames."

Now, as Brad's gaze slides over my perfectly toned body and the black bikini that covers only what absolutely needs to be covered, all the way up to my plump lips and luxurious auburn hair, I'm secretly grateful that my mother encouraged this innate vanity in me.

He wants me. I can tell by the beginnings of a hard-on I spot growing behind his patterned swim trunks. It only becomes more obvious when his gaze settles back on my breasts.

BACK IN CHICAGO, all of my mother's worrying about looks felt pointless. She's been
reminding me since I was old enough to hop on a treadmill and pronounce *probiotic* that it was my duty, as the Leone family's second child and only daughter, to entice men. Not just any man, but one with the appropriate wealth and family connections to earn the right to slide a diamond onto my finger, preferably as close to my eighteenth birthday as possible. Never mind that I had ideas about things like *going to college* and *sexual exploration* and *travel and independence*. My family—like every other crime family in the upper mid to northeastern States and probably beyond—is permanently stuck in the era of marriage alliances and using their daughters as bargaining chips. I didn't see the point in my dinner portions being rationed out or the long workout sessions, the biweekly yoga classes, or the countless hours at the spa for facials, manicures, and hair extensions. Why go through all that trouble and wasted time when the man picked for

me wouldn't be marrying me for my looks. He'd be doing it for the association with my family name, our ties to Sicily, and the considerable wealth that would come with me.

I might still be a virgin, but I already know how predictable men can be.

I tilt my glass, letting the last of the creamy drink drip into my mouth, leaving the smallest bit on my lower lip. Brad watches, his gaze glued to my mouth, as I lick it away.

"So, uh—" he swallows, "How *are* you here, anyway? I mean, who—"

To my other side, I hear Claire stifling a giggle.

"Who do I know?" I look at him innocently. It's such a crass question, and it's a clear reminder of the divide between me and everyone else here, that difference between new and old money. My family goes back generations, to some of the oldest Sicilian mafia ties, but that wouldn't mean a thing to these sons and daughters of Silicon Valley venture capitalists, tech billionaires, and celebrities. They talk about content and cryptocurrency and markets like it really matters, like all of that hasn't made their families rich overnight.

Like it couldn't all disappear just as easily.

That's why I like it here, though—part of why I was so quick to jump on Claire's offer. Here, I'm not the daughter of a mafia boss; I'm just Claire March's friend, tagging along for her spring break adventure in Ibiza, lucky to be asked.

Also, considering my family's recent misfortune, I don't have such a high horse to ride on any longer.

"She knows me." Claire pipes up, rolling onto her side and propping her elbow up. I see Brad's gaze slide to her—surreptitiously, and only for a brief second. Claire's boyfriend is never all that far away, and Brad knows better than to get caught checking her out. Although, with her knife-sharp blonde bob, yoga-taut figure, and perfectly sculpted cheekbones, Claire is worth getting into a bit of trouble to look at. "I invited her. My mother went to college with—"

I let the sound of Claire rattling off her family connections drone into the background briefly, while I take another look at Brad.

Could he be the one?

I made myself a promise before coming here that Ibiza would be where I'd find someone to unburden me of the virginity that I've been forced to cling to for so long.

I didn't dare to lose it in Chicago out of fear that the lucky guy I picked might brag, that word would spread back to my family. It was too risky. But here in Ibiza-

Here, no one is going to tell. I can do as I please.

"Do you travel a lot?" Brad scoots a little closer to the edge of his lounge, near enough to me that I can smell his lemony cologne and the scent of sunscreen. "What do you think of Ibiza?"

"I've been to Italy a few times. My family has property there." I stretch out, arms up over my head, arching like a cat in the sun. I can see the twitch of Brad's cock under those too-thin boardshorts he's wearing, and I know that he's mine if I want him. I'm not sure yet, though. *You've only been here a few days,* I remind myself. *No need to jump too soon. There's still most of the vacation left.* "But nothing so crazy as this. I had to sneak out, can you believe it? But I couldn't pass up Claire's invitation." I reach for the piña colada that he brought me, pursing my lips around the straw.

"Your parents don't know you're here?" Brad's eyes light up a little —he likes the idea of me being a little rebellious, clearly. *If only he knew.* "What, you snuck out through the window?"

"Basically." I laugh, shading my eyes with one hand as I look at him. "I don't know if my mom has seen through my excuse or not. But I haven't been looking at my phone, so—" I shrug.

Brad looks briefly confused. "But how—oh, you're probably saving all the pictures to post on social media when you get back." He nods sagely. "One of those girls who doesn't do candids and selfies. All planned." From his tone of voice, I can't tell if he thinks that's a good thing or not.

"I don't have social media," I tell him flatly.

He stares at me for a moment before he realizes I'm not joking. "What? Wait, you're serious—"

I shrug again. "Not allowed. My parents are super strict. And it just never bothered me that much. You've got to pick your battles, right?"

"Um—yeah. That makes sense." It's clear that Brad's three brain cells are all struggling to grasp what I've just said, and I sit up a little, taking another drink. *He's not very smart,* I think as I watch him out of the corner of my eye. *But does he need to be?*

I don't entirely know what I want out of my first time, exactly. I know I want it to be good—as good as it can be. I know I don't want my partner to know I'm a virgin—I don't want to make a big deal of it. But other than that—

I almost think I'd prefer someone a little older. Someone closer to thirty, at least—not so close to my own age. If I had to guess, I'd put Brad at twenty-three or so...still the age when I'm pretty sure guys don't really give a shit about anything beyond their own pleasure. When I go home, the specter of an arranged marriage will still be haunting our house, waiting for someone to give my mother the win she so desperately needs. And when that happens, I doubt there will be very many thrills in my marital sex life.

Those thrills are going to have to happen now, in this place of pure hedonism and vice, if they're going to happen for me at all. Which means I have to be careful about my choice.

Or I could pick more than one. I bite my lip, considering. There's merit to that, too. If I fuck Brad tonight, it could be someone else tomorrow. My 'slut era,' as Claire so eloquently put it when we talked about this on the flight over. *A brief one, for sure, but shouldn't I take advantage of the little freedom I have?*

"How do you know Claire?" Brad's voice cuts in as he steers the conversation back to what is, apparently, the most comfortable territory for him. "Your parents, or—"

"College. We're both art history majors. She's better at note-taking than I am, so...here we are." I flash him another smile, just as Claire gets up from her lounge chair, unfolding her lanky, slim body and turning to look at me.

"I'm going to go get us shots," she says with a grin. "We'll be going out to dinner in a few hours—we should pre-game! And then the club after that." She glances at Brad. "You're welcome to come if you want."

The invitation is given off-handedly, as if Claire couldn't care less if he comes along or not, which is the absolute truth. She's just giving me a chance to seal the deal if I want, which I appreciate. At the very least, it'll give me more time to decide.

"Anyway—" I shrug, laying back down. "We studied together a few times and really hit it off." *Hit it off* is an understatement—Claire is the first close friend I've ever had. I grew up around the other mafia daughters, but there was always an underlying competition there. As the daughter of one of the more prominent families, there was always the question of whether or not they were just using me to get closer to what my connections could offer them. But for Claire, there's none of that. Her goal as my friend became to find ways to temporarily break me out of what she called my "claustrophobic life," and over the past year, she's accomplished that in a number of ways. "Studying" was always an excuse that got me out of the house. After that, it was just a matter of slipping out of Claire's house with her undetected by my security, and out to whatever party or concert or event she decided I needed to experience. But this—

Ibiza is something else altogether.

I take the last sip of my piña colada just as Claire sways back up with two shot glasses in her hands. I feel a little fuzzy around the edges already—the most I've ever had to drink when I've snuck out with Claire back home is a couple of beers, for fear that I'd be hungover the next day and my mother would figure it out.

Claire hands me one of the shots—pointedly, she didn't bring one for Brad—and tosses hers back as I take a sip of mine. "Do the whole thing at once!" she chides; another one appears out of nowhere that she tosses back just as smoothly as the first, and I try not to make a face as I try to do the same.

It's lemony and sickly sweet, with a sharp burn at the back of my throat, but somehow I manage not to cough. Claire grins, flinging herself back onto the lounge chair, her gaze somewhere off in the distance, watching the others spread out across the deck of the yacht.

My gaze drifts back over to Brad, now ensconced in conversation with two other guys by the railing, and I wonder if anything will come of it tonight.

I wonder if I want it to.

—

One nap and a luxurious, eucalyptus-scented shower later, I find myself jostling for space on the bathroom counter with Claire as we get ready for dinner. I borrowed more than a few things from her closet for this trip, and I'm so in love with the dress I borrowed for tonight that I want to keep it. It's a jewel-blue minidress, tight in the front with a loose, draped back, coming just to the tops of my thighs, with delicate silver chain straps at the shoulders. Claire is running a straightener through her sharp bob, the candy-sweet smell of hair gloss filling the humid room. My heart flutters in my chest, every ticking minute bringing me closer to whatever tonight will bring.

I don't ever want this week to end.

We end up seated outdoors at a tapas-style restaurant, the warm, humid night air wrapping around us as laughter and conversation fills the air. I don't know most of the people at the table—some of them I saw on the yacht today, and some of them I've never seen before in my life—but I don't care. A model-gorgeous girl across from me with a mane of tightly curled black hair is asking me about my art history degree, and I answer the questions without really thinking. *What does it matter if I tell the truth?* I think with a sort of giddy glee that almost feels like a high. *I'll never see her again anyway.*

I reach for a carafe of sangria, refilling my glass, and hand it to Claire. There's fruit floating on the top of it, and I catch one of the lemon pieces with my teeth at the rim of my glass, enjoying the sweetness as it bursts over my tongue. I can feel Brad's eyes on me, his hand grazing along the side of my bare thigh, and he leans over, whispering in my ear.

"Claire said you're all going out dancing after this. Mind if I come along?"

I turn my head to look at him. He's close enough to kiss, and I have a wild thought that I could do that right here. Not exactly my first kiss—that was some drunken band member at an underground show in Chicago that Claire took me to—but close enough.

"Do whatever you like," I tell him flippantly, letting my gaze flick from his ocean-blue eyes down to his mouth and back up again. Playing hard to get is fun, I'm finding, especially with someone so willing to chase. I want to make him work for it a little more, even if I decide to let him catch me in the end.

I have no idea who pays for dinner. A pile of credit cards are thrown into the middle of the table, and I avoid tossing mine into the mix this time—I've tried not to use mine too often, in case my mother checks the transactions. Claire grabs my arm as I get up, steering me towards the waiting car.

"Is he gonna be the one?" she asks me in a hushed whisper, a giggle behind the words. "You can take him back to our room later if you want. I'll go stay with Jean. But you *have* to call me if you need anything, okay? Don't let him push you into anything—"

"I don't know yet." I keep my voice low, too, resisting the urge to glance back. "Maybe I'll meet someone else at the club tonight. Who knows? I'm not ready to decide—"

Claire giggles again. "You're not *marrying* him, silly. Just let loose and have fun. Besides—"

She lets out a squeak as Jean slides into the car next to her, his hand sliding up her thigh despite the fact that the rest of us are *right* here. I can see his fingertips dancing along the inside of it, just under the hem of her dress, and Claire's already alcohol-flushed cheeks blush deeper.

Jean leans over, murmuring something in her ear, and she lets out another gasping squeal as he pulls her into his lap. Next to me, Brad is pouring champagne, handing me a flute as he nestles closer. I'm next to the door, and there's precious little space. I can feel the heat of his broad body seeping into my skin, the lemony scent of his cologne filling the air as his hand lands on my leg, squeezing just above the knee.

"You're gonna like this place we're going to," he tells me, draining his champagne flute and filling it again. "It's the best club in Ibiza. There's a whole light show—you've never seen anything like it. And plenty of spots to sneak off to." His hand slides a little higher, and I glance over to see that Jean has Claire facing forward on his lap now, her hands on his shoulders as she squirms a little. My own face flushes as I realize that I'm pretty sure he has his hand up her skirt— that my best friend might be getting fingered right now in front of me. I don't know whether to be embarrassed or aroused, and I suddenly, desperately want some air.

Brad's fingers are making circles on my inner thigh, his voice droning on in my ear about what he considers to be the top five party spots in Ibiza, but I can't take my eyes off of Claire and Jean. She's kissing him, her knuckles almost white where she's holding on to him, and as her hips move, I know for sure that I'm watching him get her off.

That could be me. I could put Brad's hand up my skirt, and he'd do the same thing, if I wanted him to. I sit there frozen, feeling an insistent pulse between my thighs that makes me ache in ways I've never felt before, and I'm suddenly very certain that I'm going to sleep with *someone* tonight. I'm still not sure if it's going to be Brad, but it very well might be.

Jean looks over Claire's shoulder, breaking the kiss as she buries her face in his neck. His eyes lock with mine for just a moment—just long enough to see the smirk on his face as he realizes I'm watching. I see her hips shudder, see his other hand clamp around the back of her neck as he drags her mouth back to his—to stifle the sounds, I realize with a fresh wave of desire and embarrassment—and I realize she's coming, just as the car rolls to a stop in front of the club.

We all pile out as the doors open, but Jean and Claire hang back. I get one glimpse of her sliding to her knees on the floor, her hands reaching for the front of his shorts, before he shuts the door, and the wave of my newfound "friends" carries me inside the club.

"I'll get us drinks!" Brad's voice carries over the noise, as I glance back towards the entrance.

"I should wait for Claire—" I bite my lip nervously, feeling suddenly thrown off. I hadn't expected her to not be here with me the whole way—there's no one here that I know as well as her, not even the few other friends from our Chicago group who came along. The club feels huge and a little scary, and I take a deep breath, trying not to be upset with her for leaving me like this.

"Don't worry, she'll be back in no time." Brad grins at me. "I bet Jean won't take long to get his dick sucked. Come *on*, Lia. I'll buy you whatever you want to drink."

"It's Amalie." I glare at him, emphasizing it, but from the look on his face as he draws me towards the bar, I don't think it sank in.

He was right about one thing. I barely have my drink in my hand —some kind of sugary, fruity concoction—when I see Claire making her way towards me. She's dabbing at the corner of her mouth with one hand, and she grabs me the moment she's within reaching distance.

"Come with me to the ladies'," she says, peeling me away from Brad, who looks more than a little miffed. I follow gladly, drink still clutched in my hand. Claire shuts the door behind her as soon as we're inside the luxuriously appointed ladies' room.

"Sorry about that," she murmurs breathlessly, looking in the mirror as she takes her lipstick out of the small clutch she's holding. "Jean likes to watch and be watched—it gets him off, you know? He was feeling a little frisky. I didn't want to leave him hanging."

"It's fine." I laugh tightly. "If anything, I'm a little jealous."

"Well, that's why we've got to find you someone!" Claire grabs my hand as we head back out of the bathroom, towards the bar and dance floor. "Someone who'll do all the crazy things you can imagine this week, where everything stays here and nothing matters." She grabs a glass from a passing shot tray, downing it and dropping the glass on a nearby table. "Come on!"

Claire loves dancing. We've ended up at concerts and clubs more than anywhere else when she's convinced me to sneak out with her back home, and Ibiza is no different—just a more frenetic pace and more freely flowing vice. The crush of bodies on the dance floor is warm and pulsing, and Claire and I lose ourselves in the middle of it. The heat flows through me, making my dress cling to my skin and my hair stick to the side of my neck, a cloying feeling that I find strangely exhilarating. Claire spins around, gyrating against me as she flings her head back against my shoulder, her blond bob tickling my neck as I look around the seething dance floor.

Who am I going to pick? Brad is seeming less and less like the option I want to go with, but he's been monopolizing so much of my attention that I haven't really noticed anyone else. As Claire and I break away from the dancers, going in search of some water for her, I scan the bar, my pulse beating a little faster in my throat as I consider the possibilities.

And then I see *him*.

At the end of the bar, surrounded by three, no, *four* other women, is a man more breathtakingly gorgeous than anyone I think I've ever laid eyes on. In a club full of men in shorts and t-shirts and tank tops, half of them shirtless already in the thickly hot air, this man is wearing suit trousers and a button-down with the top two undone, his sleeves rolled up to showcase muscled forearms darkly inked with tattoos that I notice from all the way down the bar. He has thick, swept-back dark hair, a sharp jaw, and chiseled cheekbones, and even though I can't see the color of his eyes, I'm willing to bet they're every bit as gorgeous as he is.

"Claire." I tug on her arm and gesture to the man. "Do you know who he is?"

Claire peers forward, a little unsteady on her heels, and shakes her head. "I don't know *everyone* in Ibiza, Amalie," she says teasingly. "Now come *on*. I need water, and Brad and Jean—"

But I'm not listening any longer. Something went through me when I saw him, like an electric jolt down to my toes, and I've forgotten about Brad. I've forgotten about anyone else I've met since I've been here.

I shake off Claire's hand, and I start to walk to the end of the bar, with only one thought in my head.

I need to meet him.

2

DAVID

I almost don't see the drop-dead gorgeous girl walking towards me through the crowd, but when I do, she takes my breath away for a moment.

It's a strange feeling, one I'm not sure I've ever had before—not like this. I can't remember anyone ever making my heart stop in my chest for a second, or my breath catch, or a jolt of pure, electric lust shoot through me the way this girl does. There are endless women in this place—four of them hanging off of me already—but for a minute, I almost forget that they're there.

The girl is a knockout—thick auburn hair cascading in loose curls around her face and shoulders, a bright blue dress that looks like it's painted on the front of her, and the most perfect body I've ever seen. Even in the heat of the club, I can see the outline of her nipples against the silky fabric, and my cock instantly twitches, my entire body on alert and interested in whoever this girl is.

It doesn't take me long to find out.

She walks up to me with the kind of confidence that catches my attention right off the bat, swinging that thick auburn hair over her shoulder as she smiles at me. The smile makes my heart trip in my chest again, that buzz of desire tingling over my skin as she walks up to me. I catch a whiff of what I feel sure is her perfume—berries and vanilla filling my nose over the musky warmth of the crowded room.

I nudge one of the girls who is nearly on my lap to the side—one of the blondes, I don't actually remember any of their names—and flash a smile at the approaching redhead. "Hey, there. You look like you need a drink in your hand."

"I wouldn't say no to one." She hesitates, glancing at the brunette sitting to my right, and I motion to her to get up. The brunette pouts, but she does, sliding off the barstool to come and hang off of my arm.

"What's your pleasure?" I arch an eyebrow as I ask, waiting to see her reaction. She flushes lightly, her porcelain skin turning pink at the high points of her cheekbones, and laughs softly.

"Something sweet." There's a lightly flirtatious lilt to her voice, and I grin, motioning to the bartender. Despite the crush of bodies at the bar, he comes over immediately—likely because of how much I've been tipping all night.

"A lemon drop for the lady, please." I hand him a folded bill for the tip, and he pockets it, nodding. "And another round of what the other girls here were having, too."

"You're popular tonight." The redheaded girl smiles at me. "I wasn't sure if there'd be room over here."

"Always room for one more. I'm David." I nudge her drink towards her as the bartender sets it down.

"Amalie." She reaches for the drink, taking a small sip of it. "It's nice to meet you. Is this your first time in Ibiza?"

Her smile almost seems a little shy around the edges, like she's not quite sure if she's flirting right. It's charming, especially paired with the confidence that seemed to radiate off of her when she approached. "No, it's not," I tell her. "I haven't been here often, though. Just once before."

"Where are you from?" Her tone seems genuine, although I can't tell if she's really interested, or just making small talk. I don't plan to tell her all that much about myself—there's plenty she doesn't need to know, not when she'll be a fling at best. But a little chatting won't hurt.

"New England. Near Boston. Thus, the vacation." I laugh. "It can be cloudy and chilly there even this time of year. I needed a break from my responsibilities and a little sunshine. And some good company." My arm slips around the brunette girl's waist, emphasizing the last part.

Amalie's gaze flicks to the girl, and then back to me. She takes another, tentative sip of her drink, tossing her hair again as she tilts her chin up a little. "You definitely have plenty of company." Her tongue flicks over her lower lip, catching a drop of lemony vodka clinging to it, and I have a sudden urge to lean forward and capture her chin in my fingers, drawing her in for a kiss. I want to pull that full lower lip between mine and hear the soft gasp that I know she'd make for me.

I have the sudden, intense feeling that I can't let her get away. That I *need* to have her in my bed for the night. I've never felt anything quite like it before.

It's the stress, I tell myself. The pressures and responsibilities at home have been mounting by the week—by the day, really. I wasn't meant to be in the position I'm in now. I was never meant to be the heir, the one holding up my father's legacy as he slowly fades into the background. But it's where I am now, thanks to my brother. He couldn't keep his shit together, and now I'm shouldering all his burdens.

I've been shouldering them for a long time.

But there's none of that here. Boston and the crumbling Rhode Island mansion and the pressures slowly wearing me down are an ocean away. Here, there's nothing but sunshine, good booze and drugs, and beautiful women lining up for the chance to get down on their knees or bend over for me. I've had more sex in the four days I've been here than I've had in years, and I don't remember a single one of their names. I hardly remember what they looked like—to tell the truth, one of the four here with me right now could have already been in my bed, and I probably wouldn't remember.

I know for certain that I haven't seen Amalie before, though. I have the distinct feeling that I'd remember her—that even if she walked away right now, she's the sort of girl I wouldn't forget. It's a little unsettling, to tell the truth—but not enough to make me brush her off.

"After another drink or two, I was planning to make this a more private party." I take a sip of my own drink, keeping my gaze fixed on Amalie. "You're welcome to join us. I have a penthouse suite; there's plenty of room."

Her gaze flicks over the women around me again, and I see that tiny hint of uncertainty on her face once more. "I think it seems like it'd be a little crowded," she says softly. She raises her glass again, tipping the last of the drink back, and sets it down with a finality that sends a shiver of disappointment across my skin. "But I appreciate the drink, David. It was nice meeting you."

She hesitates for just a moment as she gets up, just enough to let me know that it's not me she's not interested in. It's the women around me. There's a flicker of disappointment in her eyes, and I catch the quick way her teeth graze over her lower lip, but she looks at the brunette standing next to me again, and turns away.

Fuck. I'd been looking forward to a night spent sinking into as many women as I could crowd into the king-sized bed in my suite. Still, every instinct in me is driving me to get up and follow her. I move almost without thinking, getting up and taking two quick strides towards Amalie, reaching for her arm before she can disappear into the crowd again.

"What—" She spins, her eyes widening, and for half a second, I think she's going to slap me for touching her. I see the moment of recognition, and she pauses, her brow creasing a little as she looks up at me in confusion. "What is it?"

"Come dance with me." I step closer, and I have the uncanny feeling that the press of the crowd around us vanishes, that for a moment, it's only her and I as I slide my hand up her arm, tugging her closer. The air around us is thick and warm, perfumed with the scent of a thousand or more drunken, moving bodies in this space, but all I smell is that sweet vanilla scent of her perfume. It makes me want to drag my tongue across her skin, nibble at her ear, and taste every inch of her until I find out if she tastes just as sweet.

"I only like dancing with one person at a time." She bites her lower lip, and the innuendo is unmistakable—as is her meaning. She's interested, but only if it's just her and I.

I should be more concerned with the fact that I'm considering this. I've never met a woman who could make me want to change my plans for her, who could make me want her enough that I'd pass on the chance of a foursome for the night just to get her in bed. But something about Amalie makes me feel as if I'll regret it if I let her go.

"Just the two of us, then." My fingers brush over her arm, and I feel the slight shiver that goes through her. "Do you like dancing?"

She nods. Her gaze is fixed on mine, and I see the flutter of her pulse in her throat. I want to run my hands all over her, feel that silky fabric under my palms, and then the soft skin underneath. From where I'm standing, I can see a glimpse of her cleavage in the tight blue dress, and I can imagine her breasts in my hands, soft and small against my fingertips.

I tug her towards the dance floor, and she follows. The music is a heavy beat, vibrating against the soles of my feet and up through my body. Amalie is already swaying to it before we've even made our way into the crush of bodies on the dance floor. Once there, it's all-consuming—there's no chance of hearing anything over it, no chance of doing anything other than letting it flow through us, the colored lights weaving over the bouncing, swaying, grinding people crammed together as the music intensifies.

Amalie turns her back to me as she moves against me, and my hands go instinctively to her hips. The way she moves is intoxicating, more so than any drink I've had tonight, the curves of her ass rubbing against me tantalizingly as she moves to the beat. Within moments, I've forgotten about any other woman I had here with me tonight—I've forgotten about *anything* other than her, the way she feels, the sweet smell of her perfume, the way her hair drifts against my neck as she tilts her head back, briefly resting it on my shoulder. She dances like she was born to be out here, carefree and confident, and all I can think about is what it would be like to have her in my bed. Every movement of her hips has my cock twitching, hardening, a slow, hot ache spreading through me, more intense than anything I can remember feeling in recent memory. She feels fucking incredible against me, and all I want is to get her back into my room.

"Let's get out of here." I lean down, murmuring it against her ear, and for a moment, I don't think she's heard me—until she turns, her chin tilting up as her arms wrap around my neck. She presses against me, hips writhing against mine to the beat until I'm so hard it fucking hurts. I can tell from the way she's moving that she knows it, that she's purposefully teasing me.

Amalie goes up on her tiptoes, her fingers scratching lightly against the back of my neck as she presses her lips close to my ear, sending a hot shiver through me. "Bored already?" she whispers, and a surge of desire floods me, my hand gripping her hip hard. For a moment, I think it might be *too* hard, that I might frighten her, but I could swear that even over the pounding music, I hear her gasping moan.

I catch her jaw in my other hand, thumb caressing the side of it as I hold her gaze. "Not even a little bit," I assure her. And then, there in the middle of the teeming crowd, I crush my mouth against hers.

She tastes like lemon and the sharp bite of vodka; she smells like sugar. It's enough to make my teeth ache with the sweetness of it; the rest of me aches with a need more intense than anything I've felt before. My hand on her hip holds her there, her body still moving to the music, against me, and I have the sudden, driving desire to take her here, to push her up against the nearest surface and fuck her where everyone else can see. Her lips are soft and warm against mine, and if her kiss feels a little clumsy, I don't think anything of it. We've both had a little to drink, and I take control of the kiss, sliding my tongue into her mouth as her lips part and devouring her exactly the way I want to.

I *feel* her moan this time, the sound vibrating against my lips, and my hand slips into her hair, around the back of her head, holding her mouth to mine. "Come back to my suite with me," I groan against her lips. "Let's fucking get out of here."

I grind against her once more, driving the point home, and I feel her shiver at the hard pressure of my cock against her thigh. She nods as she breaks the kiss, clearly breathless, and I grab her hand, steering her out of the crowd and towards the entrance of the club. I already have my phone out, texting the driver I rented for the week, and I see Amalie has her phone out, too.

"I'm just telling my friend where I'm going," she explains as we step out into the warm, humid night air. "Where are you staying?"

I give her the name of the hotel, glancing around for my car. "Tell your friend you'll be back in the morning." I reach for Amalie, pulling her against me as I say it. I have the deep, aching feeling that I can't bear to not have her skin touching mine for more than a moment. "Maybe we'll even have breakfast before I send you back."

"Is the breakfast me?" She giggles, her lips finding mine again, and I don't know what's come over me. I don't spend the night with women, not since—

I shove the thought away as the car pulls up to the curb. I'm not interested in entertaining ghosts, not tonight. *Especially* not tonight, not with a warm, flesh-and-blood woman in my arms who makes me feel things I didn't know I was capable of.

The moment we're in the car, I waste no time. "Take us back to my hotel," I tell the driver, putting up the partition, and I reach for Amalie, pulling her across the leather seats towards me. There's no hesitation now—she melts in my hands as I bring her mouth back to mine, and I feel assured, unequivocally, that I made the right choice in leaving with only her.

I'd rather have her in my bed tonight than any other woman in Ibiza.

3

AMALIE

My head is spinning.

As David kisses me, his mouth hard and hot against mine, I try to scramble to organize my thoughts, to make sure this is what I want before I'm in his room and in his bed. I feel as if I've been quite literally swept off of my feet, and his kisses make it hard to think.

I didn't want my first time to be an orgy—which is exactly what it looked like he was setting up for himself, with all of those women around him. It wasn't that I objected to a three—or more—some on principle, but the idea of being the only inexperienced one was so daunting that it took all I had not to quite literally run away. So I finished my drink, thanked him, and went to leave.

I didn't expect him to follow. And I didn't expect everything that happened after that.

His kisses take my breath away. I feel as if I quite literally can't catch a breath as he pulls me across the leather seats and onto his lap, so that I'm straddling him in the back of the car, my dress pushed up high on my thighs as his fingers slide up my leg.

It's a mirror of what Claire was doing with Jean earlier, and if I had enough presence of mind to think about it, I might find it ironic.

No one has ever kissed me so expertly, his mouth dragging over mine, teeth grazing over my lip before his tongue slides into my mouth, hot and insistent as his fingers wind through my hair. It feels *good*, so fucking good, until I'm throbbing with a desire more intense than I've ever felt. I lose myself in the kisses, in the sharp taste of alcohol on his tongue, the spicy scent of his cologne mingling with the sweet smell of mine, mixing with the scents of warm skin and cool leather in the car until I'm dizzy with all of it.

His hand slides higher on my thigh, fingers brushing against the soft skin, and I moan. I can't help it. I feel myself clench with desire, my hips rolling of their own accord as his hand climbs up my leg, and I wonder if I should stop him. Kissing is as far as I've ever gone— should I be letting this happen *here*, in the back of his car? Should I ask him to wait until we get to his room? Pretend to be shy because of the driver?

I don't want him to know I'm a virgin. But more than that, I'm not sure that I really *care* about any of that. I don't care if the driver hears. I'm not sure I want to wait until we get to the room, for any reason other than that I think I'm *supposed* to want to wait.

I'm in fucking Ibiza, I think as David's hand tightens in my hair and his mouth crushes against mine again, his groan vibrating against my lips as his fingers graze against the front of my silky panties. *I have my whole life to do this in a bedroom. I want the full experience before I can never have it again.*

So I give myself over to it. I cling to his shoulders, my tongue tangling with his as his fingers nudge my panties aside, and the gasp that I let out when I feel his fingertips slide over the outside of my folds shudders through my entire body.

"*Fuck.*" David rubs his fingers back and forth, not quite delving inside yet. "All soft and bare. You *were* looking to get fucked tonight, with a bare pussy like this, weren't you?" He drags my mouth back to his. "Dirty girl," he growls against my lips, and then his fingers slip between my folds.

I'm drenched. I know the moment that he feels it, that hot wetness coating his fingertips, from the sound he makes as he kisses me. I feel him tense under me, the muscles in his thighs tightening as his hips rock upwards too, and I can feel the hard ridge of his cock against me as his fingers slide up to my clit.

"So fucking wet," he murmurs against my mouth. "It won't take long for you to come for me, will it? I bet I can make you come before we get back to the hotel."

His fingers start to circle my clit as he speaks, soft, tight circles that leave me gasping and trembling. He finds it instantly, zeroing in on the spot that makes my thighs quiver and my nails dig into his shoulders, and I know he's right. It won't take long for me to come, not like this. He knows *exactly* what he's doing, and the fact that we're in the back of his car, fully dressed, my arousal dripping down over his fingers while the driver can hear the wet, filthy sounds that they make as they rub against my clit, turns me on even more.

My hips rock against his hand as he kisses me, grinding down against his fingers. I slide one hand behind his head, bracing myself as I feel his fingers move faster, rolling over my clit as he sucks my lower lip into his mouth. "Good girl," he murmurs, feeling the flood of arousal that drips down over his hand. "Come for me. Come all over my fucking fingers."

I'm utterly lost in it. The way he's taken control, the filthy things he says in that low, growling voice, the expertise of his fingers and mouth—*god*, I can't wait to find out what that mouth feels like between my legs. I can't wait to find out everything with him, and that's the thought that sends me over the edge, my entire body seizing with the strongest orgasm I've ever had as I buck and writhe against his hand, clamped between my thighs as I moan into the kiss and come every bit as hard as he wants me to.

"*Fuck*." David breathes the word as he slips his hand free. I watch in a fog of dazed lust as he raises his fingers to his mouth, flicking his tongue over the tips. "I was going to wait until I had you in bed to find out how you taste," he murmurs. "But I don't think I can wait with you all over my hand like this."

His fingers are fucking coated in my orgasm. He licks them again, groaning as if I'm the sweetest thing he's ever tasted. Then he touches my lower lip, his already dark eyes even darker with lust.

"Taste yourself, *bellisima*," he murmurs, his voice thick with desire. "You taste so fucking good."

I part my lips without thinking, letting him slide two slick fingers into my mouth. His other hand squeezes my hip, pulling me down hard into his lap, against the thick ridge of his cock. I know I must be making a mess of his suit trousers right now; my arousal smeared all over the fabric as I grind helplessly down onto him, his fingers pushing into my mouth as I suck on them with a whimper. David groans as I suck, his hips rocking against me, breathless with his own lust now.

"God, I want your pretty mouth around my cock." He tugs his fingers free, pulling my lips back to his. "I want to be inside of you. *Fuck.*"

The car rolls to a stop, and David fumbles for the door handle, slipping me gently off of his lap as he opens it. He helps me out of the car, and we're barely on the sidewalk before he kisses me again, pulling me against him with a kind of raw hunger that takes my breath away.

I hadn't expected this—this *need*. It makes me feel unsteady, but I don't want it to stop. I kiss him back, trying desperately not to seem inexperienced, not to seem clumsy. I don't want him to know that he's my first, and suddenly that seems of paramount importance. If he did know, I have no idea if he'd still want this.

"I need you in my bed. God, I *need*—" He kisses me again, growling the words against my mouth, and then we're stumbling towards the glass doors leading into the hotel, through the mosaic-tiled lobby, to the elevator at the end of it. David breaks the kiss long enough to press the button, and the moment the doors open and we're inside, he has me up against the mirrored wall, his hips pressed hard to mine. His fingers thread through my hair, and he's kissing me all over again as he fumbles with his other hand to slide the black matte key for the penthouse into the key slot.

My lips feel raw and swollen, my body throbbing with desire. I'm too far gone to think now, beyond anything except sensation, the feeling of his broad hands sliding over my body, one cupping my breast as his thumb glides over my nipple through the silky fabric of my dress. I catch a glimpse of us in the opposite mirrored wall, my hair a wild tangle around my face, David's hand cupping my flushed cheek, his hair falling into his eyes as he kisses me again. His other hand slides down to my waist, holding me there, and when one of my hands slips between us to graze against his cock, I feel him groan against my mouth.

He feels *huge*. I have a moment's concern about how all this will work, but we're beyond that now. *At least he won't think you're a virgin because it's a struggle to get it in*, I think wryly as he breaks the kiss for a moment, his lips dragging down my throat and taking my breath away. I think any woman would feel tight to him, first time or not, and that feels like an odd relief, despite my concerns about whether it will work at all.

The elevator chimes, the doors sliding open, and David leads me out. There's only one door up here, and we go straight to it, my heels clicking on the wooden floor as David holds his key card up to the light. The door clicks open, and as we step inside, I'm blown away.

I'm used to luxury—I've grown up in it. But this is something else. I can't take it in all at once, not when he's behind me, his hands sliding down my dress with a hungry urgency, but I see the expansive living room with the huge windows overlooking Ibiza, the soft-looking couch and pillows strewn everywhere—and most importantly, an open door that leads to a bedroom that I can see just a glimpse of.

"I thought about fucking you up against that window," David murmurs in my ear from behind, his hands working my skirt up my thighs. "I'd have you completely naked, pressed against the glass, that whole fucking view in front of us."

The skirt slips up, over my hips, and he drags the fabric upwards, sliding it over my arms and head and tossing it to the wooden floor. I had very little on beneath it, and in a matter of seconds, I'm bare except for my panties.

"We'll start in the bed, though, I think," he murmurs, turning me to face him. In one swift motion, he picks me up, my legs wrapping around his waist as he carries me to the bedroom, kissing me the entire way with his hand wrapped in my hair.

The room smells like citrus. It's the only thought I have before he spills me back onto the huge bed, made up with cool white bedding that chills my flushed skin as he follows me, leaning over me as I'm pressed back into the mounds of pillows. The heat of his mouth sears against my lips as I reach for his shirt without a thought, wanting to see *him*, too. I fumble with the buttons, my fingers trembling as I try to get them undone, and when one pops loose, I gasp softly.

David laughs, the sound vibrating over my skin where his lips are pressed against my jaw, at that soft spot just behind my ear. "Don't worry, *bellisima*," he murmurs, his fingers replacing mine as he nimbly undoes the rest of his buttons. "It's just a shirt."

Bellisima. I wouldn't have guessed he was Italian. He called me that once before, and if it had been closer to the start of the night, it might have put me off—a reminder of all the men back home that my mother is trying to convince to accept my hand in marriage, men who might once have tripped over one another for the chance to get closer to my family name and wealth, and the power that being so closely tied to the mafia would bring them. I didn't come here looking to fuck a man like the ones I know in Chicago—but David seems different, all the same. He doesn't know who my family is or the Sicilian mafia ties that the Leone name has. None of that matters here.

And it doesn't matter now, because his hands are on my waist, his mouth on my throat, his shirt falling open to reveal a leanly muscled chest dusted with dark hair and inked with tattoos, and I *want* him. I slide my hands up his abs, my fingers catching on the ridges of muscle as David reaches for his belt, and my heart hammers in my chest.

This is really happening. I'm really doing this. He leans back on his knees, between my spread thighs, his gaze raking hungrily over my bare breasts as he undoes the front of his pants. I don't feel as shy or embarrassed as I thought I might, almost entirely naked in front of someone for the first time. I think it has something to do with the way he's looking at me, like I'm the most beautiful thing he's ever seen. He had four women all over him back at that bar, but I feel certain from the look on his face that all he's thinking about right now is me.

When he pushes his pants down his hips, his cock springing free, I bite my lip as I feel my eyes go wide. He *is* huge—long and thick, the throbbing length framed by muscled thighs that flex as he looks down at me, his cock twitching eagerly. My entire body feels tense, aching to be touched, and even though a quiver of nerves goes through me as I look at him, I'm not as scared as I thought I would be.

"God, you're fucking gorgeous," David groans, leaning down to stroke his fingers over my hips. "Let's get these off of you, *bellisima*. I want to taste you."

His fingertips hook in the edge of my silky panties as he says it, sliding them down my legs as his gaze fixes between my thighs. I got a wax the first day here at the spa with Claire, and my skin is soft and bare, everything visible for his hungry eyes. The moment he tosses my panties to the side, his hands slide up my inner thighs, opening me up for him as he spreads my legs, and as he leans down, I suck in a soft breath of anticipation.

I want to know what this feels like. His mouth—

"Fuck!" I cry out the instant his tongue touches me, wet and hot, sliding up through my folds and centering on my clit. My hands twist in the sheets, and my hips buck upwards, and I hear David's low chuckle as he holds my hip with one hand, pinning me down against the sheets as he presses his mouth tighter between my thighs. "Oh god, *god*—"

"That's it." He slides his tongue around my clit, fluttering it as his fingers dig into my hip, and I let out another shuddering moan. "Moan for me just like that. *Fuck* yes."

I couldn't help it if I tried. His mouth feels incredible, better than anything I ever imagined. His tongue drags over me as expertly as his fingers did earlier, finding every spot that sends sensation after sensation crashing through me, my muscles tightening as I feel that knot of pleasure starting to unfurl in my belly.

I've made myself come before with my fingers, even with a small vibrator that I bought at a toy shop out with Claire and hid in a drawer, but it's never been as good as this. I feel like I'm coming out of my skin, like my body can't contain all the pleasure coursing through it as David's mouth tightens around my clit, licking, sucking, his fingers stroking through my folds as he focuses all his effort on making me come. A stream of sounds spill from my lips, moans and high-pitched whimpers, and when I feel the pleasure crest, my entire body arching as his tongue flicks over that one perfect spot once more, I think I'm going to die from how fucking good it feels.

His fingers slide into me the moment I start to come, and I cry out from the surprise of the sudden intrusion. The sharp pain that follows—but it's indistinguishable from the cries of pleasure, and David doesn't stop or falter. He keeps going, his tongue fluttering over my clit in that perfect rhythm as I come hard on his face, and for a moment, I think I might black out from the sheer intensity of it.

When he pulls back, a shudder of pleasure goes through me at the sight of him, his lips reddened, his mouth and chin glistening with my arousal. His cock is pressed against his belly, and as he leans over me, one hand brushing my hair away from my face as he bends to kiss me again, I can feel the desire tightening every inch of him.

He nudges my thighs wider with his knee, and I wrap my legs around his, urging him closer. My heart is beating quick and fast, my pulse fluttering in my throat, and I'm nervous—but I also want this. I *know* I want it, and when I feel his hips arch forward, his cock nudging against my entrance, I tilt my chin up to kiss him again.

I can taste myself on his lips, an echo of his fingers in my mouth earlier, and it sends a flood of arousal through me. I'm drenched, and I can feel the tip of his cock slipping between my folds, sending another eager quiver through me.

He doesn't ask if I'm ready for him—but why would he? He doesn't know this is the first time that I've felt any of this, which is exactly how I want it. There's no hesitation, no questions, nothing but him pushing inside of me as he kisses me again. His swollen, thick tip pierces me as a shock of pain washes through me —but it's swallowed up in all the other feelings. His mouth on mine, the heated weight of his muscled body, his hands sliding over me as he thrusts. I feel his groan against my lips as I gasp, my body jerking at the sudden intrusion. He *is* too big, just a little, and I feel as if he's splitting me open.

"Oh!" I cry out, shuddering, and David goes still.

"*Fuck.*" He hisses the word through his teeth, shuddering with pleasure as his hips roll against me of their own accord. "God, you're so fucking tight. Is it too much?"

I can hear how much he wants me to say no, how desperately difficult it is in this moment for him not to keep going. I sink my teeth into my lower lip, trying to breathe.

"Just give me—" I feel him twitch and throb inside of me, the strange feeling of being touched from the inside, *filled* so thoroughly, chasing away the pain. "I'm fine," I breathe, tilting my chin up. "You're just—"

"I know." He chuckles softly, kissing me again. His hips start to move, long, slow thrusts that burn and feel incredible all at once, and with every movement, the pain is chased further away by the growing, building pleasure. His hand slips between us, his fingers finding my clit again with that same quick expertise, and I moan as he starts to rub me there in soft, quick circles that push me toward the edge again.

He thrusts again, groaning, and then stops. "Fuck—I forgot—"

I see his jaw tighten as he pulls out, his cock stiff and throbbing, glistening with my arousal. It's the most erotic thing I've ever seen, his muscled body tense with interrupted pleasure, the sheer sexuality of it making me tremble with need as I reach for him again. "Why—"

"Hang on." He leans over, rifling in the pocket of his discarded pants, and I see him pull out a foil-wrapped packet. "Shit, I got so into it I almost forgot this. I nearly came in you without one."

That shouldn't turn me on, but it does. I have a moment's disappointment that he stopped, followed by a flood of arousal at the idea that I managed to turn this man on so much that he threw caution to the wind to be inside of me—followed by the sobering realization that it's a good thing David remembered. *I don't want a souvenir from tonight,* I think darkly as he rolls the condom down his stiff length with a groan, his hand tightening reflexively around himself before he leans down again, pressing himself into me.

It doesn't feel as good with the condom—a little strange—but still better than anything I've ever felt before. He picks up as if we never stopped, his mouth trailing a hot line down my throat as his fingers find my clit again, matching the rhythm of his thrusts as I gasp, my head falling back into the pillows. I thought him stopping would mean I'd lose my second orgasm, but his fingers quickly bring me back to the brink, my body tightening under his as I feel his hips quiver and jerk against mine.

"I'm close," he murmurs against my skin. "*Fuck,* you feel so fucking good—come for me, Amalie. One more time, come for me—"

My body obeys as if he flipped a switch, the climax tensing every muscle in my body as it jolts through me, my lips parting on a high-pitched cry of pleasure as I clench and ripple around him. I hear him groan, feel him thrust into me once more, and then the sharp buck of his hips as he swells and hardens in me. I want to *feel* him come, feel that hot rush inside of me that I've imagined, but this is nearly as good—his hand clutching the pillow next to my head as he shudders above me, kissing me once more as he comes.

"*Fuck,*" he breathes as he slips out of me, pinching the condom as he slides it off. He's still mostly hard, and I have a moment's desire to have him inside of me again as he gets up, walking to the bathroom with a slight hitch in his step that makes me flush with pleasure.

I made him feel like that—a little weak in the legs. There's an odd sense of pride at seeing how good it was for him, too, and I watch as he comes back to bed, enjoying the sight of his naked, muscled body, the inky tattoos patterning his skin. I wonder if he'll want to go again, and a tingle of anticipation flutters through me.

"Was that good for you?" He asks it teasingly as he lays down next to me, still gorgeously naked. I would have thought I'd be more shy about being naked like this in front of someone afterward, that I'd want to cover up, but I don't feel bothered by it. I like the way he's looking at me, his gaze lazily sliding over me as if still enjoying the view, even now that we're done.

"God, yes," I breathe, laughing a little. "It was incredible."

"Good." His hand smooths over my hip, stroking down my thigh, and I can't repress the shiver that flutters over my skin. I wonder if he'll want to do this again, if he might be my Ibiza fling—and if that's what I want, or if I want to explore my options. It's hard to think of wanting anyone else—the idea of going to bed with someone like Brad after this sounds less than appealing. I have a feeling that David has set the bar high for anyone who comes after him.

Not that there'll be that many. Once I go home, everything will go back to normal. The next man in my bed after that will be whoever my mother manages to convince to marry me, and any excitement I might have hoped for will vanish.

"How long are you staying for?" His fingers are still idly tracing a pattern on my hip, his cock half-hard against my thigh, and I see it twitch lazily as his gaze drifts down the length of my body. My heart flutters a little in my chest at the question—I want him to want me again, I realize. I want this to not be the last time.

"A week." My voice is breathier than I'd like it to be, giving away more than I'd like of how this makes me feel. "It's spring break for Claire and me and our—group of friends."

"Mm." His hand slides up my waist, and for a moment, I think he's going to slide it higher, initiate a second round, but instead, he gets up and goes to the minibar across the room, giving me a fantastic view of his muscled ass from behind. "I'm still a bit jet-lagged, to be honest, even after being here a few days." He opens a small bottle of gin, pouring it into a glass with tonic, and I have the sudden feeling that he wants me to go.

David turns back towards me with the glass in hand, and it's obvious to me that he's not offering me one. "How long are you staying?" I ask tentatively, and he shrugs.

"I've left it open-ended. I'll have to go home soon, but there's no firm date, you know?"

"Of course." I *don't* know—I definitely need to be back in a week, and I feel a flutter of jealousy at that, at the idea that he can just go as he pleases and do what he wants. I'd love to have that kind of freedom, and I never will. Even this was only achieved by sneaking out.

There's a brief, uncertain silence, and I bite my lip. I can feel the self-consciousness creeping in, and I sit up, looking for where my dress fell. *Out in the living room,* I remember with a nervous flutter, and I glance at David.

"Should I go?" The question comes out a little more bluntly than I mean it to, but I don't know how these things are talked about, exactly. On the way here, he'd mentioned breakfast and made it sound as if I'd stay the night, but everything about his demeanor now makes me think that he wants me to leave.

There's the briefest moment's hesitation—just a second where I think that he might say no, that he wants me to stay. And then he nods, his face smoothing out so that there's no emotion there that I can read.

"That's probably best," he says neutrally. "I'm sure your friend will want to know you've gotten back safe, anyway."

Claire is probably in bed with Jean right now, I think—a little glumly —but there's no point in saying that aloud. I don't think David *really* cares about whether or not Claire is concerned about me. I think he's just saying what sounds good to get me to go back to my hotel, and my chest tightens a little with hurt, even though I know it shouldn't. This was always a fling, and probably always going to be only one night.

"I'll just call an Uber, then." I get up, doing my best not to seem self-conscious about the fact that I have to walk out into the living room naked to retrieve my dress. My phone is in my clutch purse somewhere out there, too, and I toss my hair over my shoulder, striding towards the bedroom door.

"No, of course not. I'll get my driver to take you back." He's reaching for a pair of joggers as he says it when I look back, and I get one more glimpse of his perfect lower half before it's hidden behind the dark grey material, which rides low enough on his hips as he turns around that it doesn't make him any less appealing. It might even be more so—I can see the cut of muscle disappearing into the waistband, the sharp points of his hips, the dark trail of hair running down from his navel. I want to touch all of it, to sink down to my knees and run my lips and tongue over those muscles, that soft hair, slide his joggers down his hips and find out what it would be like to take his cock in my mouth.

My cheeks flush at the thought, and I wonder if he notices, but he's already typing something out on his phone. I know for sure then that he wants me to leave, and I find where my panties were lost among the sheets, slipping them over my hips and giving myself a modicum of decency before I walk out into the living room to retrieve the rest of my things.

I hear footsteps a few minutes later—fortunately, after I've gotten my dress on—and David walks out, still looking far too handsome shirtless. I hope he can't see just how much I wish he'd take me back to bed instead of sending me home.

"My driver is downstairs." He leans against the couch, watching me, and I manage a smile.

"Thank you. That's very nice. I'll just—" The awkwardness is as thick as the tension had been earlier tonight, and I grab my clutch, pausing for just one moment to see if he's going to say anything else —try to give me a goodbye kiss...*anything*. He doesn't move, and I make a beeline for the door, hurrying out into the hall.

There's a riot of emotions in my chest as I walk to the elevator in my high heels. I don't regret it, not at all—but he seemed so different afterward. *Maybe that's just how men are,* I think to myself as I step into the elevator and hit the button for the lobby. From what I know of men, it doesn't seem like so much of a stretch to think he might have wanted one thing beforehand, when he was thinking about getting me into bed, and something else afterward once the high of it all had worn off.

I think about it all the way back to my hotel, riding in the back of the car where, just a few hours ago, I was in David's lap while he introduced me to things I'd never done before. He doesn't know that, of course—and that's just how I want it—but it makes me feel a little strange, now that it's over. I'm not in as much of a hurry to try it with someone else as I thought I would be.

As expected, Claire isn't in our room when I let myself in. I shed the dress and heels, putting my hair up in a loose bun on top of my head so I can get in the shower. Some of the soreness from earlier has started to settle between my thighs, and I can feel the stickiness from my own arousal and the lubricant on the condom.

Shit. I'm reminded, in that moment, of how long he was inside of me without one. I'm not all *that* worried about having caught something, although I should probably make a gyno appointment when I get home, but—

Isn't it technically possible to get pregnant even if he didn't come in me? I bite my lip as I step into the hot water, feeling a twist of anxiety. Surely, just that bit of pre-cum can't get me pregnant. *What really matters is that when he finished, he had a condom on.* I tell myself that I'm just looking for something to focus my anxiety on, that it's not really anything to worry about until the nervous flutter in my chest calms down. However, I still don't feel entirely at ease.

When I hear the door to our room open, it's a relief. Claire is going to have questions, but I *do* want to talk about it. She'll let me talk about it in a light-hearted, unserious way, which is exactly what I need right now.

"Amalie?" Her voice rings through the room, and I quickly turn off the shower, wrapping myself up in a fluffy towel. "Are you back yet? I hear the shower—"

"I'm here! Just a second." I dry off quickly, reaching for one of the hotel robes on a series of wall hooks. I see the lights in the room come on underneath the door, and when I step out, Claire is sitting cross-legged on the bed in a silk romper, her blonde bob a little more rumpled than usual. I see a dark purple mark under her jaw, and I feel a tiny flush of jealousy—David was careful not to leave marks. Before he was so eager for me to leave, I might have thought it was him being gentlemanly, but now I think it might just have been because he didn't want to leave a reminder.

"Where *were* you?" Claire's eyes are glittering with interest. "I know you didn't leave with Brad; I saw him pouting by the bar."

"No, not Brad. Someone else." I sit on the bed opposite hers, feeling a small flush of excitement return at the idea of gossiping with my best friend about this. "Remember that man I saw? The one that I asked you if you knew him?"

"Oh—" Claire perks up. "He was gorgeous. But he had all those women around him—wait. You didn't—" Her eyes go round, and I can see her trying to imagine me going off and participating in an orgy for my first time.

"*No!*" I laugh, shaking my head. "I didn't think anything was going to happen because of that. He bought me a drink, and he did try to talk me into joining him and the other girls. But I basically said thank you for the drink and left—and he followed me."

"He *didn't*." Claire gasps. "Like—he left the other girls and just followed after you?" She grins. "I told you that dress was going to mean you got lucky tonight."

"It might not have *just* been the dress."

"It was definitely the dress." Claire leans forward eagerly, and I can feel my misgivings about the night slipping away. Talking to her about it now, like this, it doesn't seem so dramatic or upsetting. *It was a one-night stand, that's all. You're in Ibiza. That's how this was supposed to go.* "So then what?"

"We danced for a little while, and he took me back to his hotel, and we—" I trail off, biting my lip. "I did it."

"You did it!" Claire squeals. "I knew you'd find someone. Now you've gotten past that first time, you can just enjoy flirting and fucking your way through the rest of the vacation." She grins. "Or are you going to see him again?"

"I don't know," I admit. "He seemed pretty eager for me to leave, after. I think it might have just been the one time."

"Well, fuck him." Claire waves a hand dismissively. "I mean—fuck someone else. He was just the first one, and if he doesn't want to come back for seconds, that's on him." She gets up, crossing to the minibar to get us drinks, and I have a momentary flash of David earlier, naked and gorgeous, going to get himself a drink on the other side of the room. I wonder what he's doing right now—if he went back out, or if he's asleep, if he regrets just taking me back with him instead of the bed full of gorgeous women he could have had.

And then I remind myself that Claire is right, and it doesn't really matter.

"We're going day-drinking at one of the pools tomorrow," Claire says, handing me a fruity-looking drink in a glass tumbler. "There'll be *tons* of hot men there. If you don't like Brad, ignore him. Just have *fun*, Amalie. We're on vacation. The best vacation of your life, probably, and now you don't have that whole virginity thing to worry about. You're *free*. That part's over. So tomorrow—we party." She grins, holding her glass out to mine. "To Ibiza!"

Her enthusiasm is infectious. And I know, deep down, she's right. David doesn't matter, and how he feels about the night one way or another doesn't, either. What matters is how *I* feel about it—and I don't regret it. I don't want to let it control the rest of my time here, either.

I clink my glass against hers, returning her grin. "To Ibiza," I say firmly, and toss back the drink.

I have a whole week, and I plan to make the most of it.

4

DAVID

The first thing I notice when I come back to bed is that there's blood on the white sheets.

Not a lot—a few drops, really. But a cold feeling lurches down my spine for one instant, as I wonder if there was something Amalie wasn't telling me.

Don't be ridiculous, I tell myself, crossing the room to call down to housekeeping to change the linens before I go to bed. There's no way a virgin would have been so quick to come back to my hotel, so eager in the back of the car with the driver only a thin partition away, so willing once I got her into bed. I hadn't seen any reticence or fear or even pain—a little surprise, maybe, when she saw my size, but nothing that I'd expect from someone's first time. She hadn't been shy or nervous. I'd gotten the impression she wasn't all *that* experienced, but she definitely didn't seem virginal.

Not that I'd know, exactly—I've never been someone's first. But I feel like I have a decent idea of what a girl would probably be like if it *was* her first time in bed.

"Fuck," I mutter out loud, glancing at the sheets again. "I hope I didn't hurt her." I wrack my brain, trying to remember if she'd *seemed* hurt when I first slipped into her, but I'd been caught up in the moment. So caught up in it, in fact, that I hadn't thought to put on a condom until it was almost too late, something I'm still kicking myself about. But she'd seemed to enjoy herself—she came twice, and I definitely don't think she was faking it.

I go to take a shower while I wait for housekeeping to change the bedding, still turning the encounter over in my thoughts. I'm oddly in no rush to wash her sweet scent off of me—that berries and vanilla perfume that I might have found cloying on someone else. It seemed to suit her. But I get in the shower anyway, more to have some privacy to think than anything else. I still feel a bit guilty for sending her back to her hotel, when I know I gave her a different impression of how the night would go before we fucked. But after—

As good as it was—and *god*, it was fucking good—I felt unsettled after. I still do. I've never had a woman affect me the way she did. I don't usually *want* like that. I've gotten to the point where pleasure is more of a power trip than anything else, a way to make myself feel good by knowing I can get two or three or more of any women I want into my bed. Wanting someone like that—in a way that made me feel as if I'd regret it if I didn't take her home—makes me feel unbalanced, like she has an upper hand that I didn't want to give her. It's why I hinted that she should leave, because it felt very much as if letting her spend the night might make me feel things that I have absolutely no desire to feel.

I came to Ibiza to get laid, get drunk, and spend time forgetting everything that weighs me down back home. I don't want to get entangled with someone who will complicate my life even more— especially not a fucking *college student*. She mentioned she was here on spring break, and that was as good a sign as any that I need to put distance between us. There's no room in my life for someone like that.

Which is exactly what I have to remind myself of when I see her out by the pool the next day.

I have that feeling again—like a fucking moth to the flame— when I see her. She's stretched out on one of the cushioned lounge chairs, wearing a bright red bikini that barely seems to cover any skin at all. I touched all of that slim, lithe body last night, and yet I still can't keep myself from looking at her as if she's someone I've never seen before. The moment I catch sight of her, my cock twitches, my pulse speeds up as I remember the sound of her coming apart underneath me last night.

There's a girl next to her in a brightly patterned bikini with short blonde hair, leaning over and talking animatedly as she hands Amalie a cocktail. On the other side of her, I see a surfer-blond man with the kind of body that suggests he spends more time in the gym than literally anything else, and I feel my gut tighten with an entirely unfamiliar jealousy. I can see even from across the pool that he's looking at her with the kind of familiarity that suggests there's something between them—a flirtation at the very least, and from the way he touches her leg as she holds out her cocktail, laughing, for him to take a sip...I can't help but wonder if they might be more than just a flirtation.

I have no right to feel this way, of course. Amalie was far from the first woman in my bed since I came to Ibiza—there's been at *least* one there every night since I got here—and I have every intention of there being another tonight, and tomorrow night, and so on until I'm finally forced to go back home. And the way she's making me feel right now, I know that if I'm smart, Amalie won't be one of those women.

I need to keep my distance from her.

So I do. I force myself to stop looking at her and the pretty blonde and the surfer next to her, and walk over to the bar at the far end of the pool to get a drink. I look for a spot where I might be able to stretch out—somewhere with a good view—and end up on a lounge chair not too far off from the bar, next to a tall, tanned brunette in a skimpy white bathing suit that's clinging damply to her skin and her three friends, all of whom are varying types of gorgeous.

It doesn't take me long to introduce myself. The brunette's name is Holly, and before I know it, she's ordering a round of shots and including me in it, handing me one of the layered concoctions before winking at me and showing me just how quickly she can swallow the shot.

"Maybe we'll do jello shots next," she says with a grin as she sets the glass aside with a shiver—the shots were *severely* alcoholic, even as fruity as they were, and I return the grin.

"That would give me ample opportunity to show you what I can do with my tongue." I wait for her reaction, and I can see the glimmer of interest in her eyes, the way she shifts a little on her lounge chair as she leans closer.

"If you're good with your tongue and I'm good at swallowing...we make quite a pair." Her tongue flicks out over her full lower lip, as if she's imagining something else rubbing against it. "You should come dancing with me and my friends tonight. We're going to that new club—oh fuck, I can't even remember the name. I'm a little tipsy." She giggles, reaching for a bottle of water. "Just come hang out with us. Unless you have other plans."

Other plans. I don't. I came here alone, without the entourage of friends in tow that everyone else seems to have. I wanted the freedom of making my own plans and letting the days play out how they would, without anyone else's opinions or desires getting in the way. I've enjoyed the solitude of my luxurious penthouse in the mornings and the revelry that seems to constantly be on tap in Ibiza for the rest of the time. It's for exactly this reason—so that when a lovely brunette in a very small bikini with a penchant for doing shots asks me to spend more of the day with her, there's no chance of anything else getting in the way.

Which doesn't explain why my gaze flicks over to the side of the pool that I saw Amalie on earlier, looking for that flash of red bikini. Nor does it explain the feeling I have when I see her, and the jealousy that I can see wreathing across her face from here, just for a moment.

I've always despised jealousy in women. Nothing makes me end a fling faster than a woman who wants to know where I'm going or where I've been, who sniffs for hints of someone else's perfume on my clothes, who gets upset because she found something she shouldn't have been looking for in the first place. I've never promised anyone exclusivity, but that hasn't stopped some of them from wanting it and trying to angle for it. And while the women who end up in my bed are usually good about leaving nothing behind, no one's perfect. The reaction I've gotten from someone finding a lipstick left behind or a forgotten piece of clothing has often been enough to make me delete that number from my contacts and move on.

But the look on Amalie's face sparks something else in me. The obvious jealousy on her face, seeing me flirting with another woman across the pool, makes my chest tighten and my cock twitch. It gives me a strange urge to keep flirting with Holly, not because I really care all that much about whether or not she ends up in my bed tonight, but because I want *Amalie* to care.

I glance back at Holly, waving down one of the circulating cocktail waitresses. A petite blonde in a bright blue metallic bikini and a patterned sarong stops, and I flash her a smile.

"A round of jello shots for me and my new friends here. I don't care what flavor."

"Coming right up." The waitress lets her gaze slide over my bare chest for just a moment—just from that look, I feel sure I could have her bent over behind the bar in five minutes if I wanted to—and then sways off to the other end of the pool. She returns with a bucket painted with the resort's logo full of small plastic cups, handing them out to me, Holly, and Holly's friends as I give her my last name for the tab.

Looking over at Holly, I take the shot and flick my tongue out, swirling it around the edge of the plastic cup once before scooping the gelatin onto my tongue and tossing it back. One quick, deft motion, and I see the sly grin on Holly's face before she does something similar, pursing her lips around the cup before scooping the contents out with her tongue and swallowing it all without so much as a flinch.

"Oh, I think we would have fun together." I raise an eyebrow at her, and she returns the look with equal suggestiveness, but I can't help but notice what's missing. I certainly wouldn't mind taking her to bed—I can already imagine what her mouth might feel like on me

—but I don't feel that *need* that I felt last night with Amalie. I hadn't even known what I was missing, until I did, and now the flirtation with Holly feels as if it's falling flat. I could spend the rest of the day and evening with her, and I know I'd enjoy fucking her, but I feel like there's something missing. I almost resent Amalie a little for rousing it in me. I don't need something ruining what pleasure I'm able to get out of my life, and I don't have any real desire to examine why Amalie made me feel the way she did.

I just don't want it to get in the way of enjoying my escape.

"Only one way to find out how much." Holly flutters her eyelashes at me. "I'm going into the pool. Come with me?"

I have no reason to say no. Certainly not Amalie, who is lying on the other side of the pool, tossing back a shot with her friend and laughing at something the surfer next to her says, his hand grazing against her knee in a way that makes my gut twist with that flare of jealousy again. So I follow Holly into the pool—and later that night, after exchanging phone numbers and agreeing to meet up at that club—I find her at the bar as promised, now in a short metallic gold dress, ordering a drink.

"You made it!" She looks thrilled to see me, and it's almost enough to make me feel bad that I don't quite have the same enthusiasm. She's gorgeous—dark hair curled in soft waves and that gold dress clinging to every inch of her body that it covers, perfect legs set off by high heels that look far too precarious for dancing—but there's a flatness to the lust I feel that I never noticed until I had that spark with Amalie. It irritates me, and I go up to the bar, trying to ignore it as I order a drink for myself.

"Gin and tonic for me, and I've got the lady's drink." I hand over my heavy black credit card to the bartender, and I catch the glance that Holly gives it before she turns her wide, dark eyes back on me.

"You didn't have to do that," she breathes, moving a little closer to me. It's a bit early for the bar to be packed, but it's fairly full, the air starting to heat with the combination of the temperature outside and so many bodies inside, the fog of mingled perfume and cologne and rising lust beginning to thicken the air. I feel my pulse quicken as she steps closer, feel my cock twitch with the anticipation of what might happen later. Still, it's nothing compared to what I feel when I hear a familiar laugh over the music, and turn to see Amalie walking past the bouncer at the front door, her blond friend next to her.

That fucking asshole that was sitting by her at the pool is there too, talking to a lean, dark-haired, expensively dressed young man with his arm around the blonde. I grit my teeth, keeping just enough attention on Holly that hopefully, she won't notice my gaze continuously flicking to Amalie as she walks towards the bar.

She's wearing a black bandage dress tonight, a thick gold zipper up the back, and her wide gold hoop earrings are the only accents. She's teetering on high heels similar to what Holly is wearing, and her lush auburn hair is pulled back tonight, braided at one side, and then tied into a thick ponytail.

I can all too easily imagine wrapping my hand around it and guiding her soft lips to my cock, or holding on while I fucked her hard from behind. She didn't go down on me last night, but if I took her back to my penthouse again, there's no reason we couldn't rectify that—

"David?" Holly's voice pierces my thoughts, and I feel her hand on my arm, her pointed nails scratching over my skin. I can easily imagine those nails digging into my shoulders, clawing down my back, and I shiver a little in anticipation of the idea. *There we go. Think about that, and not Amalie's mouth on your cock.* "Is there someone you need to talk to?"

I know the moment she says it, a flicker of jealousy in her voice, that she saw me looking at Amalie. And unlike Amalie's stare across the pool earlier, Holly's jealousy makes me far less interested in her.

"Just for a minute." I'm already walking towards Amalie before I can stop myself, my gaze raking over her gorgeously slender body wrapped up in that dress. I want to slide the zipper down and peel it off of her, or better yet, bend her over and nudge the skirt up her hips. It's so short that it wouldn't take much—and I have no doubt that whatever she has on beneath it, it would be all too easy to simply slip it to one side.

Shame we're not in Europe. Amsterdam, maybe. There are a few places I can think of where I could have done just that—fucked her in public in a bar, and no one would have thought twice about it, except possibly to ask if they could join in. I've never done it person-ally, because I've never been *that* much of an exhibitionist—or even one to fantasize about it, really, until Amalie.

Now, apparently, I can't stop myself from thinking about it.

I start to say her name, but before I can, she takes her drink from the bartender and turns away without even seeing me—or if she does, she doesn't show it. She winds her way through the crowd as I watch her go, the lights glinting off of her dangling earrings, and I see her heading to a corner booth where the friends I saw her come in with are waiting. I have the urge to follow her, but I catch a glimpse of Holly out of the corner of my eye, and force myself to turn away.

My desire for Holly is simple. Uncomplicated. It might lack the intensity of what Amalie made me feel, but it doesn't come with all the extra baggage, either. I'm better off enjoying a night of flirting and dancing with this gorgeous brunette who wants me, taking her back to my penthouse and fucking her however I please, and then sending her off just as I've done with every other woman, every other night.

I can't stop looking for Amalie, though. As the evening winds on, Holly and I do a round of shots and then another, ordering another round of drinks before we finally make our way out onto the dance floor. I can't recall a single word of any conversation we had—I'm not even sure that I responded appropriately, but Holly doesn't seem upset with me, so I must have. She tosses her dark hair back as she grinds against me to the music, her hands on my shoulders as she moves her hips suggestively, and my cock wastes no time taking more of an interest in her than I've been able to summon all night.

"Mm." She leans in, brushing her lips over my neck, her breasts pressing against my chest. "You feel good." She purrs it into my ear, a taste of what tonight will bring if I get her into bed, the things she might whisper in bed, the sounds she might make. I try to focus on that, and not the glimpse of auburn hair that I catch in the shifting crowd. Amalie is dancing with the surfer, his broad hands on her hips, and I remember all too clearly how it felt to have her moving against me like that, her soft ass pressed back against me. I wanted to fuck her from behind, and I didn't. Once I was inside of her, I couldn't think about anything except not stopping. I couldn't think about changing positions, about other things I might want to do to her—anything except how beautiful she looked under me and how good she felt wrapped around my cock.

Holly's lips graze my throat again, her hips gyrating against mine, my hard cock pressed against her. She's moving against me as if she wants to fuck me right here, and I don't have a single shred of doubt that she does. She's already mine if I want her—but I can't seem to focus, and when I look for Amalie in the crowd again, she's vanished.

I have a sudden, gut-wrenching image of her in one of the bathrooms with the guy she'd been dancing on, kneeling down to wrap her lips around his cock or letting him bend her over one of the sinks. It makes me feel vaguely ill, and I tell myself it's just the heat and three days of drinking more than I'm accustomed to.

"I need some water." I lean down so Holly can hear me say it in her ear, and she nods, following me back to the bar. The bartender is swamped, at least ten people away from being able to serve me. When I glance back towards the booth where I saw Amalie with her friends before, I see that they're seated a little ways off now, on a cluster of low couches arranged in a half-circle.

"David." Holly's hand brushes against my arm, and I can hear the slightest note of frustration in her voice. "We could go back to my room. Or yours, if you prefer—"

"I'll be right back." I peel away from her, well aware that it's the second time tonight I've left a sure thing to go and try to talk to a woman who I'm fairly sure is a complication I don't need. I'm not even certain she wants to talk to *me* again, after I made it clear I wanted her to leave last night instead of staying. But I have that moth-to-the-flame feeling again, that sense of being drawn towards something even if I know just how bad it could be for me. It brings me nearly right up to where they're sitting before I see what Amalie is currently doing...or rather, what's being done to her.

The surfer is seated next to her, leaning in to whisper something in her ear, and his hand is sliding up her skirt. His fingers are tracing a pattern on her inner thigh, gliding nearly up to where just last night *I* was touching her, and that burn of jealousy floods through me again, so all-consuming that I can't stand it. I know that what I'm feeling doesn't make sense, that I'm caught up in a jealous rage—a feeling I've never had before—over a woman I barely know, but I'm moving towards him before I can stop myself.

It's the stress, I think, even as I reach for the front of the surfer's shirt, my hand wrapping in the front of it and yanking him up off of the couch. *It's the pressure I'm under*—as I haul him forward, slamming a punch into his jaw that I dimly register, has noise erupting all around us, Amalie coming up off of the couch too to lunge towards me. *It's too much for any one person to handle,* is my last thought before Amalie shoves herself in between us, knocking the surfer back as he clutches his bruising jaw, her green eyes spitting fire as she glares up at me.

"What the hell do you think you're doing?" she demands, her voice high and loud enough to be heard over the music. "What the *fuck*, David?"

"I—" I have no excuse. Nothing I can say that would make my reaction seem more reasonable. The fact that my name on her lips makes me hard isn't good enough. The fact that I feel my pulse beating hard in my veins, my throbbing cock demanding that I back her up against that couch, lay her down, and fuck her senseless, is absolutely not a reason.

"You don't own me after one night," she hisses, her eyes gleaming with a fury that nearly matches mine. And god help me, but it only turns me on more, seeing her like that. I want to grab her and kiss her, drag her mouth against mine, and I nearly reach for her before she slaps my hand away from her waist, glaring at me. "You *told* me to leave last night. You wanted to be done. So we're done. Who do you think you are—"

I glare at her, a flare of annoyance rising up to meet her anger. "Staying the night isn't a prerequisite to fucking again, Amalie. Or don't you know that?" I narrow my eyes, and I see the brief flicker of an odd expression cross her face, one that I don't entirely understand.

"You were *rude* about it," she spits. "You made it very clear that since you'd gotten off, you were done. So don't fucking follow me around afterward, and—"

This time, when I reach for her, she doesn't react in time to stop me. I grab her waist with one hand before I can think better of it, dragging her up against me as my other hand cups her jaw, my fingers aching to sink into her silky hair. I pull her closer, tilting her chin up, and my mouth crashes down onto hers.

She still tastes so fucking sweet, like sugar and apples, and I slip my tongue into her mouth, groaning at the hot slide of it against hers. I feel her freeze and then shudder, her body arching into mine for one blissful, aching moment before she suddenly twists away from me, shoving my chest hard as she backpedals towards the couch.

There are eyes on us—I can feel them. But all I can look at is her, even as she throws me one last hateful glare and turns on her heel to stalk away without another word. For a moment, I nearly follow her for the second time tonight, but I see the girl with the short blonde hair take after her, and I have a distinct feeling that I won't be welcomed.

Which still leaves me with the question that's been rattling in my head since the moment I met her—

What in the *hell* has come over me?

5

AMALIE

I can barely breathe as I dart away from David, pushing my way through the crowd towards the ladies' room. I'm almost certain Claire will follow me, and I'm grateful to have my suspicions confirmed when I push open the door and catch a glimpse of her in the mirror, just behind me.

"What *was* that?" she asks, eyes wide as I sink down onto the pink velvet couch along one wall. The lounge side of the ladies' room is papered in palm-leaf print, a long quartz countertop, and an equally long mirror along one wall. There's a handful of girls in front of it, touching up their makeup and giggling. I barely look at them before I turn back to Claire, who has perched herself on the edge of the couch arm. "Was he—"

"The man I slept with last night? Yeah." I resist the urge to rub my hands over my face—my makeup is impeccable tonight, thanks to my and Claire's combined efforts. I don't feel as if David deserves to be the reason it gets messed up. It occurs to me that I probably should have stopped to find out if Brad was alright, after David's punch to his jaw, but I'm not entirely sure I care. The truth is that I didn't particularly love having his hand up my skirt, but I also wasn't sure yet if I wanted to just go ahead and try sleeping with him, to see how it stacked up. What pisses me off is that *I* didn't get to make the decision.

I have a feeling that Brad isn't going to be quite as interested after this.

"God, I don't even know how to feel about it." Claire's eyes are lit up—it's clear that she's loving every bit of the drama. "On the one hand, having a man fight over you like that is kind of hot. But at the same time—"

"At the same time, who the fuck does he think he is, acting like I'm his wife because we fucked once?" Even I can hear the bitterness in my tone. "It's ridiculous. He can't just drag some other guy off of me when *he's* the one who told *me* to leave last night. I think he made it pretty clear that it was just a one-night thing."

"I'm not so sure he made it clear to himself." Claire laughs, and then slides down to sit next to me. "He's gorgeous, seriously. You definitely picked a good one for your first time. But he does seem a little —clingy."

"He didn't seem that way last night," I mutter, looking down at my clutch and picking at the tiny embroidered beads on one section. I hate feeling like this—like I'm upset that I didn't spend the night, when I really shouldn't care. I'm not *supposed* to care. And it just led to this, which is exactly the sort of thing I wanted to avoid.

I'm going to leave here at the end of the week. Whatever happens here, stays here. There's no point in someone getting jealous of other men when we'll never talk to each other again after this.

"I'm just going to try to avoid him," I tell Claire decisively. "He'll get over it in a day or two. He'll find some other girl—or *girls*, based on what I saw when I first met him—and none of this will matter. And you're right, I should probably go check on Brad."

"Probably—oh." Claire looks at her phone, frowning. "Jean took him back to the hotel—I guess his jaw hurt pretty badly. Should we go back and meet them there?"

A part of me wants to say no, that we should stay out and party until the sun comes up along with everyone else. I feel bad, too, bringing Claire's night to an abrupt halt. But suddenly, most of me very much wants to be in bed. I'd thought I would end the night in bed with *someone*, but right now, I think I just want to sleep.

"I'm going to go back," I tell her, getting up and feeling a little unsteady on my heels. "But you don't have to. I can just call an Uber back to the resort. I think Mandy and Blythe are still here—"

"I'll let them know we're going back." Claire loops her arm through mine, leading me back towards the door. "I'm not letting you leave alone."

There's no sign of David when we leave, not even at the bar, which I can't help but glance at as we go. I don't see the brunette in the gold dress that was with him earlier, either. I feel a twist in the pit of my stomach at the idea of him back in his penthouse with her, sliding that dress up over her body the way he did with me before taking her back to the bedroom.

This is exactly why I need to avoid him, I tell myself firmly as we pile into an Uber and head back to the resort. Those kinds of complicated feelings are precisely what I don't need.

Jean and Brad have already gone up by the time Claire and I get back, and as much as I know I probably should check on Brad, I don't have the energy to. I barely manage to get a makeup wipe across my face and my dress unzipped before I stumble towards my bed, fishing out a tank top to sleep in before collapsing on the mattress as a wave of exhaustion from the sunshine, day-drinking, and adrenaline hits me.

I'm out like a light, and thankfully, I dream of nothing at all.

—

My plan to avoid David works for about half a day.

Claire, Jean, and I grab breakfast at the resort buffet in the morning—there's a station specifically for made-to-order omelets. I get mine with smoked salmon and cream cheese, a luxury I'd never be allowed at home, before sliding into one of the leather-backed booths. Brad is nowhere to be seen, and I don't ask. After a good night's sleep, I've decided that he, at least, isn't going to be one of the notches on my Ibiza bedpost. It feels like it's for the best if we don't talk about it.

Jean, of course, brings it up. "Did you stop by to see if Brad was alright?" he asks neutrally, spearing a bite of sausage, and I see Claire wince.

"I figured he probably wouldn't want to see me." I try to keep my tone casual, but I can already feel myself getting defensive. *Men act like all they want is something casual, but god forbid you flirt for a couple of days and then change your mind.*

"I don't know about that. Maybe he needs to be nursed back to health." Jean chuckles, and Claire elbows him.

"Stop it," she whispers. "Amalie isn't interested."

Jean smirks. "Could have fooled me last night, before that other guy showed up. Claire said something night before last about you coming in late. That who you were with?"

I almost don't want to answer the question—something about Jean's assumption that I'd tell him rubs me the wrong way—but I just nod. "I guess he took it all a little too seriously. I might give the flirting a rest for a bit. Maybe one man is enough for my Ibiza experience."

It's clear from the look on Claire's face that she disagrees with me, but she doesn't argue. And I keep that resolve—all the way until we're in a poolside cabana later that afternoon, three piña coladas deep for me, and I see David with a petite blonde a few cabanas over.

She's sitting on his lap, and I immediately feel a flash of irritation. He's doing the same fucking thing that he flipped out on Brad for last night, but *I'm* not getting up, storming over there and dragging her off of him—because I have no right to.

The thought stops me. *Because I don't* want *to, or just because I don't think I have the* right *to?* Those are two very different things.

My resolve that maybe I've had enough of men for this trip frays, just in time for a tall, deeply tanned man with dark hair to walk over and sink onto the lounge chair next to mine. He introduces himself as Franc, and I catch one glimpse of David's head turning in my direction before I give Franc my full attention, introducing myself and accepting his offer of a drink.

The rest of the day—and the next—goes exactly like that. Claire and her friends are insistent on hitting up all of the best spots, and either David is doing the same, or he's following me. I don't *think* it's the latter, because every time I see him, he's with a different woman, but I also catch him looking at me more often than not. I make a point of talking and flirting with all of the handsome men who approach me, wanting to make sure David has no reason to think I'm mooning over him, but every time one of them tries to take things a little further, I find a reason to turn them down. At night, I go out dancing with Claire and Jean and their friends, and I let men buy me drinks and grind on them on the dance floor, but nothing seems to come anywhere close to the way David made me feel. No one makes me feel that electric jolt in my veins, no one makes my heart pound faster. No one makes me feel as if, just for a moment, I can't breathe.

It feels like David's ruined me for anyone else, and that pisses me off more than anything.

We'll be going home in a few more days, and I know what's waiting for me there. I wanted to enjoy my trip to the fullest before I'm trapped at home again, and it feels like that one night has set a standard that no one else can match. That would have been fine—if only he hadn't been such an asshole about it afterward.

I get up the next morning feeling slightly hungover and as tired as if I'm jet-lagged all over again. Claire is already awake and in the bathroom getting ready, and she pokes her head out when she hears me getting up, her straightener held in one hand.

"We're going for brunch. There's a place with bottomless mimosas that come in ten different flavors, and apparently, they have an *exquisite* breakfast buffet. You're coming too, right?"

I have half a mind to crawl back into bed, pull the covers over my head, and go back to sleep. The pace of our vacation was fun at first, but I'm starting to crave a day of solitude and silence, and I look wistfully out at the private pool just beyond our room. We haven't used it at all—Claire wants to party, not lay out in the quiet—and I wonder if

I could manage to get an afternoon alone there with a drink and a book.

From the expression on Claire's face, I don't think I have a chance at that.

"Sure." I flash her a smile, getting up and walking over to the closet where some of my clothes are hanging. "Just give me twenty minutes or so to get ready?"

She goes to get Jean while I finish freshening up, slipping into a silk-patterned maxi dress. I braid my hair along the sides of my head and loop the ends of it underneath the base of my neck, adding long, dangly earrings, and quickly glance at my reflection. I look tired, and I once more consider the possibility of more sleep before grabbing my clutch and sandals and heading out to meet Claire.

Brunch is, as Claire promised, amazing. "We're going to run back to the room to grab some more sunscreen," she tells me as I finish my last strawberry mimosa. "Just grab an Uber and meet us at the pool we went to yesterday?"

"Sure." I wave for the waiter, considering if I want to order one more mimosa as Claire and Jean get up to leave. I have a feeling there's a reason they're going back that has nothing to do with sunscreen, and I think I probably have time for another drink before they meet me at the pool.

The waiter brings me the bill as I finish that last drink, and I slip my credit card inside of it, not bothering to look at the total. There's no limit on my credit card, even if it *is* only supposed to be for emergencies. So far, my mother doesn't seem to have noticed that it's being used in a very different place than where I'd told her I would be.

I'm supposed to be at home while she's in Boston, discussing some sort of potential marriage prospects for me—something my father would be handling instead, if he were still here. He'd be the one sorting through the sons of mafia consiglieres and underbosses, angling for the best match to improve our family's standing. He tried to achieve just that with a marriage between my brother and the orphaned daughter of Giacomo Mancini—and he failed.

Now he's gone, with my mother the only one left standing to try to salvage what's left., This particular situation gave me the chance to escape. A chance to be free and on my own, just for once.

A chance that comes abruptly to a halt when the waiter returns to my table with a frown on his face.

"I'm very sorry, ma'am. Your card was declined. Do you have another I can run?"

My heart instantly sinks. *No. She wouldn't have done that.* Cutting off my card means leaving me stranded, and I can't imagine my mother would go that far, even if she's angry. "Can you run it again, please?" I ask politely. "It must be an error."

I can tell he's not happy, but he does as I ask. And I feel my stomach clench with a sick twist when he comes back a few moments later, and shakes his head.

"I'm going to need another card, ma'am."

"Just a second. I'll call my bank. Maybe it's the international trans-actions?" I fumble for my phone, feeling my cheeks heat. "Can you just charge it to my hotel while I get this straightened out?"

"Are you staying here?"

I shake my head. *Fuck.* A hot burst of resentment towards Claire fills me, for leaving me like this to go get laid. It would have been embarrassing to have this happen in front of her—and especially Jean—but she would have helped until I could get it straightened out. "No, I'm staying at—"

The waiter interrupts me, his voice curter now. "We can only charge to a room if you're staying here, ma'am. If you don't have another card—"

"Just let me call." I turn my card over with shaking fingers, dialing the number of the bank. My throat tightens as I wait to speak to someone, and it only takes a few minutes for all my fears to be confirmed.

My card has been cut off.

"Ma'am—"

"Just a *minute*," I hiss. "Can I have some privacy, please?" I've never been so rude to someone in my life, but I feel as if I'm about to have a panic attack, and the looming, disapproving expression on the waiter's face is only making it worse. I tap my mother's name in my contacts, trying to breathe as I wait for her to pick up.

"Amalie." Her voice is smooth, as rich and elegant as ever. "I wondered how long it would take you to call."

"What's going on? You can't do this. I'm not going to be able to get home—" I sound breathless, gasping, and I hate myself for it—for how panicked I feel. I want to be calm, to deal with this more maturely, but all I can feel right now is a crashing fear that I'm stranded. Claire might help with a meal, but I don't know if I can rely on her to spot me for the rest of this trip and the flight home. Not that she *couldn't*—but her entire life is predicated on having friends who have money. I've never thought our friendship was anything but rock-solid—but I've never *needed* her like this before. I don't know what her response would be.

"Home from where, darling? Aren't you *at* home?" The tone of my mother's voice says quite clearly that she knows I'm not, and that she's enjoying dragging this out.

"Since you cut off my card, I think you know *exactly* where I am." I can hear the seething tone in my voice. "Mom, *please*. Just turn it back on, and I'll be home in a few days. You can be mad at me then. You can't *strand* me—"

"I most certainly can. Since you've decided to behave this way, you can ask your friends for help." She pauses, allowing the dramatics to sink in. "Don't think I don't have some idea where you sneak off to all the time. I thought it might be alright to allow you a few small rebellions, just to get it out of your system before you got married. But clearly, I was too lenient."

"*Mom*—" The panic wells up, sticking in my throat. "What am I supposed to do about meals? My part of the room—"

"I'm sure they'll help you figure it out. They got you there, didn't they? Now, I have to go—"

"I—"

"Enjoy your vacation, Amalie." The phone goes dead without another word, and I stare at it, acutely aware of the waiter still looking at me.

I try the bank again, trying to convince them that there's been an error and that the card should be turned back on, but nothing works. I dimly hear the waiter saying that he's going to go and get the manager, and hot, humiliated tears well up in my eyes.

I'm going to have to text Claire. I'm going to have to ask her to come back and help me. The shame of it, piled on top of everything else that's happened in the past months, feels like too much to bear.

I didn't cry when I found out my father was dead. I didn't cry when my brother was shipped off to Sicily to learn a lesson. And I didn't cry when my mother told me that I was still going to be expected to marry for the good of the family—that it might be our only saving grace, now.

But all at once, hot tears well up, and I can't hold it back any longer. They spill over, my entire body shuddering with a gasp, and I burst into tears right there at the table.

Just as I hear a voice ask behind me, with a dry sort of amusement—

"Are the mimosas here really *that* bad?"

6

DAVID

The joke might have been in poor taste. But I couldn't help it. It's felt as if Amalie has been tormenting me for days—managing to be at every party hot spot that I've ended up at, flirting with every handsome man who so much as says hello to her as if to spite me on purpose. And now I've shown up just in time to see her—for some reason I can't possibly fathom—sobbing out in the open alone at a table.

Part of me thinks I shouldn't get involved at all. She clearly didn't appreciate my intrusion before, when I pulled that asshole off of her that had his hand up her skirt. She hasn't spoken to me since, even though I *know* she's seen that we've been at the same places. And if my guesses are correct, she's been trying to make me jealous on purpose.

Not that I haven't been doing a little of that myself. But whatever is causing her tears, it's likely drama of the type that I don't want to get involved in.

You don't want complications, I remind myself as I walk toward her. *She's a college student, she said. She's probably fighting with a friend. It could be anything. This has nothing to do with you.*

So why, then, do I feel as if I'm being pulled by a magnet up to the edge of her table, as if, once again, I can't resist her allure?

I haven't stopped thinking about her since the night I took her back to my hotel. That alone is enough reason to stay away. But all the same, I find myself standing there, looking down at her as I make an entirely inappropriate joke.

"Are the mimosas here really *that* bad?"

She gasps, startled, and wipes nervously at her face. She's crying too hard for it to do much, and I pull out the chair next to her, sitting down, and handing her the only clean napkin I see. "God, this is embarrassing," she whispers, dabbing the napkin against her eyes. "I've never done this before."

"Cried in public?" I wince, hearing myself make light of it again, but she seems to bring the desire to needle her out in me, even when I know I should be kinder. "Did your friends leave you here?" I'm not even sure why I'm prying for what's wrong. I shouldn't care. But the questions seem to come out before I can stop them. "What's happened that's so awful?"

Amalie's face is tear-streaked, her eyes red, and somehow, she's still impossibly gorgeous. "I can't—" she sniffles again, covering her face with her hands as the napkin drops to her lap. "I can't even say it. It's too humiliating."

I'm on the verge of giving up and walking away—I came here for a late brunch, not to pry a story out of a girl I spent one night with— when I see a waiter walking towards the table, a man who can only be the manager in tow. It's at that moment that I spy the credit card and Amalie's phone sitting haphazardly on the table, see the unpaid bill, and get an inkling of what might be going on.

"Is there a problem with your card?" I ask quietly, and Amalie flinches, looking up at me with freshly-welling eyes. "Surely it's just an international thing. Call and sort it out. I'll even distract the waiter with banal conversation while you—"

"I tried." Her voice is a small, humiliated whisper. "It's not—it's my mother. She cut it off."

Oh, this is delicious. A spark of an idea forms in my head the instant she says it, as the situation becomes clear to me. A spoiled rich girl, here in Ibiza with her friends, probably without telling her parents where she's going. Now Amalie is finding out the consequences—and even though I know what I'm considering is wrong on so many levels, I can't help but entertain the idea. After all, it's not like she didn't enjoy the night in my bed. And I could enjoy so much more, if I let myself use this to my advantage.

"I take it you didn't get *permission* to run off to Ibiza for your spring break?" I ask her dryly, and I see her cheeks heat, flushing a bright red. She has a sprinkling of light freckles on her nose and cheeks, and the blush brings them out. I find myself wanting to graze my lips over them, an urge that I find as unsettling as the desire for her that I can't seem to shake.

"What do you think?" she asks tartly, and I chuckle.

"No need to take that tone with me, young lady," I murmur. My voice is teasing, but I see her flush deeper, and I know it did something to her. *Oh, this could be so much fun.* "I might just be able to save your pretty ass, if you're open to ideas."

She glares at me, her mouth opening as if to retort, but at that moment, the waiter and the manager arrive at the table. Before either of them can say a word, I slip my thin leather billfold out and hand the manager my black credit card.

"I'll take care of it," I tell him smoothly. "Just give us a few moments of privacy."

"Of course, sir." They're gone in an instant, and I turn all of my attention back to Amalie.

"See how easy that was?" I raise an eyebrow. "I'm guessing you planned on staying here a little longer, at least. Are your friends going to help you with your problem?"

Her teeth sink into her lower lip, and her gaze flicks down to the table. "I don't know," she admits, her voice turning small again.

"I'll be in Ibiza for another week." I lean forward, reaching out to slip my fingers under her chin, tilting her face upwards so that she's looking at me. "You can stay in the penthouse with me, if you like. I'll pay for everything, treat you like a princess—but you have to agree to one thing."

There's a flicker of suspicion in Amalie's eyes. "What's that?" she asks, her voice still trembling a little, and I have to fight the urge to run my fingers over her lower lip.

"You have to agree to do whatever I want for the week," I murmur, low and seductive, quiet enough that only she can hear. My hand brushes along her jaw, and I see her eyes widen, the struggle in her between what I'm offering and her pride. "You'll be my pretty toy for the week. Mine to please and enjoy. I'll give you anything you want, but you have to do the same for me."

She wants to resist. I can see it. Her gaze flicks towards her credit card, the indecision warring in her face, and then she looks back at me. There's desire in her eyes—for me, for what I can do for her, or both. I'm not sure which it is, but it's there all the same.

Her teeth dig into her lip. "Alright," she whispers softly. "For the rest of the week. Whatever you want."

There's a spark of anticipation in her eyes, and that, combined with the heady knowledge that she's just agreed to be mine for an entire week, has my blood rushing with excitement, my cock twitching with arousal. "Let's go back to my suite then, if you're serious." I give her a challenging look. "Right now."

Her breath catches slightly, but she nods. She stands up, and I stand with her, taking her hand as I lead her toward where I've already texted my driver to be waiting.

This time, I don't touch her in the car. The building anticipation is too good, watching her tension grow as we near my hotel. She texted her friend almost as soon as we left—with some excuse, I'm sure, although I doubt it's the entire truth—and since then, she's sat an arm's length away from me, chewing nervously on her lower lip.

"You're acting as if it's your first time," I tell her teasingly, and she flushes all over again.

"I've never been someone's sugar baby before," she mumbles, and I laugh.

"Is that what this is? I thought it was just a friendly arrangement."

I touch her arm, sliding my fingers down towards her hand, and I feel her shiver. Even that touch does something to her, and I have plans to touch her in so many more intimate ways.

But first, I have other things I want to do.

The moment we're inside my penthouse, the door firmly closed behind us, I stride into the open living room and sink down onto one of the sofas. I lean back, legs spread, enjoying the look of confused uncertainty on Amalie's face. "On your knees," I tell her carelessly, gesturing to the space between my legs. "Show me just how grateful you are for how I saved you back at that restaurant."

Her face flushes all over again, and I see an angry pinch between her eyes. I raise my eyebrows, gesturing again. "Don't make me ask twice, *bellisima*. Or would you like to leave, and go tell your friends about your little situation?"

"You're blackmailing me. Or is it extortion?" She narrows her eyes. "What *is* the right term for this?"

"It's neither," I tell her simply. "It's an offer. The rest of your vacation in luxury, without a care in the world, despite the little hitch in your plan that your mother caused this morning. And in exchange, I want you to get down on your knees and take care of my cock for me. I'm hard, and I want to come."

"That's not the only thing you want," she whispers, and her gaze flicks to the ridge in my suit trousers where my cock is pressing against my fly. I was already aroused on the drive here, but this little conversation has gotten me achingly hard. Something about seeing her standing there, entirely at my mercy, makes me harder than I've been in years.

"No," I admit. "But it's a start. Now make up your mind, *bellisima*. On your knees, or leave."

She glances towards the door, indecision still flickering on her face. And then she takes a step towards me, and another, until she sinks down onto her knees in between my legs, and reaches for my belt.

God, she's fucking gorgeous. Her hair is braided back, but little pieces of it have fallen out, framing her beautiful face and full, plush lips as she leans forward to undo my belt. My cock jerks as her wrist brushes against it, her fingers drawing my zipper down, and I groan when she slips her fingers inside, freeing my cock as her hand wraps around the taut, aching shaft.

"You're so big," she whispers, and I laugh softly.

"Flattery will get you everywhere," I promise her, reaching out to pluck a few of the pins from her hair. I start to lazily undo it as she runs her fingers along my shaft, teasing the length of it, almost as if she's getting used to the feeling of having me in her hand. *She really must not be all that experienced*, I think, as she plays with me, but I'm not sure that I mind. There's something about her exploration that I enjoy, which surprises me. Usually, I'd want a girl to get down to business faster.

That doesn't mean I'm going to be patient forever. "I put you on your knees because I want your mouth," I tell her sternly, as I slide my fingers through her loosening braids to send her hair tumbling over her shoulders. It's thick and wavy from the braids, and I wrap my hand in it, tugging her mouth towards my straining cock. "Suck my cock, *bellisima*."

Her face flushes at the order, but I see the way she shifts on the floor, her breath catching lightly. *She likes it*, I realize, storing the thought away for later. It's exactly what I hoped for, and I groan low in my throat as her lips graze over my cockhead, her tongue flicking out to lap up the beading pre-cum there.

"Good girl." I stroke her hair with my other hand, shifting as I tug her head closer, my hips lifting to push my cock against her mouth. "Open your mouth."

She obeys, her lips parting around my tip, and the soft, warm wetness of her mouth is fucking incredible. She doesn't seem to know much about sucking a cock—her teeth graze against me as she takes my swollen head into her mouth, and her suction is a little too light, her lips struggling to wrap around me—but somehow, it doesn't matter. Somehow it almost feels *better* than the expert blowjobs I've been getting from the women who have easily fallen into my bed this week. I have the fleeting thought, as she slides me over her tongue and starts to suck harder, that this might feel better than any blowjob I've ever gotten. I can't put my finger on why, but as she looks up at me with wide green eyes, sliding down another inch, I feel my balls tighten warningly.

"Good girl," I murmur, running my fingers through her hair. "Just take it a little at a time. Just like that. *Fuck*—" I feel myself brush against the back of her tongue, sliding a little into her throat, and the way her eyes squeeze shut as she chokes a little makes my cock throb painfully.

"You look so good like this. So fucking beautiful." I wrap my hand in her hair again, tugging her mouth down further, pushing myself into her throat. "Take it all, *bellisima*. I know you can do it."

She chokes again, her eyes looking up at me pleadingly as if to say *I can't*, but I'm enjoying it too much to let her go. A feeling of power surges through me, along with the aching pleasure from the heat of her mouth. I thrust up between her lips, dragging her mouth down to the base of my cock as I feel her throat muscles clench and squeeze around me. It's every bit as good as her pussy was, and I plan to enjoy both as often as I can for the next week.

I let her go for a moment, let her come up, and catch her breath. She gasps as my cock pops out of her mouth, hard and glistening with her saliva, her lips chafed and red and still an inch away from it. She looks gloriously lewd like this, her hair a mess and her mouth swollen, her eyes teary from the effort of deep-throating me.

"I don't know if I can—" she breathes, looking down at my cock again. "What if we—"

"No, Amalie." I see the way she sucks in another breath as I purr her name, her thighs squeezing together under the skirt of her dress. "You're going to make me come with that pretty mouth, and then you're going to swallow it all. Don't make me wait."

There's a warning in my tone, and she heeds it. She leans forward, her hand wrapping around the base to give her throat a break as she takes me in her mouth again, that heat enveloping me as I wrap my hand in her hair and groan. I can still feel that occasional bump of her teeth, the moments when she loses her rhythm, but it's all forgotten in the utter pleasure of the control I have over her. That, as much as anything else, drives me towards my climax. I thrust up into her mouth again, both hands in her hair and on her head as I start to fuck her face, driving my cock deeper as she gasps and chokes around my thick length.

"I'm going to come in your mouth, *bellisima*," I groan, one hand sliding to the back of her neck. "Swallow every drop for me. That's a good girl, *fuck*—"

I thrust again, feeling her hot tongue slide along the length, her lips sucking, the pressure of her throat around my cockhead. I think of how I got her here, of that perfectly executed manipulation that led to this girl who's teased me for days on her knees, choking on my cock while I fill her throat with my cum.

It sends me over the edge. A deep, almost animal noise rips from my throat as I drag her mouth all the way down, thrusting between her lips as my cock swells and hardens, shooting hot cum down her throat. I feel her choke, feel her splutter around me, but it only adds to the pleasure as I throb between her lips, flooding her mouth with my cum as my fingers dig into the back of her head.

"Fucking—*take it*—*fuck*—" I moan aloud, wanting to keep her pinned down like this on my cock forever, for the exquisite pleasure to never end. But I also don't want to suffocate her. I let go of her hair, letting her slide off of my length as she sucks in a breath, a little of my cum slipping out of the corner of her mouth and dripping down the full curve of her lip. I reach out, gently pushing it back between her lips, and the small moan that she lets out, coupled with the way her lips automatically close around the tip of my thumb, makes my half-hard cock twitch all over again.

She looks up at me expectantly, still on her knees, and I chuckle. I know the look on her face, that flush of arousal on her cheeks. Sucking my cock turned her on, and now she's hoping I'll return the favor.

I intend to eventually, in spades. But for now, this was about a different lesson. For the week that she's agreed to, I own her. And her pleasure is at *my* whim, not hers.

I reach for her, pulling her up off of her knees and into my lap, and she doesn't resist even a little. Her swollen lips part on a small gasp as she slides onto my lap, her silky skirt pushed up high on her thighs, and I see her cheeks flush deeper as she leans in, her hands on my shoulders.

With a quick movement, I stop her from kissing me, my hand pressing against her jaw as my thumb brushes over her cheekbone. "Did that get you wet, *bellisima*? Having my cock in your mouth?"

"Why don't you find out?" There's a light, teasing challenge in her voice, and her attitude sends a fresh spark of desire through me, a jolt of lust straight between my thighs. My cock twitches with renewed interest, but I ignore it for the moment, focusing on the lesson at hand.

She reaches for my other hand, and I quickly slip it free, grabbing hers and pressing it against the outside of her thigh. "Oh no, *cara mia*. I haven't forgotten how things have been the last few days. You've been teasing me on purpose; I've seen it. Flirting with other men where I can see, making sure that I know just how much *everyone* who crosses your path here wants you. But now, for this week, you're *mine*. And your first lesson is that if you want to come, you'll have to show me just how good of a girl you can be."

I brush my thumb down to her lower lip, pressing the pad of it against the full, soft flesh. "You did a good job, *bellisima*, down on your knees. So maybe tonight, you'll earn a reward."

She wants to argue. I can see it in her face, in the flash of frustration in her eyes. She wants to fight me on this. For a moment, I think she might try—and then she lets out a small breath, and I know she's remembered what I've offered her.

I could have spent my week fucking my way through Ibiza, seeing just how many women I could seduce into my bed before I inevitably have to go home to my responsibilities. But this—

I think with Amalie, I've just made my vacation *so* much more interesting. And I'm eager to find out just how entertaining she can be.

7

AMALIE

I 'm not sure a man has ever pissed me off so much with his attitude. *How* dare *he be upset with me for flirting in front of him, when he was doing the same damn thing all week?* I open my mouth to say it, to spit it back into his face—then I remember what the consequences of doing that would be.

He's offered to single-handedly get me out of the situation I've found myself in. Without that, I have no idea what I'll do. The thought of telling Claire, of begging for her help, is even worse than the thought of going along with this. At least this—

The control he has over me is humiliating, forcing me to exchange sex for his help—but I can't deny that it turns me on, too. I was wet from the moment he ordered me to my knees, and if I'm angry with him for his attitude and his tone right now, I also would gladly let him slip inside of me and fuck me senseless if he decided to. *It's one week,* I tell myself as I look down at his implacable expression, feeling myself clench at the thought of the things he could make me do and how very close his bare cock is to me, just below where I'm hovering over his lap. One week of whatever debauchery this man can think of, one week of submitting to his pleasure, and enjoying the lewd, forbidden thrill that gives me. One more week of vacation, without a worry in the world.

And then I'll go home and be the perfect mafia bride that my mother wants, and that my family name demands.

"How can I show you that I'm a good girl for you?" I whisper, leaning forward. His hand is still covering mine, broad and warm, and I so desperately want him to slip it under my skirt. "What do you want?"

David smirks, his other hand slipping into my hair, his fingers threading through it. "Well, to start—what were your plans for the day, *cara mia*?"

"I was supposed to meet Claire and our friends at the pool. She went off with her boyfriend to—" I flush. "I'm sure you can guess. She told me to head over there after I finished my drink. And then—well, you know what happened."

"I do." David's gaze slides down my face, resting on my lips, dropping lower to look at my slight cleavage in the silk dress. "Call her and let her know you're sorry for running late. Let her know you'll be right over."

I blink at him. "Will I?"

"Of course." His hand leaves mine, sliding down to the bare skin of my thigh just above my knee. "We both will."

Shit. I hadn't thought about that. Claire and her friends are still here for a few days, and she's going to expect me to hang out with them as if nothing happened—because she has no idea that anything *has* happened. I don't want her to know, either—and I *want* to spend time with her. I came here for that—getting laid was a secondary concern.

But if David is with me, that's going to raise questions. I definitely don't want her to know the situation or that, regardless of what he says, he's absolutely my sugar daddy for the next week. The idea that I would need one at all is humiliating, and I feel certain that she'll see it the same way.

I think David sees the hesitation on my face, because he raises an eyebrow.

"Are you going to fight me on this, *cara mia*?" His thumb rubs slow circles above my knee. "I want your time. I don't object to you spending it with your friends, but I'll be there, too."

"You just don't want me flirting with anyone else," I accuse, feeling a small spark of annoyance. He's agreed to pay for everything, true, and he's extending my vacation—*but does he have to be so fucking high-handed about it all.* "Isn't there anything else you could be doing?"

David shrugs. "There's nothing else I *want* to be doing," he says calmly. "So call your friend, Amalie. Unless you want to discuss the terms of this again?"

The threat is light, but implicit. I lean over, reaching for where I dropped my clutch, and his hands press against my thighs, holding me in place on his lap while I reach for my phone.

"Good girl," he murmurs, as I find Claire's name in my contacts. The moment I hear the click of her answering, his fingers slip to the inside of my thigh, and my pulse leaps in my throat as I realize what I think he's about to do.

A part of me wants to tell him to stop—and another part of me is embarrassingly turned on by the idea.

"Amalie?" Claire's voice sounds a little concerned. "Are you alright? Jean and I took longer than I expected, and we *still* made it to the pool before you. Did something happen?"

David's fingers slide up my thigh, close to the edge of my panties. I sink my teeth into my lower lip, forcing myself not to gasp, not to make a sound that might let Claire know what he's up to. "Just a little —detour. I'm fine, I promise. I had one more drink and—" I swallow hard, biting my lip harder as I feel him nudge my panties to one side. "I ran into David." *No point in hiding it; she's going to know soon anyway. Better to tell her on my own terms.*

"David?" Claire's voice raises an octave. "You mean the guy you—"

"Slept with? Yeah." I cut her off before she can say something like *lost your virginity to*, which is the last fucking thing I want David to know. "We—"

David's fingers slip between my folds, and I see the satisfied smile that spreads over his face when he feels how wet I am for him. I have the sudden urge to slap it away, as his fingers slide down to my entrance, circling but not slipping inside the way I so desperately want them to.

"Oh, I know what you did." Claire laughs. "Good for you. Are you still coming to the pool? I wouldn't blame you if you didn't—"

It's hard to focus on what she's saying. David's fingers are everywhere except where I need them to be—sliding to just beneath my swollen, aching clit, down to my entrance, over my soft folds, but nowhere that would actually give me the pleasure I so desperately want. It's taking everything in me to try to sound normal—to *breathe* normally, to not moan every time his fingers slide against my drenched pussy, and I clench my teeth.

I want to stay here, in bed with him. I want his tongue on me again. I want his cock inside of me. I want to get fucked, and I want him to be the one to do it. That's what he wants too, I'm sure of it, but I also know he intends to be as maddeningly in control of the entire situation as he possibly can be—and he's already given me the instructions he wants me to carry out.

Which makes me want to do the exact opposite, and tell Claire I won't be making it to the pool.

Remember what happens if you disobey. I can feel the jerk of the invisible leash he has on me, and I *hate* the way it makes me clench and throb, the hot ache that spreads through me at the idea of being so utterly manipulated and controlled. It makes me briefly hate *him* —at the same time, I want him more than I've wanted anyone else I've met or flirted with so far.

"No, I'm coming." I hear David's chuckle as I say it, the smirk on his face at the double entendre that I know is going through his head. "I have a bikini and sunscreen in my bag; you don't need to grab anything for me. I'll be on my way in just a few minutes."

"Okay. Just text me when you get here." Claire's voice is breezy and light, and when she hangs up, I let out a breath of relief that she didn't seem to realize that anything is wrong.

"You're not going to come yet." David's lips twitch in that infuriating smirk as he rubs me once more, letting his fingertips *just* graze my clit. And then he takes his fingers away, tugging my panties back into place before he lifts me up off of his lap and sets me to one side. He's hard again, his cock pressed against the front of his trousers, but he maneuvers himself back into his fly and zips up as if it doesn't matter to him a bit.

"I'm just going to go get changed," he says, standing up. "You should do the same. And then I'll have my driver take us." He smiles at me, and I can't resist looking at the outline of his cock as he stands, pressing against his fly. It seems ridiculous to me for us to both be frustrated when I'm right here and willing, and infuriated that I know he's doing it on principle.

That smirk passes over his mouth again, and I know he can see all of my thoughts on my face.

"This is going to be quite a week for us both, Amalie," he says softly, bending to kiss me lightly, his fingers grazing lightly over my lips as he pulls away. I can taste myself on his fingertips. "I'm looking forward to it."

As he walks away, it's hard for me to pretend that I'm not, too.

At least a little bit.

—

I can tell, when we get to the pool, that Claire has questions. But David doesn't leave my side long enough for her to ask me any of them, not until I go to the ladies' room and she follows me. She wastes no time the second we're alone, her eyes bright with that eagerness that I know means she's going to demand every bit of information she can get.

"So, are you a *thing* now? I mean—while you're here, anyway. Is it just him for the next few days until we leave? I can't blame you—he's gorgeous."

"Well—" I nibble at my lower lip anxiously. "That's the thing. I'm actually staying an extra week. And I'm—he asked me to stay with him. At his penthouse. Starting tonight."

I can see the mixture of glee and disappointment in Claire's face.

"Shit," she breathes. "Well—is that what you want to do? I mean, our girl time in the evenings is fun—it's part of the vacation. But if it was me, I can't say I wouldn't do the same. He has a *penthouse*?"

I can hear the mingled admiration and jealousy in her voice. Even Claire and her friends, with their access to their parents' money and credit cards, don't have penthouse suites here. The kind of luxury David is providing me with is beyond even the kind of vacation they expect here, and it makes me wonder, briefly, what it is that he does. He must be some sort of billionaire, but doing *what* exactly?

It doesn't matter, I remind myself. *One week of fun, and then you'll never see him again.*

"He does." I let out a breath. "I'm sorry—I can tell him no, if you want—"

I almost tell her the truth. A part of me wants to know if our friendship is close enough that she would help me, rather than telling me to rely on David's generosity—or worse still, wanting nothing to do with me if I'm no longer as flush as they all are.

But I can't bear the humiliation twice in one day. And—

I don't know if I want the excuse to turn David down.

"No. Absolutely not." Claire shakes her head vehemently. "You deserve this! We'll have more fun together once you come back to Chicago. Enjoy yourself with him. Enjoy the *penthouse*." She grins at me, and I feel a flicker of relief.

It's all going to be okay.

"What are you going to do about school? You'll miss a week of class—"

"I'll get the notes from you when I come back. It's just a week. It'll be fine." School feels like the last worry on my mind right now—there's no telling what's waiting for me at home when I get back. But that's just another reason to delay it as long as possible.

"You're going to keep living it up here, and you want me to take notes for you?" Claire clicks her tongue, shaking her head teasingly. "What do I get out of this?"

"My undying gratitude?" I look at her pleadingly, hoping she won't ask too many more questions, and she laughs.

"Of course. I wouldn't want you to miss out on this. Now come on," she says, looping her arm through mine. "Let's get back out into the sunshine."

When we've had our fill of laying out in the sun and fruity drinks, I go back to the hotel room to get my things. There's a small pang of regret in my chest as I pack up, knowing that the part of this vacation that's spending time with my best friend in paradise is over. I question, once more, if I ought to just tell her the truth. But it feels like that time has passed, and I meet David back at his car, letting him know that I have dinner plans with Claire and her friends. "I assume you want to come too?" I glance at him as I slide into the car, and he smirks.

"Were you planning on sending me off to dinner alone? Or maybe you thought I'd sit in my suite and wait for you?" His hand squeezes my thigh under the thin linen dress that I threw over my bikini. "I plan to enjoy every second with you that I've bought this week, Amalie. And I promise, you'll enjoy it too."

At first, I'm not entirely sure that he's wrong. Getting ready in his penthouse suite *is* an experience. I have the huge, luxurious bathroom all to myself, and while I don't feel comfortable scattering my things around like I had in the room I shared with Claire, not jockeying for counter space is a pleasant change.

The look on David's face when I step out of the bathroom sends a shiver of desire through me. I picked linen shorts embroidered with red flowers and a silky red camisole for dinner tonight—the neckline of the top low enough to show the edge of the cream-colored lace bralette that I have on underneath it—and high-heeled wedge sandals. I curled my hair, leaving it thick and loose around my shoulders, and the shorts are brief enough that I see David's gaze lingering on my legs. It makes me wonder if he's imagining them wrapped around him.

He steps forward, his hands landing on my waist and curling against the silk of my top as he pulls me in for a kiss, his lips hot and soft against mine. "You *have* been a very good girl," he murmurs, his palms sliding down to my hips and pulling me closer, letting me feel the swelling shape of his cock against me. "I think I might reward you, when we get back."

"You could reward me now." I can't help the words as they slip out, and I can't help the way my hips arch against him, teasing him the same way he's teasing me. I've been *aching* ever since he brought me up here earlier, and every hour laying out in the sun and looking at his tanned, muscled body in nothing but black board shorts just made me feel it even more.

"Good girls are patient." He kisses the tip of my nose, lightly, and takes my hand, pointedly ignoring the tiny whimper that I can't help but let out. "Let's go."

Dinner is at a beachside restaurant that Claire said she was dying to try out, and after just the appetizer, I can see why. The food is delicious, and the pitcher of sangria that she ordered is better. All of it combined with David next to me, his hand sliding along my thigh, makes it feel like a perfect evening.

Until Claire—innocently, I'm sure—mentions what happened this morning.

"That was quite a coincidence, you running into Amalie this morning," she says with a teasing smile. "Unless you've been keeping tabs on her. I wouldn't blame you—I don't think anyone else here could measure up." Her tone is sweet, but I wonder if she's testing him a little—making sure that he's someone she thinks is safe for me to stay with for another week. It's a gesture I'd appreciate, if it wasn't for the fact that it might mean she finds out everything I don't want her to know.

Which is, of course, exactly what happens.

"Oh, I wasn't keeping tabs." David smiles, taking another sip of his sangria. "But I saw a damsel in distress, and I like to think of myself as a gentleman. How could I not help?"

Claire frowns. "I don't know what you mean. Amalie said everything was fine." She looks at me confusedly.

There's that twitch of a smirk on his lips, the one that always makes me want to slap it away. "She was most definitely *not* fine," he says with a laugh. "But it was an easy enough problem to fix. And worth it, considering the fact that she's all mine for a week now, in exchange. I can already see how much she likes being spoiled by me, don't you, *bellisima*?"

His hand squeezes my thigh, his voice teasing, but I feel the heat burning through me that has nothing to do with desire. It's mingled rage and shame instead, feeling all of my friends' eyes on me as David tells them in so many words that I needed help—a sort of help that they can probably guess at—and makes it very clear what sort of arrangement we've made.

For one awful second, I think I'm going to burst into tears in front of all of them. I wrench away from David, nearly knocking my chair over in my hurry to get up, and rush away from the table.

The tears start almost as soon as I turn away, and I rush towards the bathroom, needing a moment of privacy. I hear Claire call after me, but I ignore it. The moment I'm inside, I go straight to the sink and turn on the cold water, splashing it over my face as I try to breathe normally.

A moment later, I hear the door open.

"I just need a minute." I grip the edges of the sink, not looking up. I assume it's Claire, and normally, I'd be happy to have her here to talk this out with me, but I don't think I can stand it under these circumstances. She's going to have questions, and I don't want to answer any of them.

"That was rude." David's voice is low and flat, and I gasp without meaning to. I hadn't expected him to follow me in here, and I look up sharply.

"Get *out*," I hiss, glaring at him. "You're not supposed to be in here."

"I don't see anyone stopping me." He smirks at me, walking closer, and I can see the hungry, predatory gleam in his eyes. He's angry with me, but he still wants me—and that excites me more than it should. "What, are you mad that your friends out there know what this really is? That I'm spoiling you in exchange for getting to use your body however I like?" He steps up next to me, reaching out and pushing a lock of my hair behind my ear. "I could have told them *everything*, but

I didn't. They don't know about your money problems, or how your mother abandoned you here."

"And I'm supposed to be grateful for that?" I glare at him, seething, and he laughs. It's a low, dark sound, deep in his throat, and it sends a ripple of desire down my spine that I tell myself I don't want.

"You *should* be grateful for what I'm offering you. You might be embarrassed about our little deal, Amalie, but you embarrassed *me* out there by storming off. And I don't appreciate that one bit." His gaze darkens, and my breath catches in my throat. "Pick your skirt up, *cara mia*. All the way to your waist."

I stare at him, feeling my cheeks flush hot. "Someone could walk in," I whisper, and he shrugs.

"And if they do?"

"You can't—I'll be—we'd be kicked out. *That's* embarrassing—"

"No, *bellisima*. No one is throwing me out of anywhere. You can trust me on that."

There's a certainty in his voice, an arrogance that tells me that what he's saying is absolutely true—or at the very least, he believes that it is. *Who is he?* I think with another shudder, my pulse beating wildly in my throat.

"Undo your shorts and slide them down." The order is clear in his tone. "Or you can go back to your friends and tell them the truth, and see how you fare."

This is blackmail. That must be the word for it. It's wrong, and it's humiliating. My teeth clench with fury at his arrogance and manipulation—but my hands reach for the button of my shorts anyway, undoing it as David turns off the running water, anticipation hot in his eyes.

"I told you that you would need to be a good girl, *cara mia*. Now I think it's time for another lesson."

His hand touches the bare curve of my ass, slowly rubbing over the smooth flesh. I wore a thong under my shorts, and I feel my face burn red as they hit the floor, leaving me nearly bare from the waist down. I've never been exposed like this, and I'm painfully aware that someone could walk in at any moment—Claire, or one of our other friends, or a complete stranger. I'm not sure which option would be worse.

"Don't be afraid to let me hear just how much you enjoy this, *bellisima*," David murmurs, pure satisfaction in his voice—and then his hand comes down with a sharp *crack* against my bare ass.

I almost let out a yelp. My teeth sink into my lower lip, hard enough to draw blood, my hands clutching the side of the sink, the air sucked out of me as I gasp. No one has ever hit me in my life. I'm not at all prepared for the pain of the slap—but I'm also not prepared for the way the burn that follows it seems to jolt straight between my legs, sending a flush of a different kind of heat through me.

"Such a pretty shade of red." David's hand comes down again, and I close my eyes. It hurts, and it feels good, and with each subsequent spank, I feel the heat between my legs growing, the ache building. I want to reach between my legs and rub my clit while he spanks me, but I feel absolutely certain that doesn't fall under his definition of *being a good girl*.

If he doesn't fuck me by the end of the night, I think I might actually die.

I let out a shuddering gasp of relief when I feel his hand slip between my thighs, his fingers finding my clit with that same expert quickness that they did in the car. "I promised you a reward," he murmurs, his fingers sliding back and forth, and I realize with a jolt that there's going to be nothing slow or teasing about this. He's going to make me come as fast as he can, and it won't take long. My knuckles are white where I'm gripping the edge of the sink, my entire body on fire, and the thought that someone could walk in and catch us at any moment only heightens everything I'm feeling.

"I want to hear you moan my name when you come," he growls, his fingers pressing down on my clit, rubbing so firmly that I think my knees might buckle. I feel that pressure unfurling, the sudden drop over the edge that makes my legs go weak, and my mouth open on a desperate cry of pure pleasure as the orgasm crashes over me. If anyone walked by at this moment, they would hear me doing exactly as he asked—moaning his name aloud as I come, drenching his fingers in my arousal.

"You like this, don't you?" he murmurs, as if he can hear my thoughts. "Knowing someone could walk in at any moment and see you like this. You'd never admit it, but it's turning you on."

I hear the sound of his zipper behind me, and his hand grips my shoulder, spinning me around while I'm still gasping and trembling from my climax. He pushes me down to my knees before I can even fully register what's happening, and I see his hard cock hovering in front of my face, his hand gripping it tightly.

"Open your mouth, Amalie," he murmurs, his voice a low, rasping growl. It sends a shiver of desire through me, and I open my mouth without thinking, looking up at him wide-eyed as the tip of his cock hovers over my tongue, and he starts to stroke.

There's a fierce, hot lust in his eyes as he does that startles me—and frightens me a little. There's an intensity to him that I haven't seen before, and when his hand goes to my hair, gripping it as he strokes himself over my tongue, I don't know whether to be afraid or aroused. I'm both, I think, trembling there on the tile floor as his hand rhythmically slides along his length, jerking himself to a climax as he stares down at my face and obediently open mouth.

"So—fucking—*gorgeous*," he growls, rubbing the tip over my tongue for a moment, his hand squeezing around himself. "God, I want to come all over your fucking face. I should—should send you back out there to your friends with your face covered in it—"

He's about to come. I can see him visibly throbbing, his cock stiffer than I've ever seen it, and I'm shaking all over with anticipation. *I don't really* want *him to do that, do I?* The thought is horrifying—but it also turns me on, making me clench. My thighs squeeze together at the thought of him painting my face with his cum and taking me back out to the dinner table like that. *What on earth is wrong with me?*

I hate domineering men. My whole life has always been filled with them. My father, a mafia underboss, the men who worked for him, my brother—who was always even more arrogant and full of himself than even my father. Everyone who moved within our inner circle, everyone who sought to find a way in, all of those men exuded power and control, and it always made me want to get as far away from them as possible.

I don't know why David makes me feel differently. The only possible answer I have is how far removed from all of that he is—how completely outside the life that I've been forced to live.

The first salty splash of his cum on my tongue jolts me out of my thoughts, his groan of pleasure reverberating through me as he pushes himself into my mouth, my lips closing around him without a thought. He moans as I suck hard, his cum flooding over my tongue, his hand gripping my hair as he bows forward, his other hand grabbing onto the sink as he leans over me, hips jerking.

"*Fuck,*" he breathes, his entire body shuddering for a moment before he straightens. To my surprise he reaches down, gently taking my arm and helping me to my feet before handing me my shorts. "You were perfect," he murmurs, pulling me close and pressing a kiss to the side of my forehead, his breath ruffling my hair.

It almost feels like a shock, the sudden gentleness after his roughness and control a moment ago. I can't help but lean in to the affection, the soft touch sending a flood of warmth through me that feels more like comfort than arousal. It's not something I've ever felt before, and when the first moment passes, I pull away, my pulse spiking with sudden alarm.

David can be as controlling and demanding as he wants in bed. As long as it's pleasurable for both of us, that's the kind of arrangement I'm happy with. But affection—something that could make me care for him—is far too dangerous.

"Your friends will be missing you," he says, turning me towards the door when I'm dressed again. "Let's go back to dinner. And no more theatrics this time, hm?"

I nod, apprehension filling me as we step back out into the warm, humid night air. I can only imagine what Claire will have to say now.

And I can't even *begin* to imagine what the rest of this week will hold.

8

DAVID

I'm not sure I've ever met a more infuriating woman than
Amalie. I've also never, in my entire life, met a woman who
could consume my thoughts so completely, and refuse to leave
my head even when she's nowhere in sight.

It should have made me put as much space between us as I
possibly could. Instead, we've ended up in this mutually beneficial
arrangement—as much as I know I should feel like a fool for
bringing her closer rather than avoiding her altogether.

I can't put my finger on what it is about her that's so different. Her
wide, pretty green eyes looking up at me as she takes me in her
mouth, her gorgeous face twisted up in pleasure, her perfect body
under my hands—none of that is so different from any other woman
I've had in my bed. I don't know if it's her bratty mouth, or the strange
mixture of conceit and vulnerability in her, or the way that I feel sure
she's keeping something to herself that she doesn't want me to know.
I've never been a man to be caught up in a mystery—my life is
complicated enough as it is—but Amalie, for some reason, has
piqued my curiosity in a way that I can't seem to shake.

"You haven't told me your last name," I mention off-hand in the
car, on the way back to my hotel. I keep my voice light, teasing, but I

notice the way she flinches ever so slightly when I say it. Another mystery.

"Maybe I don't want you to know." Her voice is light, too, but there's something forced behind it. "Maybe you'd recognize it if I told you, since you clearly must be someone important in Boston."

"What makes you say that?"

She rolls her eyes instantly. "You have a penthouse in Ibiza. Money is nothing to you. This place is a playground to you, but in a way that you make it seem as if it's almost beneath you to be here. You're *someone*."

That piques my curiosity even more. "So why haven't you asked mine?"

"Maybe *I* don't want to know." Amalie slides towards me, across the leather seats, straddling my lap as easily as if she belongs there. My hands go instinctively to her hips, holding her in place as she reaches up, trailing her fingers through my hair. "We don't have to be ourselves here," she says softly. "When this week is up, and we go our separate ways, we'll never see each other again. It doesn't matter what your last name is, or mine, or who we are back in Chicago or Boston, because it doesn't make any difference *here*. And back there—"

I silence her with a kiss, before I can say something that I shouldn't. There's a pang in my chest at the thought of letting her go when this is over. I do my best to ignore it, to focus on the softness of her mouth and the feeling of her body under my hands, how *good* she feels sitting atop me. *This is about sex, not feelings.* The two have never intertwined for me, and I've never *had* feelings for anyone. They have no place anywhere for me—not at home, where my every decision has to be made with a clear mind and a careful hand, and certainly not here, where I've come to unburden myself of all those expectations.

I can fuck her out of my system in a week. There's no reason to think that I can't. And we have all the time that we need to do exactly that.

The penthouse feels too far away, even as we stumble out of the car when it pulls up to the curb. The distance between the sidewalk and the elevator feels like a mile as we hurry towards it. The moment we're behind those doors, and I slip my key card into the slot, I press her up against the mirrored wall, my mouth crashing down hungrily onto hers.

I'll hold nothing back. I'll fuck her in every way I can imagine. I'll do everything I can possibly think of with her, indulge my every whim and desire, and then there will be nothing left to want when it finally comes time to let her go.

Amalie moans, arching against me, her hands clutching at the front of my shirt with that same fervent desire. I already know what I want from her before we even get inside my penthouse. The moment we step into the dark, cool room, I strip her shirt over her head, filling my hands with her breasts as I back her towards the floor-to-ceiling window that overlooks Ibiza from the living room.

"What—" she starts to ask, and I silence her with another kiss, my hands fumbling with the front of her shorts. She's undoing my shirt buttons as we speak, tugging them loose, and I shrug the garment off, letting it join the trail of clothing that reaches all the way to the window as her shorts drop to the floor.

I pull back for just a moment, drinking the sight of her in. She's fucking perfection, all lightly tanned skin, luscious dark auburn hair, perfect breasts behind the lace of the flimsy bralette she's wearing, her thong barely covering the apex of her thighs. I can already see how wet she is, the soft cream-colored material between her legs darkened with it, clinging to her bare skin. I sink to my knees in front of her without thinking, nearly snapping the thin straps of her thong in my hurry to slide it down her hips.

"Lean back," I murmur, gently pushing her back against the window, and she gasps. I see her turn to look at the vista just beyond it, at the long drop to the sidewalk below. I can feel the irrational fear that shudders through her at having nothing but the pane of glass between her and that drop. It would be almost impossible for it to break, but that small frisson of fear adds spice to what I'm about to do to her next.

"Take off your bra," I murmur, pressing my lips to her inner thigh, and she obeys. I see her small breasts above me, trembling as she draws in another shuddering breath, rosy nipples peaked and hard with excitement. I slide my hands up to her hips, holding her there as I press my mouth between her thighs, sliding my tongue up through her folds to her small, swollen clit.

Her entire body jerks when I drag my tongue over her. I'm not interested in teasing her just now—I want to find out how quickly she can come apart for me. I want to show her how thoroughly I can master her pleasure, and I press my lips tightly against her, sucking her into my mouth as she cries out above me, her hand sliding into my hair.

I grab her wrist, pressing her hand back against the glass. "Just like that," I murmur, moving her other hand into the same position. I see her give one more fleeting, nervous look to what's just beyond the window before I press my lips and tongue to her clit again, and her eyes flutter shut in pure bliss.

It doesn't take long to make her come. She's drenched, sweet arousal flowing over my tongue, and a shudder ripples through her as I slide one hand up her thigh, pushing two fingers into her as I flutter my tongue over her clit. She clenches around me, her body pressed hard to the glass, her head thrown back as she gasps and seizes, crying out my name as she climaxes on my tongue.

"Good girl." I press one last kiss against her clit, fluttering my tongue one more time over the pulsing flesh, and then stand up. Amalie's eyes fly open, her chest heaving as she tries to catch her breath, but I have no intention of giving her even a moment to recover.

I grab her waist, flipping her around so that the front of her body is pressed to the glass window as I undo the front of my pants, shoving them down along with my boxers to the floor. There's something deeply erotic about fucking her fully clothed while she's bare, but I want to feel my skin against hers. I nudge her ankles apart, gripping both of her wrists and raising her hands over her head as I reach between us, lining the swollen head of my cock up against her dripping entrance.

"David—" Amalie gasps my name, and I swear it's the sweetest fucking sound I've ever heard. Her back is arched, her ass pressing back against me. She wants this, wants *me*, but I can hear that fear still lacing her voice, see the wide-eyed look there as she looks down. "David—"

"You're safe." I groan as I push my cockhead into her, feeling her instantly tighten around me. "Nothing will happen. But it's exciting to think it might, isn't it?"

"I—" She gasps aloud as I thrust into her, hard, sinking to the hilt in one long, hot slide that nearly sends my eyes rolling back into my head with the sheer pleasure of it. "I don't know—"

"Yes, you do." My hand tightens around her wrists, the other gripping the side of her hip as I thrust into her again, pushing her against the glass. Her soft breasts are molded against it, an outline of her body forming from the heat of her skin. "There's nothing but a pane of glass between us and what's down there. And there's nothing at all to keep everyone there—" I nod towards the building directly across from us, "—from seeing exactly what I'm doing to you. From watching me fuck you like this. Nothing to stop them from seeing you and wishing they were the ones inside of you."

I punctuate the words with another hard thrust, sinking into her and grinding my hips against the perfect softness of her ass. "Think about that, Amalie. There might be some man over there, watching us right now, getting hard because he's seeing you get fucked. Do you think he could keep his hands off of himself, seeing you like this? I don't think so."

She gasps, shuddering and clenching around me, and I grit my teeth against the sudden jolt of pleasure. The fantasy is almost too much for me, and I want to draw it out.

I slide the hand on her hip around, in between her legs, spreading her folds open. I thrust hard, rocking her forward, pressing her clit against the glass as I start to fuck her in short, rhythmic motions that rub her drenched flesh against the chilly surface. "Look at you," I murmur in her ear, pulling her hips back as I stroke my fingers over her clit. "Exposed like this, being fucked like this for anyone to see. And you want it, don't you? It's going to make you come. You're going to come all over my fingers. All over my cock—"

Her whimper of assent, the way she moans my name as I circle her clit with my fingers, has me hovering on the edge. I manage to hang on until the moment I feel her tense against me, the moment that I feel her arch forward against the glass, all of her fears and reservations are forgotten in that instant of orgasmic bliss. I harden and throb inside of her, and it's not until the moment that I feel myself lose control, my entire body gripped in the throes of the strongest orgasm I think I've ever had, that I remember that I once again forgot to use a condom.

Fuck. Fuck, fuck—

I can't stop. I can't pull out. She clenches around me, hot and rippling along the length of my cock as I fill her with my cum, and it's the best fucking thing I've ever felt in my life. I can't remember ever having come like this before, ever having felt an orgasm that made the world go a little dark at the edges, the sound of her moans and the filthiness of fucking her up against this window as she screams for me sending me into what feels like a second climax—or maybe just the longest fucking one I've ever had.

"Shit," I breathe as I slip out of her, my legs feeling a little unsteady. I'm still dripping cum, and I can see it on her thighs as she presses her forehead to the glass, looking as if her knees might give out too. She looks absolutely gorgeous like this, flushed and disheveled with my cum leaking out of her, and my cock twitches traitorously even as I start to think about how to resolve the situation.

She turns around, her gaze flicking downwards, and I see the moment she realizes it, too.

"We got a little carried away," she whispers weakly, and I nod.

"I forgot." I rub a hand over my mouth, reaching for my pants. "It's my fault. Shit."

"It'll be fine." She doesn't sound entirely certain, but not as panicked as I feel at the moment, at least. "I'll get some Plan B. It'll be alright. It's not like no one ever makes a mistake. We'll remember a condom next time."

She flashes me that smile, teasing and seductive, and it makes me want to carry her back to my bed and fill her up all over again. And the moment the thought enters my head, I can't shake it loose.

"Don't worry," I murmur, reaching for her and pulling her close. I feel like I'm losing my mind, but my self-control is shattered around her, and I can't seem to pick up the pieces. "I'll have the concierge get it. You'll have it in the morning. And since we've already screwed up once—"

"Might as well keep enjoying it until the morning?" A wicked smile curves her lips, and as she leans in to kiss me, I have the same thought all over again that I had in the car.

I have no idea how I'm going to let her go when this week is over.

9

AMALIE

I don't know what came over me.

The shock of realizing that David came inside of me without a condom wore off more quickly than it should have. But I told myself there was an easy fix for it—and after all, it didn't matter how many more times he came in me between now and when I took the contraceptive in the morning.

I *liked* it. It was hot and filthy and made me feel wanted and utterly debauched, all feelings that I never knew could turn me on as much as they do. As he took me back to the bedroom, I almost missed the feeling of being vulnerable and exposed that I had in the bathroom back at the restaurant, and up against the glass in his living room. I didn't know what that said about me, but I wasn't sure I cared.

This week is about doing whatever I want. Being whoever I want to be. I don't need to examine it too closely.

Our week together flies by faster than I want it to. If David had held anything back at all, it vanishes the instant Claire and the others leave and he has me all to himself. Every day is a whirlwind of lavish extravagance, outrageous sex, and him spoiling me exactly as he promised. And, as he promised, everything I do that pleases him is rewarded. I wake him up one morning with a blowjob, sliding under the cool linen sheets to wrap my mouth around his cock, licking and sucking until he comes awake at the same time he *actually* comes, flooding my mouth with his hot, salty release. *That*, I discover, is rewarded with him returning the favor twice, once in bed and once in the shower together, before he orders the best room service I've ever had in my life, and we eat it together in bed. He feeds me bites of the food as we cuddle naked together under the thick covers, against plush pillows, smirking at me every time I moan in delight at how good it all is.

It's not as if I'm not used to luxury. The Leone family is—*was*—one of the most well-known and well-respected mafia names both in the States and abroad in Sicily, second only in Chicago to the Mancini family. I've grown up with wealth, with a staff to serve my needs and the best of everything, but everything here is elevated by the sheer hedonism of it all. I've had food as delicious as the smoked salmon crepes and the airy lemon pancakes that David feeds me bite by bite, the sweet and salty mixture followed by sips of perfectly crafted mimosa, but I've certainly never eaten it naked in bed with the most gorgeous man I've ever seen in my life.

And I've certainly never been rolled onto my back afterward when it's all cleared away, as he declares that he's still hungry, and dives between my thighs again.

I quickly find out that he's tireless when it comes to sex—both giving and receiving. I don't have enough knowledge to know if all men get hard again so quickly, but I'm eager to find out just how much he'll really spoil me, and I do—in spades. Going down on him and then letting him fuck me in the back of the car is rewarded with a shopping spree that leaves his bedroom loaded down with bags, enough that I'll need to buy a second suitcase to get it all home. When I let him finger me under the dinner table while we eat at a beachside restaurant, he promises me an afternoon at the spa the next day.

He keeps all of his promises, too. My frozen credit card is long forgotten, everything paid for without so much as a wince on David's part. He's clearly used to the best of everything, and I wonder more than once who he is that the staff in every restaurant, every shop, every spa, and every bar cater to any need he—or I, by proxy—might have. No meal is less than five-star, every drink is perfectly prepared, and he never has to wait for anything. All it takes is someone looking at a list, and suddenly, we're swept away to private cabanas, private rooms, private luxuries.

But every time I think of asking, I push the thought aside. I know well enough from my life as the daughter of Enzo Leone what kind of man could command this kind of attention. A billionaire of some sort, probably—with illegal wealth, possibly. But asking him questions invites him to ask his own, and I don't want him to know who I am. He might know the Leone name—might even have connections to them. He might know about my father's fall from grace, and the troubles we're now having with the Family.

I don't want any of that to spoil this. And the truth is that I don't really care, aside from a natural curiosity about the man who I've spent every night in bed with since he saved me in that restaurant.

He doesn't forget to use a condom again, which is a relief—even if a part of me is slightly regretful at not getting to feel him bare again... especially when he comes inside of me. *It's not worth the possible consequences,* I remind myself, but in the heat of the moment, I find myself sometimes wishing he *would* forget, even though it doesn't happen.

The last day we spend almost entirely at the hotel. There's a private pool on the rooftop, and David ensures that we have it all to ourselves. He fucks me once in the pool and again from behind on one of the lounge chairs, getting up to dispose of the condom and get us both drinks from the wet bar—entirely naked—while I check in for my flight this evening. It feels blissfully decadent to lay out naked in the sun, still throbbing between my legs from the series of orgasms I had, while scrolling through the app to confirm my flight. I'm relaxed down to my very bones, happier than I've ever been—until I see the notification, and the feeling is abruptly shattered.

"What's wrong?" David asks, setting a drink down next to me as he catches the look on my face. "Did something happen?"

"I can't believe I didn't think about this. My flight home was canceled. Because of the frozen card, I think—" My throat tightens, that forgotten panic filling me again. My friends are long gone, and my arrangement with David was for our time here, together. I don't know if getting me home is a part of that, and after a week of ignoring the conflict with my mother and pushing it off until I *have* to deal with it, I don't think she's going to be very sympathetic to my situation.

She can't leave me stranded here. I try to calm the feeling of panic rushing through my chest. *I'm her daughter. Her key to fixing our family's problems.* But I'm not so sure that she might not, for a little while, just to make me beg and grovel. Just to prove her point that I can be punished for my small rebellion of running off with my friends.

David looks utterly unconcerned, and I feel a sudden flash of anger at him. I'm completely at his mercy, and he knows it. *He* isn't at risk of being stranded here without money or resources. *He* isn't at the whim of his family's expectations, or the traditions of the mafia, or the relentless gender roles that have been enforced on me since I was a child.

He can do whatever the fuck he wants.

David lays back on the lounge, reaching for his drink. He's still gorgeously naked, his abs tight and gleaming with suntan oil, the dark hair on his tattooed chest soft and inviting. I want to run my hands over every inch of him—and I want to slap the careless look off of his face, all at the same time.

His gaze drifts lazily over my naked body, and his cock twitches against his thigh, thickening instantly. "I want your mouth," he says carelessly, picking up his phone. "Go on. I want my cock in between your lips before I'm fully hard, Amalie."

The order is clear—and I think I know what he's doing. This is payment for him getting me out of one more predicament, and my cheeks flush hot, a wave of embarrassment and anger flooding me.

You can grovel for him, or you can beg and grovel to your mother. It doesn't take much to know which one I'd prefer. David might know how to humiliate me, but there's pleasure in it, too. And after today, I'll never see him again.

My mother will never let me live it down, if I have to beg her to help me get home.

I slide off of the lounge chair, moving in between his legs as I reach for his cock. I learned quickly that I like going down on him like this, when he's still only partially erect, feeling him harden and grow in my mouth. I've woken him up more than once like this for that exact reason.

He ignores me entirely as I take him in my mouth, scrolling through his phone. There's no hand in my hair or groans of pleasure; the only signs of his enjoyment is the way his cock stiffens and twitches against my tongue, leaking pre-cum onto it as I suck and lick my way up and down the shaft. I can feel the steadily growing tension in his thighs, see the way his abs flex when I manage to take him down my throat for a moment, but other than that, it's almost as if I'm not even there—as if I'm just an inanimate source of his pleasure and nothing more.

It's debasing, infuriating—and somehow makes me dripping wet, all at once. It makes me thoroughly ashamed of myself, both for letting him use me in this way and for enjoying it—and makes me ache with the need to come. I feel used and dirty and horribly aroused, and I moan around his cock when it twitches and jerks in my mouth, letting me know he's close to the edge.

David taps something on his phone, typing something out as I slide my lips as far down as I can, struggling to take him into my throat again. His hips rise a little off of the lounge chair, his thighs flexing, and he taps one more thing before I feel his entire body shudder. His hand touches the back of my head, right as his cock throbs, and he suddenly floods my mouth with his cum.

I nearly choke as it shoots down my throat, still caught off guard, and I struggle to swallow it all the way I know he wants me to. A little slips out of my mouth and down my chin, and his fingers catch it, pushing it between my lips before he sits up slightly, reaching for me and pulling me upwards.

The chair reclines all the way back suddenly, and I gasp. David's hands on my waist keep me from toppling, and he lifts me up above his shoulders, so that I'm straddling his face as he sets me down above his mouth.

"You've got a first-class ticket home," he murmurs, his fingers slipping between my folds. "Purchased and confirmed. Your flight leaves at seven."

His fingers slip into me, curling as he tugs me down onto his mouth, and I cry out. My head is spinning, still trying to reconcile that my means of getting home is fixed as his lips fasten around my clit.

"So fucking wet," he groans, when he pulls away for a second to breathe, his fingers still working inside of me. "You liked me using you like that, didn't you? Making you suck my cock for a plane ticket. You filthy little—"

He drags me down onto his lips again before he finishes the sentence, as if he's starving for me. I dimly register the movement of his other hand below me, the quick motions that tell me he's stroking himself with his left hand as he fingers me with the right, all the while eating me out in broad daylight on the rooftop of the hotel.

It's enough to make me wish, as I grip the edge of the chair and come hard on his tongue, that I wasn't going to leave him tonight.

—

I can feel that something's changed when I pack to leave. From the moment we finished on the rooftop, I could feel him detaching, pulling away from me. Everything he says is clipped and cold, and he leaves while I gather my things, coming back just before it's time for me to go and sending me my flight information and ticket.

"I'll have the driver take you to the airport," he says carelessly when I bring my suitcases out to the living room. "I've already called down for someone to come and take your things. You can meet the driver downstairs."

He turns away from me, looking out of the huge window as he takes a sip of the drink in his hand, and a sudden lump rises in my throat. I don't know what I expected when it came time for us to go our separate ways—not romantic gestures or declarations of love—but this feels wrong, too. I look at the huge pane of glass in front of him, a shudder running through me as I remember him fucking me up against it, and I wonder if that's really the last thing he's going to say to me. *You can meet the driver downstairs.*

"David—" I swallow hard as I say his name, unsure what else might come out of my mouth. I don't even know what it is that I want him to do or say—I just want *something.* The way he's acting now, it's like none of the last week and a half happened. It's *worse* than the night he took my virginity, because we've spent so many more days together. He knows me more intimately than anyone ever has. Even though nothing was ever going to come of it—even though I don't *want* anything to come of it—I want to know it mattered to him at least a little.

I want to at least feel as if it's not easy for him to let me leave, as irrational as I know that is. But he just turns and looks at me, his face utterly blank.

"You're still here?"

The way he says it cuts me to my core. It's a dismissal, pure and simple. It takes everything in me not to burst into tears as I spin on my heel, grabbing for my purse as I force myself to open the door slowly, walking out instead of running the way I want to. I nearly smack into the bellboy coming up for my suitcases, and I see him look curiously at my tear-filled eyes as I make a beeline for the elevator, suddenly wanting nothing more than to be out of here.

I press my hand against my chest, trying to quell the ache there. *This was never supposed to mean anything,* I remind myself. It's not that I wanted him to fall in love with me—but I can't help feeling that the cold way he behaved, the way he didn't seem to care at *all,* means that all the passion of the last week was somehow a lie.

It doesn't matter now, I tell myself as I settle into my first-class seat on the plane, trying not to let it make me think of David. The week is over, and now I have to go home. Back to my responsibilities, back to my life, back to my mother and her expectations of me. Back to the *Family's* expectations for me, and the reality that my marriage to any mafia heir that will take me is the only thing that can salvage our family name.

The mansion is dark and silent when I get home. I found enough cash in my purse to call a cab from the airport, and as I step inside the cavernous foyer, I know my mother has probably long since gone to bed. I let out a sigh of relief as I slowly go upstairs, leaving my suitcases for the staff to bring up later. I feel utterly exhausted, emotionally and physically, and even though I've come home to a mansion, it feels horribly depressing compared to Ibiza and everything I just left.

I'm never going to have a vacation like that again. The thought weighs on me as I undress and slip into bed, casting a wayward glance at my laptop before deciding to deal with my missed schoolwork later. For now, all I want is to fall asleep and dream about salt and sunshine, in a place where, for just a little while, I could do anything I wanted.

Thankfully, as I drift off, I don't dream of David. And I have some hope that I'll be able to forget about him, just as he forgot about me before I was even gone.

10

AMALIE

ONE MONTH LATER

"**A**malie! I've been calling your name for fifteen minutes. How did you not hear me—"

My mother's voice is interrupted by the sound of me gagging and throwing up into the toilet for the second time this morning. I wonder dimly if I'm ever going to be able to enjoy food again, fumbling for the handle to flush before more comes up. As my mother knocks heavily on the door, I grab for the plastic stick on the counter in a panic, clutching it in my hand.

I don't look at the result yet. I can't. I don't want to know.

I've thrown up almost every morning for the last week. I told myself—and my mother—that it was a stomach flu. Claire came by with notes from class and my favorite Thai soup that always seems to settle my stomach, but it came right back up, too, and I've been too exhausted to do much more than give my schoolwork a cursory glance.

My mother hasn't cared about the missed class—she thinks college is mostly a distraction, and something she was only talked into because she knows Gianna Mancini was allowed to go—but she *does* care about the fact that I was too sick to go to a charity gala she wanted me to attend with her last weekend, after she'd been gone to Boston again.

This time, when she left, I had double the security trailing my every move, making sure I didn't run off again. What little freedom I had before has been heavily curtailed after I escaped to Ibiza. And when she came back—with nothing to say about whether she'd managed to broker the marriage that she's been trying to put together for me—her mood was much, much worse than usual.

"*Amalie!*" The doorknob rattles. "Why is the door locked? What are you doing?" She rattles it again, and I wince, gagging once more with nothing left to throw up. "I need to talk to you."

"I'm sick." My hand flexes around the plastic stick in my palm. *It's just the flu*, I tell myself, closing the toilet lid and resting my flushed cheek against the cool porcelain, but deep down, I think I know what I'm going to see when I look at the pregnancy test. I've been throwing up and exhausted, but I haven't run a fever. I don't have chills. My appetite is just fine—I just can't keep any of it down.

It's not the flu.

"Just give me a minute?" I hate the pleading note in my voice, but I can't help it. "I just need a minute."

My mother huffs out a breath on the other side of the door. "Fine," she says curtly. "I have an appointment to get to. But you are *not* to be late coming home today, if you go to class. Am I understood? No coffee with that little friend of yours, no going over to her house, no detour into the city to shop. You come straight home. I have someone I want you to meet."

My stomach twists for an entirely different reason. *This is it*, I realize, the last of my hope that maybe no one would take my mother up on her desperate bargaining fading away. *I'm going to end up married to a stranger. And now*—

I sit back on the rug next to the bathtub as her footsteps fade away down the hall, willing myself to uncurl my fingers and look at the test result waiting in my hand. The possible consequence of my—and David's—recklessness.

A man whose last name I don't even know.

I squeeze my eyes shut as I open my hand. It takes everything in me to open them, to see what I already know is going to be the result.

Two pink lines look up at me from the little test window, and my entire world grinds to a halt.

For a moment, I can't think. I can't breathe. Panic wells up in me, and I fling the test across the room, the plastic striking the door with an ineffectual sound as I burst into tears.

One stupid mistake, and now I'm pregnant.

What am I going to do? My first thought is that Claire might help me. She might not let me off the hook easily for being so reckless, but I think she would help me find a way to take care of it.

The problem, of course, is my security, and how much more stringent they've been since I returned from Ibiza. I don't think I'd be able to slip away to a clinic with Claire, the way I might have been able to before. And I can't go to our family doctor—medical privacy might apply to most people, but not to me—not in this situation. The doctors who are trusted enough to treat members of mafia families know who their loyalties lie with—and it won't be me, the daughter who got herself accidentally knocked up. There are consequences to keeping secrets like that.

I'll figure it out. I have time. It's only been a month—I can try to find a solution. I try to quell the panic as I peel myself off of the floor and go back to my room, intent on actually making it to class today. I want to avoid my mother when she gets home, if nothing else.

I get a text from Claire on the drive to campus telling me that she's not feeling well, and I feel a small, guilty pang of relief. She knows me well enough to see that something is bothering me, and I don't have the energy to dodge her questions—or come up with a convincing lie.

I hope you didn't catch it from me, I text back quickly, feeling that small pang of guilt again—I know very well that she didn't—and almost immediately see a text back.

Me too! You must be feeling better, though. Get notes for me, k?

Ok, I type back quickly, and shove my phone into my purse, leaning my head back against the cool leather seat. My stomach is still doing flips even though it's empty, and I let out slow breaths, trying to keep the nausea under control. This day has been bad enough already, the last thing I need is to throw up in the middle of class.

It's hard to focus. I manage to take halfway decent notes for Claire, I think, but my mind is constantly wandering, thinking about what my options are. Even with the proof of the test right in front of me this morning, it doesn't feel real. It doesn't feel as if that one passionate slip-up, that one night, could have turned into this.

I was supposed to leave David behind in Ibiza. For the last month, I've done my best not to think about him, not to miss the nights I spent in his bed, not to wish for more when that's impossible. It's *still* impossible—I have no way of finding him, even if I wanted to.

If my mother has found a husband for me, it's not going to be possible to pass the baby off as his, either—not unless we were to be married abnormally quickly. My mother might push for a quick wedding—the better to make sure the groom doesn't change his mind—but I don't think it'll be quick enough, no matter what.

Telling the truth is an option, but I don't know what happens then. I *definitely* don't like to think about what my mother's reaction will be, or what it's going to be like to have to live with it. She might want it taken care of, if only so that she can still marry me off—but I'd rather just handle it on my own, so she never has to know.

Briefly, towards the end of the day, I consider ignoring her instruction to come straight home after class—or trying to, anyway. Whoever it is that she wants me to meet, I'd rather not. I could go over to Claire's if I can slip past my security, tell her the truth, try to make a plan. But even as I think about it, I know the consequences of defying my mother, especially right now, aren't worth the momentary freedom I'd have. So I go home after my last class, and unsurprisingly, my mother is waiting for me just outside the foyer as if she's been counting the minutes until I'd walk through the door.

"I left clothes on your bed," she says curtly, shepherding me towards the stairs. "I'll meet you in the informal living room when you're dressed. Don't keep me waiting. And wear *exactly* what I left out for you," she adds, narrowing her eyes at me as she stops at the base of the staircase.

It's all I can do not to roll mine, but I go upstairs to my room. As promised, there's a dark green sheath dress with a thin belt on the bed and nude high heels set next to it, and I frown. It's exactly the kind of thing my mother likes for me to wear and that I hate—something that makes me feel ten years older than I am and far more prim and proper than I ever want to be. *This isn't the hill I want to die on,* I remind myself as I reach for it, stripping off the jeans and t-shirt I wore to class and tugging my hair free from the ponytail. There's a visible crease in it, and I go and plug in my straightener, knowing my mother will have a fit if my hair doesn't look as perfect as everything else when I come downstairs.

My stomach twists again as I slip into the dress and zip it up. I managed some wheat crackers and ginger ale for lunch, and it stayed down, but the anxiety over what might be waiting downstairs for me has my stomach on the verge of rebelling all over again. *Maybe I'll puke all over whoever she's dragged in to meet me,* I think grimly as I run the hot straightener through my hair, touching up my makeup a little and doing whatever I can to drag the minutes out until I'm forced to go downstairs and face this. *Surely, that'll make them think twice about marrying me.*

The truth is, though, that anyone enticed enough by what wealth and notoriety remain to us to look past my family's recent disgrace probably won't be put off by that.

I can hear my mother's voice drifting out past the door that leads to the informal living room, and behind it, a faint, deep male voice that sounds oddly familiar, though I can't quite place it. There's the hint of an Italian accent, tinged with that particular Boston flavor— which is unsurprising; I knew my mother was trying to arrange something with one of the mafia families in Boston. I hadn't thought she was going to actually manage to pull it off.

Here goes nothing. There's no running away from this, so I might as well face it head-on. I push the door open, and the voices abruptly stop.

As do I, the moment I step into the room and see who is sitting on the floral chintz couch in front of the fireplace.

My mother is there, of course, dressed to the nines and prim as ever, a pleased, victorious expression on her face. And next to her is a man I recognize—a man I could never *fail* to recognize, even if years passed before I saw him again. A face I don't think I could forget, even if I wanted to—and a part of me desperately has.

Sitting next to my mother, in my home as if he belongs there—is David.

11

DAVID

For a moment, I can't quite believe what I'm seeing.

This can't be. The world can't possibly be this small. I'd been told by my father in no uncertain terms to get on a flight to Chicago this morning, and I'd obeyed. A week ago, I was informed that a marriage had been arranged for me, and I'd known that there was no point in arguing. I hadn't bothered to ask the name of my future bride—it hadn't mattered to me. If my father had agreed to the arrangement, I trusted it was in the best interest of our family. I've understood all along that as the eldest son now, it's my job to provide the family with an heir to follow me. Half the reason I went to Ibiza was to put off that particular duty as long as possible—but it couldn't be delayed forever. I knew my father was working on it, and I had simply put it out of my head. I hadn't bothered to ask Marianne Leone her daughter's name, either—once again, because I simply didn't care. I'd find out by my wedding day, and that was really all that mattered.

I hadn't in my wildest dreams expected that I would see Amalie looking at me from across the room, her face reflecting the same horror that I feel at this moment.

"This is a mistake." I force the words out through my rapidly closing throat, grasping for a viable reason why. I hear Marianne's gasp and see her mouth open in protest—unsurprisingly, the woman has been working on my father for months to arrange this. "I can't marry her."

"And why not?" Marianne's hands are already wringing in her lap, and she shoots an accusing look at her daughter, as if Amalie should know why. She *does* know why, but from the stunned look on her face, I don't think she's going to be speaking up anytime soon.

"She's not a suitable mafia bride," I say bluntly, taking some small, cruel pleasure in the way Amalie's face goes white at that, except for two hot flushes of red high on her cheekbones. "She's not a virgin."

"You—" Amalie splutters from across the room, starting to find her voice, but Marianne isn't looking at her. She's staring at me now, in utter shock, horror to reflect her daughter's wreathing her pinched features.

"How do you know that?" she asks coldly, and I wince.

"Because he's the reason I'm not," Amalie snaps from across the room. "Were you planning to fill in that part too, *David*? Or were you just going to shame me in front of my mother?"

"You didn't seem all that ashamed back in Ibiza." I smirk at her, and her eyes go wide with a sparking fury that sends an entirely inappropriate jolt of lust down my spine.

Even here in Chicago, a world away from the luxurious, hedonistic week we shared, it seems she still manages to have a similar effect on me.

"I demand an explanation." Marianne stands up abruptly, glaring first at me, and then at her daughter. "You met on my daughter's ill-conceived little escape trip? How? Did you know somehow and follow her?"

Amalie lets out a small gasp, and I realize that possibility had never occurred to her. "No," I say simply, glancing back at her mother. "It was a coincidence. I met her at a bar. She was quite eager. Prowling for someone, even. I hesitate to believe her story that I was her first, honestly—"

"You fucking bastard," Amalie breathes, and the hatred in her eyes is so clear that for a moment, I wonder if she really is telling the truth. I have a flash of memory—small spots of blood on white sheets after that first morning—and a sick feeling twists in my gut. I'd told myself that it was on account of my size, that she wouldn't be the first girl who bled a little because she was just this side of too tight for me, but now everything seems called into question.

"Can you give me a moment?" I look at Marianne. "Or *us*, rather. I'd like to speak to your daughter alone."

Marianne's lips thin, going white at the edges, and I can see her weighing her options. She doesn't want to acquiesce, that much is clear, but I can tell she very much wants this marriage to happen.

"Fine. Fifteen minutes." Her voice is clear and taut, and she turns sharply on her heel, exiting the room with another glowering look at her daughter. Amalie is trembling with what looks like barely contained rage, and the moment Marianne is gone, she turns the full force of her glare on me.

"What the hell is going on?" she hisses, and I shrug, standing up and walking towards the unlit fireplace with my hands shoved in my pockets.

"You tell me. Did you know about this when you hit on me in Ibiza? Was this some way of entrapping me into this marriage regardless?" I frown, turning to face her. "Was your card *really* frozen because your mother was pissed, or was that all some scheme to get me to come to your rescue and try to get me to fall for you, so I'd be even more inclined to agree—"

"You're insane if you think any of that is true." Amalie's voice is as sharp and cold as her mother's. "One, I didn't even know your fucking last name—I *still* don't, so I don't know how in the hell I would have been able to follow you to that club to *entrap* you. And I certainly didn't know you'd be coming to that restaurant. I don't know whether to hate you even more for thinking I'm capable of all of that or be flattered that you really think I'm that brilliantly conniving, but this is all just a really, really fucked up coincidence, and—'"

She trails off, running out of breath, and I can't take my eyes off of her. Even furious, standing there practically spitting angrily as she shouts at me, she's quite possibly the most beautiful woman I've ever seen.

"I had no idea about any of this," she breathes, her chest heaving as she crosses her arms over her breasts. "This is all just as much a shock to me as it is to you. Except now you've told my mother something that I very much planned for her *not* to know—"

"Oh? Was I just supposed to keep silent? Take the ruined bride being offered to me?" I take a step towards her, and another, unable to stop myself even though I know I shouldn't. I feel drawn to her, that feeling like a moth to a flame all over again, and I want to grab her shoulders and shake her at the same moment that I want to kiss her until she's dizzy.

The moment I say it, I see her eyes go wide with rage. Her teeth clench, and I see that tremor of fury run through her again. "If I'm *ruined*," she hisses, "it's because of you. Because *you* fucked me."

"You're trying to tell me you were a virgin?" I step closer still, until I'm nearly within touching distance. She backs up, and I follow, as if she's tugging me towards her, with her, without meaning to. "*Now* you want to tell me that? Because you didn't behave like one."

"Oh?" Her upper lip curls, and she takes another step back. "How does a virgin behave, David? Please, enlighten me as to what it was I was supposed to do. Cry? Beg? I *wanted* to lose it. That doesn't mean that I wasn't a virgin, just because I didn't want to make a big deal about it."

The last words come out on a breath as her back hits the wall, and she lets out a small gasp as I close the distance between us. "David—"

"You were eager." I reach up, brushing a lock of her auburn hair out of her face, almost gently. "You wanted me. *You* approached *me* in a club, with all those other girls around me. You were confident, not shy. And the way you danced on me—" My hand drops to her hip, squeezing lightly. "You knew what you were doing."

"I knew how to dance, so I must be a slut?" Amalie laughs, tossing her head. "I go out dancing all the time with Claire and her friends, here in Chicago. I've danced with plenty of guys. That doesn't mean I opened my legs for them. You can argue with me all you want, David, but you were my first. I just didn't tell you, because I didn't want to make a big deal out of it."

"So either you lied to me then, or you're lying to me now."

"I wanted to pick who my first was." Amalie tips her chin up, glaring up at me defiantly. "I didn't think it made all that much of a difference if you knew or not. Are you telling me you would have cared?"

"I wouldn't have done it," I tell her bluntly, and I *want* to believe that I'm telling the truth. That knowing would have meant that I *wouldn't* have fucked her, that I wouldn't have used her predicament as a way to keep her in my bed, at my beck and call for my pleasure for another week. But even as I look down at her, I'm not sure that it's true.

"Oh?" Amalie's voice drops a little, soft and sultry. "Are you *sure* you wouldn't have, David? Are you *sure* you wouldn't have liked the idea of having a virgin in your bed, all eager for you to *ruin* her?"

Something about the way she breathes that last word makes something snap inside of me. I grab her before I can stop myself, one hand on her waist and the other gripping her chin with my fingers as I surge against her, pinning her to the wall as my mouth comes crashing down onto hers.

She's as soft and sweet as I remember, even spiced with anger. Her mouth is hot, her lips instantly yielding under mine, as if she wants this as badly as I do. I feel the rest of her body stiffen under my touch, and for one moment, I think she might try to knee me in the balls— but then her hands grip the front of my shirt, pulling me closer. Her tongue slides into my mouth as my cock stiffens, and as I press it against her inner thigh, I feel certain that two things are absolutely true.

There's no way this girl was a virgin a month and a half ago—and I don't think I care.

All I can think, as she kisses me, arching her body against mine and bringing back a flood of memories involving her soft bare flesh and her heat wrapped around me, is that I'll marry her if that's what it takes to fuck her again.

Even if she hates me. Even if she drives me insane.

Even if being married to one another means we might kill each other.

"You weren't a virgin," I whisper against her mouth, letting go of her chin and sliding my hand into her hair. "You weren't scared. A virgin would have been shy and afraid. Especially of *this*." I reach for one of her hands, prying it away from my shirt and pressing it between us, against my throbbing cock. "You were so fucking tight, but—"

"Believe whatever you want." Amalie's gaze is defiant, glaring up at me with her lips a breath away from mine. "I'm telling the truth."

Her voice falters a little as she says it, and it bolsters my doubt. But even so, I remember those spots of blood, and I wonder if she's telling the truth.

I truly don't think that I care.

If we're married, I'll have a lifetime to pry the truth out of her. And one way or another, I'll make her pay for it if she lied to me—about any of it at all.

Her mother wants this marriage, and she'll have it. If I find out that she and Amalie entrapped me or that Amalie wasn't a virgin, I'll use it to my advantage. I've always been good at that. The Leone family needs me more than I need them.

And I want Amalie in my bed again badly enough to risk it.

I start to lean down to kiss her again, her hand still firmly trapped against my cock with my fingers wrapped around her wrist, when I hear a hard knock at the door.

"Fifteen minutes." Marianne's warning voice comes from the other side of it, and I let go of Amalie, taking several steps back as I give her a moment to compose herself. She *looks* as if she's been pinned up against a wall and kissed—her dress wrinkled, her hair wild around her face, her cheeks and lips flushed. I see her take a deep breath, and I give her a wink that's returned with a glare as I call out to her mother.

"We're finished talking," I say clearly. "You can come in."

The door opens and Marianne Leone steps in, giving her daughter an appraising glance before turning back to me. "Well?" she asks coolly. "I hope the conversation was satisfactory?"

I smile tightly at her, the poise and calm inherent to my station in life returning to me in a moment as I let out a slow breath, ignoring Amalie entirely. "It was," I tell Marianne calmly. "And my worries have been assuaged. I'll be happy to marry your daughter, as we discussed."

I hear a small gasp from Amalie, and I see the horror on her face at the same moment that I stifle the smile that threatens to spring to mine.

She thought she'd gotten out of it.

But I already let her go once—and I have no intentions of doing so again.

12

AMALIE

I can't believe this is happening. *If he really doesn't believe I was a virgin, that he's the only one I've been with, how is this still happening?* I'd been furious that he'd challenged me on it, that he'd made such wild accusations, but a small part of my mind had been shouting that if he didn't believe me, it would mean he wouldn't want to marry me.

I'd have my freedom for a little while longer. Maybe longer still, if the news that I'm now *ruined* spread. My mother might not be able to arrange a marriage for me at all. There would be consequences to that, of course—but at this particular moment, I'm not entirely sure that I wouldn't rather suffer those.

The idea of marrying David terrifies me. I don't know him, but my body responds to him in ways that I know gives him the upper hand over me—even more of an upper hand than he would have simply by virtue of being my husband. And there's something about him—

He's different, here. Stiffer, colder, angrier. He's more like the man who coldly asked me if I was still in the room after he dismissed me, when I left Ibiza, and nothing like the man who spoiled and fucked me senseless for a week straight. That, too, frightens me—that kind of duplicity in a person. It was one thing when I thought I would never see him again.

It's something else altogether when I'm facing the prospect of being his wife.

I barely hear what else David and my mother talk about. He says something in a low voice, and I see her mouth tighten, and then she nods. "I'll speak to my daughter," she says. "If you don't mind waiting here, we'll just step outside."

When her hand closes around my elbow, I nearly yelp with pain. Her fingers dig into my flesh tightly, pinching, a clear sign of just how angry she is with me. She marches me out of the room before I can do much more than look at David, and the expressionless look on his face is almost more frightening than his anger from earlier. The door shuts heavily behind us as my mother walks us down the hall, well out of earshot of the living room.

"What the hell was he talking about?" she hisses, and I wince. My mother never curses; for her to do so now means she's more furious with me than I think she's ever been.

"He's lying." I force the words out. "He must not really want to go through with a marriage to someone from our family, after—"

The slap comes so fast that I don't even see my mother's hand move. Red-hot pain bursts over my cheek, and the fingers of her other hand crush my elbow a little tighter. My mother has never struck me before, but if there was ever going to be a first time, I suppose today makes sense.

"If *you* lie to me again, the next one will be worse," she snaps. "Now tell me the truth, Amalie Leone. *What* is he talking about?"

Briefly, I consider doubling down. But I'm not sure I see the point. David, whether he believes me or not, seems inclined to marry me anyway. *And*, I realize with a sudden flood of something very close to hope, *there might be some part of the truth that gets me out of this after all.*

"I slept with him in Ibiza," I mumble, glancing away from my mother's accusing glare. "I met him in a club, like he said. I didn't know who he was. He never told me his last name, and I never asked.

I *still* don't know it," I add with no small amount of sarcasm. "And apparently, I'm going to marry him."

"Carravella." My mother says it flatly. "That's his last name. You little *slut*. Do you have any idea what this could have done to us? This could have ruined our last chance at—"

Vaguely, I recognize the name, and my stomach turns over, until I think I might be sick with the irony of it all. I remember thinking in Ibiza that David was so far removed from my life here, the sort of man who had no ties or connections to what I'd left behind, and I couldn't have been more wrong.

Carravella. A Boston-Italian mafia family with ties to Sicily and the leading mafia family there, the Riccis. I remember vaguely hearing about some scandal related to them in the past, but I hadn't cared enough to really pay attention. They've never shown up to any of the galas or events that I've been present at here with my family, and I've never gone to Boston. Still, David and I orbited each other without ever knowing it—and now we've been abruptly pulled into a union that I don't think either of us wants.

He wants it enough to agree to marry me, even if he doesn't think I was a virgin. My stomach clenches again, and I lick my lips nervously.

"I didn't want my first to be whatever man I was *forced* into marrying." I do my best to glare back at my mother, as intimidating as she is at this moment. "I wanted it to be my choice."

"My god!" She lets go of me, shaking her head as if she can't believe what she's hearing. "How did I raise such a stubborn, *stupid* daughter? You don't get *choices*. Women in our world don't get *choices*. Do you think I chose to marry your father? Do you think I *wanted* him? Do you think I wanted to be left with all of *this* to deal with, after his machinations went wrong? Do you *seriously* think this is enjoyable for me, Amalie?"

I swallow hard. "He's not going to want to marry me," I say softly, and my mother's eyes narrow.

"You heard him." She presses her lips tightly together. "In spite of your mistakes, he still wants to—"

"I'm pregnant."

The words hover between us, and I can see that it takes a moment for the recognition of what I've said to sink in. Her mouth opens slightly, gaping a little like a fish, and then she shakes her head.

"You're lying again. You're not getting out of this, young lady—"

"I threw the test away, but I can take another one." I tilt my chin up, trying not to look as scared as I feel right now. *If this doesn't work, David Carravella will be my husband.* Something about that fills me with a dread that I can't entirely explain, a feeling that of all the men it could be, this is the one I should want the least. It feels terrifying, to imagine that I could have met him so far away, in such completely different circumstances, and end up here like this after all. "I'm not lying."

"*Christ.*" My mother hisses the word, another thing I've never heard from her before. "You're determined to ruin us, aren't you? As if what your father did wasn't enough. Is it his?" She jabs her finger towards the room where David is waiting, and my stomach flips again.

"I don't know," I whisper, and once again, her hand cracks across the other side of my face. My knees almost buckle, and I reach up to touch the burning spot on my cheek with a whimper as tears fill my eyes. I *do* know, of course—it can't be anyone else's. But the pregnancy feels like my only possibility out of this—and if he knows it's his, that possibility vanishes.

"You're telling me it could be someone else's?" My mother's face is pinched with anger, more so than I've ever seen before. "My god, Amalie. I can't believe I raised—"

She goes silent, taking a deep breath. "It doesn't matter," she says finally, and I stare at her.

"What do you *mean*, it doesn't matter—"

My mother rounds on me, a sudden determination in her face that makes me shrink back. "Make him believe it's his," she snaps vehemently. "Our family needs this, Amalie. And if he thinks you're carrying his heir, it won't matter if he believes he was your first or not. As long as he can feel certain the baby is his." She pauses, and I can see the wheels turning in her mind. "Don't tell him until it's absolutely necessary," she says finally. "Not until after the wedding. It's been what, a month?"

I nod, swallowing hard. "I took the test this morning."

She presses her lips together. "And you've been sick for a week. I should've realized—well, I didn't think I'd raised such a little whore." She says it almost flatly this time, like a fact that she's starting to come to terms with. "You can go a little while still without seeing a doctor. Long enough for the wedding to take place. You can tell him afterward, and he'll want to believe it's his."

"And if he doesn't?" I challenge it anyway out of sheer desperation, even though I know I'm playing a fool's game—the baby is David's, and no amount of pretending that there's some chance it isn't will change that. "If he doesn't want to just *believe* it? If he demands proof? A paternity test?"

"Then we'll deal with that problem if it comes up. We can make this marriage more difficult for him to get out of than to get into." My mother paces a little ways down the hall and back, clearly plotting now. "We can make it worth his while to look past it, perhaps—"

My stomach sinks, a knot of despair like ice filling it. Even if he demands proof, he won't want out of the marriage once he knows it's his baby. The only way to get out of this is to keep the marriage from happening at all—and I can feel those walls closing in. There's no escape that I can see.

"You *will* keep absolutely quiet about this," my mother hisses, rounding on me once more. "I will make you regret it if you breathe a single word, Amalie Leone. Do you understand me?"

I do. I understand her completely, and I can hear the death knell of my freedom as I look at my mother's sharp blue eyes.

"Yes," I whisper softly. "I understand."

"Good." She straightens, a little of her calm returning. "I've arranged for us to go to the church and finish the betrothal contract. We'll go and fetch your husband-to-be."

She motions for me to follow her, and I do, feeling numb. David is standing by the unlit fireplace, looking out of the window as if lost in thought, and he turns when he hears us walk in. I'm struck all over again by how handsome he is—but it's a different sort of handsomeness here. In Ibiza, there was an indolence to him, a rakish attractiveness that came from the way he carried himself, as if he was a little above everyone else around him, a little better than all of the trust fund babies and billionaires' children flooding the resorts and clubs.

Here, he simply fits in. In his bespoke suit, his face clean-shaven and his expression calm, he looks entirely at home among the antiques, vintage furniture, and expensive textiles in the informal living room. He belongs in this sort of place—old money, not new—and looking at him now, I'm not sure how I missed it before. I've grown up around men like David—like my father and brother and all of their colleagues and friends—my whole life. I don't know how I didn't see it sooner—except, perhaps, because I simply didn't want to.

"The driver will be around with the car any minute," my mother says crisply, ignoring me and speaking directly to David. "We can go to the church and finalize the contract."

He pauses, looking between the two of us. "There's one thing I need to do," he says finally. "I'll take my own driver, and return in a few hours. We can go then."

My mother looks as if she might have an aneurysm. I'm not sure anyone other than my father has ever told her to wait on their pleasure, instead of immediately jumping to obey her itinerary. "The priest—"

"Can wait," David says curtly. "I'll ride to the church with you, if that's what you prefer. But I'll need a few hours before then."

I'm banished back to my room while we wait on David. I pass the time pacing back and forth, trying to think of an out, trying to think of an escape—but there is none. There's nothing I can do, and I know it.

The three hours pass all too quickly before David returns, without a word about where he's been. He doesn't say anything to me on the ride to the cathedral. Not a word. He sits on the other side of the car, leaning back as he scrolls casually through his phone, and my cheeks burn as I think about that last afternoon in Ibiza. It's hard to believe that the cold, composed man sitting across from me is the same one who fucked me up against a glass window, the same one who whispered such filthy things to me as I came on his fingers, his tongue, his—

I squeeze my eyes shut for a moment, trying to banish the thoughts. My mother is sitting stiffly next to me, and I fold my hands into my lap, trying to calm my racing heart. It feels unthinkable that in just a short time, I'm going to be engaged to David—to a man that I thought I'd never see again.

That feeling persists as we enter the church, walking to the altar where the priest is waiting for us. My mother is holding the leather folio with the contract in it, and I feel my stomach knot and flip over, that well of nausea threatening as we approach. I feel trapped, hemmed in, like an animal in a cage. I want to scream, panic, run away—anything to get out of this, but there's no escaping.

I stare at the altar, my chest contracting as I try to breathe. The last time I was here was for my father's funeral. Closed-casket, since his body wasn't in a state to be viewed. The feeling in the church was different then, a sense of anger and frustration permeating the air from the gathered mourners and guests.

There could be no retribution for my father's death. No retaliation against the Mancini family. That was the word from Sicily, the order that Don Fontana gave. His judgment could have ruined either of the families involved—but he chose ours. He decided my father was at fault. He took my brother. And now all that's left to salvage our family name is to do *this*, to marry David, and try to repair what was broken.

"Do you have the ring with you?" my mother asks crisply, and I look first at her and then at David, startled out of my thoughts. I hadn't expected him to give me a ring—it feels almost like a mockery of all of this. No one has asked me what I want, and regardless of whether there's a piece of jewelry on my finger or not, I'm going to be forced to be his. When he slips a black velvet box out of his pocket, I almost want to laugh.

Please don't go down on one knee, I think desperately as he steps towards me. If he does, I don't know if I'll be able to stop myself from bursting into hysterical laughter.

Fortunately, he simply opens the box. And there, glittering against the dark velvet inside of it, is the most beautiful engagement ring I've ever seen. The most startling part isn't the size, though—at least five carats for the center stone alone—or how expensive it must be, but that it's not the most traditional ring. Instead of a white diamond, the center stone is a deep grey, just this side of black, with two trillion-cut white diamonds on either side of it, set on a plain platinum band.

"It's—" I swallow hard, staring down at the ring, my traitorous heart thumping in my chest.

"You're not a very traditional girl," David says quietly. "I thought you might prefer something less traditional, as well."

I look up at him in utter confusion, speechless for the first time, as he slips it out of the box and onto my finger. I don't understand him, not even a little bit. He's all hot, blazing passion one moment and then cold indifference, careless about my feelings one moment, and then thoughtful the next. His emotional whiplash formed into a person, and the thought of spending the rest of my life with him makes my head spin.

We might kill each other, I think as he slides the ring onto my finger. It fits perfectly, the grey and white diamonds sparkling in the low light of the church, and I swallow back the lump in my throat. I want it to mean something, but it doesn't. It *can't*, because I don't want this, and I don't truly think he does, either.

Numbly, I repeat the words the priest tells us to, taking the fountain pen I'm handed and signing my name to the contract. David does the same, and then, as the priest confirms our engagement, he takes my hand and steps closer, his fingers touching my chin as he leans in to kiss me.

It's nothing like his kisses in Ibiza, or the searing way he kissed me up against the wall this afternoon. His mouth ghosts over mine, the barest brush of lips, and my body tightens as I remember with a sudden, inappropriate flood of desire all the ways he's kissed me before. All the places on my body that his mouth has touched, all the sounds I've made because of it.

When he steps back, I instantly want to feel his mouth on mine again. I hate it—hate that he has that kind of control over me, that he can make me *want* like that. I press my lips together, stepping away from him, the ring suddenly feeling like a shackle on my hand, weighing me down.

"I'm going back to Boston tonight," David tells my mother curtly. "I'll be back to collect her in two weeks, to go back to Boston for the wedding."

He doesn't look at me again. He doesn't speak to me as he turns away, striding down the aisle and out of the church. And I realize, with a dawning horror, that this means I'll be moving to New England in two weeks.

Sudden tears spring to my eyes. I've never been there before, but I have an idea in my head that it'll be cold and bleak and isolated, and my chest clenches with panic. *You're not moving to fucking Alaska*, I tell myself as I follow my mother out to the car, trying to reason with myself, but it doesn't help. It's not even the prospect of leaving my mother and my family home—that part doesn't seem so bad—but all of my friends are here. My only ties to a normal life are here. It's all going to be ripped away from me, and I'll be alone with a husband who I barely know, and certainly don't trust.

I don't even know if I'm going to be able to finish school.

The weight of it all sinks down on my shoulders as I slip into the car, and I look down at the ring on my finger, still glimmering in the dim light. It's beautiful, but I'd do anything for it to disappear.

Once, I wanted the week with David to stretch out for longer, to have more time with him.

Now, I desperately wish I'd never see him again.

13

AMALIE

I get my answer about school the next day, when my mother abruptly tells me over breakfast that I've been withdrawn from my program.

"What?" I stare at her, dropping my grapefruit spoon against the china plate with a *clink* hard enough that it sounds as if it might have chipped the porcelain. "You can't—"

"What's the point of continuing?" My mother shrugs, elegantly scooping up a bit of cottage cheese and diced peaches on a teaspoon. "You're going to New England in two weeks. Why bother wasting time in class when you can be getting ready for your wedding, and the move? There's shopping to do—you'll need some new clothes. I've been careful with money since your father's death, but I can't send you off to the Carravellas without—"

She keeps droning on about clothes and shoes and jewelry, about what I might need for a wedding rehearsal, and I hear absolutely none of it. I'm still stuck on the part where she told me that she withdrew me from my classes, and I slap my hand down on the table without thinking, startling her out of her rambling.

"*Amalie.*" She glares at me. "If there was ever a time for you to start learning how to behave like a lady, it's now—"

"*How* were you allowed to just withdraw me? Without my consent? How is that possible?" I swallow hard, trying to force back the tears springing to my eyes—tears that are more of anger than anything else. I'd had ideas that I might be able to study remotely, that I could switch to online classes—anything to finish the degree that will be the *only* thing I'd have that was entirely mine—and now that's been taken away from me, too.

"I'm your mother," she says stiffly, picking her spoon back up. "All I needed was to sign a few papers. You're still my dependent, whatever you might like to think, Amalie. And beyond that, there is still *some* respect attached to the Leone name, even if it's more for our money than anything else. Trust me when I say there's nothing you can do about it. And as far as your little friend—" My mother pokes the spoon in my direction, her eyes narrowing. "I've taken your phone and laptop. You won't be contacting her or seeing her again. You have two weeks to change your ways of thinking, Amalie, and come to terms with your new situation. Seeing that friend of yours won't help that. It's time you focus on the future that you were born for, and not these idiotic, modern ideas of independence that you have. Claire March has nothing to do with our world, and she has no place in your new life."

I stare at my mother, entirely speechless. I can feel everything crashing down around me, and the tears well up completely before I can stop them, dripping over my eyelashes and down my cheeks.

My best friend won't even be there to help me choose a wedding dress. She won't even know *why* I've stopped talking to her, although I think she might suspect. The sudden isolation feels crushing, and I bite my lip, trying to stem the flood of tears. It's utterly useless.

"Stop being such a child." The irritation in my mother's voice is clear. "You've managed to get yourself *pregnant*, for god's sake, so it's time to grow up, Amalie."

My stomach chooses that moment to revolt, the reminder crashing into me as I shove my chair back and rush from the dining room, ignoring my mother's protests as I fling myself into the nearest bathroom.

If this keeps up, it won't take long for David to figure out the truth, no matter what my mother says.

—

Not even shopping and picking out my wedding dress can lift my spirits, although I didn't really expect that it would. My mother makes us a private appointment at a bridal salon, where I'm whisked into a dressing room and handed a satin robe while a sales associate brings a rack of dresses that have been pre-selected for me to choose from. There's no browsing through the store, no chance for me to think about what I might want for myself. Instead, I sip nervously at the sparkling apple juice someone put into a champagne flute for me, cursing the fact that I can't have any actual alcohol—and the fact that at my wedding reception, of all days, I won't be able to either.

I'm not entirely sure how I'm going to get through it all sober.

There's a fairly wide array of styles, although they're all very modest. I end up choosing a dress with a full silk skirt and a lace-overlaid bodice, with three-quarters sleeves that end in the same fringed eyelash lace that is appliqued at the hem of the gown. The addition of a fingertip-length veil with the same style of lace perfects the bridal look, and my mother is pleased with it, which makes my day a little less miserable.

But looking in the mirror as the saleslady pins and tucks for alterations, I can't fathom that I'm really going to be wearing this in two weeks—walking down the aisle to marry *David*. It all still feels like some strange dream that I'm going to wake from at any moment. I push my ring this way and that with my thumb, feeling the points of the diamonds under the pad of flesh, digging in just hard enough to hurt a little. I feel like I'm losing my mind.

None of this feels real. But it is.

My mother pays for the dress and sweeps me off to another store, choosing shoes and jewelry to go with it. I don't have very many opinions about any of it, but that doesn't really seem to matter—my mother does, and I don't think mine would have been heard, anyway.

She picks sapphire and pearl earrings, telling me that they'll match her strand of pearls that she'll give me to wear—*something borrowed and blue*—and goes back and forth endlessly over just how high of a heel I ought to wear walking down the aisle.

Privately, I hope that they're high enough that I might trip while dancing, and break my neck. That seems like it might be the best outcome for all of us.

I might be miserable, but my mother makes no secret of the fact that she's having one of the best days she's had in a long time. She might not have liked my father very much, but she's always loved the trappings and traditions of the mafia life, and this lets her fancy herself exactly what she would like to be—an important woman outfitting her daughter as she's sent off to a marriage alliance.

My mother truly was born several centuries too late.

Even stopping for lunch isn't much of a reprieve. As if to add insult to injury, we go to one of my favorite small bistros in the city, but I end up ordering the blandest thing I can think of on the menu —a strawberry and goat cheese salad with chicken and dressing on the side—since I have no idea when my meal will decide to come back up to say hello. After lunch, all I can think of for the remainder of the shopping trip is how best to keep my nausea in check. I've sipped more ginger ale over the past week than I ever wanted to— and I suspect that after this, I'll never want to taste it again.

The two weeks before David comes to collect me drag by. Without class, without Claire or any other diversion except my mother's endless lectures on how to behave myself around David's family and which mafia families in Boston I should know the names of, I almost start to look forward to the wedding. At least then, I'll have something to occupy my attention, even if it's not *good*.

Part of my time is spent wondering which version of David I'll get when he comes to collect me, and I find out the minute he walks through the door. Peevishly, I chose to wear all black for this trip— black cigarette slacks and a black silk sleeveless blouse, with simple diamond studs and a diamond solitaire necklace I was given for my eighteenth birthday. I'm waiting in the formal living room with my mother when he walks in, and I see his gaze flick to the engagement ring on my left hand, as if to make certain I'm still wearing it.

His face is cold and impassive as he looks at my mother. "Is she ready to go?" he asks bluntly, and I'm instantly seething.

"I'm *right* fucking here," I spit out, starting to stand up, and my mother grabs my elbow in that same pinching grip, yanking me back down onto the couch.

"*Language*," she hisses, and I almost burst out laughing, thinking of some of the things that David managed to pry from my lips while he drove me mad with pleasure in Ibiza—things that would make my mother's head explode if she ever heard me say them.

"You can ask me questions, you know." I ignore her, still glaring at David. "Or is that one of the mafia customs for Boston that I'm supposed to learn? Do all questions between husbands and wives go through a third party?"

I'm being sarcastic, but the way he continues to ignore me almost makes me wonder. "Are her things ready?" he asks. "Most of her luggage should be shipped to the mansion, but a few bags can go on the plane. I can only imagine how much there must be."

The derogatory way he says it, as if I'm the most spoiled creature in existence, makes me want to slap him.

"I've already arranged to ship most of her things," my mother says calmly. "Her other bags are by the door. Amalie, are you ready?"

I'm almost shaking, I'm so angry. Her tone is dismissive, as if she's finally deigning to speak to me, and I wonder what would happen if I flat-out refused to go along with any of this, if I put my foot down and said no.

At least a small part of me knows that it's my own cowardice that keeps me from doing it, because I have no idea what my life would look like if that happened. I would be alone, without resources, and I've never had to be on my own like that. Claire wouldn't help me—I believe she's a good friend, and she has genuine affection for me, but she has her own status and wealth. If I fell that far, she wouldn't reach out a hand to pick me back up.

My future is terrifying no matter what I choose—but at least with this, I know what to expect.

I stand up slowly, and this time, my mother doesn't yank me back down. "I'm ready," I say calmly, even though inwardly I'm on the verge of panic, and David motions to the door.

"Let's go, then."

He doesn't say a word to me as the driver loads my bags into the back of the black town car waiting outside. I wonder if I might get some small show of affection from my mother—a hug, a kiss on the cheek, *something*—but she only grabs my wrist before I can step away, pulling me closer for a moment as she speaks in a low voice.

"Remember why you're doing this," she says sharply. "Don't embarrass our family any more than you already have, Amalie. And for god's sake, keep your secret until after the wedding."

She whispers the last quietly enough that there's no way David could have heard it, but my stomach twists all the same. I turn when she lets go of me to see he's already in the car, and I slide inside to follow him as the driver holds open the door for me, sitting across from where he's seated. The quiet persists as the car pulls out to the highway, and I twist my hands in my lap, trying to hold back the biting words until I can't any longer.

"Is our entire marriage going to be this silent?" I snipe, and David looks up abruptly from his phone.

"Maybe not all of it." He raises one eyebrow, his lips twisting in a knowing smirk, and my cheeks flush hot. I know *exactly* what he's referencing, and I hate that, at this moment, he's decided to remind me of just how susceptible I am to his charms when he chooses to use them.

"It's not my choice anymore." I look away from him, out of the window to the scenery passing by. "So maybe I won't enjoy it as much."

"After how you kissed me in the living room? I can't say that I think that's true." There's a satisfied certainty to David's voice that makes my palms itch all over again with the urge to slap him, a feeling that's becoming more and more familiar to me with every passing day we spend together.

"I would have rather not found out, but here we are." I move as far away from him as I can, towards the window on the opposite side, my jaw clenched. The fact that he's still thinking about that kiss makes my blood heat and my pulse beat a little faster, but I refuse to let him know that he's affecting me that way, even now. I don't *want* him to know that he can still arouse me, even when he's being an utter asshole. It's more power than he should be allowed to have—or allowed to *know* that he has, anyway.

David makes a small, noncommittal noise in the back of his throat, and the car falls into silence again. It stays that way until we reach the hangar where the private jet is, the car stopping on the tarmac. The driver opens the door, and David slips out, not bothering to wait for me as he strides towards the jet.

"Are you grabbing my bags?" I look at the driver, uncertain, and when he nods, I go after David, cursing my high heels. My mother has a particular vendetta against flats, especially for occasions like this, but I promise myself that if there's one freedom I'm going to avail myself of when I'm away from home and living in New England, it's the ability to choose my own footwear.

David is already on the jet when I board. He's saying something to the pilot, and he glances over at me as I take the final step into the cabin, motioning down the aisle.

"Choose a seat," he says flatly. "It'll only be us on the flight."

I nod, wondering if it's too much to hope that he might be sitting somewhere else, *not* next to me, for the duration of it. It'll be a short flight—only about two hours—but even that is more than I want to spend in David's chilly company right now.

Unsurprisingly, I'm not so lucky.

I settle into one of the soft, beige leather seats, fishing a black cashmere cardigan out of my tote bag—I've committed to the all-black bit for today, despite how much I know it angered my mother—and slip it on as I hear David's footsteps. As if he's fully aware of how much I'd prefer space, he settles down in the seat directly across from me, his cool, dark gaze meeting mine.

"Two hours," he says thoughtfully, his gaze raking over me. I hate how handsome he is, how, even now, the way he looks at me makes me shiver in a way that has nothing to do with the faint chill in the cabin. "How should we spend it, Amalie? What do you think?"

"I brought a book," I mumble, ignoring my body's traitorous reaction to the clear insinuation in his voice. "I think there's a new album out from a band I like, so I brought earbuds too—" Too late, I remember that I don't actually have a phone any longer, but from the way David is looking at me, I don't think it's going to matter.

He gives me a cool, appraising look that's somehow still full of lust, and it reminds me of the way he looked at me that last afternoon in Ibiza, when he bought that plane ticket for me. That was one of the most humiliating experiences of my life in a week that had had several of them—and yet my stomach clenches at the memory, my thighs squeezing together as I feel a familiar throb between them. My breath catches in my throat, heat flooding me, even as I prepare to argue with him if he really tries what I think he might.

"Take the cardigan off, Amalie," he says casually. "It's not very flattering. I like seeing more of you on display for me. In fact—undo the top two buttons of your blouse, while you're at it."

I stare at him, desire momentarily forgotten in the flare of anger I feel at his arrogant tone. "You can't talk to me like that—"

"Oh, I can." David leans back, looking at me with that same careless expression on his face. "Or would you rather I tell you to strip off completely, here where anyone could walk down the aisle and see? I do have two attendants on this flight, you know. Would you like to spend the next two hours sitting in that seat naked, spread out for my viewing pleasure? I can only imagine what they would think of *that*, if they saw."

My face is burning hot, and I can see the pleasure in his face at having riled me up. He *likes* that he can get that reaction out of me, that he can take me from arousal to anger so quickly—and back again, if I'm being honest with myself.

I don't want to obey him. But I also believe that he'll do *exactly* what he's threatening, if I refuse. And that, I think, would be one humiliation too many.

Slowly, I shrug off the cashmere cardigan, laying it over the tote in the seat next to mine. Quickly, before my fingers can start to tremble too much, I undo the top two buttons of my silk blouse—just enough for David to get a glimpse of my small cleavage.

"Very nice," he breathes, shifting in his seat. A glance downwards is all I need to see that he's aroused, the visible ridge of his cock pressing thick and hard against the fabric of his suit trousers. His gaze slides over me again, taking his time, and then he nods to the space between us. "On your knees, Amalie. You've gotten me hard, and I think I'd like my cock sucked for a little while, until I decide what else I'd like to do with you."

I stare at him, momentarily torn between hatred and desire, the whiplash of feelings leaving me speechless. "We're not married yet," I protest, the words coming out choked. "We can't—"

David snorts, already undoing his belt as he looks at me. "You sucked my cock a dozen times in Ibiza," he says as he draws his zipper down. "The change in time zones doesn't make you a virgin again, Amalie. On your knees, before I think of something more entertaining to tell you to do."

My cheeks are burning hot. He nods again towards the floor, spreading his legs a little wider to make room for me. I feel that same awful sense of humiliation that I felt that last afternoon by the pool—and arousal, too. As I obey, sliding out of the leather seat and sinking to my knees in front of him, I can feel that I'm wet. The silky fabric of my panties is clinging between my thighs, damp with that aching need, and I have no doubt that he'll find out before this flight is over. That thought is enough to bring embarrassed tears to the corners of my eyes, just as he slips his thick cock free, his fist wrapping around the base as he motions for me to come closer.

"I'm not in the mood to be teased," he murmurs, reaching out to slide one hand to the back of my head as he guides me to his cock. "Open your mouth, *bellisima*."

The Italian endearment is enough to remind me of what a fool I was in Ibiza. An idiot, to hear his voice, his accent, and not suspect that his wealth came from the same sort of source that my family's did. To never, even for a moment, consider that he might be mafia.

I hadn't *wanted* to consider it, and so I'd pushed the possibility out of my head entirely. Now, I'm finding out the consequences.

His hand is heavy on the back of my head, guiding my lips to the swollen tip of his cock. I can already see pre-cum beading at the tip, begging for me to flick my tongue out and taste it, swirl my tongue around the straining flesh, tease that soft spot just beneath it the way I know he likes. I did that to him in Ibiza, learned what he likes, tried to repeat those things to please him—but at this particular moment, I have the rebellious urge to do anything *but* the things that I know he likes the most.

He said he didn't want to be teased, and so I decide that I simply won't.

I slide my lips down over the tip as his hips lift up, his hands guiding his cock and my mouth exactly where he wants them. He was never this controlling, even in Ibiza, and I hate the way it turns me on, that the forceful press of his fingers against the back of my head makes me tighten with a throbbing need. I wish he would touch me—god, even just give me permission to touch myself, but I have a feeling that I know *exactly* how that would turn out if I tried it.

The last thing I want is to end up splayed out over his lap while he spanks me in full view of anyone who might walk by, even if there's a part of me that clenches with unwanted arousal at the thought.

Even in the month since Ibiza, I've lost the trick of being able to fit him easily into my mouth. I struggle as he slides over my tongue, pushing to the back of my throat, and I realize quickly that he's not going to give me much of a chance to get used to it again. This is about what *he* wants, not making it easy on me—or even all that plea-surable, for that matter.

It makes me wonder if this is how he plans to delineate between what we were in Ibiza, and what we'll be now, as a mafia husband and wife.

"Good girl," he breathes, pressing my head down further. "Take all of it. *Fuck*—"

The way he groans aloud sends a jolt of arousal down my spine, pooling between his thighs. I moan around his cock before I can stop myself, and the satisfied way he chuckles as he threads his fingers through his hair, clearly pleased with himself, makes me hate him even more.

I hate him, and I want him, and he's going to drive me insane. This is going to be the rest of my life, and I have no idea how I'm going to make it through. How either of us are going to be able to exist together, with the way things are now.

I choke as he pushes himself further into my throat, his fingers pressing into the back of my head as he groans with pleasure. I can feel him throbbing on my tongue as I brace my hands against his thighs, struggling not to choke. The tears in my eyes well hotter at the corners, and I feel his hand fist tighter in my hair. "*Fuck*," he breathes again, his hips jerking as my throat convulses tightly around him, and then he pulls me back off of his cock, one hand fumbling in his pocket.

"Take your pants off," he groans, ripping at a foil packet. "*Now*, Amalie—"

I almost laugh, seeing the condom. I want to tell him how fucking ridiculous that is, how useless, that the time for remembering protection is long past. But my mother's voice chiding me to keep the secret echoes in my head—momentarily dampening my arousal—and I keep my mouth shut.

It won't get me out of this now, anyway. The baby is David's, and all that revealing it will do is tie us together even more tightly. I fumble with the button of my pants, feeling that hot embarrassment creep up my cheeks again at the thought of one of the flight attendants coming down the aisle and seeing me this way. David doesn't seem to care—his cock is jutting up hard and throbbing from his open fly, stiff in his hand as he rolls the condom down his length.

He barely waits for me to step out of my pants before he grabs my hip, pulling me forward. I stumble, and he jerks me into his lap, pushing my thighs apart as I straddle him, his fingers slipping beneath the edge of my panties. I gasp as his fingertips graze my clit, a jolt of pure pleasure arcing through me, and I can't stop the whimper that escapes my lips when the sensation disappears. I want more, and I grab onto his shoulders as I feel the pressure of his cockhead against my entrance, his hand still hard on my hip as he drags me downwards onto it.

I cry out. I can't help it—he's too thick, and it feels as if he's splitting me open at first, even the lubed condom and my own wetness not enough to entirely take away the burn of that first hard thrust. He sinks into me to the hilt, his hips snapping up to bury himself inside of me as he groans, both hands on my hips now as he starts to fuck himself into me.

"You're so fucking wet," he groans, one hand moving to drag his fingers through my folds, over my taut and aching clit. My flesh is stretched around him, swollen and pulsing, and I let out another gasping moan, hating myself for it. I want to be silent, to not give him the pleasure of knowing how he's affecting me, but I can't stop the sounds that spill out of my lips. He feels so good, filling me up like this, fucking me hard, *using* me. I don't know why I like it so much, or what that says about me, but I can't deny how it makes me feel.

David pulls me forward against his chest, his lips at my ear as his hips roll relentlessly up into me. "Just think, *bellisima*," he murmurs. "Once we're married, there will be no more condoms. Nothing between us. I'll fill you full of my cum every day, just like this. Do you like the sound of that, *cara mia*? Dripping with my cum all day, that pretty pussy stuffed full?"

I refuse to answer him, but I don't have to. He laughs as I tighten around him, my body betraying *exactly* the way that makes me feel, the shivering desire that ripples through me as I press my lips to his shoulder in an effort to stifle another moan. He's taken his fingers away from my clit, deliberately teasing me, but I don't think it matters. I'm going to come anyway, just from the feeling of having him inside of me like this, fucking me out in the open. I can feel that tight pressure inside of me starting to unfurl, my body tensing and shuddering as my back arches. I hear him groan deep in his throat as I squeeze around him, rippling down the length of his cock.

"Oh *fuck*—goddamnit, Amalie—" he moans my name, sending another shudder of pleasure through me as he thrusts into me one final time. Even through the condom, I can feel the hot throbbing of his cock, the way he hardens and twitches inside as he spills his cum inside of it instead of me, and for one insane moment, I wish it *was* inside of me instead. I hate him, and I want him, and for just one moment, I wish there was nothing in between us.

He holds me against his chest, and briefly, I think there's almost tenderness in the way he touches me, his fingers brushing against the back of my neck. I can feel myself still fluttering around him, the last aftershocks of pleasure still rippling through my body, and I have that brief feeling of longing again, of wanting to stay like this.

And then he moves, lifting me off of his lap so that I'm standing, weak-kneed and nearly bare from the waist down, forced to fumble for my pants on the floor as David pinches the condom and slides it off of his softening cock.

Hurt and embarrassment fill me at the same time, and I yank my pants back on, fumbling numbly at the button as I turn away. I hate that he made me come, that I want him even when he treats me like this, that I know I'll fall for it again. He doesn't speak to me as he tucks himself away and gets up to dispose of the condom, and I know he's finished with me for the night.

This will be the rest of my life, at his beck and call.

And there's nothing I can do to escape it.

14

DAVID

The night before the wedding, I introduce Amalie to my family.

We spent the preceding night in separate hotel rooms, hers well-guarded by security—both for her own safety and to ensure she didn't get any ideas about trying to run off. I know her penchant for trying to wriggle her way out of things—I met her when she was doing just that in Ibiza, after all—and I'm well aware of the sort of eye that needs to be kept on her. It's my plan to keep so much security on her at all times that there won't be the slightest chance of her running away.

I'd considered sharing a bed with her, for that same reason, but I needed space. I needed to remind myself that things are different now—that how we were in Ibiza isn't how we can be here, as husband and wife.

Amalie for a week, was intoxicating. For the rest of my life—

She could make me fall for her. She could draw feelings out of me that I've kept locked up, carefully, because I don't *want* to feel them. For that to happen, as far as I'm concerned, is unacceptable.

I lost control with her at her home, that afternoon when her mother left her alone with me for a few minutes. I'd come far too close to pushing that boring dress she'd been wearing up her thighs and fucking her up against the wall, hand over her mouth to stifle the moans that I knew would have been dripping from her lips.

The same way *she* would have been dripping for me, if I'd done that.

It's clear that she wants me, that she can't help it, even when she tries. I shouldn't find that as satisfying as I do. I shouldn't be *aroused* that I can manipulate her so thoroughly, that I can draw her to me easily, no matter how much I try to push her away in between.

I considered, for the rest of last night and all of today, trying to find a way out of the marriage. But ultimately, there's no way out that I can see. The time for that passed when I signed the betrothal contract—breaking such a thing has far-reaching consequences. Our family has been through too much already for me to take that risk.

If I wanted to avoid marriage to Amalie Leone, I should have said no back in Chicago, and dealt with my father's frustration at his attempt falling through. But I'd thought with my cock, as I had her pressed up against that wall and writhing against it, and now I'm going to have to deal with the consequences.

She's breathtaking when she comes downstairs to meet me in the hotel lobby. For a moment, all I can do is stare at her. She pauses at the top of the stairs, her gaze catching mine. I'm instantly reminded of the moment I first saw her in that bar in Ibiza, that moment when I felt a jolt of something no other woman has ever made me feel.

I have to look away, in order to regain my composure, turning away as if I need to clear my throat. Tonight, of all nights, I need her to understand that she is not the one with the upper hand here. That here, in Boston, in my family's home—everywhere from now on, for that matter—I am the one in control.

When I let myself turn back towards her, Amalie is nearly at the foot of the stairs. She's wearing a floor-length cream gown spangled with silvery threads, the straps at the shoulders thin enough to snap with a finger, the front of the dress sharply cutting downwards to reveal the slightest bit of cleavage at each side. I catch a glimpse of her creamy thigh in the slit at one side of the dress, and her dark auburn hair is piled up atop her head, leaving her collarbones and shoulders beautifully bare. There are a few tendrils left artfully loose, and they make my fingers ache with the desire to push them back away from her face.

All of her makes me feel that way. The ruby and diamond teardrops hanging from her ears make me want to trace the shape of them, and then the shell of her delicate ear on each side. The matching fine gold chain that drapes over her collarbones, ending in an egg-sized ruby surrounded by diamonds, makes me want to follow the line of it with my tongue. She looks like a present waiting to be unwrapped, a beautiful sculpture that only I'll be allowed to defile from this moment on, and all thoughts of escaping the marriage flee the moment I see her. The feeling is replaced with a sudden, possessive desire that I've never felt for any woman, and that alone *should* make me want to flee even more.

Instead, it makes me want to grab her, kiss her, claim her in every way—and never let her go.

"David." Her voice is soft and cool as she steps up next to me. "Are you ready to go?"

There's the faintest, dripping thread of sarcasm in her voice, and I know she's mimicking what I said before we left her home yesterday. I ignore it, slipping her hand through the crook of my arm as I lead her through the Art-Deco-styled lobby and out to the waiting car.

"My parents are very formal," I warn her, as the car pulls out into traffic. "You'll want to mind your tongue at dinner, and not say anything that might offend them."

Amalie's eyes narrow. She chose a burgundy lipstick for tonight that nearly matches the shade of her hair, and all I can think about is what her full lips would look like wrapped around my cock. "Or what?" she purrs, defiance coloring her tone, and that image only intensifies, until I feel my cock lengthening against my thigh with anticipation.

"Or I'll have you on your knees on the drive home," I tell her carelessly, and her eyes widen just a little. She glares at me, but I can tell from the small, quick hitch in her breath that she doesn't hate the idea as much as she wants me to think that she does. "I might just do it anyway," I add, unable to shake the desire to do exactly that, and Amalie sniffs.

"What's the point in behaving, if you're just going to do it anyway?" she asks archly, and I grin at her, a hint of a predatory smirk curving my lips.

"Because if you behave," I murmur, lowering my voice until it's a thick whisper in the air between us, "I might let you come too, *cara mia.*"

She looks away sharply. "I hate you," she hisses, not meeting my gaze, and I laugh.

"You still want me to make you come." I shrug. "Hate me all you want, but you can't pretend that's not true."

The stubborn set of her mouth as she looks out of the window tells me that she's going to try. I can think of a dozen things I'd like to do to her before the car makes it to my parents' mansion, beginning with her on her knees and ending with her skirt pushed up and her legs around my head while I lick her to a screaming climax that the driver won't be able to help but hear—but I leave it, for now.

I need to prove to myself, if nothing else, that I can avoid indulging my every whim with her. I control her desire—not the other way around.

Dinner at my parents' mansion is set in the formal dining room—a little ridiculous, I think, for a meal that consists of five guests. The table stretches on for a good length beyond where we're sitting—my father at the head, my mother at his right, and me at his left. Amalie gracefully takes her seat next to me, opposite my sister Bianca. She smiles at Amalie, her dark hair swinging around her face as she tosses her head back.

"You didn't tell me my new sister-in-law was so *pretty!*" she exclaims, her smile only widening as Amalie flushes that particular shade of rosy pink that only redheads seem to manage. "Good for you, David."

"Bianca," my mother chides, shaking her head as she looks over at Amalie. "I'm sorry about my daughter. We keep trying to teach her manners, but it's so hard these days." Her grey-blue gaze slides over Amalie, and I know what she's thinking. "I'm sure your mother and I could commiserate over that."

"Well, you'll get a chance at the wedding." Amalie's voice comes out a little more biting than I think she means for it to, and I touch her thigh warningly under the table. The way she twitches at just my touch sends a jolt of desire through me—the power that I seem to have over her is intoxicating.

I have to make sure I keep space between us, after the wedding. Separate bedrooms, maybe. Even as I think it, I can feel myself rebelling against the idea. I want to keep Amalie in my bed always, naked and ready for me whenever I please, and my cock twitches against my leg, wanting her all over again.

"Your mother is quite the formidable woman," my father says to Amalie, jolting me out of my thoughts just as the soup course is brought in. I tear my gaze away from her, trying not to notice how the jewels at her ears and throat glitter under the light from the chandelier above the table, how she seems to glow in the dress she chose. She's stunningly beautiful, and I can't seem to think straight when I'm around her. "She wasn't going to take no for an answer, in regards to this marriage."

"I wouldn't know anything about it," Amalie says coolly. "I wasn't consulted. Just told where to show up, where to stand, and where to sign."

My fingers tighten against her thigh, another warning as I reach for the decanter of wine, half-filling my glass. I expect her to do the same, but she ignores it, and I glance curiously at it. Of all the times for her to *not* have a drink, this particular choice surprises me. *Maybe she just wants to avoid slipping up in front of my parents,* I think, but even that doesn't entirely make sense, given her sharp tongue so far.

"Well, that's how things are, isn't it?" My mother's tone is breezy as she dips her spoon into her soup. "We ladies do as we're told, and keep the traditions going. And in exchange, we live quite a comfortable and pleasant life. I'll have to think of some ways to help keep you occupied, dear, once the wedding is over. I'm sure you'll need it, until the first little Carravella comes along."

Amalie winces, and I fight to keep the frown off of my face. *Surely she can't expect that I'm going to do anything other than get her pregnant as quickly as possible?* My entire goal, in fact, is to accomplish that as speedily as I can, so that I can turn my attention to other things—and to other women. The sooner I resolve the grip that she seems to have on my mind and my desire, the better—and I can't think of any better way to accomplish that than to handle the task she's meant for, and then put as much space between us as possible. A long business trip overseas, maybe, until the baby is born.

"—just thrilled for grandchildren," my mother is continuing on, her face wreathed in a polite smile. "Bianca hasn't made a good marriage yet, so until we manage that, David is our only hope."

The look that my mother casts my way makes me uncomfortable, knowing what's behind it, but I try not to let it show. Amalie had her secrets in Ibiza, and I have mine here. There are things that, if I have my way, she'll never know.

She doesn't need to.

"The wedding is all planned," she continues. My father glances at her, but says nothing, preferring to remain quiet while my mother goes on. "I've quite enjoyed putting it all together."

"I can't wait to find out what *my* wedding will look like." Amalie's voice is *just* this side of polite, her tone smooth, but I know her well enough to hear the needling sound just beneath it. I squeeze her thigh once more, but I can tell she's ignoring me.

"Well." My mother's voice is tight and formal, the way it always is. "We couldn't allow your family's recent disgrace to tarnish your wedding to our son. No one will even *think* of it, with something like this being thrown to celebrate."

I can feel the vibration that goes through Amalie's body at that.

"Like I said." My father looks at her, his face impassive. "It was quite the deal your mother struck for us to take you on. She spared nothing in convincing me." There's an edge of bitterness to his voice that makes me wonder *exactly* what it was that

Marianne Leone said, which of our family's skeletons she threw in his face. "Our families have had dealings in the past. This seems to be a good move for both of us, but especially for you, dear."

"I never heard of any of those dealings." Amalie licks her lips, reaching for her water glass as the soup course is swept away and replaced with salads. "I can't recall having heard the name Carravella at all, actually."

"Well, you haven't gotten out much, have you, dear?" My mother has that same taut, polite smile plastered on her face. "Your family kept you quite sheltered."

"Maybe I can show you around Boston, before you leave." Bianca pipes up, clearly trying to break some of the tension around the table. An admirable effort, but not one that I'm sure will have much of an effect. "There's *so* much to see, and—"

"Well, that will be up to David." My mother smiles primly, and I feel another shudder of anger go through Amalie. "I'm sure he has plans for them, after they're married. You're probably eager to get back to the mansion, aren't you?"

"Where is your home?" Amalie interrupts, and I give her a warning look. Her etiquette is abominable, and I make a mental note to talk to her about it before she's required to be on my arm for some dinner or gala. "You haven't said anything about it."

"I thought I'd keep it a surprise for after the wedding," I tell her smoothly, my hand still resting firmly on her thigh. "Now, why don't you tell me about dinner, *mama*? You said something about a new cook—"

My mother is *more* than eager to go into detail about how she planned the menu for tonight. She has two great loves in her life—spending my father's money and planning dinner parties. I know that she must have spent days, if not weeks, agonizing over exactly what to serve tonight. Amalie has probably barely noticed any of it, which irrationally irritates me, but my mother is thrilled that anyone has taken an interest in it.

"I did replace the cook," she says, taking a small bite of salad.

"The last one kept making so many substitutions and changes! Just so difficult to find good help that can follow instructions—"

"I can't imagine," Amalie says dryly. "After all, isn't that why someone goes to culinary school? To have someone else who's never been given their opinion about the recipes?"

"Amalie!" I growl her name under my breath, fortunately just as the courses are switched again. I catch a glimpse of my mother's face —she never lets her composure slip, but I can tell Amalie's comment upset her.

She goes silent, but I can feel the tension around the table thicken. The main course is served—a lamb roast with crisply roasted root vegetables and whipped garlic potatoes—and Amalie sits there quietly through it, her frame tense. I can tell from her expression that she's unhappy, and I feel a wave of bitterness wash through me.

The moment dinner is finished, I take her arm, leaning towards her. "I want to speak to you alone," I murmur, and I feel her stiffen, but she nods.

"We'll have dessert and drinks in the living room," my mother says with a forced brightness, and I stand up along with Amalie, giving her a tight smile.

"Go ahead," I tell the others. "We'll meet you in there shortly."

Amalie follows me as I lead her down the hall, opening the door to a powder room and stepping inside with her. I lock the door behind us, rounding on her instantly as she leans back against the countertop, her eyes narrowed as she looks at me.

"Well?" She crosses her arms over her breasts. "What is it that you want to yell at me about? I can see that look on your face. Go ahead."

"Your attitude is entirely inappropriate." I don't shout it, but she glares at me as if I did. "You can't speak to my family like that. You can't *behave* like that. Not if you want to be—"

"I don't." She says it curtly, tipping her chin up. "I don't want to be your wife. But *your* family, and *my* mother, and *you* decided that I would be. So please, forgive me for not simpering and smiling over your mother's idiotic conversation, and pretending like this is the warm family reception I always dreamed of."

"I haven't said anything rude about your mother—"

"Feel free to!" Amalie throws up her hands. "I can't stand my mother. And I don't like yours. She's selfish and arrogant, and I'm beginning to wonder how much of that is in you, too, since it seems like I don't know you at all."

I frown at her. "What the hell does that mean?"

She scoffs, shaking her head at me. "You know what it means. You're not the same person I met in Ibiza. Hell, if I didn't have eyes, I wouldn't be sure that you *are* the same person. You don't speak to me the same way, you don't treat me the same way, you don't even—" She breaks off, her cheeks flushing, and I smirk.

"Go on. Finish what you were going to say." I raise an eyebrow, knowing *exactly* what it is that she's about to say. But I want to hear her say it out loud.

"You don't fuck me like you did before, either."

"There it is." I lean back against the door, crossing my arms in a mirror of her stance. "Do you know why that is, Amalie?"

"Why don't you enlighten me?" she shoots back. She's not giving an inch, and it irritates the hell out of me that it's turning me on as much as it is.

"Because things are different now," I tell her flatly. "You're not some air-headed co-ed on vacation, and I'm not an ocean away from my responsibilities. Here, I'm the Carravella heir, and soon, I'll be your husband. Your *only* job is to do as you're told, marry me without complaint, and give me heirs. Your duty is my pleasure and the future of this family—and yours, I'll remind you. Or don't you know exactly how much trouble your mother has had finding you a husband after what your father did?"

She looks away, and I can see the red staining her cheeks—from both anger and shame, I think. "You know exactly the sort of situation you're in, and you know that you can't afford to talk your way out of this—even if I was inclined to let you out of it."

"Why?" Amalie's gaze whips back to mine, and she narrows her eyes. "Why did you agree to this, if you have such a low opinion of my family? Why do you want me?"

Because you drive me insane. Because every time you open your mouth all I can think about is how it feels on mine. Because I want to bury my hands in your hair right now and fuck you until neither one of us can think straight.

I bite my tongue against saying any of that. "Because your family is wealthy, Amalie. Money talks, even if your reputation is tarnished. There is room for your family name to be rehabilitated, in the future, and my father has decided that he wants to aid in that. His reasons are his own—and I am as much a subject to what he wants of me as you are."

"I don't believe that for a second," she snaps. "I think you do what you want. *Your* card wasn't cut off when you jaunted off to Ibiza on an *open-ended* vacation."

"One of the privileges I do have." I smile tightly at her. "You need to learn your place, Amalie. The sooner you do that, the more pleasant this life can be for you."

"Oh?" She tosses her head, a few more of those auburn strands falling loose. "What is my *place*, David?"

The last thin thread of my self-control snaps. I take two quick strides toward her, all it takes to close the distance between us, and I spin her around to face the mirror. "As my wife," I growl in her ear as I take a handful of her skirt in my fist, "your place is on the end of my cock. And I'll begin demonstrating that to you now, so you're reacquainted with it."

Amalie gasps as I shove her skirt to one side, draping it over her hip as I slip my fingers under the edge of her panties, pulling them to the side as well. I'm already rock-hard, stiff and aching for her in an instant, and I keep her pinned to the counter with my hips as I yank my zipper down, freeing my cock with one swift movement.

"Keep quiet," I warn her as I press my swollen tip to her entrance, gritting my teeth against my own moan of pleasure. "Unless you want my entire family and the staff to know what we're doing in here." She's hot and wet for me, and I laugh darkly, sliding my cockhead through her folds before I push inside of her. "Does fighting with me get you wet, *bellisima*? I think there will be no shortage of arguments in our marriage, so I'm glad to know you'll always be ready for my cock."

I thrust into her then, hard, pushing her forward over the sink as I wrap my hand in her hair. It's soft and thick around my fingers as I plunge them into her updo, and Amalie cries out, abruptly covering her mouth with her hand as my cock sinks into her to the hilt.

"David, my hair—"

"You can fix it after," I growl, thrusting into her again. *Christ*, she's tight, and so fucking wet. I can feel her dripping around the base of my cock as I rock my hips against her, and I slide my other hand around the front of her thigh, finding her swollen clit. She doesn't deserve to come, not really, but at that moment, I don't care. I want to feel her come all over my cock, want to prove to her once again that it doesn't matter how much she hates me or how much she fights me. She's mine, and her body will submit to me whether she wants to or not.

She presses her palm tightly against her mouth, muffling the whimpers of pleasure that escape as I fuck her hard. I feel her hips pressed against the granite counter with each thrust, and I know she'll be bruised tomorrow. The thought spurs me on even more, the idea of the marks left behind to remind her of tonight, and I thrust again, harder and harder, as I feel her start to shudder against me.

"Oh god, David—" she moans helplessly from behind her hand, looking at me with wide, glazed eyes reflected back in the mirror. She looks impossibly gorgeous like this, flushed and wrecked, her hair a mess, and her cheeks stained red, pupils dark with lust. *I* make her like this, and I feel my cock swell and throb at the thought, at the exquisite pleasure that ripples down my length with every slide into her hot, wet depths.

"*Fuck*," she breathes again, her back arching, and I know she's about to come. I see her other hand grip the edge of the counter, feel her buck against me. I roll my fingers over her clit, teasing the spot that I know she likes the best as she bows her head forward, doing her best not to scream as I tip her over the edge into an orgasm.

The way she clenches down around me feels like heaven, like hot, wet silk twisting around my cock as I thrust into her. I'm on the edge, too, and I think she realizes it, because her gaze catches mine in the mirror, wide-eyed with sudden horror as she gasps.

"Shit, David—a condom—"

I ignore her, and she lets out another whimper. "You promised," she breathes raggedly, each word punctuated by a small intake of breath as my cock pounds into her. "Not until after the wedding—"

"I changed my mind," I growl, my hand tightening in her hair as I rock forward, groaning at the sensation of her squeezing my length again. "I'd rather think about you sitting in my family's parlor, having drinks with them while you're full of my cum. Your panties are going to be *soaked* with it," I hiss, grinding myself into her as deeply as I can. "You're going to be dripping with it."

"David, *please*—" She's begging me now, her cheeks burning red at the thought of being forced to sit through the rest of the evening with my cum soaking her panties, but I don't care. The fantasy has taken hold, and I grab onto her hip with one hand, enjoying two more long, hard thrusts before I let myself go.

"Be a good girl, Amalie," I moan against her ear as I feel my cock go stiff inside of her, throbbing on the edge of my release. "Take my fucking cum."

She moans behind the hand pressed to her lips again, her eyes filling with tears as her entire body starts to tremble, and I feel her coming again, too. I feel her spasm around my cock, and I laugh, my teeth grazing her neck as the first hot spurt erupts inside of her. "That's right. Come on my cock, *cara mia*. You want every last drop, don't you? Get all of that cum, *bellisima*."

Amalie slumps forward, still shuddering with pleasure as I fill her with my cum, the pleasure dizzying. She feels so fucking good, so perfect, and my hand slides out of her hair to grip the back of her neck as I thrust my hips against her once more, groaning as I fuck my cum as deeply into her as I can.

"If you keep complaining," I whisper in her ear as I slide free, feeling the hot drip of my cum leaking from her overfull pussy as I do, "I'll make sure that you're like this before you put your wedding dress on, too. Think about if that's what you want, *cara mia*. To walk down the aisle dripping cum. I'll be happy to oblige."

Gently, I tug her panties back into place, lightly patting her folds as I do. She lets out a humiliated whimper even as she arches back into my touch, and I chuckle, taking a step back as I tuck myself away.

"Fix yourself up," I tell her as I reach for the doorknob. "You look like a mess."

She gives me a tearful glare from over her shoulder, still gripping the edge of the counter. "I hate you," she whispers, and I laugh.

"Fortunately for you," I tell her calmly, "feeling otherwise isn't a requirement for marriage in our world. In fact—it doesn't matter how you feel. Not even a little, Amalie. You should get used to that sooner, rather than later."

As I step out and close the door, I think I hear her let out a small sob. It tugs at something deep within my chest, something I've tried very hard to keep locked up tightly.

And if I know what's good for us both, I'll keep it that way.

15

AMALIE

I'd half-hoped my mother wouldn't make the trip for my wedding day, but I should have known better. This is her crowning achievement—her success in marrying me off despite everything—and there's no way she would miss it. She's in my hotel room bright and early, opening the door with a keycard that I didn't give her, throwing the curtains open as I press one hand to my face and groan.

"Get up, Amalie! We have a few hours before you need to be at the church, and everything needs to be *perfect*."

My only consolation in all of this is that if my mother is here, at least David won't be able to come in here and make good on his threat to leave me full of his cum for my walk down the aisle. My face burns every time I think about the humiliation of last night, sitting on the couch next to him with that wetness between my thighs, reminding me of his control over me. Not just to leave me like that—but to do it and make me *enjoy* it. I don't want it to feel as good as it does, but every time he fucks me, it feels like I come harder than I ever have before. It feels incredible, and a part of me thinks that it *is* how much I hate him, how much he embarrasses and shames me. I think I get off on it, and that makes me hate him even more.

It's a never-ending cycle—one that I know I'm partially trapped in of my own volition.

Room service is sent up—pointedly, only a fruit cup and cottage cheese for me, and plain orange juice instead of a mimosa. It was hard to get out of drinks last night at David's parents' house—I begged off of the port that they served with dessert, telling them I'd recently had the flu and that my stomach was still sensitive. His mother had sparkling apple juice brought up for me instead, but I saw the sideways look David gave me. I don't think he suspected, exactly—I would have heard about it from him if he had—but I think that he assumed I was just being purposefully difficult.

I don't care, I tell myself as I unwrap the lingerie that I bought on the pre-wedding shopping trip—or rather, that my mother insisted I get and I reluctantly chose. It's pretty enough—a pair of white lace cheeky-cut panties with a small satin bow in the back and satin ribbon bisecting the lace in the front, and a smooth white silk bustier to give me a little extra support under my wedding dress...not that I really need it. I leave it on the bathroom counter as I shower, lingering a little bit too long under the hot water, my hair tied up to keep it out of the way. I was informed last night that there would be a professional hair stylist and makeup artist coming to get me ready— courtesy of David's mother's planning—and god forbid I do anything to my hair before then.

I know I'm supposed to be grateful for all of this—for all of the lengths that have been gone to in order to make this a lavish wedding, when my family has fallen so far. But I don't trust it. I think there's some ulterior motive as to why *Signore* Carravella agreed to my mother's pitch to have me marry his son. It infuriates me that no one has consulted me or discussed any of it with me. I feel confident that even David knows more than I do—that everyone expects me to just be a pretty porcelain doll, dressed up and marched down the aisle, and then laid down on her back with her legs spread until a baby comes of it.

Which will be sooner than he realizes, I think darkly as I finally get out of the shower and dry off, slipping on the lingerie and throwing a robe over it all.

The stylists are already in the room when I step out. My mother gives me a pointed look that clearly says I took too long in the shower, as I'm maneuvered and plopped down in front of the vanity mirror while two sets of hands pluck and primp and curl and paint until I'm the very picture of the catalog-perfect bride on her wedding day. Soft, airbrushed makeup that covers up my light freckles without really looking as if I'm wearing anything at all, a light rose stain on my lips, my hair artfully curled and pinned up with pearl pins into a chignon that will come tumbling down with just a few quick tugs here and there, a couple of pieces left loose around my face. My mother drifts over to the closet, getting my wedding dress out, and I shrug off the robe as I go to meet her in front of the other, full-length mirror.

It all feels a little like a dream, much like that afternoon when David turned out to be the man my mother wanted me to meet. A dream that, no matter how I try, I can't wake up from.

I step into the dress, standing there mutely while my mother buttons it up, hooking the strand of pearls around my neck and sliding a vintage comb into my hair to hold the veil as she arranges it around my shoulders, finally draping it over my face. I look every bit like the doll that I feel like. I look exquisite—and I look miserable.

"Try to put a smile on your face," my mother snaps irritably. "You're acting as if you're going to your death, not simply marrying the sort of man that you were always meant to marry. This is your *birthright*, Amalie, and it's the only one you have left, since your father ruined the rest."

I feel my eyes well with tears a little, at that. It's not that I miss my father being here today—we were never very close, and he was never the kind of man that anyone could get close *to*. But it's a reminder of how thoroughly our family has fallen that no one other than my mother is here today. I've never particularly *liked* my family—but she's all I have left.

"Don't forget how lucky you are," she chides me once more as the car pulls up in front of the church. "You're fortunate that David Carravella wants you as his bride. Don't ruin this."

"I'll do my best." I can't keep the hint of sarcasm out of my voice as I slide out of the car, the heavy silk skirt pooling around my feet as my mother hands me my bouquet. The wide doors of the church open up, and I hear the strains of music as I walk inside. It should calm me, but it only frays my nerves even more.

When the second set of doors open and I see David standing at the end of the aisle, my stomach twists in a way that makes me wonder if I'm going to make it down the aisle without puking. My pregnancy nausea seems to have lightly abated the last few days—as long as I've stuck to a few "safe" foods, I've mostly been able to keep them down. But the anxiety that floods me as I start my slow walk down the aisle makes me wonder if I'm going to ruin that streak today.

It feels very lonely. I haven't spoken to Claire since my mother took my phone, and I have no idea if she's made any effort to contact me, or simply gave me up as a lost cause. I don't have any brides-maids, and there's no comfort from my mother walking with me down the aisle. Nor is there any comfort from David taking my hand as she turns me over to him, my stomach sinking all over again as I see the expressionless look on his face.

There's no feeling in his voice as he recites his vows. My voice quivers as I repeat mine, but I make it through, trying to breathe as he slides the matching band onto my finger alongside the grey and white diamond ring that he chose for me. He doesn't move as I slide his onto his finger—he might as well be a statue, unmoving, unfeeling, repeating only what he has to. And when the priest tells him that he can kiss his bride, he barely touches my waist, his mouth ghosting over mine the way it did the evening that the engagement contract was signed.

There's no hint of the man I met in Ibiza. No hint of the man who violently fucked me over the counter at his parents' mansion. I wouldn't recognize him if I couldn't see, right in front of me, that it's the same man.

And now this capricious, mercurial man is my husband.

I feel numb as we walk back down the aisle, hand in hand. *It's done*, I think to myself, sucking in the fresh air in quick gulps in the space between walking outside and getting back into the car. *There's no going back. At least I don't have to dread it any longer.*

David is silent on the way to the reception. These long silences in the car are something that I'm beginning to get used to, and at least he's not trying to fuck me. I keep quiet, too, not wanting to give him an excuse to punish me in some way, to make sure that I'm humiliated for our reception.

The room that we walk into is decorated as lavishly as I could have imagined, based on what his mother said at dinner. There are pink and white flowers everywhere, roses and peonies, and every other flower in that color scheme that I could imagine, the tables draped with silk, elegantly dressed guests already mingling at the open bar. Once again, when David leads me to our sweetheart table, I ignore the decanter of wine, and he looks at me curiously.

"You don't want a drink?" he asks, and I shrug, biting my lip.

"I'm overwhelmed," I tell him, reaching for my water glass. "And my stomach is upset. I think wine would just make it worse." I see him wince at the mention of my upset stomach, but I shrug it off. Maybe if he's disgusted by the idea, he'll leave me alone tonight.

I have to pick at the dinner, which feels like adding insult to injury. It's exquisite, an entire menu themed around various French foods, all perfectly cooked and brought out on a series of small tasting plates. I don't dare indulge in it as much as I want to—it's all prone to upsetting the delicate balance I've found with my pregnancy nausea—and I pick at a piece of rabbit thigh with cherry compote, cursing the night that David decided to forget to use a condom. If I have to be married to this man, I'd like to at least drown my sorrows in rich food and plenty of wine, but I can't even do that.

"Try not to look so miserable," he murmurs at one point, as our plates are whisked away and replaced with a piece of sous-vide fish with lemon butter sauce. "You're going to spoil everyone else's appetite, too. You could at least manage to look *grateful*, if not happy."

"Are you happy?" I look at him, trying to read *something* beyond the blank, emotionless mask that he's kept up all day. "You can't be. Not really—"

"I'm pleased that I have a means to do my duty to my family, produce an heir, and preserve our line and our traditions." The words come out almost as a recitation, and he barely looks at me as he says it. A chill goes down my spine, turning my stomach, and I set my fork down.

There's no cutting the cake together—David's mother apparently thinks it's a vulgar tradition—so instead, delicate china plates with slices of lemon sponge are passed around, a warm berry sauce and vanilla custard accompanying it. I pick at that, too, the resentment slowly building as I taste a sliver of the cake and wish I could immediately devour it.

David's mother might be a self-absorbed bitch, but she *does* know how to curate a menu.

I wonder if I might feel some heat from him when we dance, but that coldness persists, confusing me even more. If there's one thing I've always been able to count on, it's that being so close to me, *touching* me, erodes David's control. It makes the way he can so easily manipulate *my* reactions almost bearable—but tonight, there's none of that. He holds me stiffly as we move across the dance floor, barely looking at me, his hands resting lightly on my arm and on the small of my back. It's as if he wants to touch me as little as possible, and I don't understand it.

The reception seems to drag on forever. I'm almost relieved when David finally takes my hand and escorts me out to the polite cheers of our gathered guests. There's still the wedding night to get through, but after that, at least, I'll be able to sleep. And tomorrow, I'll deal with whatever comes next.

I expect him to take us to some luxury hotel in downtown Boston, and I look at him confusedly when I realize the driver is headed *out* of the city. "Where are we going?" I ask, trying to remember if he at some point mentioned a honeymoon, and I just forgot about it. I can't imagine I'd forget something like that, though, and I very much doubt David has arranged some kind of elaborate surprise for me.

Although—I glance down at my ring, remembering how that startled me. There's always a chance, but I'm not getting my hopes up.

"We're going home," David says flatly. "To my mansion. I'd like to spend my wedding night at home."

My wedding night. Not *ours*. I don't miss the pointed way that he says it, and I clench my teeth, trying not to snap back at him and to stay calm. Tonight, of all nights, I don't think I have the energy to fight with him. I don't have the energy to deal with whatever he'll do to me in return.

"Where is your mansion?" I ask curiously. We're outside of the city limits now, and I think I see a tarmac and hangar in the distance. "It's far enough away that we need to *fly* to it?"

"Newport," David says, shrugging. "A quicker trip, this way. A thirty-minute flight."

The minute we're on board the jet, I start to head towards the back bedroom. David grabs my wrist, his eyes narrowing. "Where are you going?"

"I was going to change." My wedding dress isn't horrendously uncomfortable, but that doesn't mean I want to stay in it for the flight to Newport, and then the car ride home after that. "Is that *okay* with you?" I can't keep the sarcasm out of my voice, and I see his expression darken.

"No, it's not," he says flatly. "I intend to take it off of you myself— in *our* bedroom. Sit down, Amalie."

I stare at him. For one brief, heated moment, I consider rebelling, telling him to go fuck himself and stalking back to the bedroom, locking myself in there so that I can change and maybe get a half-hour's peace. "You have got to be kidding me," I finally manage, and David smirks, shaking his head as he steers me towards one of the soft leather seats.

"I'm not," he says smoothly. "Now sit down, Amalie, and be grateful that I've decided I want to wait to take it off until we're at home, in private."

The threat is clear—not unlike the one he made last time we were on a flight together—and I obey before he tells me to do something else, like go down on him for the thirty minutes we're in the air. I settle for giving him a seething glare as I sit, looking out of the window and refusing to speak to him as the plane begins to take off.

Although, for the rest of the flight, he doesn't speak to me either.

I have no idea what his home looks like. I imagine a luxurious mansion, something over-the-top and ostentatious—and that makes the reality all the more startling when the town car pulls up in front of David's home, and stops.

It's old. That's the first thing I can see—it must be on some historical register, from the architecture and the shape it's in. Only one light illuminates the heavy, dark-wood front door, making the mansion look particularly ominous as I step out of the car and look up at it. The stone path is cracked and in need of repair, and as David opens the door to let me in, I can immediately see that goes for the rest of the house as well. Even in summer, there's a heavy chill to the air inside, and I shiver as I follow David down the hall.

He's clearly in the middle of renovations—or repairs, or both. I see places where the wallpaper has been peeled away, floors in need of refinishing, bare walls with the outline of art that once hung there. I almost ask him why it all looks like this, but I'm too tired to hear the answer—or to risk him throwing the question back in my face in some way.

The mansion gives me the creeps; I know that for certain. And David, as cold and aloof as he's been since last night, is beginning to as well.

He takes me up to the third floor, unlocking a pair of double doors with an old-fashioned key. "The master suite," he says as he pushes the doors open, and I step hesitantly inside, looking around.

This room looks to be in some of the best shape in the house—although I don't think for a second that it's for my benefit. The walls are done in dark green wallpaper edged in a muted gold, with a white-washed brick fireplace on one wall, the hearth still in need of some repair. There's a four-poster bed along one wall with glass

French doors to the left of it that appear to lead out to a balcony. The floors in this room are finished—a gleaming dark wood that matches the furniture. It's equally as cold in here, and I glance at David, wondering if he's going to light a fire. I don't want to be the one to ask.

He slips his jacket off, draping it over one of the wing chairs in front of the fireplace. His tie is next, and I don't miss the way his gaze slides over me as he undoes it, anticipation beginning to show in his eyes. When I look down, I can see his cock starting to stiffen against his thigh, pressing against the light wool of his suit trousers, and I wonder if there's any way I can get out of this tonight.

"I'm tired," I say softly, biting my lip. *Is there anything in there that I can appeal to?* "Maybe we can—do this in the morning? It's not as if I'm going to leave blood on the sheets for anyone to see, you know that. Please—"

His jaw tightens imperceptibly at the mention of blood, and I wonder if he still doesn't believe me that he was my first.

"We are going to do this," he says slowly, that hard look still on his face as he gazes at me, "properly. Turn around, Amalie, so I can undo your dress."

My heart sinks at that. "David—"

"Don't argue with me." His hands touch the back of my dress, just where the lace meets my skin, and I shiver. I can't help it—my skin heats instantly at the touch of his fingers, and as he sweeps the hair away from my neck almost gently, I close my eyes, wishing I could not want him. Wishing that he didn't make me feel this way.

He leans forward as he begins to slip the buttons loose, his lips grazing the shell of my ear. "Do you want to deny me my pleasure on our wedding night, *cara mia*? Is that how you want our marriage to start?" His breath is warm against my skin, and I swallow hard, trying to fight off the waves of desire that are already flooding through me.

He's seducing me—and he does it so easily. Button by button, his fingertips trailing a slow, molten path down my spine, sending shivers over my skin. His hands smooth over the silk of the bustier underneath it, and I press my lips together, suppressing a moan when his hands slide beneath my dress to grip my waist for a moment.

David pulls me back, my ass pressed tightly against him, and even through the layers of fabric, I can feel the hard shape of his cock pressed against me. "No one will care about the sheets, Amalie," he murmurs, his fingers returning to my buttons. "Your family is far too disgraced for that. No one would be surprised that you weren't a virgin on your wedding day. Anyway, I'm the one who *ruined* you, isn't that right? If your story is to be believed."

I feel his fingers curl into the shoulders of my dress, and he pulls it down with a quick yank, the sleeves slipping free as the bodice pools around my waist. "This is pretty," he says, his voice low and thick with desire as his hands slide around to cup my breasts, molded into the silk of the bustier. "But I prefer you naked."

He undoes the last of the buttons at the back of my dress, sending it cascading to the floor. Then I feel the sudden, hot press of his lips to the back of my neck as he begins undoing the hooks of the lingerie. "I can make this good for you, Amalie," he murmurs. "You know I can. If you're a good girl."

"What do you want?" The words come out in a hiss, and I blink back frustrated tears. "I married you, as I was told. I'm standing here letting you undress me, as I was told. Do you want me on my knees? What do you fucking *want*, David—"

"Your submission." He spins me around suddenly as the bustier falls away, leaving me bare except for the lace panties, standing there in front of him with him still fully clothed. "I want you to admit that you want this," he murmurs, leaning in close again to graze his lips over my throat, his fingers hooking in the edge of my panties. "Ask me for what you want me to do to you. *Beg*, and I'll give it to you."

He yanks the panties down, discarding them as if my wedding night lingerie means nothing—just something to be ripped off of me. A flare of anger burns in my chest, and I sink my teeth into my lower lip, stopping myself from doing exactly that. From begging, because there's so much that I do want from him.

I want his hands all over me. I want his mouth between my legs. I want him to make me come, over and over again, while I gasp and shudder and scream his name. I want all the pleasure and passion that we had in Ibiza, and none of the coldness that's invaded what we have now, none of the hurt, none of the complications.

I want to go back to a sun-drenched hotel room where we had a week of nothing but each other, and it didn't matter that we'd never see each other again at the end of it.

Not this. Not a cold, forbidding mansion and a husband who doesn't even feel like the same man.

He backs me towards the bed, my heels catching in the pile of silk and lace at my feet. I feel the backs of my thighs brush against the soft comforter, and then I'm tumbling back, my hair loosening from its updo as I land atop the bed. I feel David looming over me, and as I look up, I see him sink down to his knees, his broad, long-fingered hands spreading my legs wide.

"God, you're fucking wet," he breathes, his fingers pressing hard into my flesh. "My filthy little bride. You can't wait for my cock."

To my surprise, I feel his hands slide down instead of up, briefly cupping my knees and then gliding down my calves, all the way to the straps of the high-heeled sandals I'm wearing. I feel him deftly undo the buckles, loosening them and then slipping my shoes free, and I let out an involuntary moan as he presses his thumbs into the arches of my feet.

"See how good I can be, when you stop fighting me?" he murmurs, his fingers massaging along the curve of each foot. It feels like fucking bliss, and I hear him chuckle, low and deep in his throat, as he bends to press a kiss to the side of one arch.

He leans up again, his hands gripping my inner thighs as he drags his lips over the soft flesh. There's the barest hint of stubble on his chin, and I can't help but gasp when I feel it graze over my skin, sending shivers over every inch of me. His breath is warm against my damp flesh, and my breathing quickens as I feel him brush his lips over my folds.

I want his mouth, his tongue—I want him to devour me. I want him to make me come like that, sucking and licking me to a messy, all-consuming orgasm the way I know he can.

But I refuse to beg him for it.

When he slides his tongue over me, hot and soft in all the right places, finding those spots that he knows will make me shudder and moan and cry out, I hate him. When he presses his lips tight against me, sucking my swollen flesh into his mouth as he pins my hips to the bed, I hate him. And when he pulls away just as he knows I'm about to come, his lips glistening with my arousal as he leans over me and starts to unbutton his shirt; I hate him more than I think I ever have before.

My entire body is wound tight, throbbing on the edge of release, and frustrated tears burn at the corners of my eyes. He knows what he's doing—he *knows*; I can see it in his eyes as he shrugs off his shirt. *I won't beg,* I think fiercely as my gaze rakes over him, my body responding helplessly to the sight of his bare, muscled torso, the ink patterned over his skin, the dark hair that makes me itch to run my fingers through it. He's impossibly handsome, a perfectly sculpted man, and he knows exactly how to use it against me. He knows how much I want him.

He undoes his belt, pushing his suit trousers down his hips, and it's all I can do not to moan when his cock springs free, hard and thick against his abdomen. I can see the pre-cum pearling at the tip already, his length straining with arousal, and I feel myself clench with anticipation, my pulse beating hard in my throat.

I gasp when his hands grip my hips, pulling me sharply to the edge of the bed as he nudges his cock between my thighs. Even as wet as I am, it's still always a tight fit, and he groans as he starts to push inside of me, my body tightening even more as I feel the sharp jolts of pleasure through me.

"*God*, you feel so fucking good," he growls between clenched teeth, wrapping my legs around his hips as he starts to thrust. "So fucking tight—"

He pushes himself into me, hard and deep, all the way to the base, as the sudden pleasure tears the air from my lungs. "You'll come even if I don't touch your clit, won't you?" he murmurs, bending to whisper it in my ear, hips grinding against me. "You want that cock so fucking bad."

I look away from him, hating that he's right. The pressure of him inside of me, the fullness, the friction, is nearly enough to tip me over the edge even without the extra stimulation. He feels incredible, just as he always does, and I bite my lip against a moan—but it slips out anyway as he thrusts again, my legs tightening around his hips as if to pull him deeper. I know he feels it when he laughs, dark and low in his throat, and he rolls his hips slowly against me again, letting me feel every inch of him.

"Tell me the truth, Amalie," he murmurs into my ear as he thrusts again. "Was I really your first? I've already married you, you can be honest."

I want to slap him. I want to push him off of me. I want to tangle my arms and legs around him and keep him inside of me until he makes me come. I've never known that it was possible to feel so many conflicting, awful feelings about one person, and I glare up at him, my body trembling on the verge of orgasm as I spit the words into his face.

"You were the first," I hiss. "You're the only one. And *god*, right now, I wish that weren't true."

David's hand fists in my hair, his mouth crashing against mine in the first kiss he's given me since the chaste one at the altar, his thrusts turning hard and relentless again. I feel the moment that I spill over the edge, his tongue tangling with mine as he growls something against my lips that almost sounds like my name. I feel him swell and harden inside of me, the hot rush of his cum prolonging my orgasm as I cry out against his lips. The force of the pleasure brings tears to my eyes, and I shudder and arch underneath him, my fingers clawing against his shoulders hard enough to draw blood. I don't care if I do —I almost hope I hurt him. I want *something* to hurt him. I want him to know how this feels.

He pulls out of me, breathing hard, and turns away. I watch dizzily as he strides to the bathroom, not looking back as he shuts the door hard behind him, and I see the light turn on from the other side as I hear him start the shower.

I shove away the urge to wonder what I did wrong as I crawl up the bed, sliding under the covers. It doesn't matter. I don't think I've *done* anything—I think there's something that David wants that I haven't—or can't—give him, and I'm not sure I'll ever know what that is.

I'm not entirely sure I care.

The bed is frigid, and I shiver under the thick comforter, listening to the spray of the shower from the bathroom and hoping that I can warm up quickly. This mansion feels like a tomb, and I wonder if it will be better in the morning, in the light of day.

I wonder if anything will.

16

AMALIE

Nothing feels better in the light of day. I wake up in bed alone and sore, the blankets tugged up on David's side, with no sign of him—not so much as a note to tell me where he is or what he might want me to do. I sit up, rubbing sleep out of my eyes, and immediately realize that the mansion feels just as cold as it did last night.

It's summer, and this house feels as frigid as a tomb.

The only solution that I can see for it is a hot shower, and I slide out of bed, wincing at the soreness in my hips and the stickiness on my thighs as I walk across the room. The bathroom is as unfinished as the rest of the house—there's a space that looks as if it's meant for a jacuzzi tub that's empty, the tiles pulled up around it, and there's one sink in the dual counter. The shower stall is the one part that looks as if it's been completed—it's large, big enough for *several* people with a granite bench on one side of it and dark mosaic tiling, niches shaped into the walls for things like shampoo and soap.

The shower itself is blissful. I wash all the product out of my hair from the day before, nearly moaning as I rub my fingers across my scalp and soothe the soreness from the pins holding it in place—and

David's hand roughly grabbing it last night. A shiver runs through me at *that* memory, and I shake my head, trying to dislodge it.

I have to stop wanting him. He's always going to use it against me, and it's always going to make things harder. *Surely it can't be like this forever,* I tell myself as I scrub the remaining traces of him away with honey-scented soap, trying to bolster myself with that thought. It's lust, which has to wear off eventually. He'll grow bored with me, and I'll get tired of him. Then we'll slowly put more and more space between each other until we become one of those married couples that simply exist in each others' orbit, instead of being—what we are now.

I just have to wait it out. I try to take some comfort in that thought as I towel off and get dressed, wrapping my damp hair up in a loose bun atop my head, and opting for leggings and a long tank top with a cardigan for the morning. Normally, I wouldn't need a sweater this time of year, but the chill in the house is pervasive, and I shiver as I head downstairs the two flights to the main floor. My stomach is growling from hunger and twisting with nausea all at once, and I hope that there'll be something I can eat that won't make me throw up.

To my dismay, I find David at the kitchen table. Like most of the house so far, I see signs of renovation in progress, and I sink down at the edge of the table, looking at him apprehensively.

"Good morning." He sets his phone down, appraising me with a single look. "Cold?"

"It's chilly in here." I push the sleeves up a little, and the hair on my forearms prickles. "Something to do with the house being so old?"

David nods. "Stone is good insulation, but with all the damp especially, it keeps the chill in as well as it keeps the heat from going out. It's not outfitted with central heating yet, and with so many workers in and out, I haven't bothered keeping the fireplaces going. I also haven't been home in a while," he says pointedly, and I feel my cheeks heat with the reminder of Ibiza.

"How does breakfast work here?" I ask, and instantly regret it when I see him smirk.

"Go to the kitchen and see what you can find. I'm sorry I don't have a staff just yet to wait on you hand and foot, but I'll see what I can do about—"

I'm up and out of my chair, storming out before he can finish his sentence. *How dare he*, I fume as I stalk in the direction that I *hope* is the kitchen, anger suffusing every part of me until I feel certain steam is going to come out of my ears. I *know* he must have grown up with a household staff, too, that it's perfectly normal in families like ours, but of *course,* he would turn it around into something to make me feel bad about myself.

I nearly trip over a stack of boards going into the kitchen, and curse aloud. "Fuck!" I hiss into the echoing, empty air, heading for the refrigerator. That, at least, looks shiny and new, as does the stove —but I don't have the slightest idea how to use the latter. That is, I know how to turn it on, but I don't know how to actually *cook* anything.

I don't want to admit that to David, so I poke through the refrigerator instead, hoping to find something I won't have to prepare. I find yogurt that's not out of date—strawberry and vanilla, and hunt for a spoon. I hate strawberries, but everything else looks as if it needs to be cooked.

Spoon in hand, I lean back against the counter, eating it in small bites. I have no desire to go back into the dining room with him, and I hope he won't come and find me.

Unfortunately, he does. I'm eating the last of the yogurt when I see his shadow stretch across the tiled floor, and I look up with a sigh.

"Don't worry, I haven't run off. Although I wouldn't even know where to run *to*, out here." The mansion appears to be a little ways away from the civilization of Newport—I can see the water off to one far side, and a half-cultivated garden behind it, but not much else. Whatever neighbors David has, they're out of seeing distance.

"I see you found something you were capable of preparing for yourself." He points to the yogurt cup, and I briefly consider throwing it at him, but manage to contain myself and toss it in the trash instead. It's not really enough for breakfast, but I don't trust myself to keep anything more down.

"You should really think about hiring staff." I push myself away from the counter, starting to walk past him, but he grabs my elbow. Not hard enough to hurt, but hard enough to let me know he wants me to stop and talk to him.

"I was going to give you a tour," he says in a calm, neutral voice. "Or don't you care to see your new home?"

I don't, not really. The entire house has an uncomfortable feeling to it, and it's not at all what I thought David would be bringing me home to. I thought, at the very least, that the home I'd be living in would be *finished*.

"Sure." I give in anyway, because it's not worth the inevitable fight. "Show me around."

"Well, you can see the garden from here." He guides me towards the large window on one side of the kitchen, where I can get a better view of it. "It needs some landscaping and for the fence to be fixed, but I have some people coming in for that."

"It needs a lot more than landscaping," I mutter, and he gives me a glowering look.

"Is this not up to your standards, Amalie? I promise you, at one point, this place was stunning. A mansion every bit as luxurious as the one you grew up in, but with history behind it. My family relocated to Boston some years ago, and it fell into disrepair, but I've taken it upon myself to fix that."

"The army of workers you've hired, you mean." I toss my head back, looking up at him. "I can't imagine you've lifted a single finger or hammered a single nail."

David frowns at me. "I'll have you know I have done some small things myself," he says flatly. "I enjoy working with my hands."

The last is said with just the smallest hint of lasciviousness, just enough to remind me of the things he can do to me, how quickly he can bring me to my knees—quite literally. I narrow my eyes at him, trying not to take the bait.

"But," he adds when I don't say anything, "I find it's usually better to let those with actual experience do the job. Come with me, I'll show you more."

His hand touches the small of my back as he guides me out of the room, and I try not to react. I try not to let him see the heat that floods through me at that simple touch, the way I want to lean into him. I follow him into the hall, and he leads me into the formal living room—which right now is just a huge room with the walls stripped bare and a fireplace with no hearth or stonework around it, dustcovers thrown over the furniture. "My brother started repairs on it," he says, gesturing around the room. "That's why so much of it seems half-finished. I decided to take it over shortly after—"

He pauses, and I look at him curiously. It's the first time in a while that I've heard any hint of emotion in his voice, and he clears his throat, looking away.

"He passed away two years ago," David says shortly. "I started looking into finishing the repairs after that. But it's taken some time. A lot has—happened."

I feel a pang in my chest. I know what it's like to lose a family member, even if my father wasn't someone for whom I felt the loss too deeply. "I'm sorry," I say softly. "Were you—close?"

"To a point." David's jaw tenses. "We don't need to talk about it. But I did want to explain to you why the place is in such a state of—disarray, I suppose you could say."

I open my mouth to say something in response—I'm not even sure what, yet—and I'm hit with a sudden surge of nausea that sends me spinning on my heel, rushing for wherever the nearest bathroom might be. I fling open two separate doors that lead to the wrong rooms, on the verge of throwing up before I can make it to one before I finally find the doorway that leads to a half-finished bathroom and collapse in front of the toilet, heaving.

Yogurt isn't on the list of safe foods, I think dizzily as I cling to the edge of the bowl, tears dripping down my cheeks as I empty my stomach entirely.

There's a knock at the door, and I wince. "Amalie?" David's voice comes through it, sounding more than a little confused. "Are you alright?"

"Keep it up, and I'll start to think you care," I mumble, before a fresh wave of nausea sends me lurching forward again.

He lets out a heavy sigh. "Are you sick?"

"Yes." I sit back, trying to gauge if it's safe to rinse my mouth out and leave, or if I'm going to end up right back here. "I'm sick."

I haven't really thought out when to tell him about the pregnancy. My mother made a point of saying *after the wedding*, and here we are. We're married—but she also said to wait as long as possible. Long enough, I suppose, for him to think it might be a result of sex post-marriage, and not before.

The thing is, I don't think there's anything that will make David divorce me. If there was, I think I'd try to use it just to get out of this hell of a marriage. I think, with the endless years of *this* stretching out in front of me, that I might do just about anything to stop this from being my entire future.

Slowly, I stand up, flushing and then cupping my hand under the running water to rinse out my mouth. I want to get upstairs to my toothbrush; I want to go back to bed. Instead, I know I'm going to have to deal with David, who I can tell is still hovering outside the door.

I snatch it open, and the way he briefly recoils back, startled, is somewhat satisfying.

"Amalie?" He looks at me warily. "You didn't seem sick last night. Did something at the wedding reception not agree with you? We ate the same food—"

"Maybe the wedding night didn't agree with me." I start to push past him, and once again, he stops me. "Are you going to dictate my coming and going *everywhere*, all of the time, or just when we're in close proximity? I want to go upstairs."

"And not finish the tour?" David is looking at me suspiciously.

"Do you have food poisoning?" He reaches up suddenly, pressing the back of his hand to my forehead. "You don't feel warm. What's going on, Amalie?"

I glare at him, fresh anger welling up. I suddenly feel entirely too frustrated with all of this—with his arrogance, his high-handedness, his need to control me. I jerk away from his hand, feeling the rage loosen my tongue until I can't hold back any longer.

"I'm pregnant," I spit at him, and I have one satisfying moment of seeing the utter shock on his face before his expression hardens into distrustful suspicion.

"You're pregnant." He says it slowly, narrowing his eyes at me. "And if you know that now, *right* now, then that means you knew it before the wedding."

"Maybe I took a test this morning." I cross my arms over my chest. "You certainly weren't in bed with me to know one way or another."

"You conniving little bitch," David breathes. "You and your mother. And don't tell me you *wanted* me in bed with you this morning, because we both know that's not true."

"Weren't you just telling me two nights ago not to talk about *your* mother like that?" I snap, taking a step back to put more space between us. David comes after me, his glare is predatory, and I take another step.

"You said you didn't care how I talked about your mother." David's jaw clenches. "Oh, for fuck's sake, Amalie, that doesn't even matter! You're sidetracking this on purpose. What the *fuck*? You knew you were pregnant before the wedding, and you didn't tell me. And I know you kept it from me on purpose, too." He shakes his head. "And you had the nerve to get upset at me for not using a condom! As if it would have fucking mattered—"

"It was the principle of the thing," I hiss. "You promised."

"And you promised me you were a virgin before me! Not that I ever believed you. I'm even less likely to believe you now—" His lips thin, and I see him take in a deep, shuddering breath. "Is it even mine, Amalie? Or were there other guys that you let fuck you raw in Ibiza?"

I try to slap him before I can stop myself. I feel my cheeks flush hot, my entire body simmering with rage, and the only thing that *does* stop me is his hand grabbing my wrist before my palm can connect with his face. He spins me effortlessly, backing me up against the wall as his hand grips my wrist.

"Nice try, Amalie," he growls. "Now, let's try this again. Is it mine?"

"Yes, you insufferable son of a bitch!" I hiss. "It's your baby. Happy? I told you that you were the only man I fucked, and I meant it. But I'm *really, really* starting to regret it!"

He glares down at me, his dark eyes burning with rage. "No," he growls. "I'm not happy, because I don't believe a fucking word you say. I'm not convinced that it's my baby, not even a little. I'm not convinced that mine was the first cock in you, because it's just my luck that I end up with a lying little slut for a wife. But we'll find out, eventually. And if it's not mine—" The muscle in his jaw leaps as he looks at me with a coldness that makes me shiver down to my toes. "You'll be begging me for mercy then, Amalie."

David lets me go with a jerk, spinning on his heel and stalking away from me down the hall. I reach for my wrist where he grabbed it, massaging the joint as I watch him go, shivering all over from more than the cold now.

I don't really want to go back to our bedroom, but it's the most finished room in the house, and the only one where I can be even slightly comfortable. I shut the doors, leaning back against them as I close my eyes, trying to calm the panic that's churning inside of me.

It doesn't matter, I tell myself as I walk to the bed, sinking down on the edge of it and trying to gather my thoughts. *It is his, so whether he believes me or not, he'll find out the truth eventually.* But it's not so much the thought of that question that frightens me.

David has a side to him that scares me. A cold, dark side that is nothing like the man I wanted in Ibiza. And every time I see it, it feels colder. Darker. If I let myself think about it for too long, it terrifies me. I know very well what a man like him—a man steeped in mafia traditions and expectations—might do to a wife they hate...or worse yet, distrust. There is no sacredness of life in the mafia, no belief that anyone is above vengeance. If anything, a wife is easier to get rid of. To dispose of. These men keep each other's secrets, no matter how dark. If David wanted to make me disappear, he could. I have no doubt of that.

This was the worst yet. I'm afraid to find out how much worse it could be—and at the same time, I don't know how to stop egging him on. He knows how to get under my skin, how to make me lose my temper, and my common sense.

I listen for a long time for his footsteps to come upstairs, and when I don't hear them, I finally relax long enough to take a nap. I curl up in the huge bed, pulling a thick knitted wool throw blanket over me, and close my eyes.

—

The house is silent when I wake up, and relief washes over me at the idea that I might be alone. My head aches a little, and I rub a hand over my eyes, blinking at the sun coming through the glass doors that lead out to the balcony.

Pulling on a cardigan, I pad across the chilly wooden floor and tug the doors open, stepping outside. It's warm and a little humid out, and I fling the doors wider, hoping some of the warmth will make its way inside. On this side of the house, I can see the wide stretch of partially-kept lawn—it's not overgrown, but nothing particularly special has been done with it. Past that is a line of trees, and I wonder if there are any neighbors on the other side of it—if anyone ever comes over. If David has friends here, or if he keeps to himself.

Men in his position, in my limited experience of my own father and brother, don't have *friends* so much as they have colleagues. Some bosses make friends with their enforcers or underbosses—back in Chicago, it's well-known that the leader of the Irish Kings, Theo McNeil, is as close to his enforcer as a brother. My father was always an arrogant and reserved man, so perhaps that was part of the problem—but then again, so are most mafia men that I've encountered.

Friends of David's means the possibility of other mafia wives—and I find that I don't mind the thought of that so much as I might have in the past. It would be, if anything, a bit of a salve for the loneliness that I can already feel creeping in.

In Boston, I would have had more ways to keep myself occupied. Here, I feel isolated and cut off, and there's a sense of panic that's already beginning to settle in. *Surely he's not going to just keep me here,* I tell myself as I stand there, gripping the edge of the balcony railing. *Surely we'll go to Boston. Other places. This can't be my life now.*

I tug my cardigan around myself as I walk back into the house, leaving the doors open for the warmth. I still don't hear any signs of life, so I slip out of the bedroom, padding down the hall barefoot to peek into the other rooms.

Most of them are unfinished guest rooms, and a large library with a fireplace that's in disrepair, as well as some faded velvet furniture and empty bookshelves that are mostly in need of replacing. The room—like most of the rest of the house—makes my skin crawl a little, and I quickly dart back out.

The only other thing I find is a staircase that appears to lead up to a partial fourth floor. I look at it uncertainly, wondering if I ought to go poking around anywhere else without David's permission. I can imagine him being angry about it—and in the end, that's what pushes me to do it anyway. *He can't control every move I make,* I think bitterly as I start to go up the staircase, gritting my teeth against the anxious feeling that has settled in my stomach.

When I reach the landing, I realize there's only one door up here. The rest of it is an empty, open room with a water-damaged wooden floor and a filthy window, and I bite my lip, looking at the door. It feels like a room that I'm probably not supposed to go into, even though David didn't explicitly tell me that there's anywhere in the house that I'm not allowed to go. But the feeling just makes me want even more to find out what's inside.

It's locked, which doesn't surprise me—but it also doesn't deter me. My first thought is that the key might be hidden somewhere, and it's easier to find than I might have thought. My initial instinct turns out to be the right one—when I go up on my tiptoes to feel along the top of the lintel, I feel a thick, heavy key. It's old-fashioned, the kind you might expect to find in a historic house, and it fits perfectly into the lock.

For the briefest moment, I wonder if it's a trap—if David left the key in a place where I wouldn't have to look too hard to find it, in order to see if I'd go into a place I'm clearly not meant to. And then, as the lock clicks open, I decide that I don't really care.

If he's going to keep me in this decrepit old place, then I at least want the chance to explore it.

The door creaks when I nudge it open, and I immediately smell dust and mothballs. There's a light switch on the wood-paneled wall next to me, and I flick it on; the only light source is a bare bulb hanging from the ceiling.

The room is, essentially, an attic. There are some old pieces of furniture, some stacked, framed art against one wall, and a stack of boxes. My curiosity gets the better of me, and I walk over to the boxes, knowing that I probably shouldn't be snooping and unable to find it in myself to care.

The first box looks like it holds some old family paraphernalia— recipe books, and some old photographs that I give a perfunctory glance. Some of them appear to be fairly old—the sort of family photos that someone probably gathered together in one place to eventually turn into a scrapbook or photo album, and never did. It's clear that David was at least telling the truth about this being his family home—several of the pictures are taken out in front of it, dating back a few generations. I can vaguely recognize a few of the rooms, too, although I can't be certain that they were taken here. I'm no architect, and most of the features of the house look like any other old home to me.

I stuff the pictures back into the box. If this is all that's up here, I don't really know why it's locked. None of it seems particularly inter- esting, just photos of long-dead family members and recipes for stews, pies, and bread that probably haven't been looked at in decades. I can't imagine any self-respecting mafia wife cooking her own family meals now.

Sitting down on the dusty floor where I've been crouched, I reach for the next box, expecting more of the same. Truthfully, I'm already bored by it—but the only thing worse than sitting here poking through David's ancient family history is sitting downstairs with absolutely nothing to do. So I open the box—and instantly pause, staring down into it.

THE BELONGINGS inside look like they must have been a woman's—someone who must have owned them fairly recently. There's a silver-backed hand mirror, a matching brush that still has strands of dark brown hair clinging to the bristles, several pieces of jewelry that look fairly valuable, a silk blouse neatly folded at the bottom, and a ceramic dish hand-painted with roses that looks like the sort of thing that would sit on a side table to hold jewelry or keys. I immediately feel strange looking at the items, like I'm touching things that were once very personal to someone, and now have been shoved away into this dusty old attic.

But it's what's in the other two boxes that really makes my stomach drop.

They're full of children's things. Clothes, toys, a few smaller odds and ends like a crib mobile and pacifiers. And again—they don't look old, like they belonged to David or his brother as children. They don't have the musty smell of clothing that's been boxed up for years, and the fabrics don't look aged at all. The toys look like things that might have been purchased recently—I even see one small picture book that's from a fairly new children's cartoon.

I feel a crawling sensation down my spine as I look at the contents, almost immediately closing the boxes up and shoving them back into the corner. I shake my hands quickly the minute they're out of reach, as if to get the feeling off of my fingers. But I can still smell the faint scents of floral perfume from the woman's things, and the hints of baby powder from the child's clothes.

Something about this feels all wrong.

He mentioned a brother who had passed away. I tell myself that maybe it has something to do with that, that the knotted feeling in my stomach is just because of the utter upheaval that my life has gone through in the last two weeks. That I'm being paranoid.

I know I shouldn't mention it to David at all. I'm upstairs in the bedroom when he comes home, curled on the bed under a thick blanket and trying to focus on a book. I hear the door open and nearly jump out of my skin, and he gives me a quizzical look.

"Awfully jumpy, aren't you?" He raises an eyebrow. "Come downstairs. I got takeout from an Italian place in Newport. It's good; you'll like it."

I press my lips together, wracking my brain for some reason to beg off and stay upstairs, and David rolls his eyes.

"You can't hide in the bedroom forever, Amalie. Just come eat. I'm willing to bet you haven't eaten all day, and that's not good for the baby."

He says it so casually that it makes my heart leap oddly in my chest. "So you believe me now?"

David frowns. "I believe you're pregnant. Whether it's mine or not is another matter." He shrugs off his jacket, walking to the closet to hang it up. When he starts to unbutton his shirt, my heart gives another traitorous leap in my chest, and I do my best to ignore it. He's fucking with me—I know he is. He knows exactly how I react to seeing him undressed, and he wants to prove to me, once again, that it doesn't matter how he behaves or how he makes me feel.

I'm going to want him regardless.

I grit my teeth, marking my spot in my book and tossing it aside. "I'm not really hungry," I tell him, just a hint of defiance in my voice, and David lets out a long-suffering sigh, reaching for his belt.

"Just come down and eat, Amalie. A little time in my company won't kill you."

My breath hitches in my throat at that. It's foolish, but something about the way he says it makes my stomach knot. *You're being paranoid,* I tell myself as I get up. He glances over at me and frowns.

"That's what you're wearing around the house?"

I look down at my clothes. It's just a pair of black leggings and a long black tank top with crocheted lace at the neckline, my cashmere cardigan still wrapped around me. "Yes? It's cold in here, and I wanted to be comfortable."

"You can't put on something nicer for dinner?" David is dressing as he speaks, taking out a pair of folded chinos and a henley. I glare at him.

"Is the queen coming to eat dinner with us? Because otherwise I can't see a reason to get dressed up. It's takeout in your half-destroyed dining room, not a banquet."

Sudden ire leaps into David's expression, and I see that small muscle in his jaw leaps again. We got along so much better when all we did was fuck and shop and go out to dinner, when there was an expiration date on our relationship. Now, I feel certain he hates me as much as I think I hate him. "It's being renovated," he says icily. "It's not destroyed. Fine. Come down to dinner in whatever you want. Just stop being such a child about it."

He strides past me, slamming the door behind him, and I resist the urge to pick up the nearest thing to hand and fling it at the door. *He'll really think I'm being a child then,* I tell myself, and instead go to the bathroom to run a brush angrily through my hair, flinging it up onto my head in a loose bun. *Now I can really look like I don't give a shit.*

The thought of what I found in the attic today is still lingering with me. I don't want to go downstairs—in his already creepy house that's now been made even more so by those discoveries—and pretend that everything is alright. It's not—and I don't know that it ever will be.

I can't just ask him about what I found, either. At best, he won't give me a straight answer. At worst, he'll be furious with me, and we'll have a repeat of the fight this morning—or worse.

David is already in the half-*renovated* informal dining room when I go down, two of the windows cracked to let in the warm, salty evening breeze as he takes containers of takeout out of paper bags and arranges them on the table. "Have your pick," he says, setting out two plates as well, and a glass of water for me. He sets down a glass of wine by his own plate. "There's ricotta in the lasagna, I think—you probably shouldn't eat that."

I frown at him as I sit down, wondering how he knows so much about what pregnant women should and shouldn't eat. I think of the boxes I found in the attic again, the children's clothes and toys that were packed away. That same unsettled feeling knots in my stomach again as I put a couple of small forkfuls of fettuccine alfredo on my plate. Everything smells incredible, but I don't trust my stomach.

David puts a little of everything on a plate and sits down across from me, reaching for his glass of wine. He doesn't say anything else, and I bite my lip, feeling the oppressive silence wrap around us both.

"You can't just push it around your plate," he says suddenly, the snap of his words shattering the quiet. "For fuck's sake, Amalie, I'm not keeping you prisoner."

I look up at him sharply. "I explored the house a little more while you were gone," I tell him, suddenly unable to keep quiet about what I'd found a moment longer. "I found some interesting things in the attic."

There's a flicker of an expression that crosses his face, but I can't quite read what it is, even though I make a point to watch him carefully as I say it. He takes another bite of his food, letting the moment stretch out, and I feel that knot of apprehension in my stomach tighten. "What sort of "interesting" things?" he asks finally, a hint of sarcasm in his voice, and I grit my teeth. It always feels like he's toying with me, and it just makes me angrier with him.

"I did." I stab a bit of pasta, swirling it around my fork. "There was a whole stack of boxes that I spent some time going through. Not what I would have expected to find up there." I'm being purposefully vague, hoping he'll incriminate himself with a look, a reaction, something that will tell me that my feeling was right. That there is something ominous about what I found, and that I'm not just being paranoid.

"Oh?" There's still no recognition in his tone, and that pisses me off even more.

"A woman's things. Jewelry, a mirror, stuff like that. And *children's* clothes. Toys. They all looked new—I recognized a cartoon from ads I've seen that hasn't been out all that long." I narrow my eyes at him. "Didn't you say this was your family's home? They didn't look old enough to have been yours, or—" I start to say, *or your brother's,* but the sudden flash of irritation in David's eyes stops me. Even I know better than to pick at a wound.

"That's none of your business." He stabs his fork into a piece of veal parmesan, and I wince.

"I live here now." I press my lips together, sucking in a breath. I know I'm pushing him, but it's so fucking difficult not to. He makes it so difficult. "We're married now, David, or did you forget? This house is mine now, too. What happened here is my business. Especially if I'm going to raise your heir here—"

David looks up, silencing me with a glare that sends a chill down to his toes. His jaw clenches, and I go very quiet.

"Whether or not you're carrying 'my heir' remains to be seen," he says tightly, his voice carefully quiet. Far be it from me to tell you where to go wandering and poking around. But don't expect me to entertain you with stories about whatever it is that you find."

I bite my lip, and I'm startled to feel tears suddenly burning at the back of my eyes. I don't know how to reconcile this cold, emotionless man with the man that I spent a week in Ibiza with—a man who enjoyed playing games with me, true, but who was passionate and full of life. This man feels as implacable and unyielding as a statue.

The dining room goes silent, quiet enough that I can almost imagine that I can hear my own heartbeat thudding in my chest. "Have you thought about a honeymoon?" I ask tentatively, trying to change the subject to something more pleasant. *Maybe it's this house, maybe it's being home, being near his family again,* I think desperately, still twirling my fork around pasta that I haven't yet taken a bite of. All I can think is that maybe, somehow, if we go far enough away to some place that will remind him of Ibiza, I'll get a glimpse of the other side of him. Maybe I could find some way to connect with him that will make life together less miserable.

David makes a noise that's somewhere between a laugh and a scoff, and any hope of that possibility vanishes.

"Wasn't the vacation we just had enough?" he asks, his voice heavy with sarcasm, and the way he looks at me as he says it tells me that he's trying to make me snap. He's trying to push and push, so that I'll lose my temper, and then he doesn't have to feel like he's the bad guy in this situation.

"Of course it was." I press my lips together, dropping my fork. Suddenly, even the sight of the food is making me nauseated. "Is there *anywhere* in this house that has a working bathtub?" I desperately want to slide into hot water and soak, and the fact that there's no tub in the master bathroom yet feels like adding insult to injury.

David shrugs. "Maybe in one of the guest bathrooms," he says flatly, and then goes back to the sliver of lasagna on his plate.

I shove my chair back, leaving my untouched dinner there as I stalk away. The house smells of dust, raw wood, and wallpaper glue, and I wrinkle my nose. I hate this place more and more with every passing moment that I'm here, and the fact that I have to *hunt* for a bathtub makes it feel worse. David's way of treating me like that makes me spoiled is just the awful cherry on top.

The guest bathrooms haven't been touched in the "renovations" yet, and one of them is clean and nice enough that I hide in there, closing the door firmly while I run a hot bath. I don't find any bubbles or bath oils to add to it, but the hot water is enough, and I sink into it with a sigh, closing my eyes. All of my muscles are sore from how tense I've been, and I let some of it seep away, hoping that if I stay in the bath long enough, David will be asleep by the time I go up to bed.

I refill the tub twice when the water cools off, prolonging it until I'm wrinkly and pink and I feel waterlogged. I dry off and wrap a robe around myself, scooping my clothes off of the floor and tiptoeing up to the master bedroom. To my relief, when I nudge the door open, I see that the lights are off, and David is on his side of the bed, unmoving.

Slowly, I find a pair of sleep shorts and a tank top, slipping into them, and sliding as silently as I can into my side of the bed. I can feel the heavy weight of him lying next to me, and I lay there stiffly, wondering how I'm going to endure this for the rest of my life.

We can't avoid each other forever. And I'm very afraid of how much worse this might get before he gets tired of me and we simply drift apart.

I've never felt so alone. And now I'm frightened, too.

17

DAVID

In the forty-eight hours since I said *I do* to Amalie, I feel like my life has become even more complicated than it was before.

This was a mistake. I haven't stopped thinking that since I brought her here for our wedding night, and every moment since has just underscored that feeling. My desire for her constantly wars with my irritation about how unwilling she is to try to settle in to her new home, to try to do anything for herself, to not constantly *pout* about having been pulled out of her former life. *This was always going to be her future,* I think on repeat, every time she seems unhappy. *Was she really that deluded to think she wouldn't end up married to someone she didn't necessarily want?*

The pregnancy was just another wrench thrown into a situation that I already regretted allowing myself to get tangled up in. I haven't been sure if I believed her story that she was a virgin when we first slept together in Ibiza, and this makes me wonder even more. And it *matters* if the baby is mine or not, for reasons beyond just my own ego.

Our children will have my name and inherit the Carravella family fortune, homes, and legacy. I refuse to have that passed on to the child of some trust-fund asshole that Amalie fucked on vacation, whose name she probably doesn't even remember...who likely doesn't remember hers, either.

When I came home last night, I brought home some things that she'd be able to eat without having to learn how to cook, in hopes that would at least improve her mood. She's right that I need to hire some staff, but I simply haven't needed to until now. I've been fine on takeout when I haven't been out of the country, and I'm reminded that now I have someone else besides myself that I have to worry about. Not to mention—I like the privacy and solitude of not having housekeepers and cooks and gardeners bustling around. It's bad enough having the workers who are renovating the house in and out constantly, and I'll never be free of the security detail that's a requirement for a man in my position. That security detail has increased now, too, because of Amalie and the need to be certain she's safe.

Amalie has turned my life upside down in a matter of days. I had my life carefully arranged the way I liked it. Now, her presence combined with that disruption has only added to my resentment towards her. I knew I would have to marry—but I had hoped it would be someone who understood that it was meant to be a marriage of necessity. Someone who would keep to herself, manage her own affairs, and only interact with me when necessary. Possibly even someone self-sufficient enough to not need a household full of staff to attend to her every need as soon as possible.

All of this would be much easier if she could just take care of herself, but I'm not entirely sure that she's capable of it. On the other hand, though, I think to myself as I dress, hiring staff might mean she finally leaves me alone. They could provide a buffer for me, taking care of her needs and wants so that I don't have to hear about them. It might be the only way I'll manage to live the separate lives I'd hoped for, while existing in the same house.

There's only one way *to find out*, I think grimly as I come downstairs for breakfast. She came to bed last night after I'd already fallen asleep, and to my surprise, she was gone this morning when I woke up. I'd had the thought that she might have tried to run off, and the sharp prick of fear that I felt at that idea startled me.

I told myself that it's only the prospect of how utterly furious and disappointed my father would be that made me feel that way, but I'm not entirely sure. Amalie has a way of making me feel things that I normally don't. It's one of the reasons I didn't want to get too close to her in Ibiza—and one of the reasons I should have said no to marrying her.

She's at the table when I walk in with my oatmeal and a cup of coffee, picking at what looks like a bowl of yogurt, granola, and fruit.

"I see you managed to handle a kitchen knife without hurting yourself," I say dryly, sitting down across from her. I know, of course, that I picked up whole strawberries from the store, and I know that the comment is going to get under her skin. It does—I can see it immediately from the glare she throws in my direction.

"I'm not helpless," she snaps, digging her spoon into the bowl and pushing it around. It's clear her appetite leaves the moment I enter the room, which irritates me to no end. I've never hurt her. I've done nothing except marry her, the thing that her family desperately needed to do, and yet she's treating me as if I'm some kind of villain.

"I didn't say you were," I smirk, taking a bite of my own breakfast. I see Amalie give my coffee a longing look, and I take a pointed sip, enjoying the frustration on her face. Especially after the nonsense about the attic last night, I'm enjoying making her a little uncomfortable.

What is upstairs in that attic is none of her business, exactly as I told her—and for the thousandth time since I said I do, I wish my father had chosen a woman for me who knows when to leave well enough alone. Surely, there are any number of women who would find a locked door and leave it that way—but not Amalie.

It's at least partially my fault for not taking that goddamned key and putting it elsewhere. But that doesn't change the fact that there is, apparently, nothing that Amalie doesn't think she's entitled to answers about.

It doesn't matter, I think grimly, taking another sip of her coffee. If I have my way, she'll never find out a single detail about any of that.

"I'm going to Boston for a few days to see my family and take care of some business," I tell her flatly, setting down the cup. "I want you to stay here. And I mean *here*, as in on this property, near or in the house. I don't want you to go off on your own. Is that understood?"

She narrows her eyes at me. "I thought you said you *weren't* keeping me prisoner."

I let out a slow, heavy sigh. "They're guidelines for your protection, Amalie, not *keeping you prisoner*. You don't need to be so dramatic all of the time."

"Then give me something to do." She leans back in her seat, anger wreathing her features. "I'm bored to tears, David, and it's been two days. And you want me to just stay here in this awful house, alone? I could be working on my college classes remotely right now, but my mother withdrew me without my consent."

I grit my teeth. It pisses me off to no end when she insults the mansion—*my* family home—just because it's not in the same perfect condition that hers is. But her comment about school startles me. I had no idea that her mother made that decision for her, and *that* makes me angry, too.

"I had nothing to do with you being pulled out of school, Amalie," I tell her curtly.

"Except for the fact that you married me." She purses her lips. "But, of course, it's not at all your fault. Nothing is."

"I would have had no issue with you continuing your classes from here. That was your mother's doing—nothing to do with me or my family. If you want to re-enroll, feel free."

Amalie glares at me. "And who is going to pay for my tuition? Not my mother, now. Are you going to? I don't have the ability to make that call myself."

I resist the urge to reach up and rub my temples. "We'll discuss it when I come back," I tell her finally. "I don't have time to figure this out right now."

"You don't—" Those high points of red are on her cheekbones again, a clear sign that she's about to blow up at me. "David—"

"You really need to learn to control your temper," I tell her evenly. "That kind of high blood pressure is probably bad for the—"

"I swear to *god*—" She jumps up, shoving her chair back before I can say *baby*, and is gone in an instant. I hear the heavy clatter of her footsteps on the stairs, and I lean back, closing my eyes against the headache that I can feel building.

We can't spend more than five minutes in the same room together without getting into a fight. *How are we meant to stay married*? I know most mafia couples don't particularly enjoy each others' company. After a while, they tend to simply avoid each other as much as possible, putting on the necessary face when there's an event. But Amalie doesn't even seem willing to do that. Part of the reason I'm not bringing her to Boston is because I don't trust her not to cause more problems with my family than it's worth.

She infuriates me. She complicates everything. She drives me mad—and even so, she makes me want her with a ferocity that almost hurts. I realize, sitting there as I watch her storm out with her face gorgeously flushed, her anger shimmering around her like a heat wave, that I'm rock hard, my cock straining against my fly.

I want to fuck her as much as I want to scream at her.

Shoving my own chair back, I stalk after her, up the stairs to our bedroom. She had a headstart, and I fling open the doors just in time to see her stripping off the loose t-shirt she had on, her hair tied up on her head as if she's about to get into the shower.

She whirls around, the t-shirt pressed to her chest, and I smirk.

"Don't mind me." I cross my arms over my chest, nodding in her direction. "Finish taking the rest off. I'll watch. And then be a good girl, and bend over the side of the bed for me."

Her eyes go wide. "Don't you have something better to do?" she snaps, turning away. "I'm going to take a shower. Just—leave me alone."

"No." I watch her stiffen, and my cock throbs against my thigh. "Finish undressing, Amalie. Unless you want me to come over there and take the rest of it off for you. Or maybe you'd like a spanking, when you finally come to terms with the fact that you *will* be bending over the bed for me, just as I told you to."

I can *see* the tension, the anger running through her. "Why is it always *bend over* somewhere?" she hisses. "Over the sink in that bathroom in Ibiza. Over the counter at your parents' mansion. Over our bed. Do you have a particular fetish for fucking me from behind, David?"

That does make me laugh, just a little. "No," I tell her carelessly. "But at least that way, I don't have to worry about you spitting in my face."

"You fucking—" She hisses the words between her teeth, and I laugh again.

"Hurry up, *bellisima*. I have a flight to catch. Luckily, it's my own private jet, so they'll wait for me. But your attitude is turning me on this morning, and, well—I really need to come. So be a good girl, and do as I say, so I have somewhere to put it."

I reach for my belt as I say the last, and Amalie stiffens again when she hears the sound. I see the t-shirt drop to the floor as I undo my zipper, slipping my cock free. I'm so fucking hard it hurts, my balls already tight with the need to empty myself into her, and I wrap my hand around my length, letting out a hiss of pleasure at the much-needed contact.

"Don't make me drag you over there and strip you myself," I warn her, groaning low in my throat as I slide my hand down my cock in a loose stroke. "You'll wish you hadn't. Or would you rather I put you on your knees and come on your face?"

I can see her grit her teeth as she shoves her leggings down her hips, every movement telling me exactly how angry she is about this. In moments, she's stripped bare for me, her perfect body exposed to me entirely, from the curve of her waist to the heart-shape of her ass. She strides over to the bed, refusing to look at me as she bends over the side of it. Her fingers curl angrily into the blankets, and I stride towards her, my cock aching.

I'd be willing to bet that when I touch her, she's dripping wet.

I reach for her hair before I do anything else, yanking the velvet hair-tie that's holding it up free and tossing it aside. Her thick auburn hair cascades around her face and shoulders in messy waves, and I wrap one hand in it, pulling her head back as I slide my fingers between her thighs.

As I'd suspected, she's soaked.

"So much fight for nothing," I breathe into her ear as I stroke her entrance, rubbing my fingers along her drenched, swollen folds. "You clearly want me, Amalie. You want my thick, hard cock fucking you, making you come. You want my cum inside of you, so you can't help but think of me while I'm gone. You *want* all of this. If you weren't so stubborn, *cara mia*, this would all be so much more enjoyable."

"Fuck you," she hisses, twisting her head around to glare at me. "I don't want to think about you at all."

I chuckle darkly at that, nudging my cockhead against her entrance as I press two fingertips against her swollen clit. "Even if that's true, Amalie, you're going to anyway. You're *mine*. My bride. My *possession*. Mine to fuck. Mine to have however I please."

I thrust hard when I say it, shoving every inch of my cock deeply into her, down to the base. She lets out a cry that's half pain, half pleasure, sending a burst of satisfaction through me as I thrust again, and she moans helplessly.

"That's it," I murmur, my lips grazing over her ear. "You love getting fucked like this. You want me to think that's not true, but I can feel it. You're fucking *squeezing* me, *bellissima*. You can't get enough of my fucking cock."

It's true, and we both know it. I can *feel* it. The sensation is exquisite, the way she clenches and ripples around me, like her body wants to drag my cock as deeply as it can inside of her and hold me there forever. I feel sure that nothing has ever felt as good as this, and that nothing else ever will. She can claim all she likes that she doesn't want this, that she hates me, that she wishes she was rid of me and our marriage. But the tight clench of her pussy around me, the arch of her back, the way her nails dig into the bedding as her mouth drops open on a soundless moan—all of those things tell me a very different story.

"Fuck you," she gasps, even as I feel her writhe on my cock as I slide out of her, her ass pushing back against me as if she can't bear to lose those thick inches filling her up for even a moment. "*Fuck you, you fucking—*"

I take that moment to roll her clit between my fingers, rubbing her exactly the way I know she likes it best, that spot near the top of her hood that makes her come almost instantly. I hear her breathless gasp, feel her entire body seize—and then my cock is drenched with her arousal as she comes, her back arching as she collapses forward on the bed, the tight clench of her almost unbearably good.

"That's right, *cara mia,*" I growl, my hand on the back of her neck as I press her face down against the bed, my pace picking up as I fuck her hard and fast. "Come on my fucking cock. God, you feel so fucking good—"

She cries out, lost in pleasure as I slam my cock into her again and again, heedless of how roughly I'm fucking her. I've never been so angry and aroused all at once in my life, and I take it out on her with every brutal thrust. My fingers left her clit with her first orgasm, my hands occupied now with holding her by the neck and hip as I ruthlessly pound into her, but I feel her come again anyway. Her cry of pleasure fills the room, her entire body shuddering with wave after wave of release, and I don't let up. I keep fucking her, as hard as I can, until I feel my balls tighten and my cock swell, and I push her down hard against the bed, flat on her stomach as I lean over her and whisper in her ear.

"I could pull out and come all over you. I *should*. I should drench you in my fucking cum and make you wear it, so you remember who you belong to. But I'm going to fill you up instead." I thrust again, pressing myself tightly against her, rolling my hips. "I don't care that you're already pregnant, *bellisima*. I'm going to keep you dripping with my cum anyway."

Amalie cries out, and I resume my pace, driving my cock into her with two more hard strokes that push me over the edge. The sound that comes from my lips as I sink into her for the last time is nearly primal, the pleasure rippling through me with an intensity that's close to pain as hot cum spurts from my cock, filling her with a flood of it as I pin her there and hold her down for my release.

I don't want to slip out of her, even as my orgasm recedes and my cock softens. I'm still throbbing with the aftershocks, and I find myself wanting to stay buried in her wet heat, to remain there until I'm hard all over again and can fuck her for a second time.

That feeling—that urge to stay close to her—is what makes me pull out abruptly, stepping away to put distance between us as I tuck my cock quickly back into my pants. Amalie doesn't move for a long moment, her eyes squeezed tightly shut, and then she finally pushes herself off of the bed, refusing to look at me as she sits on the edge. Her legs are clamped tightly together, and she wraps her arms over her breasts, looking pointedly away.

Something about it infuriates me. I'm not sure exactly what it is or why, but I stalk towards her, closing the distance between us in two quick strides as I grab her chin and turn her face to mine.

I feel her gasp when I crush my mouth against hers, my fingers gripping her jaw—and I don't know what's come over me.

I've barely kissed her since our wedding. I've made a point of *not* kissing her. I don't want there to be anything romantic between us—and this isn't meant to be a romantic kiss, either.

But somehow, it feels like one. And she feels it, too. I can tell from the way she turns towards me, softening into my touch, her mouth parting under mine. For a brief moment, we're both lost in the kiss, and I have the sudden urge to spill her back into the bed, to run my hands over every inch of her the way I did in Ibiza, to keep her there with me for the rest of the day.

I pull away, releasing her with a sharp twist of my hand that sends her reeling back a little. Her eyes are wide as she looks up at me, startled, as if she wasn't expecting me to kiss her like that. I *know* she wasn't expecting it.

"I have a flight to catch," I tell her coldly, turning away. "Don't leave the immediate grounds of the house, Amalie. I'll be very upset if I come back to find that you've disobeyed me. I'm leaving security here, and they'll keep an eye on you."

Her face tightens instantly, any softness gone as her expression turns mutinous. But she just nods, her arms still tightly crossed over her chest as I reach for my leather duffel and walk out of the room.

—

On the short flight to Boston, I do my best not to think about my wife. It should be easy—I don't *want* to think about her, and I have plenty of other things to consider, since my father wants me there to discuss business. But I can't seem to shake Amalie from my thoughts.

She's different here from the girl I met in Ibiza. There, she was carefree and flirtatious, wild, and a little reckless. Here, she's anxious and petulant, angry and suspicious by turns, and seemingly intent on infuriating me constantly. Every time I think back on that afternoon in the library, I feel certain that I should have refused to marry her. My father might have been frustrated with the failure of the arrangement, but I'm rapidly beginning to think I'd rather have faced that than the frustration of having been pushed into marrying Amalie Leone. She's far from the kind of girl I would have chosen for a wife.

I wanted someone who understood my expectations, who would want peace and security above all else. Those things I can provide, so long as I'm given my own peace in return. But Amalie—

Maybe I should have brought her with me. The problem of the attic pokes at the back of my mind, and I grit my teeth, realizing I should have re-locked the door and taken the key. If she continues to snoop around—

I have to hope that she'll be bored with that particular line of investigation before it becomes more of a problem. But I already know that's decidedly not the sort of woman Amalie is. She's stubborn and persistent, and I can tell from even this short time that she's not going to simply smile and put on a pleasant face for dinner parties and charity events, and then return to us ignoring each other at home. She's going to keep poking, prodding, and insisting that I answer her questions until things blow up between us. At this point, I half-hope the baby isn't mine, so I have an excuse to be finished with her.

Is that really what you want? That nagging question lingers in my mind, taunting me. No matter how much I insist that I want a gulf of distance between my wife and me, to only be closed when we lower a mutually agreed-upon drawbridge, I don't react that way when I'm near her. I can't figure her out, and it's making me feel obsessive. The opposite of what I want.

Truthfully, I don't know what it is that *she* wants. And we can't seem to stop fighting with one another long enough for us to figure that out.

I know my father is going to bring up my marriage from the moment I take a seat in his office that evening, after dinner. There's a cautious but knowing look on his face that I recognize, and I wince as I take the glass of port he offers me, waiting for him to say whatever it is that's on his mind.

It doesn't take him long.

"You need to get your new wife pregnant sooner rather than later," my father says without preamble, and I have to force myself not to choke on my port. "Don Fontana isn't thrilled with the arrangement I made. He didn't disapprove enough to step in, obviously, but I think he wants the Leone family permanently ground into the dirt for the trouble they've caused, not rehabilitated. He's still got the Leone boy under house arrest. I wouldn't be surprised if he disappeared one of these days and was simply—never heard from again."

The idea isn't shocking. I wouldn't put it past Fontana to do such a thing, if he thought it was for the good of the Family.

"Don't worry," I say dryly, taking a sip of my wine. "I'm doing my best to make sure there's an heir sooner rather than later."

I try to keep my expression tempered, but the conversation makes me angry with Amalie all over again. For all that she keeps insisting that she was a virgin the first time we slept together, that the baby *must* be mine, I'm not entirely sure that I believe her. If the baby is mine, then the issue of an heir is already solved. But if it's not—

Then Don Fontana will make *absolutely* certain that the Leone family never recovers from this final shame. If Amalie's family were the only ones affected, I might say it serves her right for trying to pass off another man's child as mine. But the disgrace of having been tricked into arranging a marriage with a ruined bride carrying an illegitimate child might very well be the final nail in the coffin for our family, too.

My father chuckles as he sits back down, thankfully not noticing anything amiss with my mood. "I'm sure you're quite the enterprising groom in that regard. It will be a happy day all around once we know that the Carravella family has an heir to carry on after my sons once again."

I wince at the plural. My brother is gone, but my father often makes references that make it seem as if he's still here. As if his mistakes aren't the reason that I've been put in position after position that I want no part of. As if they're not the reason I've been forced into marriage when I could have otherwise remained a bachelor, a second son with fewer responsibilities and more freedom, the life that my order of birth earned me.

"You'll be the first to know," I tell him evenly. "And then *mama*, of course."

My father smiles, finishing his glass of port and sitting back. "I'd like to send you to Sicily in my stead next spring," he says slowly. "But it will all depend on timing, of course. If your wife is pregnant, you might bring her here to stay with us, and you can go on the trip alone. I think you'd prefer that." He looks at me knowingly, and I take a slow breath.

He's right, of course. While a trip to Sicily isn't as pleasant as carousing through Ibiza, it's still far from here, and there's plenty in and around it to amuse myself—especially if I'm there without Amalie. But, of course, Amalie should have had her baby by then. She'll have a newborn, which is even more reason for me to want to leave her here with my mother to supervise and take off for Sicily alone.

Amalie, I know, will throw a fit at the prospect.

"I'll certainly think about it," I tell him, finishing my own drink and getting up to refill the glass. "After all, time apart makes the heart grow fonder, doesn't it?"

My father chuckles at that. He knows as well as anyone the dynamics of a mafia marriage, and the difficulties and pitfalls that come with it. It might not be the mark of a good family man to leave my wife and newborn child—if the child *is* mine—with her in-laws, but few mafia men could be called good at *family*. What we're required to be good at is dealing with *the* Family, the organization that, to some extent, controls us all. We're responsible for keeping up appearances, always—something Amalie will have to learn to be better at...something she should already know how to do. Who can blame us if, when we're not dealing with the pressures of managing these empires, we like to blow off steam somewhere other than our own households, if we prefer *not* to spend our evenings with wives we don't love and children who have been sired for a purpose?

I certainly don't blame any man who does, myself least of all. Amalie should have been raised to expect a marriage of convenience, not one of trust, companionship, or fidelity. And whatever ideas she might have gotten in her head, she'll learn differently soon enough.

"It might." My father cocks his head slightly, as if thinking. "Are you not happy with her?"

"She'll do. She's good enough for what we need, isn't she?" There's a wealth of things that I'm hiding under those words—my doubts about Amalie's truthfulness, the outrageous lust that she provokes in me every time she's near, the way I'm not entirely sure if it's possible for us to make it out of this marriage without killing each other. But I force a tight smile, and my father seems to take it at face value.

She'll get used to it, I tell myself as he turns to other matters—our businesses in Boston, finances, shipments, the things he wants me to help him run out of Newport. *She'll stop fighting me, and we can find some peace. A truce, at least.* And there's the baby to consider.

If the baby is mine, then the matter of an heir will be settled, so long as Amalie gives me a son. She'll be distracted with our child, and

I'll be free to go on about my life as I please. And if the baby *isn't* mine—

In that case, I think, teeth gritted against the very idea as I try to focus on what my father is saying, *she'll go the same way as the rest of her family.*

And in that case, I tell myself I'll be glad to see her go.

18

AMALIE

There was never a chance in hell that I was going to actually listen to David, and stay in the house.

If anything, I was thrilled at the chance to get out of the awful, creepy mansion for a little while. David's company does nothing to warm the place, figuratively speaking, but being alone there is somehow even worse. The night after he leaves, it takes me hours to fall asleep, every creak and groan of the old building making me jolt awake. I'm not foolish enough to believe in ghosts, but the ancient, dark atmosphere combined with my discoveries in the attic and the feeling of being utterly alone is enough to make me so jumpy that I don't rest well. Which is a shame, because I would have enjoyed having the bed—one of the few luxuries in the mansion right now, plush and huge—to myself.

David has security posted all around the mansion, but they're good at making themselves scarce. It makes the house feel empty, but it also means that once I've made up my mind to slip out and explore, slipping past them isn't all that difficult. I don't know if they expect me to try and make a run for it or not, but all that time dodging my own security detail in Chicago to spend time with Claire has paid off. The driver is apparently the one staff member who hasn't been told that I'm supposed to stay close to home—I think David assumed the security would be buffer enough—and he defers to me when I ask him to take me into Newport for the day.

I have no idea if David will get a call from security once they realize I'm gone, but I can't bring myself to care. The feeling of abrupt freedom and being out to explore all on my own makes any consequence feel worth it.

THE GIDDY BLISS of freedom is only marred by the reminders of just how caged I am. No phone, and no credit card either. I found some cash in David's office—left unlocked, as if he really thought I wouldn't dare to snoop— and stuffed it into my clutch to get me through the day. It's more than enough to shop and eat on, and I let my worries drift away as I walk down the sidewalk, the skirt of my sundress ruffling around my knees as I try to decide where I want to go first.

There are plenty of shops—some cute and kitschy, others touristy, and some more elegant. Nothing is as fancy as the sort of thing I can find in downtown Chicago—there's nothing designer here, but I decide to lean into the charm of it instead of being put off by the idea. I've never set foot in a thrift store in my life, but I duck into one that's housed in a small whitestone building that's nestled between a coffeeshop and a jewelry store, curious as to what I might find.

The small bell over the door makes a chiming sound as I step in, and a middle-aged woman with greying blonde hair looks up from a ledger that she's poring through at a glass counter. I can see that the inside of the counter is filled with all sorts of things—mostly jewelry, but some other odds and ends, too, and I wander over toward it.

"Can I help you find anything, love?" she asks, her voice kind, and I glance up at her. There's a casual friendliness to her that I'm unused to. It takes me a second to realize that here, to her, I could be a local or a tourist—but certainly not the wife of a mafia heir.

There's a certain pleasant freedom to that, too.

"I'm just browsing. I haven't been in a store like this before." The moment it comes out of my mouth, I realize it might seem rude, but the woman just chuckles.

"No, you don't look like you have."

I bite my lip. "I just meant with so much—variety."

She laughs again, but pleasantly, without any rancor. "Well, look around. You might find something you like."

I'm not so sure about that, but to my surprise, I find that there are more interesting things in the shop than I might have expected. The antiques and household goods are all a bit quaint for my taste—even if they do look like they'd look right at home in David's crumbling old mansion—but near the back of the shop, I find a surprising treasure.

On one of the clothing racks, draped over a silk-wrapped hanger, I find an old fur stole. It's in remarkably good condition, definitely vintage, and I run my hand over it, marveling at how soft it is. The rich grey color, flecked with black, would look beautiful with my dark auburn hair, and I immediately decide that I want it. The fact that my mother would be horrified if she knew I was purchasing something from a thrift shop only makes me more determined to buy it.

The price shocks me—only fifty dollars. "Are you sure this is genuine?" I ask the woman behind the glass counter, and she chuckles again.

"Of course. Got it at an estate sale. Lovely piece. I'm sure you'll put it to good use." She takes my cash and wraps it up in paper, slipping it into a plain brown paper bag. I stifle a small grin, thinking of a future opportunity to wear it—to the first gala or party David takes me to as his wife, maybe. There's a thrill to the idea of wearing something that would embarrass him if he knew were it was from.

The purchase makes me feel rebellious enough to try something else new. My whole life, I've either eaten the meals our culinary expert of a cook has crafted, or dined at five-star restaurants. Ibiza was no exception. The first time I've eaten food from anywhere that might be called an 'ordinary' restaurant has been the takeout David has brought home, and even that was exceptional. I keep an eye out for where he might have gotten it, but nowhere jumps out at me, and I start to wonder where I might want to get lunch.

There's a small restaurant towards the end of Thames Street that I notice—a little terracotta building that clearly serves Mexican food. It smells amazing—rich and spicy, and I wander inside, wondering if I'll like it. Once again, I feel a little rebellious, going to a place I normally never would, that my mother would *definitely* disapprove of...that David might disapprove of. It's that same reckless feeling that sent me to Ibiza, but on a much smaller scale.

The moment I'm seated, a bowl of salsa and a plastic basket of chips are set in front of me, along with a laminated menu that's a little cracked at the edges. It's a far cry from anywhere I've gone in the past, *but that's the point*, I remind myself. I'd passed any number of fancier restaurants, but I wanted to try something different.

Maybe that's why David lives in that mansion, I think suddenly, as I peruse the menu. *Maybe he wants something different from what he's used to.* I reject the idea almost as soon as I think of it—I don't want to excuse him living there, or get used to it. I hate the old, crumbling house—I have since the moment I walked into it. And I definitely don't want to spend the rest of my life there.

I look longingly at the list of margaritas, and when the server comes back, I order the thing on the menu that seems the most familiar—street tacos with shredded chicken and some sort of sauce that I'm unsure of. The only tacos I've ever had have been deconstructed, some kind of upscale fusion dish, and I wonder if I'll like these.

What if I could talk David into moving back to Boston? I dip a chip into the salsa, surprised by how much I like it, and consider. He seems to tolerate his family, and surely, his father would prefer having him close by to help with their businesses. And once David is sure that the baby is his, his mother might want her grandchild closer. As much as I dislike his mother—and the idea of having her in such proximity—I'd rather live in a newer, more modern home close by her than isolated in the cold and dreary mansion out here.

There's the possibility that, once he knows I'm telling the truth about the pregnancy, he'll be warmer with me. More agreeable, at least. And surely, it makes his life easier if his wife is happy.

I demolish half the basket of chips before I realize I've gone through them, and I'm startled to also realize that my stomach doesn't seem to be rebelling so far. Whether the worst of my pregnancy nausea has passed, or whether it's the sun and fresh salt air, I think I might actually be able to keep a full meal down.

When I take my first bite of taco—better than any deconstructed one I've ever been served—and swallow it without incident, I decide that this might be one of the best days I've had in a while.

It starts to give me hope that maybe, things won't always be as bad as they've felt since my wedding.

Maybe, just maybe, I don't have to feel like my life is over.

—

The hope lingers into the evening when I get back to the mansion with my few purchases from the day. I can't bring myself to think of the place as *home*, but I feel a little less despondent than I did when I snuck out this morning. I slip in the back door the same way I slipped out, and no one seems to notice or say anything to me.

It seems like I got away with my small rebellion, and that makes me feel a little happier, too.

I sit down in the half-finished dining room with a takeout Wagyu burger that I got from a bistro before leaving—this one fancier than my lunch, with tomato jam, caramelized onion, garlic aioli, and arugula. I managed to keep my lunch down, which made me both brave and ravenous—I can't remember the last time I was able to eat anything other than the blandest food without feeling sick. I nibble at the burger and accompanying sweet potato fries, once again feeling victorious when I don't feel as if it's going to come back up, and decide to go upstairs for a bath after. The silence of the house feels more relaxing now instead of frightening, and I haven't thought of the attic or any of my worries about this place or my marriage all day.

By the time I go to bed, sleepy and relaxed from the bath, I almost miss David a little. With him gone, my mind keeps drifting back to the way he was in Ibiza—demanding and a little controlling, yes, but also passionate and attentive. I shrug off the robe that I'd tossed on after my bath, feeling daring as I slide into bed atop the covers and let my hand trail downwards.

The thought of Ibiza, and David, already has me wet. I can feel it, sticky between my folds even before I slip my fingers between my legs, and I moan softly as my fingertips graze over my clit. Being alone in an essentially empty house makes me feel bold, and I spread my legs wider, imagining that I'm back in Ibiza, in that penthouse suite where David brought me after rescuing me in the restaurant. I close my eyes, arching my back, spreading myself open as I imagine him standing at the foot of the bed, urging me on.

He'd be half-dressed still, his shirt unbuttoned and open to reveal his muscled chest inked with tattoos and dusted with dark hair, his pants undone, and his fist around his cock. I moan again, soft and breathy at the thought of it—at the thought of his cock, thick and long and hard, and how perfect it feels inside of me. I'd been spoiled, having him as my first. I can't imagine that any other cock would ever feel as good.

Good girl. I can imagine him groaning that as he strokes himself slowly, without any hurry, enjoying the show. I can imagine him telling me to spread myself wider, to let him look at me, and I fold my knees to either side, a fresh wave of arousal soaking my fingers as I imagine him standing there. He'd be able to see every wet, swollen bit of flesh between my thighs. I rub my finger lewdly over my slick clit, rolling it back and forth until I can feel how swollen it is, how visible.

I can imagine opening my eyes, seeing his hand tighten around his cock, his eyes dark with lust. *Rub that sweet, wet pussy for me,* he'd murmur, his thumb sliding over his wet cockhead, letting me see how much he wants me, too. His cock would be dripping with pre-cum, slick and wet for me, his jaw tight with the effort of not climbing onto the bed and fucking me. The restraint of waiting, and enjoying the show.

I never would have thought I was such an exhibitionist, but I've never come harder in my life than I did when he had me pressed up against that glass window. I have no idea if anyone really was watching or not, if there was some other man stroking his cock to the sight of my naked body pressed to the glass, my arousal streaked across it as David rubbed my pussy. It doesn't matter, really—one way or another, the thought made me come. Just like imagining David watching me now is on the verge of making me come faster than I want to.

"I want your cock." I breathe the words aloud, startling myself with them, with the *yearning* in them. I slide my other hand down, slipping two fingers into my aching pussy, but it's not enough. I need more. I need to feel David inside of me.

Fuck. I'm so close, but I don't want to come like this. It won't be enough. I pull my hands away with some effort, rolling off of the bed and walking naked across the room to dig through one of the boxes I tucked away in the closet, hoping David wouldn't care enough to look. The last thing I wanted was to endure his teasing—or his irritation—if he came across my sex toys. He's already having enough trouble believing I was a virgin.

But *that* man isn't the one I'm fantasizing about. All I can think about is the version of David that I met in Ibiza. That version is so different from the man I married that it almost feels like I'm cheating on my husband. It's enough to almost make me feel as if I'm imagining another man's cock in me altogether when I slip a dildo I purchased after coming back from Ibiza out of the box, walking quickly back to the bed. I managed to get it by shipping it to Claire's house and having her bring the box to me at school, and now I'm glad I did.

I start to lie back again, but then I bite my lip as a different, wicked thought fills my head. I roll over onto my stomach, pushing my hips up and back into the air, just the way he likes to fuck me so often. Except this time, I'm imagining that he's watching. Stroking his cock as he watches me slide the thick dildo into myself, almost as thick as David, stretching me wide as my fingers quickly find my throbbing clit again.

This makes it easy to imagine I'm in Ibiza again, back in that licentious, warm place where I could be anyone I wanted, do anything I wanted, and not feel any shame about it. I imagine David groaning as he watches me, promising to come all over my ass, urging me on as I fuck myself with the dildo. *You're imagining it's me, aren't you?* he growls from behind me, the hard slap of his fist against his cock echoing the wet, slutty sound of my toy sliding in and out of my pussy. I feel myself clench around it, imagining seeing his cock stiffen in his fist as he watches, all of my taut, soaked flesh aching for him as I frantically rub my clit, suddenly desperate to come.

I wish it was him. I want it to be him, his cock that I come all over when my entire body tenses, my back arching, my scream of pleasure muffled by the pillow. My legs splay wide, my hips thrusting as I shove backward onto the toy, fingers still rolling over my clit as I try to wring every last drop of sensation from the orgasm that I can. I feel my arousal gush over the toy, and I imagine David coming on my ass, the hot splash of his cum on my skin as he groans out my name, some of it dripping down onto my fingers and pussy. I imagine it coating the toy, pushing it inside of me as I thrust once, twice more, another helpless moan slipping from my lips as a flutter of aftershocks course through my body.

Breathless, I slump down on the bed, slipping the toy free and dropping it to one side as I collapse against the pillows. I feel my face flush with a moment's embarrassment—I'm used to pleasuring myself quietly, under my covers late at night, careful that no one can hear me. I've never done anything like this before—but I tell myself it doesn't matter. There was no one here to see, no one to judge me. No one will ever know about it except me.

I get up, weak-kneed, to clean the toy off and carefully hide it away again. I slip back into bed naked, enjoying the feeling of the luxurious sheets against my skin, the sensation another reminder of Ibiza. I close my eyes, hoping I'll dream about it. About that version of David, and not the one I'm trapped with now.

I never notice, not even for a second, the small, blinking red light in the corner of the room.

19

DAVID

I didn't know until it was too late that Amalie slipped out of the house and left the grounds, *exactly* as I told her not to. I spent the entire morning and afternoon, after breakfast, busy with tasks that my father said he needed help with. No one called me, or notified me. She managed to quite thoroughly give my security the slip, and I hadn't bothered to warn the driver. I truthfully hadn't thought I would need to.

I was, unfortunately, very wrong.

It's not until I'm upstairs in my room at my parents' mansion, changing for dinner, that I realize my mistake. I make a habit of checking my security cameras when I'm out of town, made easy by an app that lets me scroll through the footage, and it only takes seconds for me to realize what Amalie has done. Or *did*, rather, by the time I find out. I see her coming back, too—there's that footage as well.

I don't want to admit that the fury that ripples through me is out of more than just anger that she disobeyed me. I want to leave it at that—that it's just her insolence and stubbornness and clear lack of respect for *my* wishes that has me wishing I could reach through the cameras and shake her until her teeth rattle. But there's more to it.

She's pregnant. And while I don't entirely believe that it's mine—

there's still a distinct possibility that it might be. That chance is enough to send a wave of fierce protectiveness through me as I see her getting into the car to leave, my jaw clenching as I watch her go.

Anything could have happened to her. She was walking around downtown in an unfamiliar place, alone. Her recklessness makes me want to shout at her, an urge I only just manage to curb by reminding myself that she's not actually in the room. I file away everything I want to say for later, when I get home—which will be sooner than she expects.

I had planned to stay through the weekend for the charity gala that my parents are throwing. Now, after this, I intend to fly back in the morning, fetch Amalie regardless of what protestations she might have, and bring her back here. I don't trust her to be alone after the stunt she pulled today.

As soon as the footage shows her coming back into the house, I stop skipping through it, seized by a sudden desire to see what her evening was like after her ill-conceived adventure. I watch, my irritation growing as she sits down with her takeout as if nothing is wrong, nibbling her way through the burger and fries without a care in the world. I know I should be glad that she doesn't seem as sick as she has been while eating, but it feels like a personal affront—like she's being dramatic on account of me when I'm home, and everything is better when I'm gone.

It's irrational, but I can't help it. Everything she does seems designed to either make me angry or aroused—and what follows after her dinner only makes that seem more true.

For a moment, I think she's going to go back up to the attic and snoop again, while she has the house to herself. I'm almost surprised when she disappears into the guest bathroom, where she'd found the tub for a little while. I skip forward through the blank footage until she emerges, hair up and a thick terry-cloth towel wrapped around her. It's not the most exciting view, but the moment she walks into the bedroom—*our* bedroom—that all changes.

I feel my breath catch when she slips the tie of the robe loose, letting it fall carelessly to the floor. She's naked underneath it, and I'm suddenly more grateful than ever for the money I spent for the best possible cameras, with the clearest view. This is no grainy black-and-white footage—I see every inch of her, as beautiful as she's ever been, as she walks to the bed. There's a small stab of disappointment when I realize that she's just going to slide into bed and go to sleep, but when she stretches out atop the bed, my mouth goes dry.

When her hand drifts downwards, over her still-flat stomach towards the soft, bare skin between her thighs, I can hardly believe what I'm seeing. I convinced her to do any number of things with me in Ibiza, but this wasn't one of them. She never let me watch while she touched herself. And now, knowing that I'm watching in real-time while she has no idea I'm there, I feel myself instantly grow hard.

I reach down as she shifts on the bed, rubbing my palm over my stiffening cock as I watch her slip her fingers between her legs. I have a perfect view of her from where the camera is situated, aimed so that I can see her two fingers slide in between her folds, starting to circle her clit. The sound isn't as good as I might have hoped, but I can imagine the slick, wet sounds that her fingers are making, and I fumble for my zipper. The thought of stroking myself while I watch her has me far too close before I even touch my cock.

When she moans softly, I *do* hear that. "*Fuck,*" I whisper aloud as I free my cock, groaning as I wrap my hand around my shaft. And when she spreads her legs wider, the camera giving me the exact view I want of her spread-open pussy, I feel my cock throb dangerously.

She arches her back, her fingers moving more quickly, and I grit my teeth. I don't want to come yet, not until she does. Her eyes are closed, her full lips parted, and I can see her breasts heaving with every breath as her fingers circle her clit, her other hand keeping her nether lips spread for me.

Except she doesn't know it's for me. She doesn't know I'm watching, has no idea that there's a camera recording her, that I'm going to have this footage fucking saved on my phone for every trip that I might need to jerk off on for the foreseeable future. I've forgotten about other women, about that much-vaunted freedom my father and I talked about. I've forgotten about everything except Amalie and the way she sounds when she moans, the sight of her pussy wet and spread open as she rubs her clit for an unseen audience.

Wider, I think, stroking my hand along my throbbing length, and as if she can hear me, she does exactly that. Her knees drop to the side, her folds parted, her slick, swollen flesh on full display for me. Pre-cum drips from my cock, easing the slide of my hand as I rub my palm over the tip, hissing through my teeth at the sensation. I'm aching to come, and it takes every bit of self-restraint that I have not to spill over the edge too soon. I can see her swollen clit, can imagine how it would feel under my fingers, my tongue, stiff and pulsing with her arousal. I'm suddenly aching for the taste of her, and when she dips her fingers into herself, sliding two of them into her entrance as her hips arch upwards, I feel almost desperate to be able to suck them into my mouth and lick her arousal off of them.

"I want your cock," she breathes aloud, and the words jolt straight to the object of her lust, throbbing dangerously in my fist. My balls are so tight they ache, and I shift in the chair I sat down in, half-tempted to strip naked, just to give myself some relief from the snugness of my trousers.

But I can't take my hand off of myself, or stop watching long enough to do so. I don't want to miss a second of the unwitting show my beautiful wife is putting on for me.

Her fingers thrust inside of her to the same pace that her other hand keeps against her clit, but I can tell that it's not enough. It's clear from the restless way her hips shift, the way she keeps moaning, the sound full of as much frustration as desire. *You need my cock,* I think with satisfaction, an echo of her moan a few moments ago. *Nothing will ever be as good now that you've had it.*

I'm so close, trembling on the edge, when she suddenly yanks her hands away from her pussy. I catch one glimpse of her spread open, her pink flesh wet and swollen, before she swings her legs off of the bed. I let go of my cock as if it were on fire, feeling the tip flare as more pre-cum drips down the shaft, well aware that I'm only a second away from my own orgasm. A hiss of frustration escapes me as I watch her walk toward the closet.

She can't possibly be done, can she? She was close—I know her well enough to know that, even from the other side of a camera. For a moment, I wonder if she did know about the camera—if she thought I might be watching and decided to fuck with me. The thought makes me momentarily furious—the idea that she might have purposefully been teasing me, setting me up with no intent to follow through—so much so that I miss what it is that she's doing in the closet until she re-emerges, still naked and with something gripped in her hand.

When I realize it's a dildo, almost the same thickness and length as mine, I very nearly lose control of my orgasm again.

I'm not sure I've ever seen anything as maddeningly erotic as Amalie lying back on the bed, her legs spread as she runs the tip of the dildo between her folds, moaning as it rubs over her clit. She slides just the tip into her entrance, her fingers starting to stray towards her clit again—and then I see her hesitate.

Before I can fully register what it is that she's about to do, she rolls onto her stomach, her hips pushing back as she shoves her ass into the air and spreads her legs wide, the tip of the fake cock finding her entrance again.

I squeeze the base of my own cock, *hard*. It's a last-ditch effort to keep myself from coming before I'm ready, and it only just works. I grit my teeth, unable to believe what I'm seeing as Amalie starts to fuck herself with the dildo, her fingers finding her clit as she starts to thrust. I'm almost certain I can hear her moaning my name.

I can't stop myself as my hand starts to move over my cock again, pushing me quickly towards the inevitable end. I've never watched anything as good as this. No porn that's ever been filmed could compare to this, to spying on my wife as she fucks herself from behind with her hidden toy, her ass and pussy spread open for my gaze. I *can* hear the sounds now, the wet slap of the cock as it fills her again and again, and I have the sudden image of her doing just that as I push my own cock into her ass, stuffing her full as she screams out her orgasm between the two cocks. I'd never let another man touch her, but a toy—

That I could enjoy sharing her with.

I can see when she's close. My own balls are painful from the delayed orgasm, my cock stiff and straining, a steady stream of arousal leaking over my fist. I thrust up into my hand as I see her body stiffen, her back arching, and I hear her scream of pleasure as she comes hard on the toy. I can see her arousal dripping off of it onto the sheets, see her clenching around it. The desire to be the one inside of her is so strong I groan her name aloud as I start to spurt hot cum over my fist, hips jerking as I come with her.

I want to come in her, on her, all over her. I want her drenched with it, inside and out. I want to be the only taste she ever remembers on her tongue. If there ever was any other man, I want to fuck the memory out of her and then wipe him off the face of the earth. I've never felt such a fierce, possessive desire for any woman.

Amalie thrusts back onto the toy, whimpering as she shudders through her orgasm. My cock pulses in my fist, more cum dripping over my fingers, and I groan as she slumps back onto the pillows, suddenly aware of what a mess I've made both of my hands and my suit trousers.

I can't bring myself to care. I've never seen a more erotic show in my entire life. I get up at the same time she does, to clean myself up, but I still can't get her out of my head. And I realize, as I step into the shower, that I'm missing my wife.

Not just the pleasure of being buried inside of her, or the exquisite sensation when she makes me come. I have the strange urge to curl up beside her and fall asleep, a sort of aching disappointment that when I walk out of the shower, she won't be in bed waiting for me. I've always preferred sleeping alone, but just now, the idea of an empty bed feels cold and lonely.

The thought makes my heart race with a sudden panic.

I'm not going to fall for her. I shove the thought out of my head, forcing myself to stop thinking about it entirely. I said I would keep my distance from any woman I married, and that includes Amalie. *Especially Amalie.* What I feel for her is too strong already, too volatile.

I'm not going to repeat my brother's mistakes. There's a time and a place for passion, and it's not here, not in my marriage. What Amalie and I have is a shaky foundation for what I need to build our family's new legacy on, and I won't allow anything to risk it crumbling.

She's already pregnant. If she has a son, and it's mine, I intend to touch her as little as possible after that. If my father really does want to send me to Sicily, far away from Amalie and these feelings, so much the better.

I don't want to be in love. Not with her.

Not with anyone.

20

AMALIE

When I wake up the next morning, the first thing I think of is that I want to sneak out again. I'd like to explore more of Newport, feel a little bit of that sense of freedom again, but I know better than to press my luck twice.

Which is how, after breakfast, I end up back upstairs in the attic.

I took the key with me after I left, the last time. I wondered if David would look for it—maybe with the idea of taking it himself and preventing me from going back in—but if he did try to find it, he didn't let me know about it. I hid it in one of my toiletry bags in the bathroom, and evidently, that was not a place he thought to look.

The attic is just as dusty and dirty as before, and I start to sneeze the moment I walk in. Maybe this was a bad idea, I think as I walk around the edge of it, looking for anything I might have missed. It doesn't feel quite as ominous as it did before, and I wonder if all my apprehension was just the difficulty of settling into a new place—especially one as isolated and lonely as this is. I feel a little foolish for being so worried, and I bite my lip, wondering if I should say something to David about that when I see him next. Maybe it could even be a little bit of an olive branch between us—me admitting that I overreacted.

There's a wooden writing desk by one wall, surrounded by framed artwork that's covered in dust, with a half-open box in front of it full of tangled Christmas lights. I step around the box, nudging it out of the way as I start to open the drawers.

The first two that I open are empty, with a layer of dust inside. I shut them, half-wondering if I'm wasting my time—but it's not as if there's something better for me to be doing downstairs. I open a third, finding a book that looks like it's just a ledger, with scattered notes about various businesses—and then in the fourth, I finally find something interesting.

There's a thin manila envelope tucked inside. I know I shouldn't open it—it's undoubtedly something personal, but my curiosity quickly gets the best of me. When I open it, I find a few glossy photos, slipped inside in a neat stack.

They're recent, that's for sure. Maybe a couple of years old, judging by the clothes that the woman in the picture is wearing. She's very beautiful in a neat, elegant sort of way, with shoulder-length brown hair and a pleasant smile on her face. In each of the photos, she's with a dark-haired man that I don't recognize—in one, leaning across a table at a restaurant, in another, standing at a front door. It's clear that the pictures were taken by someone watching her from afar —probably photos taken without her knowledge.

Something about one of the photos catches my eye, and I look at it three or four times before I realize what it is. The necklace that she has on—a long, lariat style with a teardrop ruby, hanging down over a chic sweater—is familiar.

It's familiar because I saw it in the box on the other side of the attic, just a few days ago.

I can feel my pulse beating hard against the side of my throat. I push the drawer shut, still holding the photos and envelope in one hand, as I walk across the room to the stack of boxes that I'd found on my first visit up here. *I'm imagining things,* I tell myself as I sink down in front of the boxes, tucking the photos back into the envelope as I set it down on the floor. *I saw something else. It can't be the same necklace.*

But when I open the box, I see it there, in the tangle of jewelry nestled atop the silk blouse. A white gold lariat necklace, the ruby at the bottom of it glinting in the dim light, the exact match to the one that the woman in the photo is wearing.

For a moment, I have the horrible urge to take it and put it on, to be wearing it when David gets back. *He wouldn't be able to hide his reaction then,* I think darkly, reaching down to touch the ruby. Surely, *that* would shock him enough for me to catch a glimpse of what his real feelings are, if there's something really wrong with all of this, or if I'm being paranoid. *It would almost be worth his anger,* I think, tangling my fingers through the necklace.

And then the blouse underneath shifts, and I catch a glimpse of rusty red on the fabric.

For a brief second, I feel my heart stop, chills rippling through me. *It's not that. It's not what I think.* I sit back hard on the floor, dropping the box, my fingers feeling numb. I stare at the dislodged sleeve, the stain on the edge of it around the gold button, and tell myself that it's not blood.

But I know what blood looks like. It's not the sort of thing that's easy to mistake.

There's an explanation. There are a number of reasons why a bloodstain could be on a woman's blouse. It's not a huge stain—something from a cut, maybe. An accidental injury. I nearly cut my finger just this morning, slicing strawberries in the kitchen.

There could be an explanation for it. Just as there could be an explanation for the photos of the brunette woman—the woman I feel certain this blouse belongs to—taken without her knowledge. An explanation for the necklace being packed away up here, along with the bloodstained blouse.

An explanation that doesn't point to my husband, the man that I've married and followed out to this isolated old house, a man with the power and wealth of the mafia at his back, being somehow involved in that bloodstain and those photos.

With shaking hands, I close the box, sliding it back where it was before. I want to take the necklace, but I don't. I leave it there, and I tuck the photos back where they were before, in the desk drawer where I found them. Until I have a better idea of what's going on, I don't dare risk David finding any of this in my possession—or coming up here and finding any of it gone.

But that doesn't mean I'm not going to ask him about it, just as soon as he comes home.

———

He returns home sooner than I expected. It's not until I hear the click of the door opening and his footsteps walking down the hall that I have even the slightest inkling that he might be back.

A strange mixture of fear, disappointment, and elation fills me. Fear, because I'm still not entirely sure that I got completely away with my little trek into Newport—and because of what I found today in the attic. Disappointment, because I thought I had two more days of peace before he returned—two more days to come to terms with my discovery, and how to broach the subject with him. And elation—

I don't know why I feel that. I shouldn't. I don't want him here. But my heartbeat picks up in my chest as I hear him walking into the informal living room where I'm sitting.

I keep flipping through the interior decorating magazine I found. I don't actually care about it, but I'm bored to tears here, and almost out of books to read. And I don't want David to see the fearful expression on my face, so I don't look up until he's nearly standing in front of me.

"I thought you'd be more surprised to see me home." His deep voice sends a shiver down my spine, and I hate it. I hate the way my body instantly rouses to the sound of it, my hands starting to tremble a little where I'm holding the magazine. I feel like a stringed instrument, tuned to immediately respond to him, and I wish he didn't have that power over me. I don't want *anyone* to have that kind of power over me.

"I'm never surprised for you to do something unexpectedly without telling me." I keep my voice cool as I set the magazine aside, finally looking up at him as if it doesn't matter to me what he does. "After all, you don't exactly care about my opinion, do you?"

His jaw is already tight, his stance stiff, and I see his expression darken at that. His gaze sweeps over me, and I find myself suddenly glad that I put on nicer clothes today. A pair of slim black pants and a cream-colored sleeveless silk blouse under my cardigan. I hadn't known he was coming home, so I'd had some idea that I might try to slip out again.

It's a good thing I didn't.

"Get on your knees." The order is swift and sharp, but there's a growling arousal in his voice that leaves absolutely no doubt as to *why* he wants me down on my knees. It sends an answering jolt of desire through me, and I sink my teeth into my lip, repressing the moan that threatens to surface. "*Now*, Amalie."

Almost without meaning to, I obey. I'm reminded of that day in Ibiza, after he helped me at the restaurant, when he brought me back to his penthouse and put me on my knees there. It was the first time I'd ever had a man's cock in my mouth.

I wanted it, then. I wanted *him*. And against all my better judgment and in spite of everything that's happened since, I still do.

As I sink to my knees, he pushes the cardigan off of my shoulders, sending it fluttering to the floor. I reach for his belt, seeing the hard ridge of his cock already straining against his fly, and I want him in my mouth. I don't care that I know he's doing this to demand my submission, that I'm giving him exactly what he wants, that this is meant to be some kind of punishment. I want him.

David groans as I slip his cock out, my hand wrapping around the hard, thick shaft. "Good girl," he murmurs, threading his hand through my hair as I press my lips to his cockhead. "Except you weren't such a good girl while I was gone, were you?"

I stiffen, and he presses my head forward a little, pushing his cock between my lips. "Don't stop, *cara mia*. You can suck my cock and listen at the same time."

A small ripple of defiance goes through me at that, and I toss my head back, glaring up at him. "I can't answer you like that, though."

"Ah, there's the wife I left behind." There's a dark, humorous gleam in his eyes. "Open your pretty mouth then, Amalie, and tell me the truth. "Were you a good girl?"

"That depends on your—" I nearly choke as his hand fists in my hair, holding me still as he pushes himself into my mouth. His cock slides over my tongue, the salty taste of him filling my senses, and I tighten my lips around him reflexively, moaning at the feeling of my mouth wrapped around him.

"Just like that. You're so pretty with your mouth full, *bellisima*." His thumb strokes my cheekbone, and he thrusts again, slowly, his cock sliding in and out between my lips as I suck. "That feels fucking good. I missed having you there to please my cock whenever I want. My pretty bride."

David thrusts again, deeper this time, his hand in my hair holding me down as he pushes nearly into my throat. My eyes fill with tears at the invasion, but I feel the throb of arousal between my legs, my thighs tightening as I find myself wishing he would put me over the couch and use me that way instead.

He jerks his cock free, the shaft glistening in the light. "Answer me, Amalie. Were you a good girl? No, wait. I'll be more direct." His hand leaves my hair, gripping my chin instead as he tilts my head up so that I can't look away. "Did you sneak out, after I told you to stay home?"

"Why should I tell you?" I glare up at him, and he chuckles.

"Because I already have camera footage of it, *cara mia*. Just like I have camera footage of you fucking your tight little pussy for me. But I don't like to be lied to, so I want to hear it from your own lips."

I feel my face go white, and then burning red at that as I realize what he means. *He saw me. He watched me.* I'm horribly, completely embarrassed—and at the same time, I can feel a flood of arousal between my thighs, soaking my panties at the realization that he watched the lewd display that I hadn't realized I was putting on for anyone else.

But you hoped you were. And now you know.

"I jerked off watching you," he says, almost conversationally. His thumb rubs over my lower lip, pressing into the soft flesh there. "And I kept the video, of course. So you can please me whenever I want you to."

I moan helplessly at that, my lips catching around his thumb. I feel myself rock forward, my thighs tight, wanting friction on my clit. I feel so desperately aroused, my panties clinging to my skin, and I want him to fuck me.

"Answer me, Amalie. You get one more chance before I take my belt to that perfect ass of yours. And before you think that's *not* a punishment, I won't let you come afterward. I promise you that."

I'm so aroused right now that I'm not sure he could stop me. I'm not sure that the spanking alone wouldn't set me off. But I'm not willing to test that theory.

"Yes," I whisper, looking up at him, his cock still an inch from my lips. "I snuck out and went into Newport."

"After I specifically told you not to?"

"Yes," I whisper, and I see his face tighten.

"Why?"

I give him one last defiant look. "Because I wanted to."

It's honest, at least. David growls, his fingers slipping into my mouth as he forces my lips open—or tries to, anyway. He doesn't really have to. I'm aching all over, almost shivering with desire, and my mouth falls open for his cock as he slides himself over my tongue again with a low, dark chuckle.

"So hungry for my cock." His hand smooths over my hair. "Take it all, *bellisima*. All the way down. *Fuck*."

He groans as he pushes himself into my throat, hips jerking as he presses me forward, my nose nearly brushing against his abs as his cockhead slips deeper. I choke around him, but he doesn't stop, his breathing quick and hard as my throat tightens around his length.

"Fuck—*fuck*. Your mouth is so fucking good. I'm going to fuck your face now, *dolce*. Take my cock. *Fuck,* good girl—"

He moans the words as he starts to thrust, his voice so thick and dark with lust that I feel like I might orgasm without ever touching myself. I'm trembling with need, my hands clenched into fists against my thighs as he wraps his hand in my hair and sinks his cock into my throat again and again. I feel him swell and harden, that stiff throbbing that tells me he's about to come, and then to my surprise, he jerks his cock free. His thumb presses down on my lip, holding my mouth open as his other hand strokes along the length of his cock, his jaw tight with oncoming pleasure.

"I'm going to come all over your—pretty—fucking—face—*god!*" He snarls the last word, his entire body going rigid, and cum spurts out of his cock and over my cheek in a hot line that makes me moan aloud. David's eyes widen at the sound, and his cock lurches in his hand, more cum splattering across my nose and chin.

"Fucking *god*," he growls, his hand stuttering over his length. "Rub your clit, *cara mia. Now.*"

I shove my hand inside my panties before he can change his mind, his cum still spurting onto my face. My fingers slide over my pulsing clit, wet and slick, and the instant I touch it, I'm coming too. I'm that close to the edge. I cry out as the last spurt of his cum coats my lips and drips down my chin, hips bucking into my hand as I moan aloud, and David lets out one final groan as he rubs his cum over my lips with his still-swollen cockhead, pushing it into my mouth.

"Clean me up, *bellisima*," he murmurs. "Keep rubbing your clit until you're done."

It feels like I'm still coming. My hips roll against my hand, my fingers soaked as I lick David's cock clean, lapping up every trace of his cum as I moan and shudder. I slide my hand down, pushing two fingers into myself as I grind the heel of my hand against my clit, and I feel the aftershocks of my orgasm pour through me, making me whimper around his cock.

"*Fuck,*" David breathes again as he steps back, tucking himself away. I know what I must look like, kneeling on the floor with my hand in my panties, and I jerk it free. "Clean yourself up too," he says, his voice every bit as stern, and I know what he means. "Don't get up until you do."

I can see the lust in his eyes as he watches me wipe the cum off of my face, licking it and my own arousal off of my fingers. His cock is already swelling again, pushing against his fly, but he ignores it.

"Get up," he finally says when I've cleaned most of his cum off of my face. "Go upstairs and pack."

It takes me a minute to stand up. My knees feel shaky, and my face is on fire, flushed with lingering embarrassment. "What? Why—"

"Because I clearly can't trust you here alone," David says bluntly. "So go upstairs, and pack to come back to Boston with me. Bring an evening gown; we'll be going to a gala my family is throwing."

I blink at him. "A—"

"You heard me." His jaw tightens as he steps past me, sinking onto the couch. "You have half an hour before we leave."

And just like that, his mood has completely changed again. I press my lips together, fighting back a retort. On the one hand, I'm utterly sick of how hot and cold he is, how mercurial, that one moment he demands I please him and the next he dismisses me.

On the other hand, I desperately want to get out of here, even for just the weekend. Even if it means seeing David's parents.

The promise of being away from this house and in the city is enough of a lure. I'm more than a little upset that he didn't take me with him in the first place—I feel like I've been wasting away here since I stepped into this mansion, and the idea of a party sounds incredible. The idea of mingling with other people, of dancing and music and a bit of liveliness, makes me happier than I've felt since I came home from Ibiza.

Maybe I can slip the idea into his head that we might relocate back to Boston. I keep that thought close, clinging to it for comfort. This is what I know how to do, after all—what I was raised for. To be a mafia wife, to look beautiful on my husband's arm, to charm and delight his associates and friends. If he sees that I'm capable of doing all of that despite our marital troubles, if he sees how much more I flourish in the city environment, maybe he'll reconsider staying out here. Or even—

He might even be able to be convinced to let me have a home in the city. To live separately, part of his time spent with me and his child in Boston, part of it spent here in this drafty old house when he wants his privacy and his space. It's not the most traditional arrangement, but he might be able to be convinced. And I'd be surrounded by eyes and ears, his family and business associates—it's not as if I could get away with anything that might embarrass him.

Once he knows the baby is his, he'll trust me more. I tell myself that as I pack, carefully slipping a favorite evening gown into a garment bag. After a moment's consideration, I tuck the wrapped fur stole into the bag as well, feeling a small thrill at the idea of wearing something that would shock everyone at a party like the one we're going to if they knew where it was from. David will never know—no one will— but I will. It feels like a small revenge against my mother, and anyone else like her, who always tried to force me to be the perfect mafia daughter—who tried to mold me into the perfect mafia wife.

A role that I now have no choice but to embody.

My stomach knots as I close my suitcase, my thoughts drifting nervously back to my second foray into the attic. I don't want to believe the worst of what I found—I feel ridiculous and paranoid for even considering it. But my husband is a dangerous man. More dangerous than I knew, when I met him in Ibiza and imagined that he was just some oil-rich billionaire spreading his wealth around a party town. He's a man who, were I to be on the wrong side of him, could ruin my life. He could *end* my life, if he wanted to. And nothing would ever happen to him.

That could very well be what happened to the brunette woman whose remaining effects are tucked away in the dusty attic of my new husband's crumbling home.

I hadn't heard anything about David having been married before. But at the same time, I realize with that growing sense of trepidation, I also don't know that he *hasn't*. I never thought to ask—and to tell the truth, I'm not sure if I would have gotten an answer. He might have simply said, as he has about other things, that it's *none of my business*.

It's starting to feel as if it very much might be.

With no staff to help, I take my suitcase and garment bag downstairs, after changing into something that might make David less inclined to comment on my choice of outfit for the flight. I catch him glancing over me when I step back into the living room, taking in the green leaf-print sundress and nude espadrilles I chose, and his mouth twitches.

"Dressed for summer vacation, I see," he says dryly, and that furious heat nearly overtakes me again.

"Do you *ever* have anything nice to say?" I snap, setting down my suitcase with a hard *thump* against the wooden floor. "Does *everything* have to be a jibe?"

David shrugs, unfolding his long, leanly muscled body from the couch and standing. I hate him for how handsome he is, for how he makes my heart trip in my chest as he walks towards me, standing close enough that I could touch him—if I wasn't so focused on making certain that he doesn't get to know how much I want to.

"I can say nice things." His dark eyes glint with barely restrained humor as he reaches for my suitcase. "For instance, I'm impressed that you packed so lightly this time."

"We're only going for the weekend." I tilt my chin up, glaring at him. "Why would I bring more?"

He shrugs, refusing to take my bait. "The driver is waiting," he says, taking the suitcase with him. "You took longer than you should have."

Oh, for fuck's sake! I want to slap his handsome face, to snatch my suitcase out of his hand, and tell him I'll take it myself, but he's already headed for the door. I grit my teeth, suddenly questioning whether the possibility of company and entertainment for the night is worth having to spend it with David.

Unfortunately, I'm not really being given a choice. One way or another, I'm going to Boston with him.

And one way or another, I'm determined to get answers.

21

AMALIE

I manage to keep my questions about what I found in the attic to myself until we're nearly an hour into the flight to Boston, if only because I'm terrified of what the answers will be. Halfway there, I knot my fingers together in my lap, looking across the small gap between us to where David is sitting back in the plush leather seat, working on something on his laptop.

"Was your brother married?" I blurt out the question, hoping that the answer is *yes*. That David will describe her as having brown hair and an elegant bearing, that he'll mention a ruby necklace given to her as a gift. That the woman in those photos will cease to matter, because she won't have anything to do with David, beyond having been his sister-in-law.

He looks up at me sharply, displeasure instantly wreathing his face. "I don't like talking about that." His voice is flat, a clear sign that he wants the conversation to end there. But I'm not prepared to just let it go. Not after what I found the second time I went up to the attic.

I take a breath, searching for the nerve to keep pushing. "I think we should talk about it," I say, as calmly as I can manage. "I'm your wife, David. I'm going to be around your family. Talking to them. How does it look if I don't know anything about your life before me—

your *real* life? If I don't know anything about your brother, or how things were before—"

David's jaw clenches. I can almost see his teeth grinding together. "It would *look* as if my wife respects me enough not to ask questions that I don't want to answer." His lips press thinly together. "We're not *friends,* Amalie. We're not even partners, or whatever ridiculous notion that others might like to think about marriage. You are a means to an end. You provide me with what I need—the other half of the foundation of a family, and in time, if you prove that you've been honest with me, an heir. *I* provide you with the means to save your family's name, and the chance to regain your status. This is an exchange, Amalie, a business arrangement. If we both take some pleasure in it now and then, well—" he shrugs, a lewd smile crooking one side of his mouth. "I suppose that's a small bonus to what could be an otherwise unfulfilling experience."

I glare at him. "Can you just answer one question without talking to me in circles? Why is it so hard, David? Why can't you just say *yes* or *no*?"

"Is that all you want? No ulterior motive for asking?" There's a glint in his eye that makes me feel a cold knot of fear starting to form in my stomach, a hint that he might know what caused this line of questioning. "Yes. Are you happy? My brother was married."

I swallow hard. "Does she live in Boston now? Where did she go, after—"

Thin lines deepen around David's mouth at that, his expression hardening. "See? It's never just one question. You're never happy with what I give you."

"*David.*" I let out a breath, utterly exasperated. "It doesn't have to be this hard—"

"Yes, it does, when you refuse to respect my privacy. A well-bred woman, the kind of woman who *should* have been offered to me as a prospective wife, would know when to be quiet. When to *not* badger her husband with questions about things he doesn't want to discuss. What her mouth is actually for." There's that glint in his eyes again, that hint of cruel amusement, and that cold fear snakes its way down my spine. "She's gone, Amalie."

"Gone?" The word comes out as more of a squeak than I would have liked it to. I see the bloodstain on cream-colored silk, the secret photos, all flashing through my mind as I sit there looking at David's cold expression. "She—"

"Moved away," he says smoothly, his gaze lingering on mine for one more second before he looks back down at his laptop, clearly dismissing me and the conversation. "We don't speak to her anymore. Now, I'm finished talking about this."

I know there's no point in asking more questions. I'm not even entirely sure what I would ask. David makes it sound as if she left because of the loss, maybe even went back to her own family. I can't find it in myself to believe there was love in that marriage—it's a rare thing to find in our world. It's not encouraged—not even really desired. His brother was the heir before him—that marriage would have been one made pragmatically, not out of emotion. It would have been even more well-arranged than ours was.

A mafia widow without children would move back in with her family, most likely. It fits with what he said, but not the tone in which he said it. I want to ask if there *were* any children—but there must not have been. I can't imagine David's mother allowing her daughter-in-law to simply leave with a grandchild, not even if it was a daughter.

I can't stop feeling as if there's something off about all of this— but once again, I can hear David's voice in my head, telling me that I'm being paranoid. That it's simple. His brother's childless widow went back to her family—doubtless a very well-respected mafia family—after her husband's death. By now, she might even have married someone else, some mafia consigliere more concerned with an heir than a virgin bride. It wouldn't be unusual.

When the plane lands, I try to shake off the unsettled feeling. If I want a chance of convincing David to relocate back to the city, I need to prove to him that we'll be happier here, that I'll be a *better* wife. I can't do that if I'm distracted and tense, my thoughts miles away in the old house that I want desperately to leave.

"Try to be more polite with my mother," is all he says to me on the ride to our hotel. I'm relieved that we're not staying at his parents' mansion—until it occurs to me, halfway through the elevator ride up, *why* he likely has us staying at a hotel. The thought stops me with a jolt, before I can respond to his jibe.

I realize, with a feeling that's half-nervousness, half-anticipation, that he wants to be somewhere that he can enjoy me without caring who hears.

"Welcome back to modern luxury," he says, his voice full of dry sarcasm as we step into the hotel's penthouse, the scents of cool leather and gleaming wood filling my senses as he closes the door behind us. "I know this is more your speed than the old house in Newport, Amalie, so no need to pretend otherwise."

"I hadn't planned on it." I *do* instantly feel more at home here, with my feet firmly on polished hardwood and standing in a room full of modern furnishings, inside an entirely finished structure. There's a huge window on one side of the living room overlooking the Boston skyline, and I feel a momentary twist of anticipatory desire in my stomach, remembering Ibiza all over again.

I wouldn't mind if he made a habit of fucking me against a window in every hotel we stay at, I think with a flush of heat, and then instantly feel a flood of confusion. I don't know how I can fear and hate him so much, and, at the same time, want him with an overwhelming desire that I didn't know was possible.

"The gala is tonight, by the way," David says, glancing at his watch carelessly. "We should be leaving in about three hours. You should probably start getting ready, I think."

It's all I can do to keep my mouth from dropping open. This is a test—I know it is. He could have easily told me before we left that the gala is tonight—I had just assumed it would be tomorrow evening— but he wants to see what will happen by springing it on me.

He wants to know how well I can pull myself together in a few hours for something like this. And, looking at the challenge in his eyes, I'm filled with a sudden grim determination to make sure that I pull this off so well that he's shocked by it.

I might not be the wife he wanted, but this *is* what I was taught to do, no matter how much I hated those lessons. If he wants the perfect mafia wife tonight, then that's exactly what he'll get.

"I suppose I should get in the shower, then," I tell him archly, flashing him a smile and enjoying the glimmer of surprise that I ever-so-briefly see on his face before he smooths it away. I wonder, for a moment, if he'll follow me into the shower—but he leaves me be, only silence following me as I disappear into the master suite of the penthouse with my things.

For once, I'm not inclined to linger as long as I usually might. For all that, things are tense between David and me. Despite the fact that his parents will no doubt be at the gala, the prospect of mingling and enjoying a dinner out and a party has me practically buzzing with anticipation. I make sure to take my time getting ready, putting my hair up in hot rollers instead of using a curling iron so that I get thick, bouncy curls, and using a light hand with my makeup. Just a little shimmer here, a hint of blush and eyeliner here, and I manage to pull off the look of careless elegance that's always expected of the women hanging off of the arms of the rich and powerful. It matters, especially when David will want to show off his young, pretty new bride.

The dress I brought is a deep sapphire blue, matching the jewelry I have to go with it exactly. It has chiffon sleeves that fall off of my shoulders, displaying the line of my collarbones prettily, and a scooped neckline with a built-in bustier that gives me just a hint of cleavage. The silk skirt sweeps down over my hips, gathered just a little at one side, and split up to mid-thigh. Sexy enough to draw the eye, but not so much so that I'll embarrass my husband—the kind of dress that makes other men jealous of him, boosting his ego that at the end of the night, I belong to him.

A shiver goes down my spine at the thought, and I don't entirely know if it's unpleasant or not. I'm terrified of David, of the potential of what he could do to me if I anger him enough, of the secrets that I've begun to uncover one unsatisfying and frightening glimpse at a time. But there's also a dark, twisted sort of excitement that he rouses in me every time we're close to one another, a battle of desires that I always feel as if I want to lose.

I've never met anyone so confusing, or someone who makes me feel so much—both good and bad.

David is waiting for me in the living room when I emerge. There's a second-bedroom suite in the penthouse that he must have used to get ready, because he looks perfect—so stunningly gorgeous that, for a moment, I can't help but stop and stare at him. His eyes meet mine, a small smirk twitching at the corners of his mouth, but I can't even bring myself to care that he so clearly sees how he affects me. I haven't seen him so dressed up since our wedding, and it takes my breath away.

He's wearing a perfectly tailored deep blue suit, the color such a perfect complement to my dress that I wonder if he somehow got a glimpse at what I packed. I don't know how that's possible, but I'm beginning to think that he can find out anything he wants, if he chooses to. It's an unsettling feeling to have, but I can't think about it just now. All I can think about is him.

That smirk spreads across his mouth, and I can't stop looking at his lips, full and soft, his clean-shaven jaw. He walks towards me, his gaze still holding mine, and I can feel myself starting to tremble. Desire washes through me, heavy and cloying, and I know I'm lost when it comes to this man. It doesn't matter how much we hate each other—we want each other more. And that will always be my undoing.

It's a small comfort to know that it's his, too.

"You look lovely." He says it softly, the slightest edge to his voice, and I can see in his gaze that he wants me, too. I can hear the grudging compliment, the admission that he set a challenge for me, and I passed with flying colors. For him to cede even that much, I know, is quite a step for him.

He reaches out, slowly, his finger tracing the edge of the diamond-and-sapphire necklace draped between my collarbones. My skin prickles at his touch, warming, making my breath catch. It feels like a promise of something different tonight, the possibility of gentleness and pleasure, like what we had before. His hand slides down my arm, brushing against the fur stole, and I can't help but tense a little as his brow furrows.

"That's an odd thing to wear." He looks at me, confused. "It's a little warm out for fur, isn't it?"

"I get chilly. And besides, it's going to be cold in the gala, I'm sure. Don't those places always make sure it's frigid to try to compensate for so many people?" I smile sweetly at him, inwardly wondering why I felt the urge to bring it. It's a rebellion, wearing something that I know would embarrass him if he knew where it came from, on a night when I need more than anything to please him from start to finish.

And that, in the end, is why. I'm beholden to his pleasure, forced to perform for him whether I want to or not, and this small rebellion feels as if it gives me the smallest bit of power tonight. *He'll never find out anyway,* I tell myself as his fingers brush over the fur, and he shrugs.

"As long as you're comfortable." He offers me his arm, and I take it. "Shall we?"

The car is waiting for us downstairs. I watch Boston's skyline slide by as we drive to the gala, reminded uncomfortably of my wedding night, not all that long ago, and how it felt leaving to end the night in a strange place. Everything about my relationship with David has kept me thrown off guard from the beginning, and it feels as if that will never change. Even as formal and polite as he is right now, with no hint of the anger or cruelty that I know can come out, I'm waiting for the other shoe to drop.

And I keep thinking, over and over again, about what I found in the attic—and his poor explanation for it all.

David steps out of the car as it comes to a halt and the driver opens the door, and I take a deep breath. *Perform,* I tell myself as I slip out after him, careful of my dress, taking his arm with a perfect smile on my face. *I'm happy. Satisfied. Thrilled with my marriage.* Nothing can go wrong tonight. The possibility of future happiness rests on that.

The gala is being held at the Boston Library, a huge, elegant space that is lit up brilliantly as we walk in, a string quartet already playing. The room is filled with guests moving around the opulent space decorated almost entirely in cream and ivory, tables draped with heavy brocade tablecloths and set with fine china. I feel myself relax a little—this, I'm familiar with. I've been to these before, as my father's daughter instead of a mafia heir's wife, but it's all much the same.

"David!" A tall, elegantly dressed woman with perfectly coiffed grey hair—and clearly, an excellent plastic surgeon—sweeps towards him in a gold gown that puts me in mind of an awards ceremony statuette. Her face is perfectly made up, her age seemingly having barely touched her, and she takes both of David's hands in hers, going up on her toes to kiss him on each cheek. "It's so good to see you. I didn't think you'd be here tonight. I imagined you'd be on honeymoon with your lovely new bride. But here she is! Or at least, I *hope* that's her."

The woman titters at her own joke, and David nudges me forward, a polite smile on his face. "Margary, this is Amalie—my wife, I'm fortunate enough to say. I missed you at the wedding."

I know him well enough by now to know, from the carefulness of his tone, that he is *not* disappointed that this woman didn't make it to our wedding. But she's clearly someone whose approval matters, so I smile at her, taking her hand as she reaches for mine. "I'm so pleased to meet you, Margary," I tell her sweetly. "And I'm sorry to hear that you weren't able to make the wedding, too."

"Well, didn't David mention why we couldn't attend?" She sniffs lightly. "My husband had business in France, and I couldn't miss an opportunity to go. It's so rare, after all, to have a spouse whose company you can still find pleasure in after all these years."

I press my lips together, maintaining the polite smile on my face that matches David's. I've never had my own money to gamble with, but if I did, I'd bet that this woman doesn't like her husband any more than any other mafia wife does. What she likes is his wealth, and the ability to be pampered and spoiled in Paris while he does business there. Which—I can't exactly fault her for. After all, I spent an extra week in Ibiza with David exactly that way myself. I just didn't know who he really was then.

"We should all be so lucky," David says smoothly. "Now, if you'll excuse us, I think I see my parents at our table."

It's all I can do not to wince. The last thing I want to do is spend the evening sitting at dinner with my in-laws, but it's a price I'm willing to pay to be out of that mansion. I might not *like* these people, exactly, but I know how to handle myself here, what to say and do. I don't feel as out of my depth, and here, at least, David will behave the same way.

His parents are sitting at the table with two other couples—one a man his father's age who has a woman next to him who looks to be about mine, and another man who appears closer to David's age. He's sitting next to a pretty blonde with a blank expression, another wife, I see from the sparkling solitaire diamond and matching band on her finger. David's mother gives me an appraising look, and from what I can see in her expression, she approves.

It's never easy to tell what any of these people are thinking. I've known that my whole life. It's part of the reason why I enjoyed Claire's company so much, why I felt so much happier during that first part of my trip to Ibiza. She and her trust-fund friends might be new money, they might be more crass and spoiled than anyone here would let on, but there's less deception, less artifice. There was an honesty to their licentiousness that was almost refreshing, after growing up among the machinations of the mafia.

Now I'm married to one of them. My future can be ruined just as easily as David ruined me for any other man, if I displease him. If I displease his family. I sit there, a charming smile on my face and small talk dripping from my lips, and I hope that it's good enough.

The older man across from the table is watching me. I see his eyes drift over the sapphire resting just above my breasts, his gaze darkening as it slides downwards. He leans over, murmuring something to the man sitting next to him, and I catch the younger man's gaze drifting over me, too. David's hand brushes against my thigh, parting the silk so that his fingers touch bare flesh, and I know he's seen them looking.

Let him. The idea of his jealousy sparks something in me. I meet the older man's gaze, turning that charming smile on him, and his mouth quirks upwards.

"Amalie Carravella?" He smiles wider, and I hesitate. My new name still sounds strange—I'm not used to being referred to by my married name, instead of Leone. I should be happy to be rid of my maiden name, and all of the shame associated with it now, but it feels more as if I've lost another tether that held me to who I used to be.

"In the flesh." I tilt my head coyly. "And who do I have the pleasure of meeting?"

"Vicenzo Ferretti." His smile doesn't falter. "A distant cousin of the family from New York, of course, if you're familiar?"

It doesn't ring a bell, but I never did manage to pay attention as much as my father would have liked, when he was trying to instill the hierarchy of the mafia into my lessons. I pretend that it does, nodding. It's doubtful that this man will actually want me to speak enough for it to matter if I really do remember them or not. "Of course," I say softly, and I feel David glance at me. I doubt it matters to him, either, if I really do know who any of these people are. What matters is that I pretend well enough to be believed.

"It's a pleasure, Mr. Ferretti." I reach for my wine—a sip, to keep up the pretense in front of his family that I'm not pregnant. David hasn't explicitly told me to do so, but I know very well that he would want it a secret, for now. I don't miss the way Vicenzo's eyes go to my lips as they touch the rim of my glass, and David doesn't either, from the way his fingers press against my thigh. It sends a flush of heat through me, and I let the stole slip away from my arms a little, the fur suddenly too warm.

"Your husband is a lucky man. I might have snatched you up myself, if I'd known you were on offer. A widower could only hope to be so fortunate as to marry a beautiful virgin bride for the second time in his life."

It's an insult, and I know it. If he knows who I am, who my family *was*—and he must—then to imply my father would have even considered him as a potential husband is rude. This man isn't even a consigliere, only an associate of men like David's father. He's letting me know, couched in pretty words, that he knows exactly how desperate my mother was to make *any* possible match for me in the wake of our disgrace.

"I couldn't imagine having been wed to anyone else." I tilt my head towards David, letting a sweet smile tilt my lips, and his gaze drifts to my mouth. His gaze is emotionless, a perfect poker face, but he leans close to my ear, his lips grazing the shell of it as his hand tightens on my thigh.

"Imagine if he knew," David murmurs, his voice so low that I'm certain no one else can hear, "that just this afternoon, you had my cock between those pretty lips, my cum all over your face."

My pulse leaps at that, my heart beating a quick rhythm in my chest. "Imagine," he continues, his breath still warm against my ear, "if I put you on your knees right now, just to show him that you're mine. If I covered that pretty face with my cum, just because I can, and then showed him what I do to men who covet what belongs to me."

A jolt of unexpected lust shoots through me, my thighs squeezing together beneath the table as my heart trips in my chest. *This shouldn't turn me on,* I think desperately—but it does. His fingers sliding beneath the silk of my dress, his voice whispering filthy things in my ear, the threat of my debasement and the violence, the promise that I *belong* to him and no one else—it all makes me feel dizzy, breathless, my cheeks flushing.

"I don't know if *all* of our present company would enjoy that," I whisper softly, turning my face towards his, and for a moment, his lips are so close to mine that they nearly touch. I know he can feel the whisper of my breath against his mouth, and I feel him stiffen, his hand pressing against the soft flesh of my leg. I know, if I slipped my hand beneath the table right now, I'd find his cock hard and ready for me—that with the slightest provocation, I might find myself on my knees anyway, somewhere in this huge place.

David reaches up, brushing a curl of hair away from my cheek, the gentleness of the touch sucking all the air from my lungs. "Don't you know, *cara mia*?" he whispers, his hand pressed to my cheek as he leans close to my ear again. "The only enjoyment that matters to me is my own."

But it's not true. I *know* it's not true, from the way he pleasured me in Ibiza, from the things that I know he can do to me if he chooses to. My fingers are trembling where they're wrapped around my wine glass, and I nearly jump out of my skin when I hear David's father clear his throat, jolting us both out of the moment.

"Well, then," he says, shooting his son a dark look. "Newlyweds, hm? What could we possibly have expected, bringing them both here tonight?"

Vicenzo chuckles, raising his glass to that, but I see the jealousy on his face. It's exactly what David wanted, the entire purpose of the little show that he just put on. I belong to *him*, and David wanted to make certain that any man who dared to look at me knows that. He wanted Vicenzo to see the power he has over me, how David can make me melt with just a touch.

He wants Vicenzo imagining, tonight when he leaves, what David will be doing to me later.

I can't stop imagining it, either. Just this afternoon on the flight here, I was terrified, dreading David touching me. Now my blood feels molten, my skin shivering and sensitive with every touch of David's hand against it, like I have a fever. I hardly taste dinner—I couldn't even say what it is that we're being served—taking tiny bites to keep from upsetting my stomach between smaller sips of wine. No one takes notice—anyone who sees me eating like a bird will just assume I'm worried about my figure. I feel a small flash of resentment at the thought, but it dissolves the moment I feel David's fingers wrap around mine, tugging me up from my seat as he nudges his dessert plate away.

"A dance, with my beautiful new wife?" He gives me a look that's full of desire, full of affection, even—the latter more than I've ever seen from him before. I know it's a show, that it's for anyone who might be looking, anyone else who might want me, but it's hard not to believe it. He plays this part so well.

All I can think about, as he leads me out onto the dance floor, is what we might do together later. His hand on the small of my back feels as if it sears through the fabric, my heart racing the way it did the first night we met, when I saw him and felt something that I never had before. We sway to the music, the dancing nothing like what we did together that night in the club in Ibiza, but being so close to him has me every bit as aroused. And if the way he's looking at me is any indication, he feels the same.

"Perhaps you weren't such a bad choice," David says lightly into my ear as he pulls me close, my body flush with his as we move slowly across the floor. His voice is almost teasing, his cheek pressed to mine, and I want to believe it. I want to lean into the sudden tenderness, absorb it into myself, to feel that it's *real*. That perhaps he's finally coming around. "No one else here seems to think that you were."

"And it matters to you?" It's a foolish question—of course it does —but I know I'm supposed to ask. I tilt my head back slightly, looking up into his dark gaze, feeling my chest tighten all over again at the way he's looking at me. "You're jealous of them. The other men looking at me." I shouldn't like the idea of that as much as I do, I know that—but I can't help it. And I think he hears that in my voice, because his mouth twitches in a smile as he spins me, bringing me back into his embrace.

"I want them to know you're mine." His hand tightens on the small of my back, and I feel the swell of his cock pressing against me where our hips are touching, half-hard, a promise of what he'll give me later. "*All* of you. *My* bride. My wife."

I know he can feel the way I shiver against him. I never knew what a heady combination of fear and desire could be, but I discover it then, pressed against him on the dance floor as the sweet music of the stringed instruments wraps around us. I almost wish I could freeze the moment, stay right here in the in-between of adoration and desire, where both of us have forgotten that we each hate the other for a moment. I want what comes later—but I'm also afraid of what will come after that, when we remember.

David's desire is almost palpable when we leave the gala, his fingers tightly laced with mine as he leads me out to the waiting car. The moment we're inside, he sits next to me, instead of across from me as he has been, and before I can even take a breath, his hand is in my hair, and his lips are on mine, leaning me backward on the seat as I gasp.

He's relentless. His other hand combs through my hair, too, wrapping it around his fingers as he lays me back on the cool leather, his knee nudging my legs apart. He's rock-hard, pressing firmly against me through the tight fabric of his trousers, and I can't breathe as he kisses me, his mouth tasting like wine from dinner as his tongue slides against mine. His hips rock against mine, firm and insistent, and for a moment, I think he's going to pull my panties aside and fuck me right here in the back of the car.

I also know that I'd let him, without a complaint, if that's what he wanted.

But he doesn't. His mouth slants over mine, warm and softer than it has been since Ibiza, the kiss full of tenderness along with passion. I forgot that he could kiss me like this, forgot what it felt like already, lost in our constant battle—and I find myself arching upwards against him, my leg twining with his, my breath coming quick and hot against his lips as he kisses me recklessly.

It all melts away. The moment in my home when I discovered who he really was, our brokered marriage, our awkward wedding, every fight we've had since, every shouted word. The discovery in the attic, the rough sex, all the moments when I've known that he resents me and that I hate him—it all disappears. It's gone, and all I can think of is how his mouth feels on mine, his body taut and straining with arousal, the way my heart twists with desire when he shrugs off his jacket and lets it fall to the floor of the car, his hands cupping my face as he kisses me all over again.

I gasp when his lips drift to my throat, my collarbone, tracing along the line of the sapphire necklace down to the swell of my breasts. His hands mold them through the silk, slide down my waist, and then suddenly, his weight lifts off of me as he turns me on the leather seat, pushing the skirt of my dress up and out of the way as he spreads my legs wide.

"There's no need for these," he murmurs, hooking his fingers in the edge of my panties as he slides down to the floor, kneeling between my legs. I don't realize at first that he's taking them off, I'm so shocked by the scene in front of me. David, kneeling in front of me, looking up at me with such abject lust in his eyes that it's startling, tugging me to the edge of the seat as he shoves my panties into his trouser pocket so he can spread me wider still for him. "I want to make you come, *bellisima*," he breathes. "As many times as you can come on my tongue, until you're all that I taste."

He presses his mouth between my thighs, his hands holding them apart, and my world dissolves under the heat of his tongue. I feel his lips against my clit, his tongue sliding down to circle my entrance, and then he pushes his tongue inside of me, the soft heat of it making me cry out before I remember that the driver can hear us. I bite my lip, intent on being quiet—and then David stiffens his tongue, curling it inside of me as he thrusts, and I forget to care.

Even in Ibiza, he never ate me out like this. He devours me, fucking me with his tongue until I'm trembling, the pleasure plateauing in a way that makes me want to beg for him to push me over the edge. I think that he *will* make me beg—that of course he will, it's what he enjoys—but he doesn't. He thrusts his tongue once more inside of me, as if he can't get enough. Then I let out a gasping moan of pleasure as his lips fasten around my clit, sucking hard as his tongue flutters over the stiff, twitching flesh.

The pleasure is beyond anything I've ever felt. My hand slides into his hair, gripping, nails digging into his scalp, but he doesn't stop. The feeling of him sucking my clit, tongue fluttering without stop-ping, sends me over the edge in an instant, my thighs tightening under his grip as I cry out his name in a rush of pleasure. I can feel the flood of my arousal as I come, soaking his face, but he doesn't stop. He presses his mouth more tightly against me, his tongue still finding every spot that makes the world spin and my vision blur, and then I feel him push two fingers into me, curling them the way he did with his tongue.

I come again almost instantly. It's almost too much, the unrelenting pressure and heat, the feeling as he adds a third finger, fucking me relentlessly with them as his tongue slides over my clit. There's no hesitation, not even a breath, as he hurtles me into wave after wave of pleasure, as if the orgasms don't really end, just ebb and flow until I've nearly collapsed on the seat, panting.

"I can't—" I whimper as he pulls back for just a moment, his cheeks flushed and lips swollen, face damp with my arousal. He looks overcome with lust, his fingers still buried inside of me, moving in a way that makes me whimper despite what I just said.

"You can," he murmurs, his voice so thick with desire that it makes me shudder. "Because I want you to, Amalie."

I realize, dimly, that the car has stopped. My cheeks flush hot as the rest of it comes to me, just as David curls his fingers inside of me again and lowers his mouth to my swollen, throbbing pussy—the realization that the driver is waiting on us to be finished, listening as David makes me come again and again.

Even in this moment, it's a show of power. How everyone, even me, waits on his pleasure—even when that pleasure is being given by him instead of received.

But even that realization isn't enough to make me ask him to stop. Not when it feels so good.

He makes me come once more, my back arching, nails digging into the leather of the seat and his scalp as I moan helplessly, my entire body shuddering with the onslaught of sensation. My clit feels swollen, too sensitive, the pleasure is almost painful by the time David draws back again, taking my hand and pulling me up off of the seat. For a moment, I wonder again if he's going to fuck me here, in the car, while he makes the driver wait, but then I see him rap sharply on the screen, separating us from the front of the car.

A moment later, the door opens. I can't quite meet the driver's eyes as David helps me out, feeling my cheeks flush hot as I think of what he must have heard—of what I must look like, my dress wrinkled and my hair tangled around my face. I can feel eyes on me as David and I walk through the hotel lobby, and a part of me is as thrilled by it as I am embarrassed. Everyone who sees me knows what the man holding my hand is going to do to me—can imagine what he might have already done. I feel desired, valued, *wanted*, and that feeling only intensifies when David pushes me up against the elevator wall, jamming his key card into the slot as he kisses me hungrily again.

"I want to fuck you right here." He spins me around, his hand in my hair, fingers pressed to the back of my neck as he lifts my skirt. "I need my cock in you, *now*."

I gasp as he shoves my skirt to one side, dragging his zipper down. I feel the heat of his thick, hard cock against my inner thigh as he pulls my panties to one side, the swollen tip pushing between my folds, and I cry out as he thrusts up into me hard, holding himself there. His hips press against the soft curve of my ass, burying himself into me as deeply as he can, his mouth grazing over my throat and making me moan as he rocks against me. "*Fuck*," he breathes, and I clench around him, rippling along the length of his shaft and making him groan aloud. "I'm going to keep you here, just like this, until we get to the top floor."

The thought of that, of his cock buried inside of me as the elevator ascends, makes me moan all over again. "What if someone walks in?" I breathe, and David chuckles darkly, thrusting deeper as his teeth graze my throat.

"Then they can watch."

His hands settle on me, one on the back of my neck, twisted in my hair, the other on my hip. He thrusts slowly, shallowly, his lips pressed to my shoulder. "That's a good girl," he groans, rolling his hips against me. "Keep my cock nice and warm. I'll stay so fucking hard for you, just like this. *Fuck*—"

I tighten around him again, that pleasurable ache building, the feeling of him inside of me more of a tease right now than anything else. He thrusts again, each slow movement building that pleasure, until the elevator reaches the top floor and stops. He holds me there for just a moment, until I think the doors will open with him still inside of me, and then slides out, tucking his hard cock back into his suit trousers with a groan. I catch a glimpse of his erection, swollen and slick with my arousal, and nearly moan with the need to have him in me again.

"Patience, *bellisima*." David kisses me, his fingers sliding against my clit for just a moment as he adjusts my panties, making me arch into him. "I'll fuck you just the way you need, *cara mia*."

I believe him. Whatever happened tonight to change his mood, he wants my pleasure as much as his own tonight, and it makes me desperate to get him into bed. I take his hand, hearing him laugh as we hurry out of the elevator, and it's all I can do not to grab him again as he slips his black card into the door and opens it wide.

The moment it closes behind us, I kiss him again. I feel empty, hollow after he slipped out of me, and David groans, his hands finding the zipper of my dress and dragging it down. "I want you naked, *cara mia*," he murmurs, eagerly seeking out my bare flesh as the silk falls away, palms sliding over my waist and hips as he yanks my panties down. "Bare, except for that jewelry. Dripping in gems for me, and nothing else."

The words roll off of his tongue, his accent thickened with lust, and I tilt my head back as he kisses my neck, backing me towards the master suite. I see all the surfaces we could be fucking on already— the bar counter, the leather couch, up against the huge window—but David seems intent on having me in the bed. He strips off his shirt as we stumble backward, yanking the buttons free, and by the time we reach the edge of the huge king-sized bed, we're both naked.

I pull back, breathless, as I look at him. He looks like a fucking god, chiseled with muscle and tattooed, dark hair sprinkled over his chest and narrowing down into the thick line that ends just below his navel, where his massive cock strains upwards. I reach for him, wrapping my hand around his length, and fall to my knees.

"*Bellisima*—" he groans aloud, looking down at me with lust-darkened eyes. "Amalie—"

It's the first time he's ever protested me doing this, even a little bit. Usually, he demands it. "I want you in my mouth," I whisper, and I mean it. I'm aching for him to be inside of me again, but I want to taste him too, and I relish the sound of near-pained pleasure he makes when I press my lips against his swollen, sensitive cockhead. My tongue flicks out, tasting my own arousal mingled with his pre-cum, and something about that sends another flood of desire through me. I can feel myself dripping, soaked with need, and I wrap my lips around him, sliding his cock over my tongue as I struggle to take him deeper into my mouth.

"Oh *god*." David grips the back of my head, his hips rocking forward. "Your fucking mouth—those pretty lips—*fuck*. I love watching you suck my fucking cock—" His jaw tightens, and I feel his thigh flex under my hand as he struggles to let me set my own pace, not to fuck my mouth the way I know he wants to. I feel the same rush of desire that I felt in Ibiza, the desire to please him, and I slide my lips down further, trying to take as much of him into my mouth as I can.

His hand tightens in my hair when his cockhead presses against the back of my throat, and he pulls free of my mouth suddenly, his cock so stiff that it nearly presses against his belly as he steps back and pulls me to my feet.

"I need you." His voice is hoarse, almost desperate, as he grabs my waist and picks me up, laying me back on the bed. "I need to be in you. *Fuck*—"

The lust in the air feels so thick, so strong, that it makes me feel as if I can't breathe. David's mouth crushes against mine again as he pushes himself between my legs, thrusting into me so hard and fast that it knocks what little air is left from my lungs. His hands are on my hips, holding me still as he fucks me with long, slow strokes that make me arch and cry out, writhing on his cock as he drags his mouth down my throat. His teeth graze against the diamonds lying against my skin, the jewelry cold compared to the heated flush burning through me, the hot slide of his cock into me again and again. He thrusts harder, grinding against my clit with every impact of his body against mine, and I realize with a dizzying rush that I'm going to come again, every muscle in my body winding tight.

"I want to come in you," he breathes in my ear. "I want to fucking fill you with it. I want it dripping out of you, my pretty little bride. I want to keep you full of it, so that if any other man dared touch you, it'd be me all over his fingers. His cock. *Mine*." He nearly snarls the last word, hips slamming hard against mine, the fullness of his cock inside of me nearly driving me over the edge.

"You'd kill anyone who touched me," I breathe, looking up at him with lust-glazed eyes, the thought of it sending another wracking jolt of desire through me. "I know you would."

"I'd make them watch me fuck you first." David wraps his hand in my hair, drawing himself out of me slowly, until only the swollen tip is still buried between my folds. He thrusts shallowly, the ridge of his cockhead rubbing against the sensitive spot just inside of me, and then his hips snap forward, burying himself inside of me so roughly that I nearly scream. "I'd make them watch you come, over and over, screaming my name. I'd make sure they thought long and hard about how they'd never touch another woman."

There's a thick jealousy in his voice that frightens me. For the briefest moment, in between the shattering pleasure of David's body thrusting into mine, I remember the photos in the attic—clearly taken by someone else, someone following that woman. I remember the bloodstained blouse. The necklace, hidden away.

I wonder if it was really David's brother that woman married, after all.

His mouth covers mine again, swallowing my cry of pleasure as his cock slams into me again, as deeply as he can go. He bucks his hips against mine, and I feel my swollen clit rub against his skin, that last bit of friction making me arch and writhe under him, my world unraveling as another orgasm shatters me. My muscles seize, my body consumed with pleasure, and I feel my nails rake down his back as his cock hardens and throbs inside of me, spurting hot cum as David's orgasm joins mine. I hear him moan, his pleasure and mine all tangled up together. I feel the pulse of him inside of me as he comes, and I don't want it to stop.

I don't want any of this to end. I want him to fuck me, again and again, and make the pleasure go on forever.

I don't want to go back to what we had before tonight.

David pulls back, and I realize with a shock that I whispered some of that aloud, against his lips as I came. "Don't worry, *cara mia*," he murmurs, his hips moving slowly, and I realize, to my sudden shock, that he's still hard. "You can have as much of my cock as you like tonight."

He thrusts again, and I feel the stickiness of his cum on my thighs, dripping out of me as he fucks his release into me, deeper and deeper with every rock of his hips. I feel another ripple of pleasure, the slow build to another cresting wave, and I reach for him, pulling his mouth down to mine.

"We have all night," I whisper against his lips. "Just please don't stop."

22

AMALIE

H
e doesn't stop. The second time is long and slow, the third sleepy and languid, and I fall asleep in his arms for the first time since Ibiza. For the first time since Ibiza, too, I start to feel as if I'm falling for him again.

The nausea that propels me out of bed in the morning and into the bathroom reminds me of why I can't. Why I won't ever fall for him, even once he knows that I'm not lying, and that the baby is his.

David knocks heavily on the door as I flush the toilet, wiping my mouth as I close the lid and rest my forehead on the cool porcelain for a moment. *Is this ever going to stop?* I wonder dimly, pressing my other hand against my stomach. There's no real sign of the baby yet besides this awful nausea, and it's hard to believe that it's real sometimes, that this isn't just some persistent flu.

But it *is* real. I sit back on my heels, getting up slowly as David knocks again. "Amalie? Amalie, answer me!"

"Just a minute!" I snap angrily, turning on the faucet and reaching for a small bottle of mouthwash. I feel a fresh wave of anger at his demanding tone, at the way he seems to think he can have my attention whenever and however he wants, no matter what I'm dealing with. I'd been afraid last night, that the momentary tenderness between us was temporary—and this feels like the first sign that I was right.

And then I yank the door open, and see worry on his face.

"Are you alright?" He looks down at me, genuine concern in his eyes, and I stare at him confusedly.

"I was sick. The—the baby." It's hard to say it out loud, knowing that he doubts me. That he doesn't believe that it's really his, that I was really a virgin, that he's the only man I've been with. That he's the only man I've ever *wanted* to be with, which sometimes feels more like a curse now than anything else.

"Take a shower." He reaches out, brushing a piece of tangled hair away from my face, and I flinch, startled at his gentleness. But I see from the way his face goes instantly cold that he's interpreted it as something else. "I don't want to be here all day," he says, his voice turning flat. "So try not to make it a long one."

When he turns away, my heart sinks. There had been a chance—a brief one—that the way things were last night might have continued into today. Longer, even. But one small gesture undid it all, and the frustration of that makes my eyes well up with tears. *He can't give me the benefit of the doubt for even a moment,* I think bitterly, shoving the bathroom door closed as I walk to the shower. We're going to head back to the mansion today, after brunch with his parents, and I've never wanted anything less.

David is back to being quiet on the brief flight home. Brunch was nothing but small talk with his parents; any mention of David's possessiveness over me last night in front of their guests was ignored. His mother commented on my fur stole, telling me how lovely it was, which gave me a moment's sly pleasure—knowing she'd be horrified if she knew where it really came from.

I know I should try to break the silence, to make some kind of conversation with my husband, but I can't find the will to. With every minute that passes, last night feels further and further away, like some kind of fever dream that never really happened. I can feel my mood deteriorating the closer we get to the mansion, and I know David picks up on it. The air between us feels more and more tense, with anger this time instead of lust, and he doesn't hesitate to call me out on it the moment we're inside the house, the door firmly shut behind him.

"What the hell is wrong with you, Amalie?" he snaps, and I stare at him, pressing my lips tightly together.

"I don't want to have this conversation." I turn away, feeling him grab my wrist as I do, but I manage to shake him off as I make a beeline for the stairs. I can feel the oppressiveness of the house closing in around me, the isolation, the feeling that everything I say and do here is somehow wrong. That no matter what I do, there's no way out of this place.

"You can't just walk away from me!" His voice rises, and I hear him following me. My pulse spikes, beating hard in my throat as I scurry up the stairs, suddenly wanting nothing more than to put a door between him and me. I could feel him going cold ever since I flinched away from him this morning, and my chest aches. I want to stop the back and forth, to stop hating and desiring him all at once, to stop wondering when his coldness might turn into something worse.

I dart up the stairs to the bedroom, and I know he's right behind me. I don't dare look back—I don't want to see the look on his face, to see if it's anger or lust or both. I feel almost certain that it *is* both. With us, one always seems to feed the other, and I don't know how much longer I can stand it.

The moment I try to close the bedroom door behind me, David blocks it. He pushes his way into the room after me, closing the door hard as he stands in front of it, and I whirl to face him, glaring at him with all the anger I can muster.

"Just leave me alone!"

"No." His voice is hard and flat. "You don't get to just storm off in my house, Amalie. If I want to talk to you—"

"*Our* house," I hiss, and he starts to laugh.

"Oh, so now it's *ours*? But you hate it. You can't stand this place, you spoiled little thing." David glares at me, his expression hard. "You want nothing to do with it, until you can use it as a means to argue with me."

"Why would anyone want to live here?" I throw my hands up, gesturing around the room. "This is one of what—three finished rooms in this entire house? There isn't even a tub in the bathroom. Anyone would be embarrassed to live here—"

I see David's jaw tighten, that muscle twitch in the way it does when he's having difficulty controlling himself. I feel a spark of fear, my stomach twisting at the look on his face, but I'm too angry to stop, too upset at being thrust back here after a moment's respite in Boston. "This is my family home, Amalie," he says slowly, his words laced with anger. "You should have more respect—"

"Then they shouldn't have left it, if it matters so much!" I shout the words, flinging at them as if they could hurt, and in the moment that they land, I see, suddenly, that they did.

David goes utterly silent, and I know I've gone too far. I feel the tension in the air snap, settling into a cold heaviness that makes me wish I could take what I said back. I don't know *why* it upset him so much, only that it did. I know that I've taken another step down the path of irrevocably damaging whatever little tenderness there might be between us.

But he's done—and continues to do the same. The resentment I feel for that seems to outweigh anything else, every time.

"There's another party this weekend," he says finally. "One here in Newport, for a charitable board that I'm on. You'll be expected to attend with me, of course. I imagine you'll put on the same lovely show that you did last night. I was impressed with how well you played the part of a perfect mafia wife, considering the fact that deep down, this—" he waves a hand at me, "—shrewish personality is who you really are."

I swallow hard, feeling that tight ache in my chest again. *It's not*, I want to say. *It's just that somehow, I'm like this with you. Even when I don't want to be.*

"But there's an entire week until then," he continues, his voice still flat and emotionless. "I suggest you start volunteering, Amalie, or find something to do with your time. I can't always cater to you and keep you entertained."

I stare at him, feeling every word as if he's slapped me. He thinks I'm spoiled and selfish, and I don't know how to convince him otherwise. "Is that why you wanted me so much last night?" I ask softly, feeling as if the question burns my tongue when I ask it. "Because I played the part you wanted me to?"

There's not so much as a flicker of emotion on his face as he steps away from the door, walking towards me. I want to flinch back, but I hold my ground, all the way until he reaches up, pressing his hand against my cheek. "You were a good girl," he murmurs, his gaze caressing my face the way his fingers caress along my cheekbone. "You pretended so well. I thought you deserved a reward. And you kept pretending all night, didn't you?"

I blink at him, startled. "I wasn't pretending," I whisper, before I can stop myself. A part of me would rather him think that I *was*, if it meant him not realizing just how much sway he really has over me, how much command he has over my desires. And another part of me can't believe that he really thinks that—that he could have seen anything other than absolute sincerity in my desire last night, just as I saw it in him.

There must be some reason he wants to think it was pretense. I realize it in the same moment his hand slides into my hair, tugging my head back as his other hand trails down my jaw, over the length of my throat. "You're mine, Amalie," he murmurs. "My wife. If I say I want you here, then you will stay here. If I tell you to go somewhere with me, you will go. You will *obey* me, and if it takes *pretending* for you to be a good mafia wife, then that's what you'll do—"

I slap him before I can stop myself. My hand connects with his cheek, not quite hard enough to leave a mark, but hard enough to sting. I can see it in the shock on his face, feel it in the way his hand briefly loosens in my hair before grabbing it again, harder this time.

He spins me towards the bed, backing me up towards it so quickly that I nearly fall. "Is that what you want?" he growls, his hand digging into my hip. "You want it rough? You want to slap me, hurt me? Try it again, Amalie."

I stare at him, suddenly frozen with fear. I'm not sure that I've ever seen him quite this angry, his eyes dark with rage, his hand pulling at my hair until I whimper with fear and discomfort.

"Do it," he hisses, and something dark and angry rises up in me, too. All the resentment at the control that everyone seems to have over my life except for me, all of the hatred that I have for the life I was born into, how angry I am at the choices that my father and brother made that put me here, in this marriage, with this man. I raise my hand again, striking him across the side of his face, and when he shoves me back onto the bed in response, I see that he's hard.

"Good girl. See, you can take orders, as long as they're orders you want." David yanks at his belt, the ridge of his cock straining against his fly, and I feel my pulse leap in my throat despite myself. Even when I'm furious with him, I still want him.

He yanks down his zipper, his thick cock springing free, and he wraps his hand around it as he meets my gaze. "Spread your legs," he growls, his hand sliding along the length. "I want to see you."

The words are sharp, demanding, and every one sends heat lancing through me, staining my cheeks with embarrassment. I ball up the skirt of my sundress in my hands, lifting it up as I spread my legs, my knees falling to the side. I chose a pair of peach-colored silk and lace panties this morning, and I see David's eyes darken as he gazes between my thighs, his mouth twitching with amused desire. My face flushes hotter, knowing what he's seeing—the damp fabric clinging between my legs where I'm already wet for him.

"Take your panties off," he murmurs, his hand still slowly stroking his cock. "*Now*, Amalie," he adds, when I hesitate for just a moment, my gaze fixed on his throbbing length. I can see the pre-cum pearling at the tip, and I can't help the way I lick my lips as he rubs his thumb over it, pressing the pad of it into the swollen flesh.

"You want my cock in your mouth, don't you?" he murmurs, that lewd smirk still on his face as I slip my panties down my thighs. "But you'll have to earn my cock again, Amalie. You were so good last night, but I'm afraid you've undone it all. So spread your legs like a good girl. Just like you did for me while you were alone here, while I was in Boston."

I stare at him, uncomprehending for a moment. My legs snap shut as I sit up on my elbows, blinking confusedly. "What are you talking about?" I whisper, and David chuckles darkly, his hand sliding lazily along his cock once more.

"You didn't figure it out?" He nods towards the corner of the room, his hand still moving, as if pleasuring himself is just another part of the conversation. I turn in the direction he's looking, still confused— and then I see the small, blinking red light.

Horror sweeps through me as I realize what he means. "No—" I whisper, remembering that night, how I'd touched myself, fucked myself with the toy in a way that I would have *never* let him see me if he'd been there, how I'd moaned his name. I feel tears of humiliation pricking at the back of my eyes, realizing that he knows I fantasized about him when he wasn't there, that no matter how much I claim to hate him, I want him even more.

"Such a little slut." David steps closer, between my legs, his hand wrapping in my hair once more. "Fucking yourself like that for me to watch. It got me off, watching you. Seeing you like that, wet and spread open for me, not knowing I was seeing everything. I came so fucking hard, *bellisima*. I couldn't wait to come home and fuck your pretty mouth. My little whore of a wife." He shoves me back again, his hand moving along his cock more quickly. "And you expect me to believe you were a virgin?"

I glare up at him, the fury returning in a flash. " I *was*," I hiss. "You were the only one. You've *been* the only one, even if sometimes—"

His gaze sparks dangerously, and he reaches down, grabbing my knee as he spreads me open. "Careful what you say, *cara mia*," he murmurs. "Now show me how wet you are for me. How much the idea of me watching you come turns you on. You like that I was watching, don't you? Even if it embarrasses you, too."

I hate him. It echoes in my head, even as I obey him, my body aching with the need to be touched, to be fucked, to push past all of the games and fighting and just *feel*. I hate that he didn't tell me about the camera. No doubt waiting for exactly that to happen—for me to give him a show without knowing, so that he could hold it over my head. I hate that he mocks me with it, instead of making it something teasing and sweet. I hate that nothing between us can ever be good, and I hate that I don't fully understand why.

My legs fall open as if on their own accord, my body throbbing with need. I watch, breathless, as his hand slides over his cock, the length of it glistening with his arousal, as his gaze fixes between my thighs. "Spread yourself open, *bellisima*," he murmurs, his voice thick and hoarse with desire. "Let me see."

I feel flushed and hot, my skin too tight for my body. I reach down, spreading myself open with my fingers, feeling how slick and wet I am, my swollen clit peeking through even before I part my folds, letting him see every inch of my aroused flesh. I know he can see it when I tighten, my body clenching on nothing, wanting him, the way my hips arch up at the touch of my fingers, my clit twitching with the need to be touched.

"Just like that," he murmurs. "Stay just like that, *bellisima*."

I know, from the way he says it, that I'm not allowed to touch myself further. My fingers are a fraction away from my clit, holding my folds open for his view. I whimper helplessly as I watch him stroke his cock, his muscled forearm flexing below the rolled-up sleeve, his jaw clenched taut with pleasure. His palm rubs over his cockhead, spreading his arousal along his shaft, his hips jerking forward as he fucks his fist, and I so desperately want it to be me instead.

"Good girl," he murmurs, his hand sliding down to the base and squeezing, his gaze fixed darkly between my thighs. "I think you might deserve a reward, *cara mia*."

I realize at that moment, as David steps forward with his hand sliding up my thigh, that he's not as impervious to how I make him feel as he so often makes me think that he is. He wants me to think that he's doing me a favor by relenting and fucking me, that he's *rewarding* me—but the truth is that he wants to be inside me just as desperately as I want him. This is just a way for him to pretend that he doesn't need it every bit as much.

His hand grabs my hip, squeezing, his thumb pressing against my hipbone as he yanks me to the edge of the bed, dislodging my hand. I can't hold back the sound I make, the moan that slips out as he spreads my legs wide, fingers digging into the soft flesh almost painfully as his cock presses against my entrance. I can *feel* him throbbing, even like this, hard and aching for me, and I feel a sudden thrill, a burst of satisfaction that I can turn him on so much. That I can push him past the limits of his self-control.

But he pushes me past mine, too. When he thrusts into me hard, filling me with one swift thrust, I can't stop myself from crying out. I can't stop myself from wrapping my legs around his hips, pulling him closer, wanting more as I arch into him. I want all of it—every bit of sensation that he can give me, the feeling of his body against mine, my breasts brushing against his chest, the flex of his muscles as he slams his cock into me again and again, as if he wants to take out every bit of his anger on me.

And I want to let him.

He groans as he slams into me again, reaching up to grab my hands where my nails are digging into his shoulders. His fingers close around my wrists, dragging my hands up above my head and pinning them there as he rocks into me, grinding against my clit with every thrust. "You're going to come for me again," he rasps, his expression taut with pleasure, his voice hoarse with it. "You can't help it. You couldn't stop if you wanted to."

The way he says the last half makes me wonder if he's saying it to me or himself, the words filled with so much disdain that it makes my heart ache. I turn my face away, but he presses his mouth to mine, tilting his hips as he thrusts into me again so that I cry out into the kiss, the swollen head of his cock brushing against that spot deep inside of me that nearly makes me spill over the edge again.

It feels so good, every time. I feel myself arch, my muscles tensing, that delicious pressure unfurling inside of me as he pushes me closer and closer. I can feel his rhythm stuttering, his thrusts more erratic with every hot slide of his body inside of me, and I know he's close. When I tighten around him, gasping his name as my climax hits, I hear his ragged groan and know that he can't hold back any longer.

"*Fuck—*" he groans aloud, hips jerking as his fingers tighten almost painfully around my wrists, his cock harder than I think I've ever felt him as he pins me to the bed, filling me with spurt after spurt of his cum. I can feel him, hot and thick, and it sends another aftershock of pleasure through me, rippling around him as he presses his mouth to my shoulder and moans.

And then, almost as quickly as he pushed himself inside of me, he slips free, standing up and turning away from me. Something about the sudden detachment sends a pang through me, and I push myself up on my elbows, half-sitting up as I tuck my legs underneath myself. I want to shrink back when he turns to look at me, his face so expressionless that it's almost worse than his anger, but I force myself not to move. I don't want to give him the satisfaction. Even like this, standing there completely naked, his softening cock clinging damply to his thigh, he still frightens me.

He will always have the power to destroy me entirely, if he wants to.

"I feel like you hate me," I whisper softly, and I feel the prick of tears behind my eyelids, burning there in the corners. The words hang in the air between us, and I wait for him to deny it. Even hearing him say that I'm overreacting would be something. But his expression stays cold and blank, and he doesn't so much as flinch.

"It's better than being in love with you," he says finally, his voice as cold as his eyes, and turns to walk away.

I sit there in utter shock for a moment, staring at him as he leaves. He grabs his clothes from the floor as he goes, striding out of the room as if he's already forgotten that I'm there.

I know I shouldn't be hurt by his dismissal, but I am. I watch him go, those last words still cutting me down to the bone again and again; every time I repeat them in my head, I feel like I can't breathe.

It was always too much to hope that the man I married would

love me. But I had hoped, in some small part of myself, that he wouldn't despise me as much as David seems to.

Reaching for the blanket at the end of the bed, I tug it up over myself as I start to cry, curling into a ball in the center of the mattress. All of the loneliness comes flooding in, spreading through me as I lay there, my hair falling into my face as I sob. I wonder, for a brief moment, if David will hear and feel badly about what he said, if he might come up and comfort me.

He doesn't. And I cry myself to sleep.

23

DAVID

I know that what I said was too harsh the moment it came out of my mouth. And I regret it the instant that it does. I regret all of it—the look on her face when it sinks in, the realization that I've hurt her. *Really* hurt her—which tells me more than anything else in our brief relationship has.

She cares about me. For all that she fights with me as if she hates me too, sometimes, for all that she rebels in ways that make me furious—and frustrated, in more ways than one—it matters to her how I feel about her. And thinking back on last night in Boston, at her surprise when I'd softened with her, I'm not sure how I didn't see it sooner.

I don't want to have feelings for her. I don't want the complications or vulnerability. But seeing the look on her face, the shock when she realized that what I'd said was the truth—even if I did regret saying it aloud—makes me wonder if perhaps she is telling the truth about the things I've doubted her on.

She doesn't come down for dinner, and when I go up later that evening, my work for the day finished, I find her already asleep, and all of the lights in the bedroom turned off. The doors to the balcony are open, letting in the warm summer air, and I walk to where the gauzy curtains are drifting around them, intent on shutting the doors.

Why? I pause, my hand on the knob. My first instinct was to close them *because* I know Amalie wanted them open—she always seems to, for some reason—but why? Why do I want so badly to do whatever the opposite of her desires are? I push her to the edge constantly, pricking and poking at every soft spot, as if I want her to prove to me that she's impossible. As if I *want* her to make me hate her.

The breeze is pleasant, warm, and faintly salty, softening the chill of the room. I have to admit that it is nice, and I retreat to the bed, sliding in next to her. She's on the very edge of her side, as if she wanted to put as much distance as possible between the two of us before I even came to bed. I have half a mind to reach for her and pull her closer, just to prove to her that I can have whatever it is that I want, but something stops me. I'm not sure what it is, exactly, but I lie there instead, watching her as she sleeps. I remember watching her in Ibiza—how different she looked, exhausted and carefree at the end of the day. Now, she seems smaller, more fragile. I have the sudden, unexpected urge to reach for her again—but this time to soothe her. To tell her that I didn't mean it.

But you did, didn't you? I push down the thought, reminding myself of her snooping, her stubbornness, the questions that she keeps insisting on asking. All of the ways she's made my life more difficult since I agreed to marry her.

I reach for my phone instead, texting my assistant. I can do something to try to make up for what I said earlier, without letting myself slip too close to the edge of actually caring for her.

Even if my actions last night told me that I've already, perhaps, stepped too close to that edge.

—

In the morning, I wait to get up until Amalie wakes, going over a few things in bed while she sleeps in. She looks surprised when she opens her eyes and sees me there, then guarded, as if she's expecting me to demand something of her.

"Good morning," she says hesitantly, and I smile, trying to put her a little more at ease. I reach down, pushing a bit of hair out of her face as I kiss her lightly, and I feel her go still, as if she's trying not to flinch away.

I start to snap at her, to bite out something like *why do you always have to make this so difficult,* and I stop myself. If she's upset still, I can try to smooth it over. That small step might make things more peaceful for us both—and besides, I've already done something to try to accomplish exactly that.

"I have a surprise for you downstairs," I tell her, pulling back, and she looks startled.

"Oh." She whispers it, sitting up a little, and I can see that guarded expression still on her face. There's that urge to snap at her again, to tell her that it was one comment, that she's overreacting— but I take a breath instead.

"You'll see." I toss the covers back, standing up, and I see her gaze flick towards me almost as if she doesn't mean to. As upset as she might be, she still can't help but want me. I often wish that I didn't feel the same—but seeing her half-sitting up in bed, the sheet clutched to her bare breasts and her thick auburn hair tumbling over her shoulders, I feel my cock twitch with interest, my body instantly reacting to the sight of my wife. I'm as susceptible to her as she is to me, and it's a never-ending cycle that's determined to drive us both mad.

I stride away from the bed instead, going to shower. When I emerge, Amalie is dressed, wearing the leggings and loose t-shirt that seems to have become her uniform around the house. It looks sloppy, in my opinion, but I remind myself that no one is here besides my security. If she wants to be comfortable, what does it matter?

And, as she turns away to walk towards the door, I can't deny that the view of her ass in the tight fabric is an argument for letting it go.

"It's in the dining room," I tell her as I follow her downstairs, and she glances at me over her shoulder, her expression half-curious, half-suspicious. I'd expected her to ask what it is, to try to wheedle it out of me at least a little, but she says nothing as we walk through the main floor of the house, and she stops in the doorway of the dining room.

"Oh," she says softly, again, her voice a higher pitch now than it was before. I can't see her face as she looks at what's on the dining room table in front of her—a vase full of red roses and a white box— and I step up next to her, reaching for her so I can turn her to face me.

To my surprise, there's still confusion on her face, and her eyes are glimmering with tears.

"This was supposed to make you happy." I reach down, thumbing one of the tears away from where it's hovering on her lashes. "I thought you might like a surprise."

"I do," she whispers, but she licks her lips nervously, pressing them together as she looks at the table. "I just—I never know when you're going to be upset or not." Amalie tilts her head up, the words coming out in a rush, as if she's almost afraid to say them. "Last night was one thing, and now this—it's back and forth, all of the time—and I almost wish you would just..."

She breaks off, biting her lip, and I let out a sigh. My first instinct is to be impatient, to tell her she's being ungrateful, but I rein it in. *Try to be patient,* I tell myself, pulling her closer as I brush my thumb over her jawline. "Look at what's in the box. I know you've been frustrated with not having things that are already cooked for you." I lean down, brushing my lips lightly over hers. "Let's try to make today better."

Amalie lets out a slow breath, nodding. She disentangles herself from my arms, walking over to the table. I feel a strange sense of warmth when she bends down to sniff the roses in the vase, a tiny smile playing at the edge of her mouth. I've told myself again and again that I don't *care* if she's happy here, that she should be happy and grateful simply that I married her and saved her family from ruin —but I can feel something in me soften at the sight of a flicker of happiness from her.

She flips open the box, and the smile widens. There's an assort-
ment of pastries in the box, all of them from a nearby bakery that I
know is quite good, and I walk up behind her, gently resting a hand
on her lower back.

"I thought this might be something you could eat. I even had my
assistant deliver some decaf coffee. I'll go make some for us." I lean
down, kissing her lightly on the cheek, and to my surprise, she turns
into the kiss. Her hand touches my chest, almost as if she wants to
pull me in, and for a brief moment, I consider the idea of having *her*
for breakfast instead. All I would need to do is set her on the edge of
the table, and I could devour *her* instead of the pastries, hear her
moan my name over and over as I remind her that she's mine. That I
can command her pleasure whenever I wish.

Romance has never come easily to me, and it's more difficult than
ever now. But I step away from her, letting the kiss remain brief as I go
to brew each of us a cup of coffee.

There's a domesticity to it that I find oddly pleasurable. I've kept
the house mostly bare of staff for my own peace and privacy, but in
the warm light of the morning, as I fix coffee for us both, I find myself
wishing that I could talk Amalie out of her request to hire them. I
could almost enjoy this, if I let myself—if things were different
between us.

If the baby is mine, maybe they could be. I'm not sure where the
thought comes from as I carry the cups back to the dining room, as I
see her sitting there with a lemon-filled Danish in front of her,
picking at it as she waits on me. She's turned away from me, her
profile lit up by the sun coming in through the window and turning
her hair a brighter red, and she looks every bit as lovely as she did
that first night that I saw her in Ibiza. More so, even, because now she
is mine. Because seeing her sitting there peacefully in the morning
light, I see a glimpse of what I might be able to have, if it's not too late.

"I don't want you going out to look for a dress for the gala this
weekend," I tell her as I set the cups down, choosing to sit next to her
instead of across from her today. I shake my head as she opens her
mouth to argue, reaching for a pastry from the box. "You'd have to go

into Providence to have a chance of finding something decent, and I don't like the idea of that, not when I can't go with you. Here at home, I can be sure you and the baby are safe."

"David." Amalie looks at me, a thin line forming between her brows as she frowns. "You can't keep me locked up in this house forever. It's not—"

"Just humor me." I take a breath, trying to keep my patience with her. "I've asked my assistant to have a selection of dresses and jewelry delivered to the house today. You can try them all on and pick whichever you like. More than one, even, if you want—I'm sure there will be plenty more events that you'll need something for." I reach out, turning her face towards mine, brushing a finger over her lower lip. "I'll be home today, so you can even show them off for me."

I let a little of the desire that she always rouses in me slip into my voice, a promise for later, and I see Amalie's eyes widen, her breath catch. "Alright," she says softly, her lips closing lightly around the tip of my finger. "That could be fun."

"Good." I tap her lip teasingly, removing my hand. "Now eat. I've asked my assistant for a referral to a good doctor as well—we can't have anything going wrong now, can we?" I reach out, touching her thigh as I say it, and Amalie gives me a startled look. It's the first time that I've hinted that I might believe her that the baby is mine—the first time, truly, that I've let myself really hope that she is telling the truth. Everything in me rebels against that hope, against the possibility that things could be changing for me—for *us*—but I fight back the urge to lash out at her for it.

If she's telling the truth, then Amalie and I are bound together—for better or worse, 'til death do us part. If one or both of us doesn't find a way to live with the other—

The last thing I want is for those words to feel like a blessing, instead of a curse.

24

AMALIE

I don't have the slightest idea how to feel about David's change in mood. I certainly don't think I can trust it—but I can't help wanting to lean into it a little, to accept the respite that it offers me from how angry he was yesterday. So I sit there with him, eating the delicate pastry—which *is* delicious, almost as good as some of what we had together in Ibiza—and try not to think too hard about the fact that all of this is almost certainly temporary. That I'll say something wrong, *do* something wrong, and he'll be back to anger and sarcasm.

I meant what I said, when I saw the surprise. I would almost rather have him treat me as if he hates me all of the time than be so hot and cold. I could brace myself against anger and cruelty—so many mafia wives have to endure that. What I can't withstand is never knowing which husband I'm going to wake up to in the morning—never knowing if he's going to be cruel or charming, sweet or sarcastic.

The dresses are delivered in the afternoon, just as he said they would be—a rack of garment bags, boxes of shoes, a carefully packaged tiered tray of jewelry. It's all set in the informal living room downstairs—incidentally just across the hall from David's office—

and he smiles at me indulgently as the staff who delivered it arrange everything and then quickly disappear.

"I want to see them all," he tells me, dropping another light kiss on my lips. "Come show me—it'll be a nice distraction from my work."

I almost lean in for another kiss, but stop myself. He's touched me like that since this morning—carefully and with reservation, as if he's trying to keep himself from doing more than that. Ironically, it's done the opposite for me—that feeling of having some power over him and his desires has made me want him more.

"Alright." I give him a small smile, hoping that my acquiescence will encourage his good mood, and turn to the rack of dresses as David leaves the room.

They're all gorgeous. I pull a deep blue gown off first, one with a slim silhouette and chiffon draped over the silk skirt, fancier than some of the other gowns I've worn. The neckline is lower than usual, dipping in a deep v, and I think it might be *too* sexy for the sort of gala we're attending. But David said he wanted to see them all, and I slip the dress on, picking out a pair of matching silk heels with gems on the pointed toes, and a pair of champagne diamond earrings.

He smiles at me when I slip into his office, watching as I turn around slowly. "Not that one, I think," he says, frowning a little. "You wore blue to the last event. If there's a green one, don't bother with that, it won't suit your hair."

I realize as he says it that there's a certain controlling pleasure in this for him, having the power of vetoing my choice for the night. I want to argue with him purely on account of that, to fight for the dress I have on—but I don't *really* like it that much. *I can give a little on this,* I tell myself, taking a breath, and retreat back to the other room.

"Look at you," David says teasingly by the time I'm on the fourth dress—the blue and green options having been already set aside— his gaze roving over me as I spin for him in the flame-red silk dress that I chose. "All of these dresses and jewels." He reaches for me, his arm going around my waist as he tugs me into his lap, the skirt spilling over his knees. "Such a spoiled wife."

It's nothing he hasn't said before, but there's no bite to it this time. It's faintly teasing, almost sweet in the way he says it, and he taps my nose lightly, leaning in to kiss me. "You do look beautiful like this," he says softly. "Maybe being spoiled suits you."

I start to argue, to tell him that I'm *not* spoiled, but he deepens the kiss, and I find that I can't breathe enough to say anything at all. When he pulls me up to straddle him, his hands lifting the silk skirt, I don't want him to stop.

"I think we have to keep this one if you fuck me in it," I whisper, daring to tease him just a little, and David laughs, threading his hand through my hair.

"I'll keep as many of them as you like, *cara mia*," he murmurs, his lips on mine again as his hand slips between us to free his straining cock from his trousers. As he slips inside of me with a groan, I find myself wishing it could stay like this.

This man, I could be happy with. This man, I could even love, in time.

But not if I can never trust that it's really him.

———

The evening of the gala, I haven't seen David all day. It's not unusual—he's often gone dealing with various parts of his business that he doesn't tell me about—but I can feel the restlessness returning. I've stayed away from the attic and avoided snooping any further into the rooms of the house that I haven't visited yet, but the cabin fever is beginning to get to me. The only thing that's kept me from it is that David's good mood has persisted for days, and I haven't wanted to break the spell.

Since that afternoon in his office, we haven't fought. It's only been three days—but that's a record for our marriage so far. He hasn't been sarcastic or biting, and if he's often been quiet, I've preferred that to the near-constant arguing. The lack of stress has helped me, too—I haven't been sick from the pregnancy since the morning we left Boston. As I sit at my vanity getting ready for the gala, I can almost see a hint of that glow that pregnant women always talk about. My skin looks clearer, a bit brighter, and I use a light hand with my makeup. I want David to see me like this, happy, flushed with the glow of carrying his child, and hope that he's beginning to believe me when I say that it *is* his.

The dress that David liked me best in is a deep metallic grey, the fabric woven with threads that glitter in the light. It has a high waist, giving it a retro sort of nineteen-twenties style. Although I still don't have any outward signs of being pregnant, the loose waist makes me feel a little better. I don't want any sign of it showing up yet, any chance of someone commenting on how quickly David must have gotten to work—or anyone counting back and realizing that it definitely couldn't have been *after* the wedding that he got me pregnant. Tonight is another chance to show him that I flourish when I'm around other people, not sequestered away like this. I don't want anything to ruin it.

There's a knock at the door, and David steps in. He whistles low under his breath as I stand up, and crosses the room quickly to me, his hand on my waist as he leans in for a kiss. "Anything I can help with?" he asks, and I nod, handing him the strand of pearls I planned on wearing.

"Help me with this?" I sweep my hand under my hair, lifting it away from my neck, and I can't help but shiver at the brush of his fingers against the nape as he clasps the necklace. They linger for a moment, brushing against the soft hair there, and when he turns me to face him, he tips my chin up, kissing me more deeply.

"We'll be late for the gala if you keep that up," I whisper, a little shakily. He's been remarkably constrained in his desires for the last few days, wanting me only at night before we go to sleep, and never in any of the rough or demanding ways that I've come to expect. I almost miss him ordering me to my knees or insisting that I do things that embarrass and turn me on all at once. I try not to think too hard about what that says about me—that I miss his roughness, when he's making an attempt at being gentle.

"I'm the head of their board," David murmurs, kissing me again. "If I want to be late, I can be late."

"We also sent all of the other dresses back. If you ruin this one like you did the red dress, what will I wear?" The question is light, teasing, but even I can hear the thread of desire in my voice, remembering what he did in his office. The skirt of the red dress ended up torn, when he'd lifted me off of his lap and bent me over his desk, ripped in his hurry to move it out of his way so he could be inside of me again.

I liked the dress, but I didn't care. I'd liked the way he felt more, the urgency in his hands, the way he'd wanted me so badly.

"Maybe I should parade you naked in front of all of them." His hand slides down my hip, gathering the fabric lightly in his fingers. "Show them all how powerful I can be. There'd be no question then, when all those old men start looking at you, that you're mine."

"All those old women would faint." I giggle, kissing him lightly. "Or die of heart attacks. You'd have no one left to run things."

"Might be for the best." David kisses me again, his hand hard on my hip as he pulls me against him, and I bite back a moan as I feel his cock pressing against me. For the first time, I feel like a real married couple—*better* than most mafia couples, even. It's the sort of domestic banter that makes me feel as if things might be alright, at last, between us—or that they at least might be headed in that direction. "That's why I want you to volunteer with them, *cara mia*. They'll be more inclined to follow my wishes, if my wife sits on the board."

The statement is enough to distract me from the desire that he'd started to rouse in me. It's not the first time David has mentioned me volunteering on one of the various committees or for any of the charitable organizations that he has a hand in. Still, it *is* the first time he's said it in a way that hints at the idea that it might be because he values my opinion in some way—or at least finds me useful. He's always phrased it as if it's something to occupy my time, some way to distract me from whatever other girlish foolishness I might get up to, to keep me from being bored and causing trouble. But the way he's looking at me now, with a keen eye and calculating expression, suggests that he's thinking of me the way a mafia heir thinks of a wife who can help him.

Who might, in time, have influence in other ways beyond just sitting on a committee and reporting home to her husband what they discuss in his absence.

That is, after all, part of the province of a mafia wife. Beyond providing heirs and planning parties, the wives make friends with each other. They hear the gossip, hear snippets of conversations in passing, and learn how to read the men in the room even when those men ignore them. My father didn't put much stock in what my mother gleaned from the other wives, nor did he particularly respect her opinion—but there are husbands who do. The thought of David seeing me that way, of us being the sort of couple who share power instead of me always living in his shadow, sends a thrill through me that I can't entirely ignore.

But I can't let it take root. *A few days isn't enough to rely on.* I'll be happier if I manage my expectations, if I don't let myself hope that he might trust and respect me that much eventually—when right now, he doesn't even believe that I'm telling him the truth about my pregnancy.

"You want me to go sit on charity board meetings and then report back to you at dinner?" I press my hand against his chest, giving him a teasing kiss. "I'll have to think about that. It could be fun." I lean my head back as I say it, smiling at him, but I want to see his face—to see which version of David I get. If I see the man who would tell me that I'll do as he says, whether I want to or not—or the one who will play along.

"Don't think too hard." David taps me on the nose, releasing me. "It doesn't suit you."

Somewhere in the middle, then, I think as he turns away, biting my tongue against the retort that I want to make. I remember my mother telling me, long ago, that being a mafia wife is playing a role. I hated the idea of it then—and I hate it even more now, when the man for whom I have to play that role is someone who makes me desire him instead of despising him.

"Wear this tonight." David sweeps the fur stole off of the wing chair that I draped it over, holding it out. "It can get chilly down by the water, even in summer. And it looked lovely on you at the party in Boston. It matches your dress perfectly."

Somehow, I manage not to flinch, to keep the smile on my face. I *had* thought that it matched the dress—had even thought of wearing it tonight—but I hadn't wanted to risk David's good mood if he somehow were to find out where I got it. I don't want to be rebellious tonight. I just want to get through the party, to be the picture-perfect version of the wife he needs, and show him that he *can* trust me. That I haven't lied to him about any of the things that he suspects me of.

But I also can't tell him why I don't want to wear it without admitting where I got it in the first place.

I nod, keeping the smile on my face as I take it out of his hand, wrapping it around my shoulders. "There," David says, leaning in to kiss me lightly once more. "You look exactly the way the wife of a powerful man should." His hands rest on my shoulders, turning me to face the full-length mirror, his fingers skimming down my bare arms as his lips ghost over my ear. "As beautiful as a piece of art."

The flattery warms me more than it should. I *want* to please him, to make him happy, and I know how dangerous that can be. How easily I could fall into the trap of always trying to meet his every want and need, and losing myself in the bargain. It's what I've always been afraid of, why I bucked against the future that was planned for me for so long.

In this world, it's far too easy for a woman to be entirely consumed by a man.

I follow David downstairs, out to the waiting car. He sits across from me, pouring himself two fingers of cognac as he leans back in the leather seat, watching the scenery go by as the car pulls away from the house and out onto the street. I watch him, my pulse beating a quick rhythm in my throat, wondering how tonight will go. If the night will end the way our last night in Boston did, or if something will go wrong.

For all the grandeur of it, this party feels more intimate. It's held at one of the other mansions, a gorgeous estate owned by a couple who has a great deal of public-facing influence for this particular organization—a Mr. and Mrs. DeRosa. "They're the public face of it," David tells me as our car pulls into the long, winding driveway, following the line of other cars headed for the valet. "They answer to me, of course, and the DeRosa family has had ties to the mafia for generations. We keep those ties quiet, and they give us the means to funnel our money into something legitimate and respectable." David shrugs, sitting up and setting his glass aside as the car slows to a stop. "All a part of the game. So tonight, we pretend to be a part of the elite *without* the criminal connections. Although—" he smirks, his eyes glittering with dark humor as he looks at me. "There is no such thing as elite and wealthy without being some sort of criminal. It's just whether you can admit it to yourself or not."

The door opens, and David steps out, reaching to take my hand and help me out after him. The mansion in front of us is huge, lit up from within, with the landscaped trees out front strung with hundreds of fairy lights that make it look as if everything around the house is sparkling. The mansion is entirely cream-colored stone, with huge, wide stone steps leading up to the ebony double doors. I see valets posted at the edge of the steps as we get out of the car and make our way there with the rest of the guests. David has already slipped my arm through his, his posture straight and expression carefully blank, the very picture of a powerful man who wants to be certain no one else can read what he's thinking.

Once upon a time, in Ibiza, I thought that I understood him a bit —or at least his desires. Now I know better than to imagine I could ever have the upper hand with him—even though I've come to understand that David's family has skeletons in their closet, just as mine does, and that their hold on power isn't as strong as they would like others to think.

I also know that David would be furious if that were to ever slip.

Is that what happened to her? The woman in the photos? Did she discover that, and pay the price for not keeping quiet about it? Did she challenge them—or him? I feel a chill at the thought, and I tug the fur stole a little closer around me, trying not to think of it—not the woman who supposedly was David's late brother's wife, not the bloodstained blouse or the attic in the ominous mansion I now live in. I force myself to focus on the moment, on the floral-scented warmth of the house as we step inside, the sound of music, the chatter of guests in the next room.

"David Carravella." A tall man who looks to be in his late forties intercepts us, smiling and holding out his hand for David to shake. "A pleasure to see you here. My wife will be delighted to meet your new bride. I heard you'd gotten married and hid her away from all of us."

"You can't blame me for wanting to keep her to myself for a little while." David's smile is joking, but I can hear the edge in his voice, just as I can hear the same in the other man's. *Does no one in these circles ever truly like each other?* I used to wonder the same thing, at these sorts of parties with my parents and brother. They all feel like vultures, constantly circling each other, waiting for someone to fall so they can all flock together to pick the bones clean.

"Of course not." The man's gaze sweeps over me, just enough for me to see the appraising way he takes me in before he looks back at David. Someone smart enough, then, not to let David see if he finds me attractive. "Most of the guests are outside—Mrs. DeRosa thought it was a pleasant enough night for a garden party."

"We should join them, then." David keeps my arm tucked in his, his hand covering mine as he leads me through the next room and out to the French doors that are flung wide, revealing exactly that. A garden party full of guests already drinking and eating and mingling, caterers with trays of appetizers and drinks moving seamlessly through the crowd, music floating through the air. There are more of those tiny, delicate fairy lights strung through the trees and shrubbery, turning it all into something airy and beautiful, a gorgeous facade for the gossip and machinations happening behind the scenes. I can see heads turning as we walk outside to join the others, curious to see who David married. I imagine there will be gossip about it tomorrow—chatter that I won't be a part of, since I don't know any of these women. If I do as David has asked, and join these committees and organizations he has a hand in, I'll already be a step behind. They'll all have formed an opinion of me, talked about me, and whether those opinions are good or bad entirely hinges on how tonight goes.

I tuck the stole a little closer around me, and as David releases me to go and talk to a small group of men standing near the bar, I take a deep breath.

I can do this.

It's not as unpleasant as I thought it might be. The conversation is mostly banal and largely centered around their husbands and children, but it's a conversation I'm accustomed to making, at least. I stand there with a glass of champagne that I took from a passing tray, taking the occasional small sip to ward off any questions, and act as if I'm fascinated by their lives. As if I can't wait to be *one* of them, to be brought into their circle. And all the while, I listen almost without meaning to for anything that might be of interest to David. Any mention of their husbands' business, of their opinions about the organization, the charity they're involved in. And from time to time, as I glance over to see where David is, I see him watching me. Not in a way that looks calculating or irritated, but almost as if he's *pleased* with me. He looks at me in a way that could almost make me think he's wishing he were spending the evening at my side, instead of whatever conversations he's having.

It's not just that, either. It's the way he touches my hand when he comes to collect me for dinner, his thumb brushing over the back of my knuckles as he tucks it into the crook of his arm as if he *wants* to touch me. The way he looks at me throughout dinner in between the small talk and polite conversation, an almost knowing look in his eyes, one that says *this is boring us both, isn't it?*

It almost feels like a romantic night between husband and wife. I can almost picture a night like this in the future, the two of us going home together afterward—not to the crumbling old mansion we're in now, but something more like this estate—and looking in on our children to make sure they're sleeping before slipping back to our room, David's fingers sliding down my spine as he unzips my dress—

I breathe in softly at the thought, a flush creeping into my cheeks, and when he glances over at me again, I know he sees it. There's a glint in his eye that tells me he's picked up on the flutter of desire, that he feels it, too, and it only makes my cheeks pinken even more.

That happiness is the most dangerous of fantasies. The idea that David and I could have that kind of companionship, that kind of domesticity, is the most dangerous hope I could have. It's not a common thing in our world. It's not the kind of marriage I was raised to aspire to, even if it's what I would have wanted. And with a man as seemingly capricious as David—

Believing in that could make me complacent. It could make me *his*, in the ways that I'm not yet, not completely. It would make it all the more painful if, one day, he decided he no longer wanted me. If he went cold again.

And yet, when his hand brushes along my thigh under the table, when he takes me out to the dance floor after dinner, and we start to sway to the music, his gaze meets mine with a softness that I haven't seen in his face since a few rare moments in Ibiza, I could almost believe that it's possible.

"You're perfection tonight," he murmurs as he pulls me close, the sound of the string instruments and the warbling flute wrapping around us. There are other couples doing the same, dancing nearby, but it feels almost as if the room narrows down to us—as if it's only he and I, there beneath the brightly lit chandeliers. I can smell his spicy cologne and feel the pressure of his hand on my back, his fingers laced through mine as he spins me away and pulls me back in, and I want so *badly* for it to stay like this. For us to have another night like we did in Boston. For *this* David to be my husband, 'til death do us part.

"I hoped you would think so," I say softly, my free hand pressed against his chest as we move. "I wanted to make a good impression for you."

"You certainly did. Mrs. DeRosa stopped me on the way to the bar and said she *insisted* that you come to the next board meeting. That she couldn't wait to get to know you better." A small smirk curls the corner of his mouth, as if he knows exactly how unappealing that idea is to me. "She also mentioned having you over for coffee. Everyone is intrigued with my new bride. A bit of gossip to liven up their days."

"I tried to make sure it would be *good* gossip." There's an uneasiness in my stomach at that, but I ignore it. There's always talk, always gossip, always conversations about other wives behind their backs in the small clutches of friends that women make with each other. My job is to make certain that I do nothing that could reflect poorly on David.

"You've done quite the job." He spins me again, and this time when he pulls me in, I feel his hand slide low on my back, nearly to the curve of my ass, pressing me against him possessively. He leans in, cheek to cheek, his breath warm against my ear. "Maybe I was hasty in regretting my choice."

Unexpectedly, tears prick at the corner of my eyes. I blink them back quickly, not wanting to let him see me cry—not right now, not when things are going so well. I hadn't expected to hear him say *that*, and as afraid as I am to trust in this, I want to lean in to the sudden kindness that he's showing me. To believe that maybe he *has* realized that this marriage isn't as much of a mistake as he believed.

"We shouldn't stay too late," he murmurs, as the song slows, and we start to go back to our table. "I'm going to keep you up for a while tonight, *cara mia*. And you need your rest." His hand splays on my waist as he says it, fingers brushing the edge of my stomach, and I know what he means. It's the first time he's come close to suggesting that perhaps he believes me, that perhaps the baby *is* his—that he sees me as the woman carrying his heir. That small spark of hope that he set alight flares, and I bite my lip as we sit back down at our table, my pulse fluttering in my throat for reasons that have nothing to do with his promise of taking me to bed later.

"*David!*" A woman sits down suddenly next to him in a chair left empty, her wrinkled face wreathed in a smile. She's old enough to be his grandmother, with short white hair carefully styled and wearing a matronly deep blue dress. "I heard all the chatter earlier about your wife. This is your bride?"

"Amalie Carravella." He smiles, leaning back a little so that I can say hello to the newest guest to exclaim over David's marriage. "Amalie, this is Marie Montrose. She's an old friend of the family."

There's a slight emphasis on the word *friend*, which tells me that the Montrose family must do some sort of business with David's. I lean forward a little, smiling. "It's lovely to meet you, Mrs. Montrose."

"Oh, it's just Marie." She waves a hand. "My husband died years ago, so none of this *Mrs.* nonsense. My sons run everything now. They'll be along to see *you*, before too long, David, now that you're back in town. I do hope you plan to stay for a while, rather than spending so much time in Boston."

"I'm very focused on renovating the mansion now, so I plan to be around more often than not." David has that blank, pleasant smile on his face that I've grown accustomed to seeing, the one he wears when he's being careful not to show his real emotions. "Tell them to call, and my assistant will set up an appointment. I have a home office now."

"Perhaps I'll come by one of these days, too. It would be lovely to see the house being put back together. Your family did love it so, once. You're a good boy, making sure it's restored, and not letting it crumble into dust."

"The least I can do." There's a sudden tightness to David's smile, and I see an opportunity. It's very clear the conversation is beginning to make him uncomfortable, and I smile at Marie, reaching for her hand.

"You should absolutely stop by. We can have coffee, or tea—oh, and David introduced me to this wonderful pastry shop in town. I can have some delivered. You can tell me all about the Carravella family." I let my smile widen, just a little, as if there's nothing that I would like more. "But—" I turn towards David. "I'm getting a bit tired. Maybe we should head home? I don't want to be rude, but it's getting late—"

I give him a slightly wide-eyed look, just enough to imply that I'm a newlywed wife who can't wait to get her husband home. It works, because Marie lets out a knowing laugh, sitting back in her chair.

"Ah, I remember those days. I did like my husband too, once upon a time when we were first married." She winks at me. "Well, I'll let you two lovebirds get on with it. I can't be offended that you prefer each other's company, and god knows you deserve it, David." She reaches down, squeezing his hand. "It's so nice to see you happy again. We thought you might never be, after the first Mrs. Carravella passed away."

The room goes very still. I stare at her, my pulse suddenly thundering in my ears. I can't look at David, only at the sweet old woman standing there, a smile on her face as if she hasn't said anything unusual.

"What?" The word comes out almost strangled, and she looks at me quizzically, as if I should know what she's talking about. David stands up abruptly, walking away from the table with a quick, short stride, and I look from his receding figure back to Marie with confusion. "What do you mean?" I blink, wondering if I've heard her wrong.

Marie frowns at me. "He must have told you. It wasn't all that long ago—two years, but I know that can be a long time for a man of his age. It was terribly sad. He was devastated—that's why we're all so happy to see that he's found someone. None of us ever expected he would."

I can hear a strange ringing in my ears. I turn slowly, staring at David. His face has gone utterly still from where I see him standing at the bar, and I know at that moment that my suspicions aren't unfounded. He's been lying to me about more than I imagined.

"Please excuse me." I get up, feeling my hands trembling as I walk numbly towards where David is standing. I can barely speak past the lump in his throat, but I hiss the words under my breath, staring up at him as I stand close enough that no one else can hear.

"David." I can feel my voice shaking, but I can barely hear myself speak over the thundering of my own heartbeat. "What the hell is she talking about?"

25

AMALIE

Before I can say another word, David's hand is on my elbow, pulling me away from the bar. His fingers dig roughly into my skin, and I gasp as I dimly hear him apologize to Marie, turning me away from the table as he marches me towards the mansion's entrance. I try to wrench out of his grasp, but his hand tightens even more, and I bite my lip to keep from making a sound.

"David—"

"If you make a scene, Amalie, I swear to god I'll make you regret it."

My blood runs cold. I remember the bloodstained blouse all over again, his refusal to talk about what I found in the attic, and all my suspicions and fears come rushing back. My heart is pounding so hard that it hurts. I'm terrified of going back to the mansion, of being alone with this man who, only minutes ago, I thought might finally have come to truly start to care for me.

I've been so stupid. I know the kind of man David is—the kind that almost all mafia men are. I should never have let my guard down, even for a moment. I never *can*. And now I'm afraid that it all might be about to get so much worse.

"What was she talking about?" I try to jerk my arm away from

David's again as we get to the car, the urge to dig my heels in and refuse to get inside washing over me. "No one said anything to me about you being married before! You need to explain—"

"No, I don't." His voice is flat and terrifyingly cold, and he urges me forward into the car, blocking me so that I have no choice but to get in. He follows me, and for a moment, I think he's going to tell the driver to take us home, but the car remains still. "It's none of your business, Amalie."

Something inside of me snaps. It takes everything in me to stay where I'm sitting, my hands clutching the edge of the leather seat, instead of flinging myself at him in absolute fury. "What do you *mean* it's not my business! I'm your *wife*, David! Your second wife, apparently, which no one bothered to tell me about! Don't you think I should know that? Wouldn't you want to know if you were my *second fucking husband*? If the first one *died*?"

I'm nearly screaming now, but I can't stop. The windows on the car are heavily tinted enough that I know no one can see in, but that doesn't make me feel better. All that means is that no one will be able to see if David does anything to me.

Every muscle in his body is tense, his voice as cold as his expression as he speaks. "I'm not entirely convinced that there wasn't a man before me, Amalie. Who knows how many men? I did meet you in *Ibiza*, after all. You weren't married before, of course, but isn't that worse?" There's a raw contempt in his voice that infuriates me even more, and I feel my nails digging into the seat. I want to tear at the leather in lieu of him, to scream until my throat is raw. I feel as if I'm trapped in a nightmare, as if I'm going crazy.

"You were my first," I whisper, my voice hoarse. "You *were*. And the baby is yours; it would be impossible for it to be anyone else's, because there hasn't *been* anyone else. I'm not *jealous*, David—but you can't lie to me like this! I'm your wife! I have a right to know. As your wife, it's my right—"

"You're wrong." The coldness in his voice seems to burrow down into my bones—I've never heard anyone speak like this, not even my father. There's no emotion in it at all, not even anger or hate. He sounds as if he's speaking from far away, as if he's already detached himself from all of it. "I was forced into marrying you, Amalie. Your mother managed to wheedle my father into making a deal that I wasn't a part of, and I was foolish enough not to put my foot down and refuse to marry a woman that I had already fucked. No self-respecting future don would marry a woman he met in goddamn *Ibiza*, but I did, because I was convinced it was best for our family. It can continue to be good for our families, if you will learn to—"

"To *what*?" I can feel my lips trembling, the tremor making its way through my body as I look at the man I've married, a man I'm tied to for the rest of my life, who, at this moment, is scaring me more than he ever has before. "Learn to be quiet? To never ask you questions? To be—"

"To be a good wife." His jaw clenches. "Your mother convinced my family that she taught you how to do that. If I'd known she'd done such a poor fucking job—"

"Is that what happened to your first wife? Was she not *good* enough?" I'm on the verge of tears again, sinking my teeth into my lower lip to try to stop the flood that I know will break free if I let myself cry even a little. "David—"

"I don't have to talk about anything with you that I don't want to." There's a ring of finality to his tone that feels like a blow, and when he opens the car door, I have the urge to push past him, to run back into the mansion and beg for help, for anyone to listen to me. To beg for the truth about what happened, since my own husband won't tell me. Since he seems intent on tormenting me with it instead.

Or he just doesn't care enough to tell me. Deep down, I know that's the truth. He simply doesn't want to tell me. He's not torturing me intentionally—it's just that I'm nothing to him, not really, except for what I can provide. And right now, I'm providing nothing.

Just as I know that if I did run into the mansion, no one would help me. No one would tell me. They would hand me back to David and turn away.

I have no one who will help me.

David taps the divider between the seats and the driver. "Take her home," he says gruffly, and then he steps out of the car without another word, shutting the door hard. I'm left in the dim interior, shaking, still clutching the edge of the seat as the car starts to pull away.

I'm being sent home alone, and I don't know if that's better or worse than going home with David. I'm glad that I don't have to spend another minute with him, that I can sit here and grapple with the fact that it feels as if my heart is cracking apart alone, because I don't know if I could have stood it with him here.

I don't know how this man, who has so often treated me with dismissal and occasionally cruelty, can break my heart over and over. I don't know how I can keep falling for the moments when he's kind, when he makes me think that there could be some other side to him. And I don't know how I'm going to bear to keep doing this, over and over again.

The tears start to fall on the drive home, sliding down my face as I sit there trembling, with no reason to hold them back any longer. I don't care what the driver thinks of me, or David's security, if I even see them when I get home. There's no staff to hide my emotions from, nothing but that empty old house, even more full of secrets than I first realized.

I barely look at the driver when he opens the car door for me, pushing my way past him with my skirt gathered up in my hand, stumbling tearfully up the stairs to our bedroom. Every breath ends on a gasping sob, and I toss the fur stole over a chair, yanking at the zipper of my dress, desperate to be out of it. To be rid of *all* of this, every bit of this awful night. I snatch the pins out of my hair, scattering them across the top of my vanity. I feel all the anger and fear well up inside of me, exploding as I grab my jewelry box and fling it at the full-length mirror next to the bed. It shatters, spilling shards of glass over the wooden floor, and I stare down at them with my chest heaving as I stand in the pool of fabric that was my dress.

I hope David cuts himself on them when he comes home, I think darkly, tears still streaking down my face. I catch a glimpse of myself in the vanity mirror, mascara and eyeliner trailing down my cheeks, and I know David will be upset if he comes home and sees me like this.

I can't bring myself to care.

I grab the dress off of the floor, stalking to the closet and throwing the doors open, and I see all my things hanging there, all the clothing my mother insisted I buy for my new life, all the trappings of a marriage I don't even want. I grab at them, at the boxes and bags, flinging them across the floor in another swell of anger as I scream over and over, knowing no one will hear me. No one will care.

And I can't help but wonder, as I stand there crying, if David's first wife stood here and thought the same thing. If she wanted to beg for help and couldn't.

Numbly, I walk to the bed naked, crawling under the covers. I curl up into a ball as I turn off the light, seeing the moonlight glitter over the shards of glass on the floor, and I close my eyes.

When David comes home, I want to be asleep.

—

Unfortunately, I sleep too lightly to not wake up when I hear his footsteps. I drifted off, dozing through dream after dream of what I found in the attic, of David chasing me through the house, of having our baby only for him to refuse to believe that it's his, only to be jolted awake by the sound of his shoes on the wooden floor.

I keep my eyes closed, my breathing as even as I can. He doesn't flip on a light, and I can hear from the unsteady cadence of his walk that he must be at least a little drunk. My chest tightens, and I hear him curse under his breath as he stops at the edge of where the broken glass is. I can feel him standing there, looking at me.

And then I hear the sounds of him walking to the other side of the bed, getting undressed. The slither of his clothes to the floor, the thump of his shoes and belt hitting the wood, and fear and anticipation knot themselves together in my belly, wondering what comes next.

I don't move, don't give him any inclination that I might be awake.

I lie there, still breathing carefully, as I feel the weight of his body in the bed next to mine, the warmth of his bare skin. I catch a whiff of alcohol from his breath, and I know then that he *has* been drinking—and likely a lot.

His hand touches my hip. Not roughly, the way I was expecting, but almost gingerly, as if he's trying not to wake me. It occurs to me to wonder *why* he's drunk—I've never seen him drink past the point of a light buzz, not even in Ibiza. He'd been so cold back at the mansion during our argument, as if it hadn't affected him at all. It's hard for me to believe that he was so upset about it that he would get drunk at an important event, one where the perception of others matters so much.

His hand slides up to my waist, and it takes everything in me to keep my breath from catching at his touch. Even now, the feeling of his hand gliding over my skin sends a flush of warmth through me, the beginning of a pleasurable ache building between my legs. I hear him groan low in his throat behind me, moving closer as his hand slides up to cup my breast, and my pulse speeds up. I hope he can't feel it, that he thinks I'm still sleeping. I wonder if he'll care if I am or not.

His thumb flicks over my nipple, and I nearly gasp. Something about the effort of trying to remain quiet and not react, trying to pretend that I'm asleep, makes this even more arousing. I feel him brush against the small of my back as his fingers roll over my nipple once more, and I realize that he's hard. It doesn't surprise me, but what does is the flush of arousal that washes through me, my body tightening, wet with need, as his hand slides down to rest over the flat of my stomach.

It's a reminder of Ibiza—not David touching me in my sleep, but all those days and nights when I learned things about myself that I never would have imagined or dared to fantasize about. When I discovered that, it turned me on to be ordered down to my knees, for him to ignore me while I sucked his cock, to be humiliated by how much I wanted him in spite of his arrogance and his demands.

I expect to feel him nudging between my thighs, for him to slip my panties aside and take what he wants. Instead, I feel him let out a heavy breath behind me, his hand going very still on my breast as he realizes—or thinks, at least—that I'm not going to wake up.

"Fuck," he breathes, and I feel him roll over onto his back, a sudden space between us. There's a moment's silence, and then I feel him shift, and hear the shift of fabric, and his breathing quicken. I don't realize what's happening at first, until he lets out a low, muted groan, and I hear the soft sound of flesh on flesh.

I freeze, wondering if I'm imagining what's happening. I find it hard to believe that David would choose to pleasure himself instead of simply taking what he wants—me, in this case. But he doesn't move to touch me again, or wake me. Instead, I hear the sound of something wet, and then of him quickening his pace, a sound that spurs a sudden ache between my thighs. I almost roll over, wanting to see the image of him half-naked in bed with his hand wrapped around his cock, thrusting into his own fist instead of me to ease his need.

But if I do, he'll fuck me instead. And after what happened tonight, I don't know if I can bear it right now.

It doesn't take long. I don't know if he's simply that aroused or if the idea of pleasuring himself in the bed next to me as I sleep turns him on, but I hear him groan again a moment later, a strangled sound that I recognize. I feel him tense next to me, and I can imagine him spurting over his hand, his thumb rubbing at that spot that I know so well, prolonging his pleasure as he comes all over his fingers instead of inside of me.

If I reached down and touched myself right now, I could do the same. I squeeze my thighs together, knowing that if I do, I'll think of him. I can't bear that, either. Not when he confuses me so much. Not when I found out only a few hours ago for certain that my husband is lying to me.

He gets up from the bed, padding quietly to the bathroom. I lie there with my eyes closed, still feigning sleep, until I feel him lie down again and hear his breathing go soft and even.

Then, and only then, I let the tears gathering in my eyes slip down my cheeks.

I always knew that the life I was destined for would be a difficult one. But I had no idea just how very frightening it could be.

—

I'M WOKEN by a rough hand on my shoulder, shaking me awake. I open my eyes blearily to see David looming over me, fully dressed, his face creased with anger that's startling to see first thing in the morning. "What the *hell* is this?" he snarls, shoving a piece of paper into my face, and I blink, grabbing it reflexively from his fingers as I flinch backward.

"I don't—" I push myself up and away from him, dazed from being jerked so unceremoniously out of sleep. "It's—"

My stomach twists when I realize it's a receipt—and not just any receipt, but the one from the thrift store where I bought the fur stole. In the light of day, I can see the mess that I made of the room last night—the clothes and boxes torn out of the closet and scattered around, the glass still sparkling on the floor in the morning sun, the shattered mirror. "I—"

"Don't bother with excuses." David's face is a study in rage, his anger sharper and hotter than I think I've ever seen it. "I can't believe I told you last night that I might have been wrong to regret marrying you. You wore something from a *thrift store* to a gala with my fucking *parents*? To the party last night? Are you a fucking idiot, Amalie? Do you have any idea how much you would have embarrassed me if anyone had known?" His jaw clenches, the muscle leaping as he stares me down. "I can hear it now, the gossip about how the Carravella heir can't afford to clothe his wife properly, after our misfortune. They all see me renovating this mansion as a noble family gesture, but that tune would change if—"

"How would they know?" I sit up, clutching the sheet to my breasts, my anger suddenly matching his? "They wouldn't, because it was a *good* piece. I know how to choose clothing; after all, it's one of those skills that my mother taught me that are *so* in demand. What does it matter where it came from? It's not as if any of those women stepped foot in that shop—"

"And neither should you!" David bellows the words, making me suddenly grateful that we have no staff to hear it. "You were never supposed to go out in the first place! You have been *nothing* but a problem for me, Amalie, since the moment I stepped into your mother's house—"

"You don't seem to mind being married to me when you're fucking me!"

"Neither do you!" He shouts it, his hands fisting at his sides as if he wants to reach out and grab me, and I shrink back. "You moan and beg for my cock like you can't get enough. So don't pretend—"

"Don't pretend what? I haven't pretended to be *anything* with you!" I can feel hot tears filling my eyes, and I blink them back, refusing to let him see me as anything but angry at this moment. "*Neither* of us said who we were in Ibiza, but neither of us asked! We were never supposed to see each other again! I told you the truth about everything—"

"Not that you were pregnant." David's glare is withering. "You kept *that* a secret until after the wedding. I imagine because you knew I would put it off until there was proof that the baby was mine. And why not wait, if it *is*? The only reason I can think of is because you're passing off some billionaire's son's brat as mine—"

"You were the only one!" I scream it again, my hands fisting in the sheet against my chest. "And I regret that as much as you regret marrying me! My mother *made* me keep it a secret. She was worried you'd find a different bride if you had to wait. I have never had *any* choices about *anything* except the one I made with you, in Ibiza. And I wish to *god* I'd picked someone else!"

"I wish you had, too." David is breathing hard, his jaw clenched, the edges of his nostrils white with tension. "If you'd been honest with me—"

"You weren't honest with me either," I whisper. "You didn't tell me that you were married. You still won't tell me what happened. So we've both kept things from each other. You're no better than I am."

We stare at each other from across the bed, the seconds ticking away. David makes a sound like a growl deep in his throat, turning away at last, the muscles in his shoulders bunched with rage. "Don't ever let me see you wearing that again," he says finally. "And clean up this fucking mess. Even if I had staff, I wouldn't send them up here to help you."

And with that, he stalks away, out of the room.

It takes me a long time to clean up the mess, after I'm sure David is gone, and I've had a chance to get dressed. I have to wander through the lower part of the house, looking for a broom and anything else I might need to use to clean, and I can hear him in his office behind the closed door, his voice low and quiet. The anger from our argument earlier is still simmering, and I bite my lip, forcing myself not to barge into his office and demand answers. I know that won't help me get them, but the urge is still there.

The only way I'm going to get answers is by finding them myself. David's attitude toward me has turned chilly again. I don't feel the slightest bit of guilt the next day when I slip out of the house, intent on visiting the nearby church and graveyard. He's not home today—he left on business before I was even awake, and I don't bother asking any of his security to go with me. I know exactly how he'll feel about that, but I'm too angry, and too desperate for the truth to care. If he won't tell me, I'll figure it out myself.

It's a warm summer day, and the walk makes me feel a little better. I walk down the paths that lead away from the estate to the old church a few miles off, finding that being outside in the fresh air settles my stomach and eases some of the pregnancy symptoms that felt as if they were on the verge of returning. It's become very clear that they're exacerbated by stress, and there's been no shortage of that since the moment I walked into the living room in my old home and saw David standing there.

The graveyard is behind the historic church, filled with moss-covered stones, the age of it reminding me of David's mansion. I walk through the rows, looking for the Carravella plot, which is easy enough to find. There are a handful of graves, all marked with dates, and I look at each one, trying to find the most recent.

There are four, within the past ten years. *Maricia Carravella. Lucio Carravella. Bria Carravella. Marcus Carravella.*

The last one startles me more than the rest, when I look at the dates. Marcus was a child when he died—not quite four. I remember the thought I had when David told me that his brother had been married—that the family would never have sent his widow away if she'd had a child—and I wonder if that's why. But when I look at the dates again, I realize that Marcus died a little over two years ago. Lucio Carravella—whose death date matches up with what David hinted at—died two years before that.

Bria's death date is only slightly after her son's.

I sit back on my heels in the grass at the edge of the graves, my heart racing. I feel a chill despite the heat, trying to piece it all together. David's refusal to talk about it, his attempt to hide his prior marriage from me, his conflicting feelings about my pregnancy. The way he's hot and cold, the way everyone seemed so surprised and pleased to see him married again—and the things I found in the attic, the photos and the belongings that had been a woman's and a child's.

The pieces don't quite fit together, but in all the ways that I can think of, they point at something terrible. Something that might spell danger for both myself and my child.

I press my hand against my chest, trying to ease my racing heart. *Maybe he's so cold because he doesn't want to be hurt again,* I try to reason, pushing aside my fears for a moment. If Bria really was David's wife, if Marcus was their child, then to lose them so soon after losing his brother would have been a terrible blow. I can understand how he might resist any feelings he has for me, how feeling anything might make him instantly pull back. I can see how the unexpected news of my pregnancy might make him lash out. And—

Marcus was born before David married Bria, if I'm calculating the dates right. *He might not have been David's son.* There could be something to that—some other part of the mystery that explains David's paranoia about my child being his.

But the bloodstains. The photos, were clearly taken by someone following the woman in them. I don't know that the woman is Bria, that she and Lucio's wife might not be two different people. But I can't ignore that there's evidence that something terrible must have happened in that house.

Fear creeps through me again, impossible to ignore. I can easily imagine the worst—and the worst means that I'm in danger. I think of David's anger last night, this morning, and a swell of nausea ripples through me. I touch my stomach, my pulse racing again, and I know I need more answers. I need to know who these people were for certain, to try to tie the threads together before I come to any conclusions.

And I have to try to find a way to mollify David until I know.

The walk to the public library is another mile, but I manage it, grateful that I wore sensible shoes. David would hate seeing me out like this, wearing workout leggings, sneakers, and a long top, but he isn't here to see it. If someone tells him, I'll deal with it then. I wish for the first time that I wasn't so carefully trying to keep my pregnancy quiet for now—it's an excellent excuse for my appearance.

I don't have a library card, of course, which takes time to set up so I can use the computers. I also don't have any form of identification, but when I mention my married name, the assistant at the desk is quick to help me. I end up with a laminated card that I tuck into the zippered pocket of my leggings, going to one of the computers at the far end to do my research.

Much like the graves, it doesn't take long to uncover some of the answers I've been so desperately trying to pry out of David. It makes me wonder why he refused to tell me anything, but at the same time, I can't imagine that he expected me to do *this*, to dig at all. He expected me to be a meek wife, to accept his refusal to give me answers, and to know my place.

I refuse to be kept in the dark. Not when my own safety might be at stake—and especially not when my child's might be.

The first startling thing that I find is that Maricia Carravella was David's mother. I realize with shock that the woman I met in Boston, when I had dinner with his family, must be his stepmother. Her attitude makes more sense then—the way she treated me, the way she behaved as if she needed to oversee every small detail of the Carravella household and life. It occurs to me that David's father's move to Boston must have been prompted by his second marriage. I wonder if that's a part of the reason why David is so irritated by my dislike of the mansion, so easily provoked by any hint that I might want us to leave it. If he resents his stepmother for encouraging his father to do exactly that, and leave the ancestral family home for something more modern.

My suspicions are confirmed that Lucio is, in fact, his brother. There's very little detail surrounding how he died, which I don't find all that unusual—if there was anything off about it at all, any conflict or involvement of some other family, it would have been swept under the rug. It would be impossible for anyone to easily find details of *my* father's death, or my brother's exile—all of it carefully covered up by Don Fontana. I imagine that whatever happened here, it was handled similarly.

But what I *do* uncover is that Bria and Lucio were married. That Marcus was their son. I scroll through the engagement and wedding and birth announcements, my feeling of dread growing bit by bit, until I find a picture of Bria and Lucio on their wedding day, and my heart nearly stops. I have to cover my mouth with my hand to keep from making a sound loud enough to disturb the other library patrons.

The woman in the photos that I found in the attic and Bria Carravella are undoubtedly the same person. And I find, dated just over two years ago, the wedding announcement for Bria and David—two years after Lucio's death. With a little more digging, I uncover Bria and her young son's obituaries—once again, with any details of their deaths carefully absent. *How* they died is painfully unclear, just as with Lucio. To someone else, it might seem like nothing. To someone like me, who has spent my life growing up steeped in the dangers and machinations of the mafia, who knows the lengths that these powerful men will go to cover up their crimes—it feels like a physical blow.

I can see the pattern forming. David's brother, Lucio, married Bria. Their son, Marcus, was born. And then Lucio dies. David marries Bria—why? And then she and her son are both dead, two years later—and I find, in this isolated home where they lived, items that used to belong to them. Not treasured keepsakes kept for a reminder, either, but strange things shoved away in an attic like hiding evidence of guilt.

I'm being paranoid. I have no proof. But I think of what I've found in the house—the photos, the children's toys, the blouse with the bloodstains of David's anger, of his insistence that none of this is my business. I think of his moods, of his refusal to tell me the truth, and I feel that cold fear sink into my bones all over again.

If I am being paranoid, and I accuse him, he'll hate me all the more for it. And if I'm not—

I have to find a way to get out of this. The knot in my stomach tightens, a sick feeling that has nothing to do with my pregnancy spreading through me. I've never felt so in danger, so certain of the possibility that my husband might pose a very real threat to me. That if he has the slightest inclination that I might uncover all of this, that I might shame his family again as well as mine—

I'm expendable. My child is expendable. Two dead brides in the course of so short a time might raise eyebrows, but a man as powerful and charming as David could cover it up, spin it, turn himself into an object of grieving pity instead of someone to be suspected. And even if anyone *did* suspect him, what would they do? He's the heir to a powerful mafia name, with Sicily still behind him, even if the Carravellas did diminish somewhat after—

After a misfortune. That's what I was told. I press the heels of my hands against my eyes, the pieces starting to fit together at last. Lucio's death. His widow's remarriage. Her death, and the death of her son, the future heir.

Possibly at David's hand. Something to be covered up. It surprises me that Fontana would help with such a thing, especially considering how heavy a blow he dealt my family—but there's no telling what other layers there are to it, what favors were owed, what reasons there might be. The wheels of power are always turning, and the women are always the last ones to know why something happens—if we ever really know at all.

I log out of the computer abruptly, another wave of nausea washing through me. I have a long walk home and too much to think about. Too much to face, when I have no real way out of this.

I thought the mansion felt like a prison when David first brought me there.

Now I'm worried that it might be my grave.

26

DAVID

Once again, I come home to find that Amalie has ignored me, and left the house alone again. I catch her slipping back into the house through the back door, quiet as a mouse, not realizing that I already saw her walking down the long path that leads away from the mansion. I can guess where she went— probably to snoop into Bria's death, to try to find the answers that I refuse to give her. I can also guess that she won't be able to piece together much from a few gravestones. Not enough to understand what truly happened.

Which is for the best, I remind myself yet again. Amalie doesn't need to know about my past. What *should* matter to her is the future, both for my family and hers, and for the one we'll make together if she hasn't lied to me. I haven't grilled her about the things that have happened to her family—not that I would need to; I'm well aware of what Enzo Leone did, just as I'm well aware of what happened to her brother. But all the same—I haven't asked.

She closes the door almost silently, turns—and then nearly jumps out of her skin as she sees me sitting there at the table.

"David!" She presses one hand to her chest, as if to stop her heart from racing, and I see the blood drain from her face. "You scared me—"

"What do you think you were doing?" I grit my teeth, standing up and walking towards her. I haven't touched her since I came back drunk from the party and fucked her while she was asleep—a thing that made me feel more than a little guilty in the morning—and just being near her makes my cock twitch restlessly. I have the sudden urge to bend her over the table and punish her. I can almost feel the heat of her bare ass against my palm, hear the way she would whimper for me, imagine the tight, wet warmth of her clasped around my cock afterward, aroused despite herself.

"I went out for a walk." She tilts her chin up defiantly, jolting me back to reality. She crosses her arms over her breasts, glaring at me, and her rebellion infuriates me all over again.

"I told you not to leave the house—"

"I can't *do* anything if I don't leave the house! And there's nothing for me to do here in it!" Her voice rises almost immediately, then falls, her cheeks going a little more pale. It's almost as if she's afraid to shout at me, which I find amusing, considering that she's never acted like that before. "I can't stand being cooped up," she says, her voice dropping, her arms wrapping a little tighter around herself. "I feel like I'm going crazy here."

"You're being dramatic and spoiled." I grit my teeth, my frustration rising sharply. "You're acting as if I'm keeping you in a prison—"

"It feels like it!" Her voice rises again, and I draw in a long breath, trying to contain some of my anger.

"This is ridiculous." I feel my jaw clench tighter. "Just because you're not being pampered and waited on here, treated like a princess—"

"I don't need that! I just want some freedom, so—"

"So what?" I grab her by the shoulders before I can stop myself, pushing her back into the wall. I don't know if I intend to shout at her again or kiss her; my entire body is wound tight with frustration and desire, but something in Amalie's face stops me from doing either.

She looks *afraid*. I feel her shrink back, her eyes going wide and her face bone-white except for the small pricks of red high on her cheeks, and her hands drop to her stomach, protectively pressing against it. As if she's afraid I'll hurt her.

As if she's afraid I'll hurt the baby.

I drop my hands instantly, startled as I back away from her. "Where did you go that was so important, Amalie?" I try to ask it as calmly as I can, and I see her suck in a breath, still glued to the wall. I can see her trembling faintly, and I let out another slow breath, trying not to upset her more. I'm frustrated with her, but it upsets me to see her shaking like a leaf, as if she thinks that I'll truly harm her in some way.

"I went to the graveyard." Her hands are still flat against her stomach, her mouth tight at the corners. "I wanted to see their graves. Since you won't tell me anything."

She says the last almost defiantly, as if she's daring me to yell at her again, to tell her that she shouldn't have gone. But in that particular moment, as I stand there looking at her cringing against the wall with her hands protecting her baby—*our* baby, possibly—I can't find it in myself to say anything at all. My past is catching up with me, colliding with my present, and I no longer know if I recognize myself.

I no longer know if I have any idea what kind of life it is that I want to build here.

So instead, I turn around, and walk away.

—

Sequestered in my office, away from Amalie's accusing glares, I'm able to think more clearly. I sit down behind my desk, rubbing a hand over my mouth, trying to consider what to do. She won't leave it alone, that much is clear. *How much more poking and prying will she do?* My frustration with the woman I've married wells up once again—a good mafia wife, the kind I was supposed to marry, the kind I would have *chosen*, would understand to leave it alone. A wife isn't meant to dig up her husband's skeletons. She's meant to keep others from doing the same, while leaving them buried herself.

I could tell her the truth. It's not the first time I've considered it. I wonder if I would have, if I had married the sort of calm and capable woman that I imagined making my bride, when I knew I would be obliged to marry again after Bria's death. Someone who could take the information in stride, who would understand all that happened and not lose her composure. I don't trust Amalie to do that. I don't trust her to *listen*, to not throw it all back in my face, to not accuse me of secrets and lies.

I spent a week with her in Ibiza because I wanted her, but not as a wife. I never, not even for a moment, considered something more with her in those last days before we parted. Even though I wanted her, even though I felt as if I'd keep thinking of her long after she flew back to Chicago and I went home, I *knew* she wasn't a suitable partner for me. And yet I ended up married to her anyway. I tried to put space between us after the marriage, too, and yet every time, I found myself pulled back to her, magnetized by frustration and desire.

We can't stay away from each other. And in the moments when she's not driving me insane, I've found myself starting to care for her —which is the worst of all.

I don't want to get close to her. I don't want to have any feelings at all for her, which is why I've tried so hard to force myself to see her as stubborn and spoiled, rather than determined and brave enough to keep standing up to me again and again. I've forced myself not to see how she's pushed herself through the difficult beginnings of a pregnancy she didn't want, how she's done her best to please me when she can, how she's behaved admirably at the events I've taken her to. *Except for that stupid fur,* I remind myself—but when it comes down to it, I know my fury over that was more because I *wanted* to be angry with her than because I truly was. She was right that no one would have known about it. And even if they had, older wealth respects the ability to find something valuable without spending excessively. She might even have been admired for finding such a piece.

If I treated her better, if I cared for her, if I encouraged her— Amalie could be the wife I need. The wife I would *want*, even, which is precisely why I pull away again and again, because I don't want to *want* anyone.

Before I can stop myself, I slide open the drawer on the right side of my desk, reaching for a picture inside. The woman in it is laughing, her dark hair thrown back, her eyes bright. There's a ruby necklace around her neck, glittering like blood against her olive skin, and my chest clenches at the sight of it. I feel a swelling wave of sadness and resentment, the only feelings I ever have when I look at a picture of my late wife. When I remember Bria, and how much havoc this family wrought on her.

I set the photo down, tapping my fingers against the desk, lost in thought. I didn't want to get married again at all. I would have remained a bachelor if I could—but that was never an option for me. An heir needs another heir to follow him, and with my brother gone, it's my responsibility to provide that. I had simply thought that I would manage it with a woman more amenable than Amalie.

Leaning forward on my elbows, I run my hands through my hair with building frustration, a feeling that I've come to associate closely with thoughts of my present wife. I find myself wishing, more than anything, that we could have left things back in Ibiza. That my memories of her could have remained happy—memories of fun and pleasure, rather than what they've become, inextricably tied up with my real life until the good is entirely swallowed up by it.

I touch the picture again, brushing a fingertip over Bria's cheek. I can remember life with her clearly, and this picture so rarely reflects it. What I remember is her fear and sadness over Lucio's death, her crippling guilt, her refusal to look at me or touch me at first. The way she laid in our bed, stiff and still, unable to touch me in ways that made our marriage a cold one, lest I feel like I was violating her. We'd fought over it. I'd told her, again and again, that we needed another child. That Marcus wouldn't be enough for my father, that he would want our line better solidified than that.

I remember the way she turned away from me, telling me to take what I wanted, then. As if I ever really wanted her like that. As if I ever *really* wanted her at all.

The time when that picture was taken, when I remember her happy, was so brief. Brief enough that, without this to remember it by, I might not be able to at all.

I can see my life with Amalie going in the same direction. And I feel a spark of fear that, if something doesn't change, our time together might meet the same end.

27

AMALIE

David doesn't speak to me again for the rest of the day. He isn't downstairs for lunch or dinner—both of which I cobble together out of takeout leftovers that I reheat—and he doesn't come up to bed. Or at least, I'm asleep when he does, and he's gone by the time I wake up.

I have to do something to mollify him, at least a little while I decide what to do. He wanted me to go to one of his board meetings —which I obviously can't accomplish without leaving the house—so I decide to, at least this time, take some security with me. David's head of security is a tall, burly man who makes me feel miniscule the moment I walk up to him, and he looks at me as if I'm an annoyance that's interrupting his day.

"I need a car and some of your security to take with me to a meeting," I tell him, doing my best to address him as if I have the right to ask for those things. I *do*, of course—but my time as David's wife so far hasn't made me feel as if that's true. "I have a board meeting to go to on David's behalf."

It's not *entirely* true, but I manage to say it with enough confidence that he does as I ask. Ten minutes later, an SUV pulls around front with three of the security team inside—men who will, no doubt, keep an eye on me and report back to David as much as protect me. But I don't care. I don't intend to do anything today that I'll care if he knows about.

The meeting goes almost entirely as expected. I'd dressed carefully for it—a black pencil skirt and heels with a modest red chiffon blouse that ties at the throat, my hair pinned back at the sides, and delicate diamond jewelry. I can see the approval in the other women's faces, their thinly veiled excitement at having me there, an indication that David is happy with how things are going. I sit and listen to them talk about donations to various education efforts, a fundraising drive for the library, and plans for the next gala, nodding and agreeing where it seems appropriate. I listen for anything that I think David might want to know—there's nothing that stands out to me—but the part I'm here for is what comes after.

I'm here to see what they say to me when the meeting is done, and we have time for idle chatter.

It doesn't take long. I've barely gotten up to get a cup of water after the meeting is finished before a pretty woman who appears to be in her mid-thirties comes up to me—I think I recognize her from the party. "Caroline, right?" I ask, biting my lip as if I'm embarrassed that I can't entirely remember her name. "I'm so sorry, that party was a whirlwind. So many new people to meet! And I've never been very good with names. I'm better with faces." I laugh self-deprecatingly, and she smiles, waving a hand.

"I understand, I'm the same. But you got it right! It is Caroline. And honestly, I can't blame you for forgetting if you did." She lowers her voice, glancing back at the other women. "We all can't believe what Marie did, bringing up what happened to Bria like that. And on a night when everyone was so excited to meet David's new wife! It was so insensitive of her. But of course, I'm sure she just assumed you already knew all of it."

There's a keen look in Caroline's eyes that tells me she's trying to determine how much I *do* know. I take a sip of my water, letting out a small sigh. "David doesn't like to talk about it. It made me feel foolish, really—barely knowing anything about my own husband's history. But I understand it's a bit of a sore spot."

I'm counting on a penchant for gossip to encourage Caroline to tell me more. But instead, she flinches, looking suddenly concerned, as if she's said too much.

"Well—" She glances back again, but this time as if she's hoping someone will come to her rescue. "I'm sure he has his reasons for keeping it quiet for now. You've just gotten married, after all."

I can already feel her backing away from me. The other women are starting to pay attention to our conversation, and one of the older ladies walks over, looking curiously at me.

"Everything alright?" She glances at Caroline, who nods.

"I was just mentioning what Marie said at the party. But Mrs. Carra—Amalie said her husband hasn't told her much about—"

The reticence to talk about it makes me feel tense, my suspicions pricking at me harder than ever. "I think he's hesitant to talk about it. But I'm curious about his family, and that old house—"

"Well, it really is good of him to be putting so much work into it. But that's all for his brother, of course. They were close, once."

"Once?" I frown, and the other woman tenses, similarly to how Caroline pulled away.

"He really hasn't told you anything, has he, dear? Well, that's for him to say, I'm sure. He must have his reasons for keeping quiet about it."

It's almost the same thing Caroline said, word for word. I take a slow breath before I say something that I might regret—or that might get me in trouble with David, if anyone repeats it. "I'm really just curious—"

"You should ask him." The tension in the room thickens, and I know at that moment that I have to let it go. I can feel the mood of the room uniting against me, and I have the feeling that I won't be coming to any more of these meetings, if I'm not careful. David wouldn't be pleased with that.

"I understand. Thank you for having me." I force a pleasant smile, making the rounds to say goodbye before I leave, and retreat back to my waiting car. The presence of David's security feels oppressive on the ride home, and I have to force myself to stay calm. More and more, it feels as if going back to the mansion is returning to my jail cell.

As much as I'm nervous about the latter part of my pregnancy, I almost can't wait for the baby to be here—if only so I have something to *do*. I'm bored and restless, and it comes out in the way I act around the house, all of the creaks and noises making me jumpy and skittish. David notices at dinner, and I can tell it irritates him.

"Is something wrong?" he asks finally, setting down his fork. Dinner is, as usual, takeout from the nicest restaurants in Newport. A china plate with filet, grilled shrimp, rice pilaf, and roasted vegetables is in front of David, a glass of wine next to his hand. I've picked at my own dinner, a roasted duck breast with cherry glaze and sliced potatoes and vegetables. I've seen David's gaze flicking towards me more than once as we've sat here in silence. "You're barely eating again. Amalie—"

"I feel uncomfortable here. This house—I feel like there's always someone looking over my shoulder." I blurt it out without meaning to, but I can feel that crawling sensation sliding down my spine again. I know I shouldn't say anything—I can already see the long-suffering sigh that David lets out, but I still feel on edge from the meeting today, and more restless than ever. "We could visit your parents again in Boston soon. I think I'd rather find a doctor there than—"

"There's a perfectly good doctor in Providence that you can see. She knows the family already. She—" David breaks off, and I see his jaw tense. I can already imagine what he was going to say, and my mood makes me speak before I can think better of it.

"She was Bria's doctor? Maybe Marcus'? Is that what you were about to say?" As soon as the words spill out, I know it's a mistake. David looks down at his food, almost regretfully—as if he knows he won't be finishing his dinner—and looks at me.

"Go upstairs, Amalie. I don't want to see you right now."

I feel a flush of hot anger wash over me. "You can't order me to do whatever you like. I—"

"Can't I?" His dark gaze turns on me, full of a look that I know all too well, and I feel a different kind of heat flicker in the pit of my stomach. "I could tell you to do anything I want, Amalie, and you would do it."

"That's not true." Just saying that will only provoke him, and I wish I could take it back the moment the words come out of my mouth. I try to change tactics, quickly. "You're more defensive about this house than you are about me. Just because it makes me nervous—"

"You're being childish and overimaginative." There's a finality to David's voice, as if what he says is the absolute truth, without question. "But maybe I can put your imagination to better use. What do you think I'm going to tell you to do next, Amalie?"

I can think of any number of things, and I don't want to suggest any of them to him. I feel a shiver of fear follow that heat that I felt a moment ago, and I remember that I need to be *careful*. David has a way of provoking me, of making me forget every self-preservation instinct I have. *Was it this way for Bria?* I think, the heat in my stomach turning to ice. *Did he make her forget, too? Until it was too late?*

"Go upstairs," he says quietly, his voice suddenly velvet-soft. "Now, Amalie, before I think of a more interesting way for you to help me finish my dinner."

I see the way his body has tensed, the way he shifts in his chair. I've become attuned to what he wants, to the signs of his desire, and I can see it in him now.

If I go upstairs, he'll leave me alone, most likely. I could have a bath, go to bed, and spend the rest of my night in what passes for peace here in this house. But if I don't—

"Amalie." There's steel under the velvet, a clear warning.

I don't move. I *can't*. Letting him order me around like this, tell me to go upstairs like a child who's been bad, feels more embarrassing than whatever he's going to do next. I sit stiffly in my chair, my cheeks flushing, horribly aware that a part of what keeps me glued here is my curiosity about what he plans to 'force' me to do. That a part of me wants to know—and wants to do it, whatever it is that he desires.

David reaches for his wine glass, draining it. His tongue flicks out over his lips, collecting a drop there, and I feel that flicker of heat again, a terrible anticipation of what he might do. And when he stands, his gaze gone dark with lust, I feel myself start to ache.

He reaches out, turning my chair to face him. That hand sinks into my hair, fingers running through the thick strands, making a fist in it as his other hand reaches for his zipper. As I suspected, he's already hard. I can see him straining against the fly of his suit trousers. I watch in mute fascination as his fingers slide his zipper down, his tattooed forearm flexing as he takes his cock in his hand the moment it slips free. His expression is hard and cold as he guides it to my lips, but all I can think of as I look up at him is how stunningly handsome he looks in the dim light, like a chiseled Adonis, a god who could order me to my knees with a word.

"Open your mouth, *cara mia*," he murmurs, and my lips part without a thought.

He rubs his cockhead over my lower lip, smearing pre-cum over the soft flesh, and I whimper. I don't mean to, and he knows it, from the way he laughs darkly in the back of his throat. My tongue flicks out, lapping up the salty taste of him, and I feel as if I'm no longer in control of my own body. As if I'm sitting outside of myself, watching my handsome husband feed his cock between my lips, watching me look up at him with wide-eyed need as he slides himself over my tongue.

"You always want me." There's an almost vicious satisfaction in his voice, as if he *needs* to say it out loud. As if he needs confirmation that it's true. "*Always.*" His hips rock forward, pushing his cock deeper into my mouth. My lips close around him, sucking, my tongue sliding over the shaft, teasing the soft spot just beneath the tip that I know is sensitive. He groans, his hand tightening in my hair, and I feel a flush of pleasure, followed by the heat of humiliation, because everything he says is true. No matter what happens between us, I can't seem to stop wanting him. Even at this moment, sitting here in the chair, gripping the edge of the table as David thrusts into my mouth, doesn't feel like enough. I want to sink to my knees, slide my hand under my skirt, pleasure myself while he fucks my face. My other hand presses against my thigh, and I think he sees it, because he taps the side of my chin and urges me to look up at him.

"No pleasure for you yet, *bellisima*," he murmurs. "But you look so pretty with my cock between your lips; I don't think I'll be able to deny you afterward." The hand in my hair runs through it again, his fingers drifting against the back of my neck, and I shiver. "Swallow my cum like a good girl, and I'll reward you. Show me how much you want it, Amalie." He nearly groans my name at the end, as if just saying it arouses him even more.

I moan around his cock. I can't help it, and I see the way his jaw tightens at the sensation, feel the rock of his hips as he pushes himself to the back of my throat. I slide my tongue over the throbbing veins, trying to take him as far as I can as he urges my head down. I feel myself choke, my throat convulsing around him, and I hear David groan.

"Keep doing that, and you'll get your reward sooner rather than later." His fingers stroke the back of my head, urging me on. "*God*, yes. Just like that—"

I know the rhythm he likes by now, the way I can flutter my tongue against the base when I finally manage to take him deeper, the way his entire body shudders when I slide my mouth nearly off of him and tighten my lips around his tip. I suck harder, giving him the pressure I know he likes, and I feel him throb against my tongue, the movement of his hips stuttering as he hovers on the edge.

"*Fuck*—" he breathes. "God, Amalie, *yes*—"

There's a sincerity to his desire that's intoxicating. It drives me to try harder, to lick and suck until he's moaning with every other breath, his cock stiff between my lips, and I look up at him wide-eyed, begging without words for his cum. I roll my tongue against his tip, sliding down again until he rubs against the back of it, and I feel his whole body go rigid as the first wave of his orgasm overtakes him, his hand hard in my hair as he starts to come.

"*Amalie*—"

The way he groans my name sends a tremor through my entire

body. I feel the hot rush of his cum over my tongue, thick and salty, and I swallow it down. My throat works convulsively around his cock as he spills down it, not wanting to spill a drop, wanting that moment to be every bit as good for him as he whispered to me earlier. I don't stop, not even when he's leaning over me shuddering, his hips thrusting as the last of it spurts over my tongue. Not until he slides free of my mouth of his own volition, breathing hard, his thumb pressed against the corner of my lips as if to make sure that none of his cum slips free.

Without a word, he lifts me up out of the chair, moving me to the other end of the table where it's empty and bare. He picks me up as if I weigh nothing, setting me on the edge of the table, one hand already pushing my skirt up as he reaches for a chair with another, dragging it forward. There's a dark, hungry look in his eyes that sends waves of desire through me, and I'm dimly aware of how wet I am, of the hollow ache between my legs. I moan helplessly as he pushes my skirt higher, spreading my legs as he sinks down into the chair between them, pulling me to the very edge of the table as he bends down to drag his tongue over the front of the silk panties I'm wearing beneath my skirt.

He moans, the sound muffled, the vibrations shivering over my skin. "You taste—" he breathes the words, warm against my flesh, and I moan again. Both of my legs are hooked over his shoulders, his hands holding my thighs apart as he licks the silk again, adding to the wetness. I gasp as I feel him hook one thumb under the edge of the fabric, pulling them to the side, and then his tongue plunges between my folds.

There's no teasing, no dragging it out. It's as if he can't wait. His tongue slides inside of me, licking, circling, until my hips are arching, and I'm gasping out pleas that don't entirely form words. My clit is swollen and throbbing, aching for his touch, and at the same time, I never want him to stop fucking me with his tongue. I grind against his mouth, begging between every moan, and I hear his dark, deep laugh as he suddenly slips his tongue free of me and slides it upwards, fluttering it over my clit with a motion that makes me cry out.

"God, yes," he groans. "Moan for me, *cara mia*. Let me hear how good this feels."

My nails scratch against the wood of the table as I buck against his mouth, and he swirls his tongue around my clit again, the vibration of his laugh spreading over me. I can feel his delight in how helpless I am under his touch, how much I want him, and I feel his hand tighten on my thigh, holding me down hard against the table as I writhe.

I'm so close to the edge. He sucks my clit into his mouth, tongue still fluttering over my clit, and I feel like I can't breathe. Every muscle in my body is tight with pleasure, and then he pushes two fingers into me, curling them as he thrusts them hard into my pussy, and I fall apart.

There's no doubt that anyone in or around the house hears me scream his name. The orgasm shatters through me, my back arching hard as I come on his tongue, and I feel him lapping up every bit of my arousal, his fingers thrusting as he drags me through the seemingly endless climax. It keeps going, wave after wave of sensation crashing through me until it's almost too much, and I expect him to stop. To pull away from me, to say something derisive about how easily he can make me fall apart—but he *doesn't stop*.

His tongue lashes over my clit, lips fastened around the sensitive flesh, sucking as intensely as I did with him before. I feel him slip a third finger inside of me, the fullness still not quite as good as his cock, but so fucking close that it keeps that endless pleasure rippling through me. He pushes his fingers into me as deeply as he can, curling them so he can stroke me from the inside, and I feel utterly helpless under the onslaught of his touch. I feel another orgasm building, the pleasure quick and sharp this time, driving every conscious thought out of my head.

It's almost too much—and then it *is* too much, the oversensitivity making the pleasure ride the knife's edge of pain. "I can't—" I gasp out, pushing reflexively at his shoulder, but he just laughs again, that dark, deep sound that ripples over me. Something about his insistence on continuing to pleasure me, the endless flutter of his tongue, the way his mouth is devouring me until I'm swollen and sore, drives me over the edge again. Except it's no longer a climax; it's an endless ebb and flow of pleasure and pain, every nerve in my body raw and tingling. I sag back against the table, twitching under his touch as he strips me bare of every bit of pleasure that I have to give.

When he pulls back, his hair tousled and lips swollen, he's never looked more gorgeous. He looks half-mad with lust, his mouth glistening with my arousal, his fingers still buried inside of me as he looks down, looming over me. "We're not done," he growls hoarsely, crooking his fingers as I whimper helplessly, and I see that he's hard again. His cock is stiff against his belly, leaking pre-cum and visibly throbbing, and before I can say a word or move, he surges between my thighs, grabbing my wrists and pinning them over my head.

"David—" I moan his name, writhing under him as his swollen cockhead pushes against my entrance. I feel battered with pleasure, every part of me soft and sore with the endless orgasms he dragged me through, and I don't know if I can take any more. But I also don't know if he's going to give me a choice.

I don't know if I want him to.

"Say you want me." His hips rock forward, nudging just the tip of his cock inside of me, his voice a near-feral growl. "Tell me the truth, *cara mia*. Tell me you need my cock. Tell me how much you want me to fuck you."

There's something almost like begging in his voice, his eyes wide and dark with need, only the very tip of his cock rubbing inside of me as his hips shift forward. A cruel, angry part of me wants to throw it back into his face, to tell him that I *don't* need him, that I don't want him. That fucking me right now would be taking me against my will —but I know it would be a lie. Just the slight pressure of him inside of me has my hips arching, my body begging for more, for the fullness that I'll feel when he thrusts every inch into me.

"Say it." He sucks in a breath, his fingers pressing hard against the small bones in my wrists. "Say it, Amalie."

There's something almost broken about the way he groans it that makes me give in. "I want you," I whisper, my voice choked, the words spilling out on a cry as he gives me another inch of his cock. "I want your cock. I *need* you to fill me up. *Please*, please—I want it—" The rest of it comes out almost without meaning to, every inch that he slips deeper prompting more begging, more whimpering pleas for him to give me all of it. He makes a sound in the back of his throat that's nearly a growl as he slams the last inches of his cock into me, filling me completely. He holds me there, impaled on his throbbing length, as he stares down into my face with an unreadable expression.

When he slams into me again, it's ruthless. I can feel the table shaking beneath me as he fucks me hard, hear the sound of a wine-glass breaking as it tips over, and out of the corner of my eye, I see the wine running over the wood and dripping down to the floor, red as blood as David keeps me pinned there beneath him. He thrusts into me again and again, sending waves of pleasure rippling through me with every hard meeting of his hips against mine, and I realize that I'm going to come again. The sound of his name on my lips comes out half-strangled as he surges inside of me, buried to the hilt as he shudders above me, his jaw clenched as he comes. His gaze is fixed on mine, nearly black with lust, and I know my wrists will be bruised tomorrow—but I can't bring myself to care. I feel him flood me with heat, his hips rocking against me as I clench and tremble with my own climax, and his head drops forward, his chest heaving as he stays very still inside of me.

"Now," he murmurs, looking up at me after a long moment with my body still trapped beneath his, "now tell me you hate me, Amalie."

I stare up at him, shocked. His face is taut, strained with emotions that I can't begin to unravel or understand, that confuse me even more given all the pieces of information that I know but haven't yet put together completely. I don't know what to say, but I feel his hands convulse around my wrists, his cock still twitching inside of me as he softens, and I know I have to say something.

M. JAMES

"I hate that I want you so much," I whisper, and I realize as I say it that it's one of the most honest things I've ever said to him. "I hate that you make me feel this way." To my horror, I can feel tears pricking at the corners of my eyes, even as I can still feel myself fluttering around his half-hard cock. "What did I do to make you like this?"

David's head jerks up, his entire body tensing, and then he pulls free of me. He turns away, tucking himself back into his suit trousers, utterly silent.

"David." I push myself up, trying to reach for him, but he pulls away. "David—"

He refuses to look at me. I see his shoulders hunch, his muscles tightening, but he doesn't speak again. I hear the sound of his zipper as he fixes his clothing, and then he strides out of the room, leaving me there—half-dressed on the dining room table, his cum pooling between my thighs as I watch him go in utter shock.

I don't understand what just happened. And in this moment, as I stare after him, I wonder if I'll ever truly understand anything about him at all.

28

AMALIE

David doesn't come up to bed later. I have no idea where he sleeps in the cavernous house—in his office, maybe—and I don't relish the idea of wandering through it to find out. I lie in bed awake for a long time, wondering if I *should*—if going and seeking him out might help repair something between us, but I don't know if it would. For all I know, he'd be angry with me for disturbing him. His moods are impossible for me to read or predict, and as I lie there alone in bed, I wonder if he was always this way. If he was this way with *her*. I think of him asking me—almost *begging* me to tell him that I want him—and then I think of his bruising grip on my wrists at the end, telling me to say that I hate him.

There's something else there. There's a *reason* for his behavior, but I'm terrified to find out what it is. I'm terrified to discover that it's something even worse than what I've suspected so far. In the dark of the bedroom, it's easy for my thoughts to unspool out into the darkest possibilities. I press my hand to my stomach, wondering if I'm bringing a child into the world that has a monster for a father. A murderer. Someone capable of killing those closest to him.

In the morning, David is nowhere to be found in the house, and I'm glad. I slept restlessly, my dreams awful when I did finally fall asleep, and I don't want to hear anything about how tired I look or the bags under my eyes. I eat a leftover pastry and have a cup of decaf coffee for breakfast, trying to think of anything to occupy my time that might distract me from the thoughts still rattling around in my head, but there's nothing. I keep thinking of the attic and what I found there, and wondering if there's anything else in the house that I missed.

Going through the numerous rooms, at least, is something to kill time. The first floor of the house I've already mostly explored—there are the two dining and living rooms, one of each for formal occasions and one of each for more informal, the huge and mostly unrenovated kitchen that goes largely ignored without any cook on staff, a massive room for entertaining, a downstairs bathroom and powder room, and the mudroom at the back. There's also David's office, which is always locked now, and *that* key I know he also keeps on his person.

The second floor is entirely guest rooms and the adjoining baths, and I wander through each room, finding nothing interesting. A little more than half are unfurnished, empty rooms with faded wallpaper, feeling forgotten and hollow. The furnished ones are dusty and still unrenovated, all of them having a haunted, chilly quality that leaves me feeling unnerved. The house is so huge, and so largely forgotten about in so many places, that it leaves me with a feeling of loneliness as I walk through it. I think of David's efforts to renovate, and I wonder if, deep down, the house makes him feel the same way, too— if renewing this place that he grew up in is a way of exorcising the ghosts of the people who died here.

Or, alternatively, a way to erase what he did.

I feel insane every time I think it—paranoid. Every mafia wife knows her husband is capable of murder, but to murder *family*, a wife, a child—it's not unheard of, but it's also something so dark and vicious that it would be covered up immediately, pushed as far under the proverbial rug as it could go. Those are the kinds of sins that haunt someone, that make him an object of whispers, of suspicion, of fear.

I think of the mysteries shrouding David, of the reticence to talk about his history that I've seen in everyone, and I wonder if I *am* crazy—or if I have a right to be afraid.

The third floor feels almost as pointless. I wander through the library, through a study, through more abandoned guest rooms— until I find a locked room at the end of the third floor hallway, the knob refusing to turn. I reach up and slide my hand over the top of the door, hoping I'll be lucky enough to find another key left behind, but there's nothing there.

I stand there fiddling with the knob, knowing I should leave it well enough alone. But I *can't*. There are so few locked doors in this house, and the last time I snooped beyond one of them, it set me on a path to discover things about my husband's past that no one else would have told me. I know the wondering will drive me insane, if I don't find a way in.

I have no idea how to pick a lock. I've heard of ways, and I spend the next hour searching for some sort of plastic card that might help, or something else I can slide between the lock and the doorjamb. Eventually, I find two old hotel keycards in one of David's pockets in the laundry hamper, and I grab a few bobby pins off of my vanity, just in case. I don't have much hope that it'll work—but at this point, I'm bored enough and curious enough to spend time trying.

One keycard breaks, trying to slide it in and wiggle it along the doorjamb. I huff out a breath, frustrated, and turn to trying the bobby pins. It's clear that I have no idea what I'm doing—I twist and turn them in the lock, but nothing happens. The door stays resolutely shut, and as time ticks on, I listen carefully for the sound of the front door opening downstairs. The last thing I need is for David to come home and find me doing this.

I try again with the second keycard, to no avail. It occurs to me how ridiculous this looks—that I should, truly, probably just give up —but I keep going. I slide the keycard up again, this time wiggling one of the bobby pins in the lock at the same time—and I feel something give.

Shit. I suck in a breath, trying to focus as I manipulate the lock. I press my arm against the knob, awkwardly trying to turn it while I have both of my hands occupied—and suddenly, it moves, the door swinging open into the room.

For a moment, I'm disappointed. It looks like just another guest room—furniture covered in a fine layer of dust, the bedding stiff with it, the wooden floor dull. Heavy curtains cover the window, blocking out the light, but when I breathe in, I almost think I can smell a hint of a woman's perfume. I turn, looking around the room—and I see the source of it, sitting on a vanity table on the other side of the room.

The room, I realize, is still full of someone's things. There's a half-full bottle of Chanel perfume sitting on the vanity, a pair of diamond earrings next to it. As I walk closer, I see a nearly-used tube of expensive hand cream and a jaw of moisturizer, a dish containing two rings sitting near the mirror. My breath catches as I look down at them. It's unmistakably a wedding set. One ring is a diamond solitaire, the large round stone dull with dust, and next to it is a diamond-encrusted wedding band. They're both thin and delicate, as delicate as that ruby necklace that I found upstairs in the attic, and I can picture that woman in the photo wearing them. I can see the diamond glittering on her long, slender fingers, the elegance with which she'd wear such a simple set.

My heart is pounding as I walk to the closet, flinging it open. It's still full of clothes, hung neatly, boxes stacked beneath them. I feel faintly ill as I sink to the floor, reaching for one of the boxes—and when I open it, I press one hand to my mouth.

It's more children's things—these for a baby. Onesies, smaller clothes than even what I found upstairs, teething rings, a bottle. The hard cardboard books that you would give to a very small child. Stuffed animals, a soft fleece blanket—I reach in, touching the blanket gingerly, and I feel tears fill my eyes. I have a name to put to the child now. *Marcus*. Bria's son, and I suspect, David's nephew.

I push the box aside, reaching for another. When I open this one, my fingers touch something stiff, and I freeze.

Inside, there's more clothing. A pair of slim women's trousers in a cream color, and a light blue blouse—both of them bloodstained. I jerk my hand back, staring down at the clothes, and I swallow hard as I try to resist the urge to vomit.

This isn't the smaller stain that was on the sleeve of the other shirt. There's a spray of blood across this blouse, spattered over the fabric of the trousers, long since stained. Enough to stiffen the fabric, and I look at the clothing uncomprehendingly, wondering why anyone would keep this. Why it's in this closet, tucked away for god knows how long.

Gingerly, I move the fabric aside—and I feel a sharp nick of pain in my finger as something sharp presses against it.

"Shit!" I yank my hand back, peering down into the box, hoping that I haven't just stabbed myself with a needle. I haven't—but what I see underneath the clothing is nearly as bad. There's a knife, the blade still crusted with more blood, and I wince, clutching my hand into a fist and trying not to panic about the fact that I just cut my finger on a dirty knife.

A dirty, bloodied knife—tucked into a closet under bloodied clothes, in a locked room in my husband's house. I feel the sharp pang of a migraine coming on, my head aching with confusion and fear and stress, and I swallow hard, looking down at the box as if it might give me some answers.

And then, at the very bottom, I see something that might.

There's a leather-bound book. I reach for it, knowing before I even touch it that I'm almost certainly intruding on something private—but just as I couldn't stop myself from breaking into the room, I can't stop myself from slipping the book out of the box. I open it, and see that the pages are full of prim, slanted handwriting, the tops of some of the pages dated.

It's a diary—and the name on the inside of the first page makes it obvious who it belongs to.

Bria Carravella.

I close the box, pulse racing in my throat as I do my best to put the room back together the way it was before I broke in, still holding the diary. There's no re-locking the room, but from the state of the dust when I came in, no one has entered it in a very, very long time. I just have to hope that David won't decide to check and see if the door is still locked anytime soon.

There's no sign of David when I come out of the room, no sounds to suggest that he's home. It's nearly dinnertime, but I can't imagine trying to eat right now. My stomach is in knots, the nausea barely held at bay, and I try to think of where I could go to read the diary where he might not surprise me and see what I'm doing.

I end up retreating to the bath with a half a glass of wine, the little bit that I know I'd be allowed while pregnant. I'm sure David would have something to say about it if he knew, but I can't bring myself to care—I don't know how I'm meant to get through this otherwise. I lock the bathroom door behind me, stripping off my clothes and leaving them in a pile next to the tub as I slip underneath the steaming water. The diary sits on the edge of the tub, mocking me with what might be inside, and I reach for it gingerly, as afraid to find out the truth as I am to keep not knowing.

The script inside is elegant and pretty at first, looping with a steady hand. It's dated a little over two years ago, and I lean back in the tub, my breath catching as I start to read.

TODAY IS MY WEDDING DAY. *My second wedding day, which isn't something that any woman in my position hopes for. Much less that the second wedding will be to the brother of the first. I always knew families like ours were fucked up—this whole world feels like some kind of waking nightmare sometimes—but this feels even worse than the usual. I don't know how I'm meant to go to bed with him in that house, the same one I shared with Lucio. If I'm lucky, we'll go to a hotel. But I still don't know how I'm going to ever touch him.*

Sometimes, when I look down at my hands, I think I'll still see blood.

I STARE AT THE PAGE. *Why would she have blood on her hands?* Another disjointed piece of the puzzle, something else that doesn't make sense. I feel that throb of a headache again, the feeling that all of this is beyond me. With that feeling comes anger—because if David would just *tell* me what happened, I wouldn't have to do all of this. I wouldn't have to snoop and sleuth. I would *know* if I'm in danger, if my child is. I would know what happened.

I CAN'T STAND HIM. I can't stand this place. I feel like I want to scream every moment of every day. He acts as if I'm the one in the wrong, as if my coldness is hurting him somehow. Why couldn't they just let me go? I know the answer, of course—it's Marcus. My child. He'll inherit all of this one day after David. If I hadn't had a child with Lucio, I'd be free now.

I BITE MY LIP, scanning the entry again. It almost sounds as if Bria resented her child, and the thought makes my chest ache as I wonder if I might feel the same eventually. Will I wish that David and I hadn't been so reckless in Ibiza eventually? Will I see our child as just another shackle holding me to a marriage that's making me miserable?

It's not as if I wouldn't have ended up with a child eventually, one way or another. From the moment I said *I do*, it was always a ticking clock until I would provide the Carravella family with their next heir. But Bria's first husband's death meant she might have had a way out. Her child shackled her even more thoroughly to something she didn't want.

I'VE CONVINCED David to let us have separate bedrooms. It wasn't that hard; he says he hates sleeping next to me anyway, that I behave as if he's going to violate me at any moment? How am I supposed to feel, when he says Marcus isn't enough? That his father demands that I have a child with David, too? He acts as if it's hurting him to have to fuck me when he knows I don't want it. As if all men don't want a woman at their beck and call. Like he doesn't enjoy the power he has over me.

· · ·

I STARE AT THE PAGE, feeling my breath catch. The hatred flowing off the page feels almost palpable. I think of David in bed with the pretty brunette woman from the photo and feel a hot flush of jealousy—but I also think of something else. I remember him pinning me to the dinner table, his face taut with need, the half-broken way he asked me to say that I wanted him. As if it mattered to him that I wanted it, too. That I was as helpless in the face of my desire as he was.

It's the first time that some of this has really felt like it makes sense. I don't know for sure that I'm right, but as I look over that last entry, I have the dawning idea that David's obsession with my desire has something to do with this—with the fact that the first woman he married made him feel as if he were forcing her in bed.

So, is he a monster? Is he responsible for her death? Or is there something else going on here?

I don't know. And nothing has told me for certain what the truth is. I reach for the diary again, flipping to the next page.

DAVID IS MORE and more frustrated with me. He can't get me pregnant unless we sleep together, and he refuses to keep doing it like this, the way things are. I suggested a doctor's intervention, but that just made him angrier—he said it would be humiliating if it got out. If anyone knew. I wonder sometimes when he looks at Marcus if he resents him. There's no closeness between them. He's David's nephew, not his son. I wonder if that makes David hate him.

A CHILL RIPPLES down my spine, and I turn the pages faster, thinking of the graveyard. The child's tombstone next to Bria's, smaller, a reminder of a life cut much too short.

Marcus is sick. The doctor says it's RSV, a particularly bad case, that it's bad luck. That we have the best of care and they'll do everything for him. But it's my fault. I know it must be. I wished him away. I wished to be free of all of this. And now my baby is sick.

. . .

DAVID IS ANGRY WITH ME. *He says I'm being ridiculous, paranoid, that none of this is my fault. He's worried, I can tell—but I don't think it's because he cares about Marcus. He's worried about his precious family line. I heard him on the phone with his father earlier tonight. I heard him saying that he doesn't know what he'll do if Marcus dies. That he doesn't know how he can have another child with me. That's what he's thinking about right now.*

I WON'T DO *this anymore. I won't, I won't—*

THE DIARY ENDS THERE, the script trailing off in a scrawl. I press my hand to my mouth, feeling my heart beating uncomfortably hard in my chest. I'd hoped there would be some clarity from this—but there's nothing. Only more questions. Only more confusion as to *how* Bria died exactly, and what happened to her son. I'm not even entirely sure how Lucio died. It's all been shrouded in mystery, covered up, and with every new small clue that I find, I feel more and more terrified that the reason it's been so thoroughly swept under the rug is because David did something terrible.

If my baby is in danger, I have to do something to protect them. I have to protect us both.

A sudden, hard knocking at the door nearly startles me out of my skin. "Amalie?" David's voice comes from the other side, and my chest tightens with fear. I close the diary, trying not to sound as terrified as I feel.

"I'm in the bath. I just want to be alone."

There's a pause, and then I hear the sound of a key in the lock. A flush of anger replaces the fear for just a moment over David's utter inconsideration for my desire to be by myself, the arrogance of him thinking he's welcome in any room at any time, but the fear overcomes it again just as quickly as I hear the knob turn. I sit up, grabbing frantically for my clothes as I shove the diary underneath them just as the door starts to open and David steps inside.

"Are you alright?" He looks at me quizzically, closing the door behind him. His gaze drifts over me, naked in the tub with my knees drawn up to my chest, but there's not the same lust in them that I'm often accustomed to. He looks almost worried. "Do you always lock yourself in the bathroom?"

"Why do you care?" I snap, and he flinches. His expression hardens, and he leans back against the sink counter, that smooth arrogance replacing the concern I saw a moment before.

"Is it so wrong of me to want to know where my wife is?" He crosses his arms over his chest. "I like keeping track of what belongs to me."

My cheeks flush instantly, and he sees it. I *know* he does from the way the corner of his mouth tilts up the slightest bit, the hint of a smirk, but he does nothing else. For once, I'm too afraid to feel more than the beginnings of arousal. My heartbeat is fluttering in my throat, the memory of what I just read and all the suspicions it raised far too close.

"You can see I'm fine." I swallow hard, wanting to sink down into the water and disappear, wishing he would just vanish from the room. "I just wanted a bath."

"And some wine, I see." There's that flicker of disapproval on his face that I expected, and I glare at him.

"Everyone knows a half a glass is fine." I press my lips together, wishing I could just tell him to leave. But I know that doing that would only make him more inclined to stay.

He lets out a slow breath, as if he's trying to keep himself from retorting. "I could join you in the bath, if you like." His gaze slides over me again, and I could *swear* I still see that hint of concern. It confuses me more than anything else.

"Why can't you just leave me alone?" The words come out more plaintive than I mean for them to, and I steel myself for him to throw that back into my face, but he just pauses, looking at me with that even, unreadable expression.

"Maybe I wanted to spend some time with my wife. But if you'd prefer to keep the hot water all to yourself, I can stay right here."

"You never want to spend time with me." I bite my lip, moving a little further away from him. I'm painfully aware of the diary under-neath my clothes, inches from his foot, of my bare and vulnerable flesh in the heated water while he stands there fully clothed. "What —you just want to talk?"

"You were asking about my family." His voice is tense, and I flinch. "I thought perhaps I'd ask about yours."

"And I should tell you, when you won't give me anything about your past?" I glare at him, and David chuckles low in his throat.

"I know what happened with your family, Amalie. Of course, I *know*. I can't believe you would think otherwise. What I was curious about is how you feel."

I'm not sure he could have said anything that would have startled me more. I stare at him for a moment, licking my suddenly dry lips. "How I *feel*?"

David lets out a sigh, as if I'm making this far too difficult. "Yes," he says, a touch impatiently. "How you feel. Your father is dead. Your brother is in Sicily. Have you heard from him?"

I blink, trying not to laugh at the thought of Andre calling me. "No," I tell him flatly. "I'm not sure Andre remembers he has a sister. He ignored me often enough when we lived in the same house; I doubt he thinks about me in Sicily."

"So you weren't close."

"There's nothing close about any of my family." I wrap my arms around my knees, uncomfortable with David's line of questioning, but the half a glass of wine and the heat has gone a little bit to my head. *What if answering his questions makes him answer mine?* It's a foolish thing to think; I have no reason to believe that David wants to do anything other than pry more information out of me that will give him the upper hand. But I see that flicker of concern, of something almost like *interest* in his face again, and it makes me want to answer. "My family has always been very cold."

"Is that why you ran off to Ibiza?" David smirks a little. "To feel *warm*?"

"Cute." I roll my eyes at him, aware that it could piss him off, but unable to help myself. I'm so often unable to stop myself from reacting to him in ways that could go badly, and I feel another small tremor of fear at the thought of Bria, wondering if she had been the same. Wondering what she might have done to finally tip him over the edge, if that really is what happened. "If you must know, I wanted to lose my virginity in Ibiza to someone *I* picked, before my mother married me off. And I did." I meet his gaze evenly. "To you."

David is quiet for a moment. "You've really stuck to that story." He grips the edge of the countertop, looking at me. "I almost want to believe you."

I shrug. "It's true."

He takes a slow breath. "There was blood on the sheets, the morning after. I didn't know who you were—I thought you were just some co-ed, some trust fund kid. I didn't think you could possibly be a virgin, especially not when *you* approached *me* in that club. And the way you behaved in bed—"

"Not everyone has to be a shrinking flower on their first night." I glare at him, biting my lip. "Just because I didn't cry and beg you to stop—"

"No, I suppose you did want to be there." He rubs a hand over his mouth. "I just told myself it was on account of my—" David waves a hand in the general direction of his groin. "I'm aware that I'm—sizable. I thought it might have just been a bit much for you. You were —incredibly tight."

His voice sounds a little strangled as he says it, and I see the line of his cock twitch against his fly. I don't know whether to laugh or be aroused by him telling me that he thought his cock made me bleed the first night, and I press my knuckles against my lips, forcing back any possible laughter. I don't think he would take it well.

"You can believe whatever you want," I say finally, when I've managed to collect myself. "But I told you the truth. You were my first."

"And you want me to believe that there was no one after me, either." His gaze is still holding mine, his fingers curled around the edge of the countertop as he watches me intently. "That none of those men I saw you flirting with made their way into your bed. That even after I dismissed you that first night, didn't even ask you to stay, you didn't fuck anyone else."

I let out a slow breath, feeling my jaw clench. I don't want to admit this to him, to tell him how good he was, but he's leaving me no choice. Not if I want to convince him that I'm telling the truth. I feel as if I'm walking a knife's edge of danger—that if he goes the *other* way, if he's convinced I've lied, that I might truly be in harm's way.

"You made it hard to *want* anyone else, alright?" I snap, narrowing my eyes at him. "I didn't want to tell you any of this, because you're already too fucking arrogant as it is! But that first night was *good*. Better than good. Better than I expected it to be. And every time I thought about fucking someone else, I just kept thinking about you and how good that night was. I thought maybe I should leave it at that, instead of sleeping with some guy that was just going to disappoint me. I was already going to be disappointed when I got married; I didn't need to add to it on vacation!"

David's mouth twitches with humor, and somehow, that makes me even angrier. "This isn't funny," I bite out, wrapping my arms around my knees. "You were supposed to be something that I could remember, something I chose for myself, even after I went home and had to go along with the life that was already planned out for me. Instead, you became just another thing I didn't choose."

I see the way he flinches at that. His jaw tightens, and he looks down at me, the warmth in his eyes flickering out. "Are you sure you don't want me to join you in the bath?" he asks, his voice deceptively quiet. "I am *asking*, after all. So you *can* choose."

The fear I felt earlier returns, winding its way through me, making me feel chilled despite the warmth of the water. I don't know if it would be better or worse for me to say yes—if he would rather I give in to him or if, given what I just read in the diary, pretense would only make things worse. All I know is that, at this moment, I *don't* want him. Not even the desire that seems to rear its head every time he's near is enough to overcome what's happened today.

"I want to be alone," I say softly.

For a moment, I'm not sure that he's going to leave. That he's going to ignore what I've asked for, and join me anyway. His jaw tightens, and he looks at me once more, an expression on his face that almost looks sad. And then, to my relief, he pushes away from the counter and turns his back on me, walking out of the room.

I sit there for several long moments, waiting for my pulse to slow, waiting for any of this to make sense. The man I've married is a convoluted mystery, and I no longer think I have time to figure out if it's one I should unravel.

There's no easy way out of this for me. Running away from a marriage like mine is unheard of. It's unfathomable. But my gut instinct is telling me that's exactly what I need to do. That if I stay, my baby and I will meet the same fate that Bria and Marcus did.

I stay in the bath for a long time, until my skin has started to prune and the water starts to go cold, and I look at my pile of clothes next to the tub. The diary is still tucked underneath, and I know I can't put it back where I found it, not without risking getting caught. I'm going to have to hide it somewhere that, hopefully, David won't look.

Wrapping a towel around myself, I bundle the diary into my clothes, heading upstairs to our room. My stomach tightens when I see David already in bed, propped up against the pillows with a book in hand. I clutch the clothes tighter, as if the diary might fall out and give me away at any moment. The only thing I can think to do is walk quickly to the laundry hamper, stuffing the clothes and diary down inside and hoping I can retrieve it later. For the first time, I'm glad there's no regular staff that might sweep away the laundry in the morning—right now, David relies on a weekly service to take it, and that's still a few days away.

David doesn't look at me as I slip into bed, but I can feel a shift in the air, the sudden tension of his body beside mine. I slide down under the covers, facing away from him, and I'm reminded with a rush of the night he came home drunk from the party—his hands sliding over me, the way he touched me when he thought I was asleep, the way he whispered even then that I wanted him. As if it was a reassurance, a reminder to himself that even asleep he wasn't making me do anything I didn't want to do.

After what feels like a very long time, his light switches off. It's dark, only the faint moonlight coming through the balcony doors lighting the room, and I feel that prickling sensation wash over me again. I can hear David breathing behind me, his hand in the space between our bodies, and I go very still when I feel his fingers brush along my lower back, just under the edge of my tank top.

"I want you." His voice is low and quiet, and I feel my breath catch in my throat. He's never said it like that before, like he's *asking* for what he so often says is his, what he tells me that I'm always willing to give him no matter the circumstances. "*Cara mia—*"

I close my eyes, and for a moment, I want to say yes. There are so many reasons why. I feel warm and lethargic after the bath and the small amount of wine, and the way he's been tonight makes me want to give him another chance. His questions about my family, about my *feelings*, his allusion to the possibility that I might be telling him the truth about Ibiza, and now this—

It makes me want to believe that he's trying. But how many times have I wondered that before? And now, with everything I've found out, a more sinister thought slips into my head.

Is he doing this because he suspects that I've caught him? Because he thinks that if he gets me to lower my guard, I'll slip, and he can find out just how much I know? Whether or not I know too much?

My stomach knots, and I wonder if I'm being paranoid. If I'm throwing away a chance at something close to happiness with my husband on suspicions and conjecture. If I'm planning to try to run away from a man who has every means at his disposal to catch me because of something that I've pieced together without any real assurance that this is the truth.

If I'm making it all worse by telling him no tonight—the only time I ever have.

"I'm tired," I whisper, without looking back at him. I know, in that moment, as the words slip out of my mouth, that my decision is made. That I can't stay here, growing more and more afraid and isolated day by day, risking my child's safety and mine.

This life is almost impossible to leave. But I have to try.

I wonder, as his fingers go still against my skin, if he's going to ignore what I said. If he's going to keep touching me, arousing me the way he knows he can. I haven't outright said *no*, but the words hover in the air, and I wonder if he's going to pretend not to understand.

He hesitates, just a moment. And then his hand drops away from my back, leaving me feeling strangely bereft as he rolls onto his back, and the room is silent and still.

I lie there for a long time, wondering if the decision I've made is a mistake. If I've got it all wrong.

If I'll ever really know for sure, one way or another.

29

AMALIE

Over the next week, I make plans to leave. I tell myself with every small thing I do that I haven't left *yet*, that I can still change my mind, that it's not too late. That I can forget all of this, and go back to living the life I was always told I was born for. That I can decide to *not* be afraid of my husband, and the possibilities of what he did before.

I manage to hide the diary again, back where I found it. The stress and anxiety worsen my pregnancy symptoms again, and I use that as an excuse to avoid David touching me, wondering every time if this will be the moment when he decides he's had enough of indulging my whims and takes what I know he must want. I can feel the way he looks at me when we're eating meals together or sitting in bed, the tension constantly running through him, and I wait for the moment when he explodes. It feels like there's an unspoken truce between us, although not one that we arranged or agreed on. It's almost as if we're each waiting for the other to step over some unknown line, and throw our marriage back into turmoil—and it's almost worse than fighting, because I never know what that line is or what will tip us over.

That, too, drives my sense of urgency to leave before something happens that will prevent it, before I get caught. I have my first appointment with the doctor David wants me to go to in Providence in two weeks, and I use that as my marker—as the point in time by which I know I need to be gone.

All of the little rebellions that I practiced with Claire, what seems like a lifetime ago, come in handy now. How to slip away from my security after the board meetings that I go to over the next two weeks, so I can go to one of three pawn shops where I managed to find and sell some of the jewelry I've collected over the years. I'm grateful, for once, that I'm not sentimental about my family—I can only imagine how my mother would feel seeing some of her jewelry handed over to sit behind glass, sold for far less than it's worth. I collect the cash day by day, taking out small withdrawals from the credit card that David gave me—not enough for him to think anything of, but enough to bolster the small savings that I'm collecting. I hide the money in the closet, behind my clothes in my dresser, anywhere I can think of that David won't bother to look, and day by day, I try to think of how I'm actually going to pull this off. How I'm going to disappear, and how I'm going to hide when he inevitably tries to track me down.

The truth is that I don't have a good plan. I don't have much of anything beyond the fact that I know I can't use my real name or any kind of card that can be tracked. I don't know where I'm going to go, except that it needs to be far from Chicago or Boston. I can't leave the country without a passport or identification, and I don't know anyone who could make me falsified documents. It's never been more clear to me how thick the bars are that cage the women in my world—but I'm determined to not end up like Bria.

I'm determined to keep myself and my baby safe, even if I have to make it up as I go.

I plan to leave two nights before my appointment. I slip away to the library that afternoon, looking up the closest bus station and writing down the directions on a slip of paper that I tuck into my purse. It will be a long walk, but if I go at night and after David is asleep, if I'm quiet and careful, he won't know I'm gone until the morning. And by the time he's managed to track down where I've gone, hopefully, I will have managed to slip onto another bus, another train—until I'm far enough away that I can disappear.

As for the rest of it—how to survive without identification or a social security number or anything like that in a world that relies on it—I tell myself I'll figure it out when the time comes. For now, all I can focus on is getting away—and doing whatever I need to in order to ensure David's guard is down when I do.

He picks up on my mood at dinner, the night I plan to leave. We're sitting with takeout from the Italian place that he brought home the first night I was here after our wedding—a coincidence that I try not to think too much about—and I push my bolognese around my plate, unable to even touch the half glass of wine that David didn't fight me on tonight. My stomach is in knots, and no matter how much I tell myself that I need to hide my anxiety, I can't seem to entirely pull it off.

"What's wrong?" David sets his fork down, looking at me with an expression that tells me he might finally have had enough of my aloofness for the past two weeks. "You've been acting like I'm going to bite you since we talked while you were having your bath that night. I've left you alone and given you space, but this is exhausting, Amalie. What's going on?"

I bite my lip, forcing back the retort that I want to let slip out. *You're exhausting. Our life together is exhausting.* I want to tell him that and more, to let everything I've been keeping inside for what feels like so long now, but I can't. I can't risk it, and so instead, what comes out is the truth and not, all at the same time.

"I miss you," I whisper, and David's eyebrows go up before he can stop himself and mask his surprise. I reach over, almost impulsively, and brush my fingers over his wrist. "I miss—"

"I think I know what you miss." His voice sounds faintly hoarse, and I see his fingers flex against the wood of the table, his gaze flicking down toward the end of it as if he's remembering what he did to me there. I see him swallow hard, his gaze darkening as he looks at me, and then suddenly, he stands up, pushing his chair back as he reaches for me.

For a brief second, as he pulls me up out of my seat and kisses me, I forget that I'm doing this to placate him. I forget that this is supposed to be a means of making him think I'm his, to distract him so that there's no chance of him suspecting that I might sneak away tonight. His mouth is warm and firm on mine, his arm going around my waist as he kisses me with the urgency of a man who has been waiting for this, for even the slightest hint that I want him. The realization of that, of the thin thread of self-control that he must have been hanging onto, makes me feel weak with desire, my body sinking into his as his mouth devours mine.

"Upstairs," he whispers, backing me towards the doorway, our dinner forgotten. His hands are gripping my waist, his lips brushing against mine again and again with every step, as if he can't stand to stop kissing me. As if nearly two weeks of deprivation, after he'd fucked me nearly every night of our brief marriage, has been almost too much to bear.

The stairs feel impossibly long, as if there are far too many between us and the bedroom. He shoves the door to our room open, leaving it halfway ajar as we move back towards the bed, and I feel a sudden, unexpected pang at the thought that this is the last night.

My last night with him—not just here in this room, but if all goes to plan, *ever*. The last time I'll touch him, kiss him, and the last time he'll do the same. I wonder, as his hands slide over me, dragging my shirt up over my head as his mouth finds the hollow of my throat, if this isn't what I think it is. If this is a betrayal, rather than an escape.

I feel certain that he'll never forgive me if he catches me, either way.

David's fingers undo the clasp of my bra with swift dexterity, dropping the garment to the floor along with my shirt as he kisses a path down between my breasts, cupping them in his hands as his tongue slides over my nipple. "These were beautiful when I first saw them," he whispers hoarsely, teeth grazing my sensitive flesh as I gasp. "But like this—"

I've gone up half a cup size since I realized I was pregnant, my chest fuller and more sensitive than before. David's mouth sliding over the curve of my breasts, his lips fastening around one nipple as his fingers toy with the other, sends jolts of sensation over my skin. I run my fingers through his hair, the ache between my thighs building, and I remind myself that I'm supposed to be doing this for reasons other than my own pleasure tonight.

I want him so satisfied that he passes out, so thoroughly sated that he has no reason to suspect me of anything. I'm tempted to let him continue to focus on me, to drive me wild with pleasure, but I force myself to fall to my knees instead, sinking down in front of him as I reach for the button of his pants.

"I want you in my mouth," I whisper, and once again, it's somewhere between the truth and not. I can't let myself be swept up in how much I *do* want, or I'll forget what it is that I'm doing here. I'll lose my resolve, and then what happens?

I might meet the same fate that Bria did. It might be my name that the next woman finds, wondering what happened.

Even that thought isn't enough to stop me from wanting him, now that we've started. I hear David groan as I slide my hand against the thick ridge of his cock, slipping him free and wrapping my fingers around the base. He breathes my name as I press my lips against the slick head, tongue lapping up the salty taste of his arousal, his fingers tangling in my hair. When I wrap my lips around him, sliding my mouth down the rigid length, the sound he makes is half-choked with need.

"Your mouth feels so good," he breathes, his hips twitching forward with the effort to not thrust into my mouth. I'm startled by how gentle he's being, the lack of demands, the way he seems entirely willing to let me be the one in charge. *Did he miss me that much,* I wonder, *that he's happy just to have me touching him again?* It doesn't fit with what I've known of him before, and I feel that flicker of fear again, the paranoia that I'm being set up somehow.

I take him as deeply as I can, feeling his swollen head rub against the back of my tongue, trying not to wince at how hard the wooden floor is against my knees. All I can think about is how to make it as good for him as possible, sliding my tongue over the ridged veins, around the edge of his cockhead, against the soft skin beneath as I suck—all the things that I know by now drive him closer and closer to the edge.

"*God, cara mia*—" His voice is thick, his accent rasping as he suddenly pulls free of my mouth, startling me. "I need to be inside of you. I need—"

He pulls me to my feet, his mouth crashing down on mine again as he guides me towards the bed, his hands feverishly plucking at the remainder of my clothing and his. We end up on the bed with me stripped bare, his shirt hanging open, and his cock hard against his belly, his eyes dark with desire as he pins me back against the pillows. "I want you," he breathes, his lips pressing hard against mine, and I know what he wants to hear in return.

"I want you, too." I don't have to lie. I *do* want him—my entire body is taut with it, the slick wetness between my legs sticky on my thighs, my blood throbbing in my veins. "I want—" I can't quite say the words. They catch in my throat, and I push at his chest, urging him onto his back. It only takes him a second to realize, and his eyes widen. For a moment, I think he's going to refuse, that he's going to want to be the one in charge, as he so often is. It's always him atop me, pinning me against the bed, the table, bending me over whatever surface is at hand. I don't think I've been the one on top since Ibiza, when I still barely knew what to do in bed.

But he rolls onto his back, bringing me with him so that I'm atop him, his cock brushing between my thighs. I lean forward as I push his pants down his hips, kissing him with his cock trapped between us, feeling the heat of it against my stomach. I can't resist the urge to grind against him as I do, as his hips lift off of the bed to kick off his pants, and I feel more than hear him groan against my mouth as he throbs between us.

"I'll put *you* on your back if you don't put my cock in you," he growls against my lips, his fingers sinking into the soft flesh of my thighs, and I can't help but moan. "You like that, don't you? When I tell you what I want." One of his hands sinks into my hair as the other guides his cock between my legs, the swollen head slipping inside of me as my back arches and he bites at my lower lip. "Even on top, you want it like this."

I whimper as I feel him fill me, his hands on my hips again as he drags me down onto his length. I'd thought I was going to take charge like this, that I'd be the one fucking *him*, and somehow I find the strength to break the kiss, sitting up atop him as I brace my hands against his chest and start to roll my hips.

"Or like this?" I whisper as I see his gaze sweep over me, taking in the view of me riding him, my thighs splayed open on either side of his hips. I arch upwards against his grip, sliding up until only the very tip of his cock is inside of me, and then back down again, grinding along his length with every inch as David's head tips back, a low groan of pleasure escaping him.

"*Fuck—*" he breathes. "God, you feel so fucking good. So tight and wet—" One hand leaves my hip, his fingers finding my clit and circling it as I grind down onto him. "*Yes, bellisima.* Take my cock, just like that—" His voice is hoarse, rasping over every word as his hips thrust up into me, and I can see that glazed look of pleasure on his face. It thrills me, making my heart race, pushing me closer to the edge, too. When we're like this, together, everything else fades away. The things that I'm afraid of disappear, and there's only this—my husband's hands on me, his gaze locked on mine, the two of us sharing an intimacy that I never knew before him.

But it's not real. I remind myself of that, trying not to lose my resolve. I feel another orgasm building as he thrusts into me, his fingers rubbing a steady rhythm between my legs, and I close my eyes tightly as I kiss him, refusing to let the tears fall that well up in my eyes. If he sees me crying, he'll want to know why—and right now, I don't know if I can lie well enough to fool him.

His fingers sink into the flesh of my hip, hard enough to bruise, a reminder of him that I'll have tomorrow. I feel the heat of his tongue tangle with mine as his hips jerk beneath me, flooding me with a different kind of heat as he comes, and I arch against him, moaning as my climax follows his. I tighten around him, feeling him throb deep inside of me, and it feels so good that, for a moment, I can't breathe or move or think. I feel his hands sliding over me, holding me against him, and I wish for one bright, painful moment that I never met him in Ibiza at all.

But even that wouldn't help. It wouldn't keep us from ending up here, with me torn between loving him and leaving him, afraid that I'm making a mistake and terrified of what happens if I stay.

Our marriage was arranged regardless of whether I met him in Ibiza or not. Even if I'd never gone, even if I'd never walked up to him in that club, David Carravella would still have ended up standing in the living room of my childhood home, introduced to me as my future husband.

This was inevitable. Now, it's just a matter of what I'm going to do about it.

The fear is almost crippling as I lie in bed next to him later that night, waiting for him to be fully asleep. I collected the money earlier—it's tucked in my jewelry box on my vanity, waiting for me to get it out as I slip out of the bedroom. I left clothes in one of the guest rooms so that I could change without waking David up or arousing suspicion—my purse is there too, the directions to the bus station hidden inside. I go over the plan again and again until I hear his steady, even breathing, imagining each step until I'm out of the house and slip away into the darkness. What I hadn't expected, in all my planning, is how hard it is to find the courage to get up and leave.

Or how much I would wish that things were different, as I look at David sleeping next to me. The way the good memories would come flooding back in, reminding me that it wasn't always like this. That sometimes, it seemed like there was a chance we could be happy.

What finally gets me up is the thought that once upon a time, Bria might have thought that, too.

I'm grateful that David is a heavy sleeper. The hardest thing I've ever had to do is move slowly—I want to rush, to snatch everything I need and run—but that makes it more likely he'll wake up and catch me. With every slow step, I wait to hear the sound of the bed shifting, of David sitting up, asking me blearily *what the hell are you doing, Amalie?* My fingers shake as I open the jewelry box, almost slipping and dropping the lid, and I try to breathe as I take the envelope of money out from under what I have left. I consider taking some of it with me, to pawn later, but that feels like asking to be mugged.

The blinking light of the security camera flickers in the corner of my eye. David will see what I've done as soon as he looks at the tape, but that doesn't matter. I'll be gone, and I can't think of anything that he'll be able to guess from the tape that he wouldn't know simply by virtue of the fact that I've left.

I creep out of the bedroom, wincing with every step as I wait for the floors to creak and give me away. I feel as if I'm constantly on the verge of bursting into frightened tears, my throat tight with fear and my chest aching. I press one hand to my stomach as I walk, reminding myself why I'm doing this, why I'm risking so much, why I'm running away. Even if I could risk myself on the chance that I've gotten this all wrong, I can't risk my baby.

The room where I've stashed my clothes is the next floor down. I change as quickly as I can, listening for any sounds of David waking up above me. I don't know what excuse I would come up with now if he caught me—there's no pretending I woke up thirsty or needing to pee or just couldn't sleep. I'm fully dressed, and he wouldn't believe me even if I tried to lie.

I reach for my purse—an oversized leather tote that I've stuffed a change of clothes into—and carefully head for the stairs. There's no avoiding some of the creaky places in the wood, and I curse the old mansion all over again as I make it down to the first floor, breathing hard, trying to listen for any signs David is awake. I don't hear him, but I could have missed it. There's no guarantee of anything until I'm out of the house.

There's less security at the back, and they're easy to slip past, especially at night. I've done it before during the day, and I know where they are—that's not what I'm worried about.

I hesitate at the edge of the dining room, the path to the back door clear in front of me. The wood floors creak under my feet again, the bag heavy on my shoulder, and I close my eyes. The chill of the house feels like it's creeping into my bones, freezing me in place, keeping me here. I know it's all my imagination, but I feel as if I'll never make it to that back door. As if I'll move slowly, like a dream, my feet moving but my body never really making it anywhere. As if I'll never get out of here.

If I'm wrong about all of this, I'm leaving behind a life of comfort and security for the unknown. For a world that I don't know how to live in. I've never been on my own. I've never had the opportunity to try. As I stand there, working up the courage, I wonder if doing this isn't more terrifying than simply staying.

And then, just as I'm about to force myself forward, I feel a hand clamp around my wrist.

I scream. It's an ear-piercing shriek, shattering the air between me and the dark figure that I see behind me when I twist around, trying to wrench my hand free. It's David—I recognize his shape, his build, and I can see his features dimly in the moonlight shining in through the dining room, making him into something eerie and terrifying. The monster that I've been afraid he is, come to life.

Panic floods me. He says something, but I can't hear it over the sound of my blood rushing in my ears, my heart beating painfully in my chest. I lurch backward, twisting in his grasp, my shoulder burning with sudden pain as I try to yank myself free. I stumble forward, and he follows me, pulling me back, an awful tug of war that I'm suddenly certain is a game of life and death. There's no pretending away what I was doing now. He knows, and I'm going to pay for it.

David pulls me into his chest, and I lash out, screaming and scratching, clawing at his face with my free hand. I drive my knee up towards his groin, shoving, kicking, trying to get away in a feral panic that overrules any common sense or strategy. I feel him trying to subdue me with both hands as I twist in his grasp, and he trips as I kick at his ankles, the momentum of my attempt to get away taking us both down to the floor. My purse flies off of my shoulder, skidding a foot away on the wooden floor, and I feel a sharp pang of fear. I have to get to it—all the money I have is in there. Without it, I won't be able to get a bus ticket. I won't be able to leave.

"Amalie!" David shouts my name, still trying to pin me down. "Amalie, *stop*! Stop struggling. You're going to hurt yourself—the baby. *Amalie*! What the hell is going on?"

He shouts the words into my face, his expression furious and confused all at once, and the fear I feel as I look up into his darkened, angry face is worse than anything I've ever felt in all my life. It's numbing, cold as ice, so deep and all-consuming that I know I'll never forget how it feels.

"No!" I scream, thrashing underneath him, every thought driven out of my head except how desperate I am to get free. "You're going to kill me like you did Bria! Let me go! *Let me fucking go!*"

I shriek the last words, kicking and bucking against him, and it takes me a moment to realize that David has gone utterly still above me, his fingers bruising my wrists as he looks down at me with an expression of utter shock.

"*What* did you just say?"

30

DAVID

I'm not entirely sure that I've heard her right at first. I can't have. I look down at my struggling wife, see the fear on her face, and I realize that she means it.

She's afraid of me.

She's afraid I'm going to *kill* her.

I don't even know what to say for a moment. For once, the instinct to lash out at her, to tell her that she's overreacting, that she's paranoid, simply isn't there. It's entirely true for once—but all I can think is that I can't believe it somehow got this far. That my refusal to open up the wounds of the past led to *this*.

"Amalie." I try to speak as slowly and carefully as I can. "Wherever you think you're going, however you thought you were getting past my security, you're not going to now. They're alerted by now from all the noise."

"I don't care!" She bucks against me again, her voice cracking and breaking with fear. My heart wrenches in my chest, seeing her like this. I never imagined I would make her so afraid. It feels like the past repeating itself all over again, and I try to loosen my grip on her wrists just enough to avoid hurting her. She feels terribly fragile to me suddenly, and I have the overwhelming urge to pick her up and hold her to my chest, to protect her from herself. From this fear that she's whipped up until it's become a frothing, living thing that's on the verge of destroying us both.

"Amalie, *please*." I risk letting go of one of her wrists, cupping the side of her face in my palm. It hurts to see her flinch back, her eyes widening as if she thinks I'm going to strike her. "Please, just come with me and sit down in the living room. We can talk. You have this all wrong. *Please*."

I've never begged her for anything before. I never thought I would. I can see the realization of that in her face, the way it sinks in as she slowly stops struggling. When I see the tears glistening at the corners of her eyes, it feels like my heart is cracking open.

"Amalie," I whisper her name, and she goes lax underneath me, nodding slowly.

I pull back, letting go of her wrist as I push myself up to my knees and give her a hand to help her up, too. She's trembling, and I start to reach for her, but when she flinches back, I stop myself, holding my hands up to show that I'm not going to touch her.

She waits for me to step out of the doorway, and for a moment, I think she's going to make a break for it again. But she scoops up the bag that fell onto the floor, holding it close to her as if she can't bear to let go of it, and follows me into the closest living room.

It's the huge, formal room—still only partially renovated, with the half-pulled apart fireplace and only one couch not covered in a drop cloth. I'm suddenly aware of all the things Amalie said about this house that I didn't want to hear—that it doesn't feel like a home, that it feels cold and unwelcoming, like a mausoleum to people who are gone. A house filled with ghosts.

All I've been able to see is what the house will become, when I'm finished with it. But I understand, looking around, how she wouldn't be able to visualize what I always have. After all, she's never seen it the way I did growing up here.

So much of how I've gone wrong bursts into clarity, all the ways I could have done this differently, and I'm so terribly afraid that it's too late.

I don't know what I'll do if it is.

She sits very far from me, on the opposite end of the couch, her hands knotted together in her lap and her posture tense. I can see the wary look on her face, and I switch on the lamp on the side table, bathing the room in a soft golden glow that feels quiet and intimate. I want her to feel safe. I want her to see the sincerity on my face as I tell her what I have to say—what I hope she'll listen to—even if it doesn't make a difference in the end.

"I'm sorry," I say softly. "I should have told you everything, Amalie. I never dreamed you would think—"

"How?" she asks icily, glaring at me. "How would you possibly think I wouldn't come to that conclusion? When you wouldn't tell me anything, when everyone tiptoes around what happened as if it's a deadly secret, when I found their graves and Bria's diary—you must think I'm an idiot. Now you want me to believe I have it all wrong?"

"You do," I tell her, as calmly as I can manage. "I'm not saying I don't have some fault in it—in what happened before, and what's happened between us. I'm just saying that it's not what you think it is. I should have explained it all; I see that now. And I will—if you'll let me."

Her lips are pressed so tightly together that the edges of her mouth look white. She nods, a small, quick motion, and she looks as if she's poised to run at any moment. It makes my heart ache to see her like this, small and afraid, her eyes fixed on me like a terrified rabbit's.

"I told you this was our family home," I say quietly, keeping my voice as even and calm as I can. "The Carravella family has been living here since we came here from Sicily—there was no talk of moving out, until my mother passed away and my father got remarried. The house had started to fall into some disrepair by then, as old houses do, and she wanted nothing to do with it. She wanted to move to Boston, and my father gave in to make her happy." I see Amalie flinch at that, and I let out a slow sigh. "I'm not saying I was right to be angry with you for hating the house because of that. I should have made an effort to see that it was different, that you were lonely and felt isolated—not just that it wasn't 'nice' enough for you. I'm sorry. I truly am."

"So they moved to Boston." Amalie's voice is a hushed whisper. "You didn't even tell me she's your stepmother. I thought she was your mother when we visited. I felt like an idiot when I found the grave and realized."

"I'm sorry." I spread my hands out, feeling entirely at a loss for how to make this better. "I'm going to keep saying that over and over, Amalie, while I'm telling you this story. I want you to believe that I truly am—but I understand if you don't."

I pause for a moment, watching her. "My brother inherited the house after my father and his new wife moved to Boston. I stayed here too, with him and his new bride. He started renovating the house almost immediately—Bria might not have loved him, but she loved the house. She thought it was beautiful, and she threw herself into helping with it. Their marriage seemed decent enough at first— she got pregnant quickly and occupied herself with the house, and my brother wasn't particularly affectionate with her; he also wasn't cruel. She and I were friends. I—" I take a slow breath, trying to think of how to say what I need to without Amalie misinterpreting it. "I cared about her. I didn't *want* her, not like that. Lucio being married to her, the two of them having a son—it solidified my freedom. There was no need for me to get married or produce heirs; he'd taken care of all of that. But he saw it as—something else."

"Oh." Amalie looks at me, and I can see a glimmer of understanding in her eyes. That she's beginning to see where this story goes.

"He got jealous. He was—possessive of her. Lucio was a difficult man. He was never particularly kind or caring with anyone, and he tried to be gentler with her at first, but once he got something into his head—it was impossible to get it out. He was stubborn, and a hard person to be around when he was angry. He got it into his head that Bria and I had something. That maybe Marcus wasn't his at all. That maybe she'd even been with others."

"You mean the same things you accused me of." Amalie's voice cuts through the conversation, sharp and angry. "You sound just like him, then, you know that? You must, hearing yourself say all of this—"

My chest tightens with a deep pang of guilt—and regret. "I do," I say quietly. "I didn't see it at the time, just as I'm sure he didn't. But I see it now. I would never have done what he did, though. You have to believe that, Amalie. If you'd gotten the results that the baby was mine, I wouldn't have questioned it."

"And he did?"

I nod slowly. "Bria was angry with him, but she had a paternity test done. He was convinced she was still lying to him. Everything she said, he twisted it somehow. I think he pushed her into seeing someone else—or maybe it was just a friend. I still don't know who the man was—"

"The man in the pictures." Amalie swallows hard. "The ones I saw in the attic."

"Lucio had a private detective following her. Taking the pictures. He lost his temper when he found out. She came home one night while I was gone, and he was drunk and in a rage. They argued, and he hit her—nearly broke her nose. Marcus heard the noise, got away from the nanny, and came down. Lucio was—" It takes me a moment to say it out loud. Even all these years later, it's still difficult to remember. "Lucio tried to kill Marcus. His son. He had a gun—and somehow, Bria got it away from him. She swore she didn't mean to kill Lucio, that the gun went off while she was trying to get it. That might be true, but it might not. I think she wasn't in the wrong either way, to tell you the truth. Not with her son's life on the line."

Amalie is looking at me wide-eyed, her expression still distrustful. "I understand if you think I'm making this all up," I tell her quietly. "I know it's a lot to take in. I know you might think I'm trying to hide what I did by blaming someone else. But I'll admit to my wrongs. I—"

"The clothes." Amalie bites her lip. "I found bloodstained clothes in a room that I think was Bria's. Or at least had some of her things in it. That was—" she shudders. "Why would you keep those?"

"She kept them. I didn't know for a long time, not until after she was gone. She hid a lot of things well. As for why I kept them after that—I don't have a good reason for it. I suppose after she hung onto it, out of guilt—it felt strange to go against her wishes and throw them away. I can't explain it in a way that makes sense. Grief makes people do strange things."

"You're trying to tell me you grieved her? You didn't—"

"I didn't kill her." It sounds so preposterous coming out of my mouth, even now, but I know I have to take Amalie's fears seriously if I want to have even a chance of her believing the truth. "My family wanted to cover it all up—what happened to Lucio, Bria's part in his death, everything. It was made to look like an accident, and they convinced me to marry her—to ensure that she was taken care of and Marcus still had some normalcy. They thought the drama of me stepping in to care for my brother's widow would distract everyone from what had really happened, and they were right."

"I read her diary." Amalie blurts it out suddenly, her hands twisting together in her lap. "It was in the same box with the clothes." She bites her lip, still looking tense and nervous. "I saw what she said about the two of you—about you wanting children, and she—"

"Our marriage was difficult. She didn't want to sleep with me on our wedding night, and I didn't push her. She said she didn't care if I slept with others; she had no expectation that I would be faithful, and I tried that for a while. I didn't like feeling as if I were cheating on my wife, but I wasn't willing to be celibate, either. It seemed like a decent arrangement, if not a happy one exactly, until my father started to ask why she wasn't pregnant again yet."

"He wanted more heirs." Amalie's voice is a whisper, and I can tell that she's telling the truth. She did read the diary—she must have, to know this much and have drawn the conclusions that she did—and I'm not sure how that makes me feel. It feels like an invasion of Bria's privacy, who I still feel some protectiveness over...but at the same time, it might make it easier for her to believe me.

"He did," I confirm quietly. "So Bria went to bed with me, but she was always stiff and cold, and made it feel as if I were forcing her. She wanted to use a doctor instead—to do IVF—and I wish I'd handled it differently. I thought she was being ridiculous. I'd done so much, and she wanted nothing to do with me. We weren't even friends any longer, the way we'd been before, except in small moments when she broke through how depressed she was. I think she resented Marcus for keeping her trapped in a marriage that she wouldn't have been in otherwise, and she felt guilty for it. She projected that onto me, accused me of hating her son because he wasn't really mine, and being desperate to have a child of my own with her. She made me feel like a monster every time we were in bed together."

"So why not use a doctor the way she asked?" Amalie can't quite look at me as she says it. I can see her thinking, trying to sort through it all, to decide if she believes me.

"I don't know," I admit, my voice tight with regret. "I should have. I *was* resentful, but of her, not her son. I was angry and hurt, and I felt trapped, too. None of that makes up for the mistakes I made, of course. I can't ever make any of it right. And it's worse, because I see that I made some of the same mistakes with you, after we were married. That I started to repeat the past. And now—"

"Now, what?" Amalie looks up at me, and I can see the tears glinting in her eyes again. Strangely, it gives me the smallest bit of hope. She doesn't look as angry, or as afraid. I think she might believe I'm telling the truth. I think, at the very least, that she might *want* to.

"Now, I don't know if I'll have a chance to make it right," I say softly.

Amalie bites her lip, looking away. "Just tell me the rest."

"I didn't realize until after we were married that I'd fallen for Bria long before, when we were friends—when she was married to Lucio. I cared for her, and told myself that it wasn't that kind of love. But after she was mine—I realized that I did feel something for her that was beyond friendship, beyond her being my sister-in-law. I don't know if I was ever *in love* with her—but I was getting there. It could have been that, if she hadn't pushed me away like she did. What happened—" I stop for a moment, struggling to find the words once again. To help Amalie understand how awful it all was, and how much I regret the part I played in it.

"Marcus got sick. Nothing malicious or strange—a flu that he got a particularly bad case of. Bria lost her mind. She thought she was being punished somehow, that it was her fault for wanting out of the marriage, all kinds of things that made no sense. She overheard a conversation—"

"About heirs," Amalie finishes quietly. "With your father. It was in the diary."

I nod. "I was devastated at how sick Marcus was. She just couldn't see it. The conversation was pragmatism and mollifying my father, nothing more. But Bria saw it as a betrayal, as proof that I didn't care about Marcus, that I didn't care about her—only the family line." I let out a slow breath, feeling tears prick at the back of my eyes, even after all this time. "When he died, we were both devastated. Bria was, of course, inconsolable. She had every right to be. I didn't realize how bad it was, though. Not until I came home one night to find the bathroom door locked—and her in the tub, dead. She'd tried to slit her wrist—I saw some blood on her sleeve, but I suppose she couldn't go through with it that way. So she took every pill she could find."

My voice is flat, emotionless, because if I say it any other way, I know I'll break down. I still see the vision of her in that bathtub in nightmares sometimes, and I still wonder what I could have done differently. If I could have changed anything at all.

Amalie's face is a mask of horror. "That's why you barged into the bathroom that night," she whispers. "I thought you were just being disrespectful—treating me like you owned me. But you were afraid."

I nod, trying hard to control my emotions, to finish the story. "All I could think was that I'd made you so unhappy that you were going to do the same. I should have told you that, that night. I should have explained why. I should have explained so many goddamn things to you, Amalie. I've made so many mistakes."

"I would have tried to understand if you did," she says softly. "It would have helped. I didn't want things to be this way—"

"I've been cold to you. Cruel, sometimes. I see all of that now, looking back." The words come faster, my voice cracking, almost desperate for her to hear me out, to understand. "I was terrified of falling for you and something happening. That you would hate me, or leave, or be hurt. That I would care about our child and lose them. It was easier to push you away, to accuse you of things that I had no reason to believe, to pretend that I hated you. I thought it would be easier if you hated me, but that made it so much worse."

"I wondered why you always wanted to know that I wanted you," Amalie whispers. "I understood, after the diary. After—reading about you and Bria, the way you—" She bites her lip. "I knew I cared, too, because I hated reading about you in bed with someone else. Even if she was your wife then."

"I hated the idea of you with anyone else in Ibiza," I admit. "I thought I wanted you to have done something wrong, so we could hate each other. So we could never have any chance of being hurt. But all that happened was we ended up hurting each other anyway. And you thought—" I swallow hard. "I could never have hurt her, Amalie. I could barely stand to touch her when she didn't want me. Everything has been made so much worse because I wasn't honest with you."

She nods without a word, her eyes glistening in the low golden light. "You should have told me," she whispers. "Now, after all of this—"

"I know." I feel my chest clench, my heart wrenching as if someone has clutched it in their hand and twisted. "I can't make it up to you, Amalie. I can't change it. I can only tell you how much I regret it—and that I understand if you want a divorce after finding out about all of this. I wouldn't blame you. I'll find a way to make that happen without it hurting you or your family. I'll make sure the child is provided for. If—"

"If it's yours?" She bites out the words, cutting me off, and I shake my head.

"I believe you, Amalie," I say quietly, feeling my heart wrench all over again. "I'm sorry that I made you think that I didn't—that I tried to believe that I didn't—to push you away. I'm sorry that I treated you so badly that it made you think something so terrible of me. I will make sure you're both taken care of."

Amalie is quiet for a long moment, her fingers twisting together in her lap. "I have things to apologize for, too," she says finally, her voice a low whisper as she looks up at me. "I didn't understand why you were so hot and cold—why things were so different from when we were in Ibiza. The things I found made me suspicious, and I—I let my imagination run away with me. I'm sorry—"

"You have nothing to be sorry for," I tell her firmly. "Your imagination ran away with you because I refused to give you any answers. I didn't give you the space to be able to come to me and tell me what you found—whenever you tried, I got angry. I was so angry about what happened for so long—and guilty, too, in some ways. I didn't want to talk about it or bring it into our marriage, but it started to eat away at it anyway. I could have avoided so much if I'd been honest with you. None of this is your fault, Amalie."

"My family has skeletons, too," she says softly. "You know that. My father's death, my brother's exile—all because he had ambitions that he wouldn't put to rest. I don't know if I'll ever see Andre again. I don't entirely know if I want to. But I would have understood, David. And I would have tried to help, if I could. I—I cared about you, in Ibiza. If we'd started the marriage differently, things might have been—"

"I know." I swallow hard, trying not to think of the irony in all of this, that in attempting to push her away to avoid a broken heart, I've ended up with one anyway. I can feel the hurt of her leaving already, even with her sitting right in front of me. "I'll talk to my father tomorrow."

"I don't know if I want a divorce," Amalie says, startling me. "I wasn't even sure that I wanted to leave. We've had—moments. But I was so afraid."

"I'm so sorry—"

"Just let me finish." Her voice is stronger now, a little more sure. "I don't know what our marriage would be like if we actually tried, David. I have no idea. It doesn't have to be all parties and wild sex like Ibiza—but what we've had so far, so much of it has been awful. But I've seen the moments where it's clear that there's something here.

That we both care about each other, when we're not pushing each other away."

"I was awful to you on purpose, to do exactly that. I'll always regret that." I feel defeated, like a weight has settled on my shoulders that I don't think I can ever shrug off. *I've ruined two marriages.* It feels like the most terrible failure.

"The baby is yours." Amalie looks at me directly, her gaze taking on a hint of that rebelliousness that's become so familiar to me. "There's no question of that. I might have toyed with you from time to time to try to make you doubt, to piss you off because I was so angry with you—and I was wrong for that—but I couldn't bring myself to want anyone else when we were in Ibiza. There was never anyone but you. I *need* you to believe that, David. It's the only way that there can be even a chance of a way forward for us."

"I do believe you." I put every bit of sincerity that I can muster into it. "And I won't let any harm come to either of you. I will do anything you want, give you anything you need. I promise you that."

Amalie is quiet for a long moment. I see her touch her stomach, her fingers grazing over the front of her blouse. "So what now?" she asks softly, and I can see the question for what it is. It's her, giving me a chance. Waiting to see what I'll say, at this moment when she's chosen not to run away from me.

I stand up, slowly, holding out a hand to her. "Do you want to try?" I ask, as gently as I possibly can. I look into her eyes, this woman that I've married, who I've never given a chance to be what I need. Who, I know, deserves so much better than me.

Amalie looks up at me, and for a moment, I think she's going to say no. And I know that if she did, I would let her go.

I can't keep another woman who doesn't love me caged, no matter what my family says. No matter what my father might want.

She stands up, putting her hand in mine. "Yes," she says softly. And then she steps forward and kisses me, her hand against my chest, her body leaning into mine.

Together, hand in hand, we turn to go back upstairs.

31

AMALIE

When I wake in the morning, I can't help but wonder at first if everything that happened last night was some kind of strange dream. It takes a moment for it to all come back to me—my attempts to flee the house, David catching me, the long talk on the couch. The realization that the truth was both somewhat similar to what I had suspected—and very far removed from it, all at once.

The decision we both made to try.

I'd half expected him to want sex when we came back upstairs to bed, to want to make up in the way that I imagined he'd desire. But instead, he'd simply laid back down and held out his hands in the space between us on the bed, taking mine and asking me to forgive him.

I told him the truth—that it would take time. That I couldn't promise that everything would be okay in a day, or a week, or a month. That we would have to learn to trust each other. To be vulnerable.

He said he wants to keep me safe. I want to believe him. And, I suppose, only time will tell if I can.

He's not in bed when I wake up, and I feel a pang, a sudden suspicion that maybe he wasn't as sincere as I believed. And then I look up, and I see the vase of roses on my vanity—identical to the ones that were on the dining room table what seems like so long ago now, when he'd tried to apologize to me without words. I don't have to guess at the significance of it, or that he's trying to reassure me that he meant everything he said last night.

I sit there looking at them, trying to sort through my emotions, and I hear the bedroom door creak open. David steps in, already dressed, and there's a look on his face that I've rarely seen. It's softer, happier than what I'm accustomed to.

"I was hoping you'd be awake." He comes to sit next to me on the bed, reaching for my hand. His thumb grazes over my knuckles, and he lets out a slow breath. "Have you changed your mind about trying to make things work between us? Any second thoughts in the light of day? Because if not—"

"No second thoughts," I tell him gently, curling my fingers around his. "It's still going to take time. I meant that. But I—I do want to try."

"Good. Because I've booked us a honeymoon." David smiles sheepishly at me. "I know you might say that grand gestures aren't what's needed here—but you did ask me about a honeymoon once. My response to it was—unkind, to say the least."

"I don't mind some grand gestures." I smile teasingly at him, and I see his shoulders relax, the mood lightening just a little.

"I'll try to think of what others I can make then." He reaches up, moving closer as he draws me in for a kiss. "Do you want to know where I'm taking you?"

"I think I'd prefer a surprise." I let myself lean into the kiss, long and slow, and I start to feel a flicker of hope. There is, I think, a possibility that this might work. That if we both try, we can have something better than either of us expected.

"It's going to be a little while, still. I thought it would be good to go when the parts of the house that we spend most of our time in are being heavily remodeled." He hesitates, drawing back a little. "I know you hate this house, Amalie. And in the spirit of trying to make our marriage work, if you really can't bear it, we'll move to

Boston. But I want to know if there's a way to make you happy here."

I pause, trying to think honestly if there is a chance, if I won't always be unhappy. If there's a way to not always feel haunted when I walk through it, to wipe away how much misery has happened here. "It's important to you, isn't it?" I ask cautiously, and David nods.

"I know not all the memories here are good. I know for you, so many of them aren't. But—" He stands up suddenly, taking my hand. "Come with me. Please."

Startled, all I can think of to do is nod *yes*. I follow him downstairs in my silk sleep shorts and tank top, for once not paying attention to the chill as he leads me all the way to the kitchen. "I used to watch my mother cook here," he says, gesturing at the stove. "We had a household cook, of course, but she liked to come in here and try to make things herself. The only thing that ever turned out was banana bread. I still can't eat it without thinking of her."

I stare up at him, still shocked speechless. I've never heard him tell me so much about himself before. "And in here." He leads me to the smaller dining room. "We used to have small dinners for our birthdays, until my brother and I got to that age where you hate everything your parents try to do for you. My mother—" David hesitates, glancing at me. "She didn't love the mafia life. She tried to make things feel as normal for us as possible. I think sometimes that's why my father married someone so different from her, the second time around. I think he genuinely cared for her. We had holidays in the big living room—we would all decorate. My mother refused to let the staff touch anything to decorate for Christmas. My father would never participate, but he would watch, smoking a pipe and commenting here and there. It was one of my favorite times of the year."

David turns to me, reaching for my hands and pulling me closer. "We have a few good memories here, too. In the dining room. In our bedroom. We can make more. You can have as much say in the renovations as you want. Whatever style you choose, whatever would make you happy. We can do it together. I'll even buy you a second house in Boston to decorate as you please, if you'd be willing to try here. Even just for a little while—"

I can tell he's afraid that I'm going to say no. I reach up, pressing a finger against his lips. "I didn't like it here because I was lonely," I say softly. "Because I felt isolated and alone. But if things are going to be different between us—maybe I'll feel differently about the house, too. I can't promise that I'm going to love it. But I'll try—just like we're going to try to make our marriage work. And you don't have to buy me a second house yet." I smile at him, leaning up to press a kiss against his mouth. "We'll wait and see if you need to apologize for something else, later."

"You little—" David laughs, a sound that seems to break free from him in a rush, as if he hasn't *really* laughed in a very long time. We're standing in the middle of the huge living room, and he backs me against the nearest wall, his hands in my hair as his mouth crushes against mine. He tastes like sweet coffee, his lips grazing over my mouth again and again as he leans into me, and I can feel how hard he is. There's a huge window next to us, and I laugh, tugging the drapes closed before any security can walk past and see us.

"I thought you liked getting fucked against windows." His teeth catch my lower lip, and I moan, remembering what he did to me in Ibiza.

"You can fuck me against every window in our hotel on our honeymoon. But I don't think you want your security team to see me getting railed in our own home."

"I'd have to kill anyone who looked," he agrees, his hands still tugging at my hair as he kisses me deeply again, with a hunger that takes my breath away.

He falls to his knees then, tugging down my silk shorts, so quickly that I gasp. His hand slides up my leg, hooking it over his shoulder as he spreads me open with his fingers, his tongue seeking out my clit with quick, light flicks that make me arch against his mouth.

"You're being a tease," I whisper, and he chuckles, the vibrations spreading over my skin as he looks up at me, dark eyes gleaming with lust.

"I'm going to tease you for the rest of your life, Mrs. Carravella," he murmurs. "I love the taste of you on my tongue, *cara mia*. And I want you to come for me." David presses his mouth against my folds, running his tongue through them with a long, slow lick that makes me tremble. "I want to taste how much you want me."

I tangle my hand in his hair, head falling back against the wall as I moan softly. "I want you," I breathe, feeling his tongue seek out my clit again, sliding over it in the slow fluttering licks that make me cry out. "I want you to make me come. Please make me come—"

"Patience, *bellisima*." His hand grips the side of my hip, holding me against his mouth as he drags his tongue over me again. "I'll make you come."

There's no doubt in my mind that's true. His mouth tightens against me, his tongue finding all the spots that he knows I like best, fluttering and licking, firm and insistent, and then easing off until I'm writhing against him and begging. When he sucks my clit into his mouth, groaning as if he's as aroused by my taste as I am by the sensation of what he's doing, I feel every muscle in my body unwind, the pleasure tearing through me as I moan his name and buck my hips against his mouth, knees nearly buckling from the force of it. I feel him steady me, his tongue rolling over my clit until every last spasm of my climax has stopped, and then he stands up, his mouth glistening with my arousal.

"Turn around," he growls hoarsely. "God, Amalie—"

I move without hesitation, facing the wall as he steps behind me, his cock hot and hard against my ass. I feel him nudge me there, his hips rocking slightly, and he lets out a low groan that sends shivers throughout my entire body. "I want you here, one day," he murmurs. "I want all of you, when you're ready."

And then he nudges his cock downwards, the swollen head slipping into me as I arch my back, and every thought in my head vanishes as he fills me up.

I don't know what the future holds for us. I don't know how to be married to this man, how to make him happy—or myself, truly. But we've both been given the opportunity to try. And as he sinks into me, his body molded to mine as he turns my mouth into his for a kiss, I know that I'm glad we have the chance.

I want there to be more for us. A future.

And now there might be.

—

Two months later, I find myself stepping off of our private jet into warm, humid air, the smell of sea and salt filling my senses. "The Amalfi Coast," David says, gesturing widely as we walk out onto the tarmac towards the waiting car. "I thought you might enjoy it here. The beach, shopping, excellent restaurants—Ibiza, but for grownups, I think," he adds with a laugh.

"For adults about to have a baby?" I laugh, too, pressing my hand to my stomach. I'm starting to show just a little, a slight roundness to my belly that David loves. He can't keep his hands off of me, and I've often joked in the past weeks that if it were possible for him to get me pregnant twice, he would have.

It's early evening by the time we get to the hotel. David helps me out of the car, solicitous of me, which I've noticed more and more. He's careful with me constantly, as if he's afraid something might happen to me as the pregnancy goes on, and I've tried to reassure him. To my great relief, it's something I can do now—now that he's grown more and more comfortable with talking to me about how he feels.

I don't know if David will ever be a man who speaks about his feelings in great detail, but I've learned how to read him, now that he's let me in. And I can see him trying. His love language is clearly gifts—ever since the night we agreed to work on our marriage, the house is filled with roses every day. Every meal is something he knows I like to eat and can keep down, even as the pregnancy has gone on and my nausea has vanished. He's promised that when we return home from our honeymoon, we'll have a staff, so there won't be takeout for every meal any longer—even if it always has been the finest of restaurant takeout.

"I have a surprise for you in our hotel room," he murmurs as we're swept inside the gilded doors, the concierge greeting David by name.

"Everything is arranged, Mr. Carravella," he says, and David nods, taking the keycard from him.

"Already?" I whisper as we walk towards the elevator. "What did you *do*?"

"You'll see." There's a broad smile on his face, and I feel a flutter of excitement in my chest. I've never been one to pretend that I don't like being spoiled, and David excels at doing exactly that.

When we step into the penthouse suite, I don't immediately see what he's done. It's a beautiful room, but it looks like what I would expect from a five-star hotel. There's nothing out of the ordinary that I notice—until my gaze drifts to the open doors leading out to the balcony, and I gasp.

There are lights strung across the balcony and overhead, bathing the space in soft light. The table is large enough for a huge vase of roses and candles, and I see champagne chilling in a bucket, the table already set with our first course. David leads me to it, and I immediately see the view below—the glowing lights and expansive, colorful sights of the Amalfi Coast spreading out in front of us.

"This is gorgeous," I whisper, and David turns me to face him, his hands resting on my waist.

"You're gorgeous," he says, his fingers brushing over my cheek. "My perfect, gorgeous wife. I should have known sooner how perfect you were for me. But I plan to spend the rest of my life showing you exactly how much I know that to be true." His hand slides into my hair, drawing me closer, tilting my mouth up to his. "I love you, Amalie Carravella. And I will tell you every day, from now until forever."

For a moment, I can't breathe. I look up at him, stunned, tears filling my eyes. "I've wanted to say it," I whisper. "I was afraid to. But I know I shouldn't have been. I should always tell you how I feel. I love you too, David. And I can't wait to hear you tell me over and over, so I can say it back."

The smile that spreads over his face is the best thing I've ever seen. The way his lips feel against mine when he kisses me is beyond perfection. And I know, standing there on that balcony, that this is the beginning of our life together. Here, in this place—a different version of the one where we met—we can be just the two of us until we go home.

And then, in the place that we've made into that home, we'll be happy.

I have no doubt of that any longer.

EPILOGUE
AMALIE

Two years later

As I LIFT my daughter onto my hip, balancing her there as I turn away from the stove, I look towards the front door to see if David is home yet. I can hear Frances—our cook—muttering to herself about something on the other side of the room, and I have no doubt it's something to do with me being in here at all. She doesn't particularly like me taking up her space, but it was important to me to make this for David, today of all days.

I'm never going to be a good cook, and that's fine. I don't particularly have any desire to learn, and David doesn't care if I can. He's kept his promise to fill out the house with a staff to take care of it, leaving me to do the things I enjoy and take care of our daughter. But I've never forgotten what he told me about what his mother used to bake that morning. Over many long, stealthy hours while he was away, I think I've finally managed to make an approximation of it.

I hear the front door open and sweep the plate off of the counter,

M. JAMES

still holding Marcia as I walk quickly to the dining room. There's a vase of roses in the middle of the table—David has fresh ones delivered every week. I can't think of a single promise to me that he hasn't kept, or a single thing he hasn't done to try to make me happy. He's tried, every single day, since we said we would. As a result, we have something that I never would have imagined was possible for me, even before I knew David and I were going to be wed—a happy marriage.

"Amalie?" His voice rings through the house, and I set Marcia down in her high chair, settling in next to her.

"I'm in the dining room!" I call out loudly enough for him to hear me, and my breath catches in my throat as I hear his footsteps heading our way.

I've always thought he was handsome, but something changed as our relationship did. Every time I see him, I feel that rush of desire that I'm used to, but there's something else now, too. A warmth, a happiness—a sense of safety that I once would never have thought we could find together. I don't want to ever take it for granted.

It takes David a moment to see what I've made for him. He swoops down to give me a kiss and then presses one to the top of Marcia's head, dodging out of the way before she can grab onto his tie and strangle him with it. He glances over the table, as if wondering why I'm in here waiting for him—and then he sees the plate and the cups of hot cocoa next to it.

"You didn't." He laughs, a genuine sound that I've begun to be more and more used to hearing from him. "You learned to bake banana bread."

"I don't know if it's *good*," I warn him. "But I thought it might be a nice way to celebrate the house being finished. The last contractors left today, and everything has been signed off. It's completely done. And it's cold outside, so I thought the hot cocoa was a nice touch."

"It's supposed to snow tonight." David sinks into the chair opposite me, reaching for a piece. "It's really all finished?"

I nod, feeling a sense of happiness mingled with relief. The renovations were put on hold for a little while towards the end of my pregnancy—when I was truly miserable on a level comparable to the very beginning of it—and while Marcia was a newborn, since it was impossible to keep any kind of sleep schedule consistent with having people working on the house. For the last several months, they've been at it nonstop—and I've occupied what time I have with decorating, taking over the project almost completely as David has had more and more to do with the family businesses. "I hope you like it," I say softly, and he smiles as he breaks off a piece of the banana bread.

"Everything I've seen I've loved so far," he assures me. "You've kept the historic feeling of the house while still updating things. It's perfect, Amalie. Although I'll still buy you that summer home in Boston if you want," he adds teasingly, and I laugh.

"I don't think it's warmer there. Maybe one in Florida."

He chuckles at that, taking a bite, and I wait for a moment. His expression is hard to read, and I frown. "It's bad, isn't it?"

"It's great," David manages, taking a sip of the cocoa, and I make a face at him.

"You promised never to lie to me again."

"Well—I'm sure if you keep practicing—" He chokes down another bite, and I glare at him, pushing the plate out of the way.

"You don't *have* to eat it. Anyway, I have another surprise for you." I reach for Marcia, lifting her up. "I'm going to give her to the nanny, and then I'll show you. Just come upstairs when you're done with your cocoa."

Fifteen minutes later, Marcia is safely ensconced in her nursery, and I see David headed up the stairs. I reach for him the moment he's on the landing, kissing him softly. "You taste like cocoa," I tell him, and he wraps an arm around my waist, pulling me closer.

"You're welcome to taste as much as you like," he murmurs, and I laugh.

"Come with me." I take his hand, leading him down the hall to a door just down from our master suite. I push it open, walking inside with him in tow, and turn to face him as he takes it in.

"What is this?" David turns around, looking at the room. The walls are painted a pale yellow, a hooked rug on the gleaming wooden floor in the pattern of a sun, with white wainscoting all the way around. It's already set up as a nursery—a white crib with yellow bedding and a soft chair on one side, shelves and drawers neatly arranged on the other. "Amalie—"

"Our house is the perfect blend of us both now," I murmur, reaching for him. "And I wanted to make sure you didn't see this room until it was entirely finished. Marcia should have her own room, I think. And in about eight months—"

David's eyes widen. "Are you—"

I nod, my own eyes filling with tears. "This one planned for," I whisper, and he reaches for me before I can even fully finish the sentence, holding me against him as he kisses me, long and slow and deep.

"This is everything I could want," he whispers against my mouth, and when he pulls back, I can see how much this means to him. "You choosing a room in the house that you wanted to be special—you helping the way you have—another baby...Amalie, this is everything. *You're* everything. I'm so grateful you're my wife." He kisses me again, his fingers threading through my hair, and I feel tears slip down my cheeks without meaning for them to. Tears of happiness—because once upon a time, I would never have known things could be this good. "I'm so grateful you stayed."

"So am I." I lean up on my tiptoes, kissing him again, breathing in the scent of his cologne and warm skin, desire flooding me as I press myself closer to him. "I love you."

"And I love you." He backs me up towards the chair, sitting down as he pulls me into his lap. "And I'm never going to let you go."

"I'll never ask you to." I sink down atop him, taking his face in my hands. "I'm yours, David. Forever."

After all, I think, as he kisses me and I reach for the buttons of his shirt, lost in desire, *it was always meant to be.* We were always meant to find each other.

And now, our future is everything we could ever want it to be.

Loved David and Amalie's story? Meet Andre Leone... the sexy and

fiercely protective anti-hero from my next enemies to lovers romance Cruel Heir!

His love story is filled with all your favorite tropes...
✔ *Revenge*
✔ *Forced Pregnancy*
✔ *And Arranged Marriage...*
Keep reading for a sneak peek! Or click here to order it now!
And don't forget to click to join my Red Hot Diva's reader group on Facebook for exclusive sneak peeks and giveaways.

CRUEL HEIR

Andre

I've spent two god-forsaken years in this place with nothing to show for it. But now, my time to shift the game back into my favor has come.

It's been two years since Don Fontana ordered my father's execution for conspiring to make Gianna Mancini my bride, and absorb the Mancini family name into ours. Two years since the upstart Alessio Moretti decided to swoop back into Chicago, take her under his protection, and then marry her himself. Two years since my father tried to kidnap her and force her into a marriage with me, only to be caught in the act.

The price he paid was a bullet in the back of his head, delivered while he knelt between two men at Don Fontana's feet. I know, because I was there. I watched him spit in Fontana's face before he knelt. I heard his last words, delivered not for Fontana's benefit, but mine.

Just because I am forced to bow to you does not mean the Leone family will.

As I heard the muffled gunshot and saw the blood spatter over concrete, I watched my father's body slump forward towards Fontana's boots as if in mockery of what he'd just declared, I thought I would be next. I had hoped that I would die with as much courage as my father had, if Fontana chose to put me on my knees.

I had half a mind to try to take one or two of his men out, before I went down.

But Fontana had other plans. He was hesitant to kill me, clearly, though he didn't deign to share his reasons. What he *did* tell me, as two of his guards led me away from my father's body and into a waiting car, was that I was too dangerous to the stability of the Family to be allowed to do as I please. My name, my blood, and my rage at my father's fall were all points that could destabilize the structure of the Family that Fontana leads. So instead, the car that he had me bundled into took me to a waiting jet, on a tarmac outside of Chicago.

That jet brought me to Sicily, to one of Fontana's estates. And I've been there ever since, as his 'guest', under house arrest while he decides what to do with me.

Or, as I suspect, has forgotten about me.

At least, I hope that's the case.

The adrenaline that floods me when I wrap my arm around his daughter's waist and pull her close to me is better than any high I've ever had. Better than drugs, better than sex, better than the feeling of being behind the wheel of a fast car. It's a feeling of triumph that trumps anything I've ever experienced in my life, particularly when her blue eyes go wide as I lean down to whisper in her ear.

"Oh no, Lucia." I feel her stiffen when I breathe her name. "You're not going anywhere, *principessa*. Except for where *I* choose to take you."

Her chin tilts up defiantly, and I see that there's fire in the little princess. *All the better,* I think with an almost ravenous desire as I tighten my grip on her. *It will feel even better when I douse it. When I break her to my will.*

This moment is one that I've been planning, sprouted from the seed that my father's dying words planted. The Leone family will *not* fall to Don Fontana's whims, not while I draw breath. I am my father's only heir, the last hope of our family name. And the girl in my arms is the first step of my revenge.

For two years, I've gone along with Fontana's wishes. I've languished in my gilded prison without complaint, eating his food and drinking his wine, reading every book in the massive library of the estate where I was kept and enjoying whatever entertainment was on offer–including most of the maids. And the entire time, while Fontana left me there to rot in a velvet-lined coffin of a house, I planned my revenge.

I planned how I would make my father's last words a reality. How, in the end, Fontana would bow to *me*.

It was an easy plan to formulate, once I heard through the staff's gossip and the careless pillow talk of the maids I fucked that Fontana had a daughter. A daughter who would turn eighteen before too terribly long, and for whom he would throw a lavish party, one that would attract so many guests that I might be able to slip through them undetected.

I grew up in a home just a few steps below this, in terms of scale and grandeur and staffing. I knew how much security Fontana likely had, how easily I might or might not be able to avoid them. I spent two years memorizing the patterns of the security guarding *me*, so I could slip away in the first place. And after two years of my good behavior, they'd started to grow lax in how well they watched me. I'd shown no signs of trying to escape before. Why would I now?

"I'm not going anywhere with you." She hisses the words, her full, rosy lips pursing with anger. "Let me *go*! Someone is going to see you, and–"

"No they won't." I haul her around the side of the fountain, deeper into the shadows, away from the lamps illuminating the sides of the path. I know I shouldn't linger, that I could begin the next part of my plan at any moment, but *this* moment feels too delicious. I want to prolong it a little bit more, *savor* it. Her fear is the sweetest thing I've ever tasted, and I haven't even kissed her yet. "I've been very careful, *principessa*. No one saw me come in, and no one will see me leave."

"Then leave *now*." There's still a trace of that haughtiness in her voice, that sense of pride that she has from being *Don Fontana's daughter*. I want to destroy it, the urge rising up in me like a physical thing, and I grasp her chin in my other hand. I turn her face towards mine as she squirms in my arms, my thumb pressing into her soft, plush lower lip.

"You don't tell me what to do, Lucia." I murmur her name like an endearment, letting it roll off of my tongue sweet and thick. "*I* will be the one telling *you* what to do."

"In your fucking dreams." She spits the words, wrestling in my grip, and my hand slides downwards, gripping her lightly by the throat. She goes still in an instant, fear glinting in her blue eyes as I apply the slightest pressure to her windpipe.

God, I've never been so fucking hard.

"You have a filthy mouth for such an elegant, well-bred lady." I look down at her blue gaze in the near-darkness, looming over her. "Fortunately for you, I intend to do all of this *correctly*. By the book, as it were. Otherwise, I'd put you down on your knees right here, and show you what better uses I have for your mouth."

"*You*–" She chokes on the word as I tighten my grip, sucking in a sudden breath as if she's afraid I might cut hers off forever. For a moment, I consider doing just that. It would still be vengeance, if I left Don Fontana's daughter dead on the cobblestones in his own garden, while he drank and rubbed elbows with his power-bloated compatriots inside.

A life for a life. It would settle the debt between us.

But it wouldn't be *enough*.

It's not enough for me to even the score. I need to tip it in my favor. I need to make him *suffer*, the way I've suffered for two years, held prisoner far away from my family and my birthright. Kept from my rightful place as the Leone heir, while my simpering mother ran things in my absence, arranging a marriage for my sister, dragging our name further into the dirt. Prevented from setting things right.

Lucia dead isn't enough. I want her father to know that she's being kept prisoner as I was. That every night, I'm fucking his daughter, filling her until she bears my child. That I will take *everything* from him, including the right to give her to whoever he chooses.

I will take *her*. Alive is better for what I want than dead.

At least for now.

"I've been watching you all night, *principessa*." I stroke my thumb along her jawline, loosening my grip on her throat just a little. "Your father really has done an admirable job. You're the very picture of elegance. Of beauty. A bride fit for the highest rank of *mafioso*. A priceless treasure."

Her eyes flash furious sparks at me. "And this is how you treat a *priceless treasure,* then? Manhandling it with filthy fingers and rude words?"

"I like your spirit." I brush my thumb over her jaw again. "You'll make this all the more fun for me by fighting."

She makes a sound almost like a hiss, bucking in my grasp again, but all it takes is tightening my hand on her throat once more to settle her. I can see the fear in her eyes, no matter how well she tries to hide it.

She's already terrified of what I could do to her. And she has no idea what's in store for her after I take her away from here.

"My father will–kill–you–" she chokes out from behind my hand, her blue eyes going wide. "Let me *go*, and you can still get away–"

"Ah, the bargaining stage." I fist one hand in her artfully curled dark hair, feeling the jeweled pins scattered through it dig into my palm. I tug her head back, releasing my grip on her throat as I stroke my fingers lightly over her cheekbone. "It won't do you any good, *principessa*."

She stares up at me, and I think I finally see the understanding beginning to dawn on her face. This entire time, she's been thinking that any moment, someone would come for her. That any moment, security would descend on me and save her. After all, that's how stories are meant to turn out for pampered, spoiled little princesses.

Someone always swoops in and saves the day.

I stroke my fingers down to her plush mouth, pressing my fingertips against the soft flesh. I want to kiss her. I want to ravage her lips and find out how sweet her mouth is, a sweetness that would only be enhanced by the knowledge of what I plan to do to her later. But as I said, I want to do all of this *properly*.

So very properly, in fact, that there can be no question of my ownership when I finally take what's mine.

"You're coming with me, Lucia Fontana," I breathe as I lean in, ghosting my lips over her cheek. "And then, whether you like it or not—"

I drag my lips to the very corner of her mouth, looking into her eyes, and I feel her shudder. A shiver that runs all the way through her—and one that, I think, isn't entirely revulsion.

"Then," I whisper. "You will be mine."

Click here to get this full-length dark mafia standalone now!

Made in United States
Orlando, FL
18 September 2024

51665499R00214